I0671515

Gay
Grifters

His new friends will not only steal your wallet and gold, but also your heart and soul!

Revised Edition 2010

By
TJ Johnson

Copyright © 2009 by TJ Johnson
Revised Edition Copyright 2010

Library of Congress Control Number:
2009927537

ISBN 978-0-9819932-0-1

Published By
Hard Title Publishing

www.ItsFiction.com

Gay Grifters Copyright © 2009 & 2010 by TJ Johnson. All rights reserved. Printed in the United States of America. No part of this book may be used or reproduced in any manner whatsoever without written permission except in the case of brief quotations embodied in critical articles or reviews. For information, contact Hard Title Publishing at **Info@ItsFiction.com**

This novel is strictly and entirely a work of fiction. All references to real people, events, establishments, organizations, or locales are purely and solely intended to give the novel a sense of reality and authenticity. All other names, characters, incidents, organizations, or locales are strictly the product of the author's imagination, as are those fictionalized events and incidents that involve real persons and entities. Of the fictional characters, any resemblance to actual persons, living or dead is entirely and purely coincidental.

Dedication

To the parents who never understand,
but love their children anyhow.

Revised Edition Note

Many readers spotted a few errors in the type of this sequel, and I have written the rough draft for Part II of the "Eric & Tyler" series called **Crosshairs**, as well Part III called **Rock Solid**. This required a few changes to Part I to set up the new adventures. This revision gave my new editor a chance to work on the original story as well as the new additions. I hope you enjoy this story as much as I did in writing this revised edition.

Eric rebuilt his life by joining America's elite fighting force, the Navy Seals. After graduation from their grueling training programs, he quickly earned a leadership role as squad leader, and began moving up through the ranks. He excelled in his role as he led his men through one successful mission after another. However, when alone and away from his military life, Eric felt different than his mates, and it took most of his second tour before finally accepting that he was gay. After eight years of intense sacrifice for his country, wounded numerous times, and decorated often, he resigned from the Navy.

Perhaps his tough-guy image gave him the confidence to disclose his secret with the men he trained and fought with. This close-knit bonded group loved him like a brother, accepted his homosexuality, and supported him. They became the core members of the private security team Eric founded. He chose additional members by selecting only the best after receiving assurance they could work for a gay boss. His firm protected the rich, the famous, politicians on the rise, and dignitaries from many countries.

Occasionally the government hired his firm to do the things they could not. The business and income for his staff grew quickly. This afforded Eric the luxury of choosing his clients cautiously, while providing top quality security that even the FBI envied. They had the best men and women, the latest weapons, the best technical gear, and a league of trainers specializing in martial arts, weaponry, electronic communication, and proudly they excelled in every area.

Eric now led the life he dreamed of with one minor exception. He always felt that one day he would also find the man of his dreams, but though he dated from time to time, no one stood out or captured his heart. However, one night in the most unlikely place, Eric's spotted a young man he could not stop thinking about.

There was no doubt that Tyler was good-looking, but he was also a thief of pockets, wallets, houses, and bank accounts, but in the case of Eric, he also stole his heart.

Books by TJ Johnson

The War Apart - Part I
(A Josh & Zeke Story)

The War Ahead - Part II Revised 2010
(A Josh & Zeke Story)

The Will
(A Brett & Chase Story)

Stranded
(An Austin & Ryan Story)

The Raceboys
(A Jack & Thad Story)

A Writer's Fantasy
(About His Favorite College Basketball Star)
(A Shane & TJ Story)

Gay Grifters
(An Eric & Tyler Story)

The Blackfeet Boys Part I
(A Kiyo & Windtalker Story)

Coming soon:

Crosshairs
(An Eric & Tyler Story)

The War Beyond - Part III
(A Josh & Zeke Story)

The Blackfeet Boys Part II
(A Kiyo & Windtalker Story)

Rock Solid Part III
(An Eric & Tyler Story)

Web Site and Release Information
Read A Chapter
View The Book Cover
Sign Up For Advance Release Notice
TJ's Blog, News, Details
Available at:

WWW.ItsFiction.com

"A loyal friend laughs at your jokes when they're not so good, and sympathizes with your problems when they're not so bad."

Arnold H. Glasgow

ONE

Eric sipped easily on his warming beer, wondering why he wasted his time and money by coming to Washington's famous all nude bar. After his each annual visit, he swore he would never return, but some habits are hard to break. He came to Washington only once a year for business, as he held no fondness for the sea of bureaucrats, lobbyists, and dreamers that dwelled there. However, each time he returned to the land of politics, he rewarded himself by making time to visit a large gay bar that featured dancing young men that the locals called twinks. They were legal in age, but generally looked a year or two younger than they actually were. By law, they allowed the boys to dance completely nude, except they had to wear a pair of socks. He thought it was one of the most interesting and perplexing laws in the district.

Every time he came to the bar and saw the cute guys swinging their dicks while wearing just the white socks, he had to laugh at how stupid the law was. However, it did provide a nice place for the dancers to roll up their dollar bill tips since they had no pockets for the piles of cash. They danced atop a long, horseshoe shaped polished bar outfitted with numerous fireman poles. These brass pipes allowed the naked boys to swing around and around while delighting the audience as their private parts flew through the air. It also allowed the boys to hang on with one hand and lean out over the men sitting on the stools, and flirting with the shy men standing behind them. It also allowed their genitals to flop in the faces of the stool pigeons, those men entrenched closest to the boys and the bar, while providing more cash for their socks. A good-looking boy with a handsome smile and big dick could earn two hundred dollars on just one trip around the bar, sometimes over a thousand a night. He knew this because one of his friends used to dance here for special occasions like Christmas, New Year's Eve, and his favorite was the night of the Presidential inauguration.

Eight years ago, he agreed to hold his friend's tips because the place was packed. It took about forty minutes for him to make it all the way around the bar and exit into a large dressing room. Eric would meet him at the door and his friend would hand him rolls of the cash from his socks. Eric would go to a private corner and count out the dollar bills in piles of fifty. He would then go to the cashier clerk and cash in the dollar bills for hundred dollar bills. They took in almost fifteen hundred dollars for just three hours work. Eric took none of it, but for his friend, it kept his car going and the rent paid, and besides, he actually loved the ego trip of dancing naked. However, his friend failed in his attempts to entice Eric to dance naked on the bar.

Over the heads of the nude boys were video monitors displaying nonstop porn movies while the wishful men sat around the bar if they were brave, or in safely away from dancer encounters in chairs around small tables, while gleefully watching and lusting after the cute boys. Everyone had a good time, and there were never any fights, though some went home happier than most by escorting a dancer to their car.

Eric knew it had been years since he actually met a dancer that produced an intelligent conversation, though many a dancer flirted with him because he dressed in nice clothes, and considered by all to be rock solidly handsome. Of course, they were determined to rid him of all his dirty dollar bills before it was time for him to leave. He knew better than to hope or wish for a handsome stranger to walk into the bar and instantly fall in love with him. Eric knew winning the lottery was a more logical conclusion than finding true love in a nude bar, and yet, deep inside, he could not help but wonder and hope a little, as did the rest of the patrons.

Eric looked like the United States Navy Seal team member that he was, projecting both an air of confidence and strength. He was a gentleman ex-soldier that knew how to fight to win, shoot to kill, and never break a sweat in the process. His clothes appeared to mold to his well-cut body, while his face remained free of scars and smooth, and his hair, cut short like all soldiers, seem to accent his inviting eyes and radiant smile. He'd broken a few hearts along the way, but more than once, he experienced the pain of having his heart stomped on with both feet.

Although the dance club was open twenty-four hours a day and seven days a week, near midnight, the crowd grew thick around the bar. He managed to sit alone near the back wall on a riser, so he could see all the performances on the bar for fun, but more importantly, he could take note of all the gay men arriving to watch the boys swinging their dicks. It was the later group that he hoped he might find mister right, or at the worst, mister-maybe-right, but so far he'd only spotted mister no-way-in-hell.

Minutes later, his eyes followed a good-looking man about thirty years of age as he left the bar and made his way to the door. Eric hated to see him leave so soon, but since he had not been brave enough to strike up a conversation with him, there was little to be sad about. Part of Eric's problem in meeting a potential new boyfriend was that although he won a Silver Star for his bravery in battle, gathering his wits about him to just go up and say hi, often scared him shitless. Throughout the evening, he spent most of his time silently chastising himself for not making the first move. He often felt like he had stepped on a misplaced tube of glue, leaving him stuck in the corner as he was tonight.

Sometimes, he resorted to moving up to the bar and standing behind an obvious older gay couple having a grand time with a few drinks under their belt while cheerfully tipping the boys. He would make friends with them easily as he wasn't interested in a relationship, and this put him in the thick of things where he then had a chance to meet men they knew, or even a friend of one of the dancers, but tonight he wasn't in the mood for idle chit-chat with the often friendly stool pigeons.

He really wanted to meet someone fun and nice that would enjoy a good meal with a great wine, and perhaps great sex.

The very moment the stranger that had caught his eye pushed out the swinging, saloon-style doors to go home, in walked three men—one younger and far more good looking than either of the other men, but the older ones looked like former models. The younger could be a dancer or a model, and all three were handsomely dressed. Heads turned as they came in, checking them out from head to toe, and wondering. Eric caught himself doing the same thing. He dismissed the younger man at first, labeling him as a twink or maybe a dancer, but one of the other men might be promising. He wondered if they were a couple, as they weren't holding hands, and they didn't whisper with alluring smiles to each other. All three seemed to be concerned with the cast of characters throughout the bar and not just the nude men dancing. Eric managed to look away before their roaming eyes panned over his table.

Nonchalantly, he managed to see one of the men laugh as he slightly nudged the younger man forward into the crowd with a nod, as if saying time to go to work. Eric saw many friends come into the bar in the past hour, but none acted like that. He thought at first it meant for the man to go strip and get ready to dance, but the boy, as he called the lad to distinguish him from his older friends, moved directly towards the patrons at the bar.

The threesome failed to note Eric's eyes as he watched from the upper shadows, but slowly he realized as the crowd watched the handsome young man make his way to the bar, the remaining pair did not watch their friend, but instead began scanning the crowd as if looking for an old friend. Eric followed their eyes as they would lean into each other as if spotting numerous friends, but oddly, they never moved through the crowd to say hello to anyone. He realized they were not regulars to the bar, and more likely out-of-towers. The odd threesome clicked his curiosity. He thought that if he wasn't going to meet mister right, why not pass the time figuring these queer ducks out?

The handsome boy ordered a beer, but a man nearby quickly paid for the drink while introducing himself. As they shook hands, the boy leaned into the generous beer buyer while obviously flirting. His eyes never actually stared, but he kept noting the wad of money the man held in his hand as he pulled a few bills free, and put the money on the bar for the drink. In short order, they were laughing and talking like old friends, though they had only met sixty seconds ago. This fascinated him, and he could not surmise in his wildest dreams why the handsome young man would be paying this bar hugger any attention at all.

Bravely, at least in Eric's mind, the man put his arm around the boy, and the boy seemed delighted he had done so. Eric tilted his head and leaned forward a bit so he could see, but he was sure he saw the boy place his hand in the man's lap and squeeze his penis. Ninety seconds, thought Eric, how in the hell did that old man get that boy to squeeze his penis just seconds after they met? The affection continued as they leaned into each other, laughed loudly, drank some more, and then there it was again, another penis squeeze. For one

3

beer, the guy received an amazing amount of affection. Eric smiled as he shook his head in disbelief, but out of the corner of his eye, he caught sight of the other two men strolling across the room and walking up to a man sitting at a table alone like Eric. Why would they be interested in a loner, he wondered?

The three men began talking away and pointing at the boys on the bar as if they were long-lost friends on their eighth cocktail. They were laughing and ordering drinks, but Eric soon noted the man alone drank far more than the pair. Once or twice, he saw the couple spill their drinks to the floor while the single man stared at the dancing boys. They bought him another round before he finished the last one.

Puzzled, Eric turned back to watch the good-looking boy, but he had disappeared from feeling up the stool pigeon, and was now hanging with another man who freely tipped every nude boy on the bar that stopped in front of him from a large pile of cash. He bought the boy a beer, and it was then that Eric noted the young fellow had left the first beer he received on the bar across from the stool pigeon. In the flashing spinning lights, he could see the bottle remained almost full. The boy drank little, but acted as if he had consumed far more and enjoying a serious buzz. He laughed, leaned into, hugged, and rubbed their backs like they were old friends or lovers.

Eric turned his head back and forth from the two men on the left and the cute boy at the bar with great interest, and found he was having more fun than he was before they arrived. He decided to give them names just for the hell of it. He called the boy Larry, and the two men Curly and Moe respectively. He laughed at himself as he watched the two men move to another table where once again they began ordering drinks as if they were owners of the club, and most determined to make each guest as happy as possible, as if naked good-looking men on the bar wasn't enough.

By the time he found Larry on the other side of the room, Curly and Moe were at their third table. Suddenly, Eric set his beer down. He looked at the bottle and realized absently he had nervously peeled off the entire label until the bottle sat there half empty and bare. He took a deep breath and let it out slowly. He wondered why he felt so apprehensive.

He turned back to the cute boy at the bar and caught a glimpse of him kissing a man, but Eric dropped his eyes a little and saw the boy's right hand carefully remove the man's wallet and pocket it in his pants.

Suddenly a realization hit him. "They're crooks," he said to no one as the loud music easily drowned out his words. "They are looking for marks. No, they are looking for gay men to steal from. He laughed aloud. "How perfect is this? I'm watching the three stooges, Larry, Curly and Moe transform from comedy to accomplished crooks!" He laughed again at the absurdity of his thoughts, but as he continued watching the threesome, he knew he was right. His military and undercover training taught him to analyze facts quickly and make positive assumptions.

4

The two men must have found their mark and talked him into joining their pal Larry at the bar. As they made the introductions, Curly and Moe shook hands with Larry as if they had never met, though twenty minutes ago, they walked into the bar together. They laughed at stupid jokes, drank some more, and hugs were freely given while more wallets were lifted. He saw Curly, the oldest, smoothly steal the man's watch as if he were a magician instead of the obvious Fagin of Oliver Twist fame.

"What do I do?" Eric asked to no one. The smile fell from his face. "They are going to rob these marks blind." He then thought they might actually hurt someone in the process, while wondering if they were really gay like the rest of the crowd, or were they straight bastards preying on the loneliness of the audience watching the smiling boys and their swinging appendages. If the latter, he felt close to punching their lights out.

He shook his head left and right. "No, I have no proof. They haven't actually left with the stolen property—yet. Maybe it was all a joke. He moved his chair farther back against the wall and out of the light over his table. He suddenly wished to remain anonymous and hidden. Larry suddenly pulled his shirt off and tucked it in through a belt loop. His gorgeous smooth skin abruptly caused the drooling men to drop their jaws, and lick their lips like the wolf standing over Little Red Riding Hood. The boy began dancing near the men like the nude boys on the bar. He leaned into the men, kissed another, ran his hands up and down the other man, and in a flash of a few seconds, he managed to turn the heads of everyone in the bar to his beautiful bare chest. He acted like he was about to explode because he was so hot and horny for these strangers. Eric couldn't imagine what might happen next, though he thought it would be cool if the boy stripped and leaped on the bar. He'd like to see more of him, and so would everyone in the bar.

Well, almost everyone. After a few seconds of staring at Larry, Eric scanned the bar looking for Curly and Moe. They had split up and returned to visit their new friends at table one and table two. They were pointing at Larry and encouraging the men to stand and cheer with them as they began clapping. They turned left and right beckoning other men to start applauding as well. He saw Curly laugh and pretend to sort of lose his balance and fell into his new friend. In a flash, Curly lifted the man's wallet and stuffed it in his blazer pocket. A second later, he relieved the man of his gold watch right off his wrist. The victim felt nothing.

"Boy, he's good," said Eric to himself.

He knew probably no one else in the room would have known what to watch for, but his past gave him the knowledge he needed. He quickly turned and scanned the room until he found Moe. He had his friend on his feet. As they watched the young man dance, Larry worked the crowd. He realized both men had moved their marks into the shadows and away from the mini-spotlight on the tables. Larry came towards them and gave the new friend a big hug and kiss. While Moe lifted the man's wallet, Larry removed the man's watch, and passed it to Curly as fast as Siegfried and Roy could make a white tiger suddenly disappear. Eric knew they were far better than the average pickpockets he met in Middle Eastern countries that preyed on the tight crowds in the markets.

Larry suddenly pretended to be out of breath, and slipped his shirt back on. Curly and Moe were saying their goodbyes to their new friends, and steadily making their way to the door. Larry went back to the bar where he left the man with the pile of cash on the bar. He leaned into the man and whispered something in his ear. The man's eyes widened, and then suddenly he smiled wickedly. Quickly, he gathered up his cash, stuffed it in his pocket, and followed the handsome boy to the door. Together, they followed Curly and Moe out of the club while holding hands with his new friend.

Eric stood there in silence, deep in thought while wondering if he should do something, say something, yell for the police, or find a manager. He then realized there were no other witnesses, and probably no one would believe him, and if they didn't, they might blame him.

He decided it was time for him to leave so he began making his way to the door. He looked for a manager type but found no one. He asked the man at the cash register for the manager, who said he would be around in a few hours. Eric looked at his watch, and it was already two in the morning, so he wasn't going to wait for the manager to show. He went out the door, down the steps, and onto the street. He looked left and right, but could not spot a cop anywhere. He turned to see if he could spot the thieves, but he knew that if they were as good as he suspected, they would already be gone, and they were.

He turned back to the club, decided he no longer desired to go back in, and now felt mad at himself for allowing the robbers to get away, while feeling ashamed he did nothing to stop them. He tried to remind himself it was none of his business, and though he had wronged many a person when he was younger, he wished everyday he could repay the folks from whom he stole. He did not know their names nor could he recall any of the addresses of the homes he robbed. He told himself he stole for food and clothes, but he knew that was only partly true. He also stole for the thrill of it, and for the ability to buy anything he wanted.

He knew the threesome were pretty good pickpockets, but nowhere near as good as he had been. He turned to walk the two blocks to where he parked his car, being careful to walk quickly, while watching the alleyways as he passed by. He quickly unlocked the door, jumped in, locked the doors, and drove away. In this area of the district he was always afraid he might get jumped for being gay, and an easy target, because he was almost always alone, as usual. He wasn't afraid of a fair fight or even two against one, but a gay bigot in the dark with a baseball bat or a knife made him feel anxious.

Tyler was in the passenger seat of the man's car as they drove down interstate ninety-five. The man felt excited with having such a fine specimen of a young thing in his car, and yet so nervous that he couldn't stop talking. He also couldn't stop rubbing his hand up and down Tyler's thigh. Tyler glanced back to be sure his friends were still following at a safe distance. He tried asking the man questions to slow him down, including how much farther to his house.

The guy's name was Joseph, but he told Tyler to call him Joe. He was forty-eight, single, losing most of his hair, and worked as a stockbroker. He was very successful with his own firm and staff of over a hundred. Tyler noted the neighborhood improved about eight miles from the interstate, and a few turns later, they drove into a very upscale development. After a few more blocks, they pulled into his long driveway lined with incredible lighting and landscaping, and up to the front of his huge house. Joe owned a four-car garage, but he was much too horny to pull around to the garage, so he stopped the car immediately in front of the door.

Tyler stepped out and saw his friends roll up to the entrance of the driveway and cut their car lights off. He felt some relief they weren't lost, but knew the job ahead of him was going to be gross. Once inside, Tyler felt they hit a gold mine as the man's house was loaded with lots of rich and expensive things.

"My goodness, you have a beautiful house," said Tyler as he stepped inside.

Joe closed the door behind and locked the door. Tyler made a note that he would have to unlock the door. "Are we alone? Do you have servants or a boyfriend about?"

Joe laughed. "No servants on duty, and unfortunately no boyfriend, or we could have enjoyed a delicious threesome. Would you like something to drink?"

"Yes please. How about a Sex-On-The-Beach?"

Joe smiled. "That is one of my favorites, too. Walk this way." Joe took his hand and practically dragged Tyler into the large living room, which was at least thirty by forty feet, with an extremely expensive and enormous Oriental rug, and then they walked over to a bar in the corner. He began making the drinks.

Tyler carefully took a small capsule from his pocket and hid it in his hand by placing it inside one of his middle-finger knuckles. The next step caused him to sigh, but following well-rehearsed instructions, he dropped all his clothes off faster than the strippers at the bar. He positioned the clothes like a fireman preparing for a quick exit. Joe turned around and nearly dropped the drinks.

"My, my! You're even hornier than I am, and that is almost impossible."

Tyler strutted to him with a bit of a bounce in his step, making his genitals bumble along, mesmerizing Joe. Tyler held out his hands. "Here, I'll hold the drinks while you strip. I want to see you naked."

Joe obeyed instantly by handing him the drinks, and rapidly taking his clothes off. Tyler set the drinks down, secretly opened the capsule with his back to Joe, and poured the contents in Joe's drink. Quickly, he picked the glass up and made the contents swirl a little. He turned around to see Joe standing there naked with a dog to a bone look on his face.

Tyler handed him the drink and said, "I want to make a toast." He backed away as he held up his drink indicating for Joe to do the same. This was a procedure he learned the hard way when very early in his career as a grifter a mark insisted they intertwine their arms, holding the glass for their new friend to drink out of at the same time. Confused, Tyler actually drank the dope. By backing away a little, he wisely removed that possible option. He grinned wickedly and said loudly, "Let's hope this drink makes our dicks so hard we can fuck all night. Drink it down and then get on your knees, and suck the tar out of my dick!"

Tyler threw his drink down his throat and out of the corner of his eye, he watched Joe quickly do the same. The next thing Joe did shocked the hell out of Tyler. Joe flung his empty glass into the marbled fireplace, shattering it into hundreds of pieces. He then fell to his knees and took Tyler's large penis in his mouth, sucking it like a hungry newborn calf.

Tyler managed to set his glass down and glance out the front windows. He saw Jim and Stephen in the shadows looking in. Tyler indicated three minutes by holding up three fingers. He allowed himself to get his penis hard, very hard. He was lucky to have been born with a rather large penis for a small guy, and he used his tool to open many doors of opportunity.

Joe almost brought the boy to a climax, when suddenly Joe slowed down, then stopped, his face turned pale, and then he fell back to the floor unconscious. Tyler rapidly masturbated himself, and soon exploded his cum all over Joe's face. Once he shook the rest of the juice from his shaft, he began peeing all over Joe's body.

He walked to the front door and turned the lock to let Jim and Stephen in. They laughed when they saw him in the nude.

"I take it you had a good time?" They stepped inside and closed the door.

"Shit! It was all I could do to get hard. I already shot and pissed on him." Tyler asked, "Do you have the camera?"

Jim slipped off his backpack, unzipped the side compartment, and handed him the Polaroid camera.

Tyler said, "I'll get the pictures done, then dress, and join you in the search. This place should be full of goodies."

While Jim and Stephen began exploring the house and loading any items they could fence quickly, Tyler went over and took pictures of Joe with the cum and piss on his face and body. Then using a picture on the table to steady the camera, he tapped the timer button, and then Tyler quickly straddled Joe's face, turned around so his face would not be in the picture and squatted down on Larry's face.

He then rolled Joe onto his side, pulled his top leg forward, then lay down beside him, pretending to stick his dick into Larry's ass, and took another picture while again excluding his face once more.

Tyler laughed after checking the photos and turned in a circle looking for objects. He giggled when he saw a huge bowl of fake fruit. He quickly snatched up a large waxed banana, and stuck it up Joe's ass and took another picture.

Satisfied, he quickly dressed, put the pictures in his pocket, and took the camera to the front door and set it down in front of it so they wouldn't forget it.

He yelled, "Where are you?"

Jim replied first, "I'm in his study or library. It is huge. Come here."

Stephen yelled, "You're not going to believe his bedroom. I haven't found the safe yet."

Tyler ran into the office, which Joe had ransacked, looking for hidden items in books, or a safe, and already had two bags of things he thought they could fence.

Tyler turned slowly, allowing his eyes to roam the room until he spotted a large painting of a naked man lying on the beach. He went to it, studied the frame carefully, and then pulled hard on the right side. It peeled away from the wall, as the left side was on a hinge. He laughed when he saw the safe.

"I found something," he said mysteriously.

Jim stopped rummaging through the desk, looked up and laughed. "Way to go. I swear you have a nose for a safe."

Tyler yelled for Stephen, "I found the safe!"

Stephen yelled back, "Good. Leave it to Jim and come help me."

Tyler watched Jim pull his electronic equipment from his backpack and begin working on cracking the safe. Tyler smiled as he ran from the room and leaped up the stairs two steps at a time. "Where are you?"

"Here!" exclaimed Stephen.

Tyler ran into the bedroom where Stephen had been busy searching through every drawer for valuables. "I found about fifty watches, some of which are worth over ten thousand dollars, but I suspect he has something hidden here somewhere."

Tyler began circling the room as he had done before. "All rich gay men do and many poor ones. A porn collection, sex tools, photos of friends having sex, because they all fear the day when there will be no more sex, and their stash gives them something to masturbate with."

Tyler didn't find anything obvious, so he went to the bed and sat down. He looked at the nightstand, but Stephen had already gone through the drawers and found nothing but books. The man was obviously well read. He saw four remote controls on the top by the bed lamp. He leaned against the headboard with the controllers in his lap and began pushing buttons. At the foot of the bed was a table much like a hall table. When he hit the television button, the top of the table motorized upward, and a huge flat screen television began rising out of the cavity.

"Far out," laughed Tyler.

"Nobody says 'far out' since John Denver died. And don't you say 'cool' either," said Stephen.

"Yeah, you're right. Let's see…oh shit!"

Stephen laughed. "I guess that word is never out of date. Any luck?"

Tyler kept pushing buttons and was just about to give up, when he found a programmed button with no label. He hit the button and a nearby wall clicked and then spun halfway revealing a hidden hallway.

"Look at that!" exclaimed Tyler, as he leaped off the bed and entered the hallway. Motion detectors turned on the lights. Ten feet into the room his jaw dropped. Old Joe was into sadomasochism. There were all kinds of leather props, tools, weapons, straps, and a harness hanging from the ceiling. There was also a wall of videos with another big screen television. He pushed a tape in the machine, turned on the television, and instantly saw old Joe busy fucking a most likely underage teenager. It made Tyler uncomfortable, remembering what happened to him as a kid, so he ejected the tape and walked out of the room.

"We won't have any trouble with this guy. I have a tape of him fucking a teenager."

Stephen laughed. "I'm done, so let's get the hell out of here."

When they walked down to the office, they found Jim cleaning out the safe. Tyler asked, "How much?"

Jim looked blank as if something was wrong, and then slowly broke into a huge grin, "Oh, I'd say about two hundred and fifty thousand, plus lots of gold coins, jewels, and even some stocks and bonds. I'd say we hit the jackpot." He zipped up the bag.

"Let's go," urged Stephen.

Tyler ran to the still unconscious Joe and retrieved his watch, rings, and his wallet, then grabbed the camera, and together they left the house. They laughed and cheered as they drove around Washington on the expressway, being careful to avoid speeding, and then up to Baltimore and their hotel. They entered their room quietly, not wanting to gain the attention of anyone.

They packed their clothes, and then emptied their winnings onto the bed. Quickly they sorted it as to which Fed-ex box to ship the merchandise.

10

Tyler brought the prepared boxes from the corner, and they began loading the pre-addressed courier boxes and taping them shut. Tyler placed the incriminating articles in another box, and shipped it to their blind mailbox, including info pilfered from the mark's wallet.

They left the room with all the boxes on a folded cart with their luggage and carry-on bags on top. Once outside, Tyler tossed the wallet in a dumpster he spotted earlier, and any packaging from the items they took from Joe's house. They drove to an all night Kinkos and delivered the prepaid packages, so they wouldn't have to use a credit card. When the clerk asked for identification, Joe gave him a fake driver's license matching the return address on the label.

They left the rental car at the airport and managed to catch their six a.m. flight as the sun was coming up. It had been cold in Washington, but when they landed in Miami Beach it was a warm morning with the temperature rising.

They drove to their house where Tyler immediately stripped, put his clothes in a trash bag, and got in the shower and scrubbed himself clean of any possible DNA, or anything from Joe. He almost felt raped, but knew it was really he that had done the raping with his indignities to the helpless man. Once dressed, he took the bag and walked to the dumpster outside the back gate of their compound.

His home was an expensive house not far from the beach, surrounded by palm trees and lush vegetation. He waved to Marvin as he drove through the back electric gate. Marvin came in the kitchen with grocery bags and attitude. He was an older gay man Jim hired eight years ago to do a job. They split their winnings, but Jim knew Marvin was not cut out for the job. However, since he participated in a crime, his lips were sealed. Thankfully, he exhibited a better skill as an excellent chef. He also supervised the cleaning staff. The house was just over six thousand square feet, not counting the pool, external apartment, and the magnificent grounds. They had a high fence with electric gates in the front and rear, and an expensive security system.

Each man maintained their own bedroom, but they enjoyed sex together while sometimes sleeping in a large master bedroom with a huge bed. Jim and Stephen were a couple when they met Tyler. He became their white cream in an Oreo as Tyler called it, but Jim would tease and say he was the baloney in their sandwich.

"Get your asses down here!" yelled Marvin from the bottom of the stairwell. "Breakfast is ready!"

Jim and Stephen had showered as well, and now they all sat at the big kitchen table with an ocean view, while Marvin served hot crepes with sliced strawberries, freshly baked croissants with cream cheese, and freshly squeezed orange juice, with grapes on the side. He insisted they eat well and take care of their bodies.

11

They devoured the food and began talking about their plans for the day.

Jim started, "I for one think this was a successful trip. Until last night, we only made about a thousand when Tyler found the mark."

Stephen added, "I've already sent the encrypted emails to our clients," which was his word for fences, "and they should have their packages in the morning. We'll get our boxes at the same time. I suggest we put the cash in the safe deposit box in bank number four, and once we get the cash from the sale of the stocks and bonds we'll add even more to our winnings." Tyler didn't know that Stephen was actually lying, as he never trusted leaving their stolen cash in a bank. He would secure the money in a hidden vault in the wall behind his desk when Tyler wasn't around.

Tyler asked, "How much do you figure to make from the clients?"

Jim replied, "I'd say a hundred thousand after their percentage. Overall, it was a great trip. I just love Washington."

Stephen said, "I'm glad you do, but we can't go back there for about six months or more. We don't want to see old Joe."

Tyler laughed. "I don't ever want to see old Joe again—especially his tiny dick!"

They all laughed as Marvin cleared the table.

"Come on boys," said Stephen as he stood up. "Time for therapy."

"I need sleep," protested Jim.

"Not yet. Come on. I'll drive."

They drove to the expensive gym and went through their workouts, which included staring at various cute guys. They swam a few laps in the pool, soaked in the sauna, and roasted in the steam room. They finished with a half-hour massage from the staff. Feeling refreshed, they drove home.

They immediately went upstairs to the common bedroom, stripped, and began making out as a threesome. They rotated positions often, and although they were versatile when it came to tops and bottoms, for some reason, Tyler wanted to fuck them both and they gladly let him. They loved his large dick almost as much as he did. They fell asleep at the noon hour with Tyler sleeping cozily between Jim and Stephen. Life was good for this band of thieves.

TWO

Eric had been in Miami just two weeks ago, planning this weekend's appearance and speech at an electronic convention. Fifteen years ago, Larry D. Menard was a poor college student looking at ten years of loan payments to achieve his diploma. In the summer after graduation, he and his roommate wrote code for a new ATM software security program that made them instant billionaires. He also developed various software programs for personal computers that became so popular he sold over a hundred and fifty million units, achieving a top-five ranking. Last year, he released new traffic control software that was installed in eighty percent of America's major cities. Wealthy, and acted like it, he mostly lived on the water in his Baltimore house, a thirty-five thousand square foot newly constructed mansion. True to his style, the house contained every possible modern convenience and technology, and some new electronic toys not yet released to the public. All the artwork was electronic, and the digital frames changed as guests visited each room, based on a simple survey administered on a touch screen system at a kiosk upon entering the house. The background music changed as well. If you liked modern art and smooth jazz that is exactly what you would see and hear as you wandered throughout the house.

Larry, a certified electronic and software developer at the genius level, could also be stupid and juvenile, which explains why there was a sliding chute installed in his third floor bedroom that descended in a spiraling fashion and landed Larry in the pool. He liked to use it in the morning or after sex, if he was lucky, and the target date buzzed sufficiently with alcohol, inducing temporary blindness and stupidity.

Eric knew his client was a homosexual, but he never let Larry find out that Eric was as well, because he felt Larry would forever come on to him. He kept their relationship very businesslike, especially the invoices he sent twice a month for security services, averaging around fifty thousand dollars a month depending on travel and accumulated hours.

He suspected Larry accepted the speaking engagement in Miami as an excuse to get back Fort Lauderdale, and check out the hot men on the beach and in the clubs, while hoping to score. Trying to keep Larry secure in a nightclub was next to impossible, so Eric insisted he wear a high quality disguise, professionally applied by a movie makeup artist from Miami. Nothing too disgusting, just a mustache, thicker eyebrows, a hair piece, and color contacts. Eric never let on that most gay people clued in quickly that the successful multi-millionaire was a homosexual, but generally strangers found his geek attitude and overbearing personality somewhat revolting. Throwing his money around never helped, as Eric always said a troll wrapped in hundred dollar bills is still a troll.

Larry came to the Fort Lauderdale-Miami area at least a dozen times a year. A few years ago, Eric convinced Larry to buy a house in Miami, so he could set up the security, making it far easier to look after Larry and his pitiful attempts to hook up. A house was far easier for his teams to control than a suite in a fancy upscale hotel.

They arrived in Miami on one of Larry's fleet of Learjets, a larger one so that the traveling team could accompany him. The advance team went down the day before, securing vehicles, checking routes, and the convention center. After depositing Larry safely in his house, Eric met with both the regular house and advance teams, and then took two men with him for his visit of the convention facilities. He saw their evaluation reports, but he just wanted to make sure everything was ready with the local police, and the team's liaison member. He also checked their timing schedules and optional routing. He met first with the hotel's security manager, an ex-army guy with a bit of attitude, and together, they walked through the building via the route suggested by the advance team, including Larry's anticipated entrance and exit. Eric approved two more exit routes, so no one could assume Larry would go out the same hallway he came in.

He stepped up to the curtain on the edge of the large stage and peered out into an audience of over ten thousand guests in town for the three-day seminar and convention. Larry would speak in the morning at ten. Satisfied, he shook hands with the ex-army man and turned to leave. They crossed through the lobby on their way to their car, when Eric suddenly stopped and turned his head to the right. For a brief moment, his peripheral vision picked up a walking person that his brain memory cells knew. He turned and began scanning left and right, but could not find the person. After he gave up, he closed his eyes and tried to recall the image, but he had little more than a blur to go on.

"Eric? What's wrong?" asked Robert, a former marine pal, who had been with Eric's company the longest.

"I'm not sure. I think I just saw someone I have spotted before, but I no longer see him. Let's go. I'll think about it."

Tyler got off the hotel's elevator with a middle age man he picked out during the lunch break from the computer seminar. He was trying to learn more about electronics, but found the discussions way over his head. However, he did enjoy visiting the various booths exhibiting the latest electronic gadgetry.

He managed to get his mark to buy him lunch, and then offered to show his room to him. Tyler knew the hotel's cameras were recording his picture as he walked through the hallway and on to the elevator, so he was careful to act as innocent as possible. After they entered the man's room, Tyler wandered around the room looking for something easy to steal, but perhaps not easily missed for a while. While his mark went to the bathroom,

Tyler helped himself to a few large bills from the man's wallet, and scanned several major credit cards with his portable hand scanner. He had trouble scanning the American Express Card so he stole it.

Finding nothing worth risking his identity for, he decided to sell his body for a thousand dollars. When his mark came out of the bathroom, he found Tyler lying naked and hard on his bed. The mark easily paid the thousand in cash, gave Tyler a productive blow job, and then Tyler returned the favor by fucking the man hard and rough. The mark's butt would be sore for a few days.

He counted the cash in the elevator while grinning. He liked earning tax-free cash with no worries of the police chasing him, and besides, he loved having sex several times a day.

The following morning Larry Menard paced back and forth while rehearsing key parts of his speech, and changing shirts and ties until satisfied he looked fine. He came into the sitting area of his suite where Eric and his team patiently waited.

Suddenly filled with stage fright or butterflies about his speech, Larry asked, "Is everyone ready?"

"Yes, my men are ready and the limo is out front waiting. You'll be fine," he added, reading Larry's anxiety correctly. "No one in the audience knows more about electronic stuff than you do."

"Thanks, I needed that. Okay, let's do it."

Eric walked him out, while one of his men opened the door of a sleek white limousine Larry purchased last year. After Eric sat down beside Larry, he glanced back to be sure the tail car was behind them, and then spoke into his sleeve microphone, "Okay, let's go." The lead car pulled away from the mansion and hit the gate button. The three vehicles sped out quickly and picked up a waiting police escort of motorcycles. Eric had timed the route three times, and they arrived precisely in twenty-two minutes as planned. They turned down the long side of the hotel's convention center towards the delivery ramp for the hotel's large kitchen. As soon as the car stopped, everyone bolted from their cars quickly, and briskly walked Larry through the kitchen workers that were busy at various cooking stations, and then they went up a flight of stairs to a dressing room just off the stage to wait for his introduction.

Once Eric and his team had secured Larry in his room, Eric left two men guarding his door, and the rest of his men took up positions in front of the podium, two more agents off to the rear of the stage left and right, and another man to the rear of the auditorium to watch the audience for any sudden late arrivals. He also noted that Steve was sitting on the aisle about twelve rows back, looking very much like the rest of the seminar attendees, and nothing like the former SEAL team leader that he was. He was there just in case someone bolted from the audience or the back doors, and made a run towards the stage. Eric insisted the show's promoter close the entrance doors no less than five minutes before Larry's speech. He didn't care if the audience talked, but he wanted them in a seat so his men could scan their faces, looking for the one face that looked out-of-place, nervous, jittery, fidgeting, or perhaps glancing around the room quickly. They wanted to find the one really oddball in a room filled with perhaps a sea of oddballs and computer geeks.

Once everyone was in position, Eric returned to the rear of the stage and gave the promoter permission to begin. He then walked to the dressing room and retrieved Larry, who took the stage as the promoter finished his introduction. Larry walked out to a standing ovation, and Eric walked about eight steps behind him while remaining just out of the spotlight. Sully appeared on the other side of the stage about the same distance from Larry as Eric. Eric had paid the union guy running the spotlight a hundred bucks to be sure he and Sully remained in the shadows.

Larry fumbled a few opening remarks, nearly ruined a couple of good jokes, but once he got into the topic of his prepared speech, everything went well. Eric refrained from listening to the speech, while he remained focused and concentrating on his job. He began scanning the face and body posture of everyone sitting in the first row, followed by the second and so on. He always scanned the audience for potential troublemakers or assassins. As the speech finished, the audience stood once again to clap for Larry. Eric had just reached the last row with his visual scan, when suddenly, somewhere in the shadows of the dimly lit room, he once again caught sight of the face he saw yesterday. He stared intently across the floor of cheering fans, checking eyes, and then abruptly he stopped as a puzzled expression came across his face. He recognized Tyler from Washington and the bar, or the young man he called Larry of the Three Stooges gang.

Meanwhile, Larry Menard began walking towards him. Eric instantly flipped back into his role as leader, spoke into his sleeve microphone, and sixty seconds later, they were in the limo and pulling out of the hotel garage.

"What did you think?" asked Larry as he downed a bottle of water.
"About what?"
Larry gave Eric a puzzled look. "My speech, of course. How was it?"
"I'm sorry. I didn't listen. It took me the entire speech to scan every pair of eyes in the audience. At the very end, I recognized someone in the last row."
Larry suddenly became alarmed. "Someone you thought might want to kill me?"
Eric looked at him and slightly smiled. "No, this guy would only want to rob you blind. I'll have him checked out to see where he is staying. Don't worry. He'll never get to you. I'll handle it."

16

Once they secured Larry in his house, with the regular security detail back on duty, Eric took a car back to the convention center. On the drive over, he began to refresh his memory with the details on first seeing Tyler when he arrived at the strip bar in Washington. He surprised himself by suddenly remembering his first impression of Tyler. The guy was very handsome, attractive, and surprisingly, he smiled without attitude and smugness. He wondered where in his life Tyler decided to go over to the dark side and into the life of a criminal, preying on the innocent and their desire to feel loved. He recalled Tyler worked with the two other men, and while putting the car in the parking garage he began to mentally sort the pictures of the three men in his brain, along with the new image of Tyler at the speech.

He rode a glass elevator to the convention mezzanine floor, and immediately went to work scanning the crowd below him. Failing to find him, he went down to the main floor. He moved down the hallway outside the huge exhibit room, walking straight down the center and quickly looking left and right, while inspecting each face he found. Failing to once again find Tyler, he entered the large vender display room where he began making his way through the large crowd. It took a half hour to reach the last aisle, and he surmised Tyler was nowhere to be found.

He rode the elevator back down to the main floor and decided to visit his friend in the security office. He thought the young man might appear on their massive security camera program. After a bit of small talk, Eric made his request, the department boss introduced him to what he called his favorite computer geek. Eric sat down at a console where the man worked and smiled at the wall of color monitors stack eight high and twenty-four wide. Everything was live and Eric panned his eyes from screen to screen, but once again failed to find him.

Eric asked, "Reggie, do you have surveillance tape of Larry Menard's speech today?"

Reggie was only twenty-eight, chewed gum rather loudly, remained years behind in obtaining a haircut, but could do just about anything with a control board or a computer system. He smiled. "Yes, I wanted to listen in."

"I don't need to see Larry, I'm interested in a man on the last row near the doors. Do you have any footage of that area?"

"Hmmm…maybe. Give me a second." Reggie began spinning dials, while clicking quickly with his computer mouse, typing rapidly, and a few seconds later, they were looking at eight camera angles on the screens in front of him. He began fast forwarding on the first view, deemed it unworthy, and tapped a lighted button for the second and did the same on several of the feeds.

Eric began to get a headache as he strained his eyes to look at the video feeds. Suddenly he yelled out, "Hold it. Back up a few seconds.

There...freeze it! He is right there," pointed Eric with his index finger, but the picture was too dark.

"Can you enhance that view?"

"Piece of cake," bragged Reggie. He began clicking and dragging, moving lines, and in just a few seconds, he produced a clear shot of Tyler on the screen.

"Print that," ordered Tyler. Reggie handed him the printout and Eric studied it carefully. He looked exactly as he did in Washington without a hint of any disguise or change of appearance. He said nothing, but he thought the guy was beautiful.

Eric stated, "I've seen the surveillance operations in Las Vegas and they have the ability to match a face with footage. I don't suppose you can do that here, can you?"

Reggie laughed and bragged, "Anything they can do, I can do better."

Eric sat back and waited as the screens began rapidly flashing through the video footage, and almost like a slot machine, one by one they began to freeze on Tyler from separate angles, floors, rooms, and even the bar.

"Whoa, excellent. On monitor seven, in the restaurant, he has just entered the room, and he's with this middle age man. Run your computers and tell me who this man is."

"No problem." On a different set of monitors, Reggie quickly found a match for the man.

"Very good, Reggie. I'm impressed. Is this man a guest in your hotel?"

Reggie turned his swivel chair around and slid a few feet across the room, punched some keys on a hotel network computer, brought up the man's record, and printed it out. He handed it to Eric with a smile. "Room 822."

Eric grinned. Okay, now I'm going to impress you. "Fast forward the footage of the boy and man in the restaurant, and I bet you ten bucks they are going to leave together, and go directly to room 822. Do we have a bet?"

Reggie laughed. "I may be a geek, but I'm not stupid. You're a detective, aren't you?"

"Security detail, and I'm sorry I can't say anymore." Eric knew Reggie would wrongly guess he was agent with the government, maybe CIA or Secret Service.

"Yeah, I understand. Let's watch the tape, and I'll keep my money."

He rolled the tape forward at three times speed. Tyler and the man finished their meal, got up and walked out. Reggie hit some keys, punched in the time code, and picked them up in the hall. They got in an elevator.

"Go ahead to the eighth floor camera," said Eric.

Reggie punched keys, brought up the tape, punched in the time code plus two minutes, the elevator opened, and they stepped out. "Well, I'll be. You're right."

"Move on down the hall please, and see if you can see them enter the room."

Reggie switched cameras once more, and saw them enter the room. "You were dead on."

"Okay Reggie. Last request. Tell me where that man is right now. You can use your cameras, picture recognition, and maybe your computer to see if he is using the phone, paying a bill with his credit, or ordering room service. I'll time you. Go!"

Reggie spun around in the chair and started numerous computers and tape machines on the search while typing in the various computers. Twenty-three seconds later, he smiled. "Room Service. He just ordered coffee. He's in his room." Reggie was grinning from ear to ear.

Eric stood and shook his hand. "Reggie, I've worked with the best all around the country and that has to be a new world record. Thank you very much. You've been a great service to your country. Give me your card. We may need to hire you. I'm going to go up and have a chat with that man. Thanks again."

Eric left the geek's office smiling, while knowing that Reggie thought he was saving the president's life or something. He rode the elevator up and walked down the hall to room 822. He listened at the door and then knocked rapidly, "Room Service."

A voice from inside replied, "Well, damn! You are fast. I'll be right there."

Seconds later, he opened the door and Eric pushed in, shut the door, and smiled. "I'm sorry to disturb you Mister Barlow. I need a moment of your time. Eric reached into his coat pocket, retrieved a leather case, and flashed his constable badge, given to him by the governor of the state of Maryland, a client of Eric's agency. He didn't leave his identification wallet open long enough for Barlow to read anything. He also carried an FBI badge, but didn't want to alarm the man.

"What is this about?"

Eric removed the picture of Tyler from his coat pocket, unfolded it and held it up for the man to see. "It's about this young man."

"Hey, wait a minute," began a panicking Barlow, "he said he was twenty-four."

"Let's sit down a moment," ordered Eric politely as he took the chair leaving the sofa for a now pale Barlow.

"I don't care about any tryst. I just want to ask you some questions about him. Think back carefully. Did you walk up to him or did he walk up to you when you first met? I'm betting he did the walking, am I right?"

"Yes, that's right."

"You chatted for a while, found him handsome, no that's not right. You found him gorgeous."

Barlow blushed. "I'm afraid so."

"Did he tell you he was hungry, and you suggested lunch, and of course he said yes?"

Barlow replied, "Right again."

"After the meal, did he imply he would like to see your room, which you agreed, thinking perhaps you might get lucky with this young man?" Eric let the man suffer with the question before going on, "Did you leave him alone in this room at any point?"

"Yes, I'm afraid I had to go to the bathroom. I think I ate too fast."

Eric smiled knowing the truth was the man was so excited he almost shit himself. "Did you notice anything missing after he left?"

"No, we had a good..." he stopped himself before continuing, "uh, a good talk. He was a nice young man. He gave me his number."

"It's probably a false number, but read it out to me." Eric possessed a well-trained mind and a photographic memory. He stored the number in his brain immediately. "Take out your pocket money and count it."

Barlow did as told and his face became puzzled. "I cashed a two thousand dollar traveler's check this morning. I have only two hundred and change left."

"Go through your credit cards. Or there any cards missing?"

Rapidly Barlow searched through a dozen cards and realized his American Express card was gone. He told Eric.

"Do you have any remaining travel checks?"

"I had three, and each was for two thousand. I paid...huh, I mean I felt sorry for the young man and gave him a thousand dollars."

"I wonder what he gave you," replied Eric somberly. After letting the man squirm for a minute he asked, "What name did he use?"

"Tim."

Eric laughed. "I can assure it that was not his real name. He didn't give you a last name, did he?" Barlow shook his head no. "Okay, I'm going to leave. I suggest you get on the phone to American Express and alert them that someone stole your wallet so they can put a hold on our credit card. I'd also call your other credit card companies just in case he scanned your cards. I'd be more careful in the future. He is a thief and very good one, but if he had been a murderer, you would already be dead. Good day."

Eric paused long enough to see the blood drain from Barlow's face. He opened the door just as the room service waiter was about to knock.

Eric left the hotel knowing that in case of alarm, a good con like Tim would have left the property immediately, so Eric left and returned to Larry's compound. He checked on his crew and went to his room. He sat down on the bed while looking at Tim's picture, and at first, he saw him as a criminal, but after a while, he saw the young man differently, and wondered what he was really like. In time, he found himself attracted and a surprise erection formed.

Suddenly, he tossed the picture to the floor, laughed at himself, and said aloud, "This is not the type of boyfriend he could take home to momma." He laughed again, and then closed his eyes for a nap.

Tyler took a cab and left the hotel immediately. His roommates didn't attend the computer show, so his partners didn't know about his theft of the man's money and he didn't plan to tell them. Stephen's rule list plainly stated no crimes on their home turf. He stopped at his bank, put the cash in his safe deposit box, and returned to the cab. He went to a mall a long way from their house and paid the driver. He went to an electronic store and watched for security cameras. Seeing none, he went in and bought a new iPod with maximum memory that he wanted and paid for it with the mark's credit card. He left the mall quickly after tossing the credit card in a trashcan. He rode the bus over to another mall, and then caught a cab for the ride home.

At dinner, Larry announced that he wanted to go out that night. This came as no surprise, so Eric didn't protest the short notice, nor did he remind him of the danger. Unlike most of his clients, he accepted that Larry would never fully follow Eric's suggestions on how to keep safe, because his ego and libido were never quite satisfied. He assigned a driver to remain with the car while he and Sam accompanied Larry into the club. Larry wore his disguise and sunglasses, so he could stare at the boys without someone recognizing him, since they couldn't see his eyes.

The club was huge and they had been there before. Eric felt an attack, or an attempt on Larry during a surprise visit to the club unlikely, and joked that he was more likely to be killed by a person whose computer crashed repeatedly from using Larry's software. However, Eric was professional in every way, and though they tried not to look like bodyguards, he never let his guard down. They went with Larry everywhere in the club, including the busy bathrooms.

They even found themselves dancing amongst a pulsating throng of over two hundred men, jiving and laughing across the oak floor as the lights swirled about their heads. Every half hour, Eric would check his watch, but although Larry appeared to be having a great time, Sam and Eric were beyond bored, and couldn't wait to leave. Continually scanning the room, he forced his brain to keep scrutinizing the dance floor and the room for potential problems, and that helped pass the time.

About two in a morning, a face near the edge of the dance floor caught his attention. The lights were glaring into his eyes, but after moving off to the right, he realized he spotted Jim and Stephen, alias Curly and Moe, the two men Tim worked with in Washington. He studied their faces when the brighter lights hit them, and stored their facial features into his brain. He wondered if they were on the hunt, and so he continued to watch them as nonchalantly as possible.

Over the next half hour, he perceived they apparently knew many patrons of the club, as various men came up and gave them a hug, laughing at his various comments. He counted over a dozen who spoke to them. He thought about that for a while, deciding they were probably not preying for victims here, as this might be a home club or a frequently visited club.

He thought about this for a few minutes, and wondered if Tim was there. He began scanning the room looking for a match like Reggie did with his computers. There were seven hundred men and a few drag queens, but one by one he looked at every face, instantly discounted their features, and moved to the next one. He had just about made it all the way around the room and back to the two men, when suddenly as if on cue, Tim, as he now called him, appeared.

The gorgeous young man was laughing and somewhat drunk, while chatting incessantly with two men who laughed in return. He was but thirty feet away and now he could see his height, hair color, smooth skin, hairless arms, and green eyes when the flashing lights caught them just right.

He yelled into Sam's ear on the dance floor. "Keep an eye out. I have to take a leak. I'll be right back."

Sam nodded and continued pretending to dance just a few feet from a mildly drunk Larry, who was dancing with a group of overweight acquaintances, all of whom appeared to be harmless.

Eric deliberately walked right pass Tim and got a good close look at him. He heard his voice and cached it in his brain. He also glanced once or twice at the other men, so he would always be able to recognize them. He went into the bathroom, filled with men talking, flirting, making out, feeling one another, and sometimes they enjoyed a quickie in the corner. He went to a pee trough about six-feet long where men stood shoulder to shoulder and let it fly.

Eric began urinating when he heard Tim come into the bathroom. He loudly spoke to a few friends, and then abruptly walked over to the trough, standing right beside Eric. He kept his eyes to the front, but Tim was swaying with the music and the alcohol. Eric glanced down as Tim finally started peeing, noting a large penis.

To his surprise, Tim laid his head over against his shoulder. "What's a tall good looking fellow like you hanging out in a club like this? Where's your husband?"

Eric looked over and smiled at him, but didn't remove Tim's head. Tim might remember him if he stomped out of the bathroom, having said nothing, or cursing away at Tim before leaving, so he did the opposite and played along. "Hi, I'm afraid there is no partner."

Tim moved his head downward looking directly at Eric's penis as he finished peeing. "How come?" asked Tim and then loudly, "You've got a great dick!"

Eric knew he blushed as he shook the dew from his lily and put it back in his pants.

"Wait a minute. I wasn't through looking," said Tim as he reached inside his pants and held Eric by his member, which began to swell. "I like the feel of this, but we haven't been properly introduced. Tim took Eric's right hand, placed his larger penis in it, and squeezed his hand around it. "That's better," laughed Tim. "My name is Tyler. And you are?"

Eric felt funny while standing at the trough holding his suspect's dick in his hand, but it also felt wonderful to him, and it had been a while since someone held his dick in their warm hand. He noted the softness of Tyler's hands. "I'm Eric. It's nice to meet you."

"The same here and I really like your dick. Can I tell you a secret?"

Eric replied, "Sure."

Tyler took his free hand and pointed with his index finger, signaling for Eric to bend his head down towards him, so he could whisper something. When Eric followed his finger down, Tyler leaned in and Eric could now smell him. Tyler started to whisper, but suddenly turned his head and kissed Eric on the mouth.

Eric wanted to pull back, but the enticing warm mouth and instant penetrating tongue weakened him. They held each other dicks, while swirling their tongues in and out and around each other's mouth, and Eric loved it. Tyler had done this same scene many times at clubs around the world, and once got thrown out of an upscale club because of the dick holding. Most folks just smiled and laughed, while wishing the handsome boy was holding their dick instead. However, in spite of the alcohol, he found himself kissing longer and harder than ever before.

Tim finally broke the kiss. "I'm sorry. I would like to get to know you, now that I have held your big cock. Can we go talk in the lounge?"

"Sure," replied Eric, as reluctantly he let go and they both zipped up. Tyler took his hand and let him through the crowd. They made their way to the front of the club, found a couch, sat down close together, and began talking. Amazingly, Tyler almost immediately appeared sober, giving Eric an indication that perhaps Tyler had been faking intoxication, so he could ask forgiveness for his forward behavior, or perhaps it was a disarming disguise while selecting a mark to rob of their cash.

Eric and Tyler began chatting, with Eric steering the conversation to learn more about Tyler, who said he lived with two roommates and worked for a doctor by managing his insurance billing. Almost immediately, he followed up his occupation and living arrangement statement, by saying he could not have guests over. Eric didn't believe he worked as an insurance clerk, but suspected the other two thieves were his roommates.

Eric laughed while telling him they had occupations in common, as he was an insurance adjuster, a cover he had used many times. He had business cards in his wallet for this career if needed, with a telephone number that went to an answering service. He kept a fake office and apartment in Baltimore at the address on the card.

Eric easily let Tyler do most of the talking, while picking up bits of information here and there, and wondering which points were true. The good-looking man said that he was an only child, and did two years of college study before having to drop out because his mother got sick and died. He said his dad split not long after he came out of the closet and told them he was gay.

Eric wanted to ask about his friends, but the subject never came up, and he knew better than to show any interest in someone he supposedly never met.

Tyler surprised him by leaning into him and kissing him again. "Let's go to your place," he whispered seductively into his ear.

Eric wished he could have said yes. "I can't. I'm in town with friends."

Tyler quickly asked, "How about tomorrow night?"

Eric thought quickly. "That would probably work. Is there a number where I can call you?"

"I'll give you my cell number."

Eric thought this was too easy, as he could trace the number in a few minutes, get the address, his correct name, and more, but Tyler did an odd thing. He took a pen from his pocket, opened Eric's hand to write the number, but then he couldn't remember the number. He flipped opened his cell phone, because he had written the number around the edge and copied it to his hand.

"There you have my number and if you don't call me, I'll assume you thought I was ugly and smelled bad."

Eric laughed. "Well, I didn't think you smelled bad."

Tyler pretended to hit him. "So you think I am ugly."

Eric pulled him into his muscled arms. "I think you are gorgeous, but there is something mysterious behind those amazing green eyes. I can't wait to get to know every square inch of you—inside and out."

"That sounds like fun. I'll look forward to your call."

They kissed several times more and then said goodbye.

On the way back to Larry's house, Eric remained deep in thought about his encounter with Tyler, alias Tim, alias Larry. Why did he have to look up his cell number? Then he smiled because he knew the answer. He would trace it in the morning, but he was confident Tyler's cell phone was one of those throwaway untraceable phones, and that he must have just purchased this one, as he couldn't remember the new number. He thought, these guys are pros, and they are very careful.

THREE

The rest of the security detail flew back the next morning with Larry, their client. Eric said he needed a few days to follow-up on a lead on the face he saw in the back of the auditorium. No one questioned him, and so he left the airport and returned to the hotel. He set up his laptop and went to work on the information he accumulated thus far from Tyler. He was correct on the phone being a throw away, but one of technical guys at the home office traced the phone number, obtained a serial number from the actual phone, that led to a brand name and a distributor, and an hour later, he managed to find out what store sold Tyler the phone.

It was only ten blocks away, and it was a Radio Shack. He took Tyler's picture with him and visited the store. He spoke with the clerk behind the counter who didn't recall Tyler. He was just about to leave, when the owner of the store came in with a box of donuts, and asked if he could help. Eric showed him the picture and the guy laughed.

"Do I remember him? He was the biggest SOB I have ever had in here. He asked me if I had a rainbow phone. I didn't catch on to what he meant, but after taking a second look at him, I realized he was a faggot. He wanted a phone painted like the gay flag. I said no, I didn't have one like that, but I had a pink one. That's what pissed him off. He settled on a gray one. He bought two thousand minutes."

"Do you require any personal identification for this phone?"

"No, the point of a pay advance phone is there no paperwork."

Eric asked, "How did he pay for it?"

"He gave me cash in the form of a hundred dollar bill. I screened the bill to make sure it was good and that got his dander up once again. As he left, I wished him a nice day, and he said for me to go fuck myself."

Eric sighed. "Well, if he comes back, will you call me?"

"Sure, but what's this all about?"

With a hint of a lie Eric replied, "His sister is dying in Omaha and they sent me to find him before she goes. Thank you for your trouble." Eric gave him his card and a fifty-dollar bill.

Eric drove around the block checking the streets, hoping to spot Tyler. He widened his circle and continued doing so until ten blocks out from the store. He then pulled under a shade tree. He dialed Tyler.

"Hello?"

Eric smiled. "Did I wake you up?"

Tyler yawned. "No, I was just resting my eyes."

"You didn't have to work today?"

"Work? Uh, no, I had the day off, as I had to work last Saturday," he lied. "How are you?"

"I'm horny and was just thinking of you. How about dinner tonight?"

Tyler smiled as he played with himself. "Sounds good. What time and where?"

"Can you meet me at Apollo's Restaurant at 827 Robertson Street at 7?"

Tyler grinned. "Hell yes I can. That is an awesome, but expensive Italian restaurant."

"Don't worry, I'm buying. Meet me there at seven. Do you think you can wake up by then?" Eric was teasing, but there was some truth in his question.

Tyler laughed. "Yeah, I think so." He yawned. "I can't wait to see you and uh, taste you."

"Same here and I'll see you then."

Eric went back to the hotel and booked another room. After securing the keys, he took a few clothes, toiletries, and moved into the other room leaving behind all his valuables, his laptop, rings, and necklace, took two hundred dollars out of his wallet and left it in the room. He went back downstairs and got change for his large bills. He asked the clerk to hold his key to his first room.

He drove to the restaurant, and began scoping out the area until he found a spot where he could see all the arrivals to the restaurant. Satisfied, he drove back to his new room and took a nap. He woke at six, dressed, and left for the restaurant forty-five minutes early. He parked his car in the restaurant's parking lot, went in and reserved a table for seven. He left saying he had to do a little shopping.

Once out of sight of anyone in the restaurant, he crossed the street and made his way to the small corner market, where he could stand inside and observe traffic coming and going. He bought a pack of breath mints. Everything he did was something he had done many times while doing security surveillance. He forgot nothing.

When a cab rolled up, Eric spotted Tyler in the back paying the bill, noted the cab number, and then he stepped out and walked up to the restaurant and went in. Eric looked up and down the street for Tyler's partners. He waited ten minutes and failing to find them, he crossed the street and entered the restaurant. Tyler was waiting on a bench feeling a little disappointed.

"Hey, Tyler, how are you? I'm sorry. I arrived early and went down the street looking for a store. Do you want a breath mint?"

Tyler smiled. "Are you trying to tell me something?"

Eric laughed. "No, I'm not brave enough to tell you your breath stinks. Come on let's sit down. I'm starved, and I bet you are hungry?"

"I haven't eaten all day."

The waiter led them to their table in a corner.

Eric stole glances at Tyler while they were both looking at the menus, and marveled at how naturally handsome Tyler was. He was fair skin with a little bit of tan, and his green eyes seemed to sparkle with excitement. The sun had whitened his blond hair, and his medium length hair just naturally fell in place. Tyler caught him looking and instantly smiled. A pair of dimples fell inward in his cheeks. He winked at Eric. "So what do you think?"

Eric laughed. "I think you look different from what you did in the club."

"And that's bad?"

"Hell no, you're better looking in broad daylight. I just love your eyes."

"Thanks, you're good-looking, too. Why don't you order for both of us? This menu has too many Italian words for my brain."

"Okay, I'll pick out something special for us." Eric nodded towards the waiter and began rapidly telling the man what they wanted. He then chose a wine and gave the waiter the menus. He came back with the wine a few minutes later, performed the usual approval ceremony, and poured two glasses of wine.

After he left, Tyler tasted the wine. "Oh my, this is really good."

"Just sip it as it is strong. Hold it in your mouth a minute to savor the flavor," instructed Eric.

Tyler laughed. "Are you talking about the wine or sex?"

Eric grinned. "The wine you rascal. Are you already horny?"

Tyler asked, "What time is it?"

Eric looked at his watch. "About a quarter past seven. Why?"

Tyler smiled slyly. "That means I have been horny for fourteen years, six months, 12 days, and nine hours."

"Or in other words, since puberty, huh?"

"Yep. I learned to masturbate early on. I think I was born with a large dick, and I did all I could to encourage it to grow."

"Do you live around here?" asked Eric as the waiter brought an order of mozzarella cheese sticks and sauce to the table, and refreshed the wine glasses. Eric took a bite of a stick and tried not to be seriously interested in Tyler.

"I live with two friends, a gay couple. I rent a room from them," he lied.

Eric noted he did not say what neighborhood or street, but to avoid suspicion he asked an unrelated question, "I bet you're a good dancer. You have a hell of a body."

"You haven't seen all of my body, at least not yet," teased Tyler.

"I could tell when we were kissing and I was holding you."

"You were holding my dick," grinned Tyler.

Eric laughed. "Yes, of course, but it was so...muscular!"

27

Tyler laughed as the waiter brought their salads to the table, and added a twist of fresh ground pepper with a bit of flair. "Do you live here?"

Eric anticipated this question and told Tyler his cover location. "I live and work in Baltimore. It's a great old city," he added as if he had always lived there with great pride. It has the most savoring seafood in the world, and I just love the smell of the sea. It also has a huge gay population, but I rarely go out at home anymore."

"Baltimore sounds nice. I flew in there once when there was a problem on the runway at Reagan National. They bused us to D.C. and I got there exhausted at two in the morning."

"You'll have to give Baltimore another try. I could show you around. You'd love it."

The waiter took away the salads with Eric noting that Tyler devoured every morsel of his salad except the radishes. The waiter quickly returned with their dinner. Tyler smiled as he set down the steaming lasagna that took up the third of a huge platter, along with portions of chicken Francesca and chicken Parmesan. The waiter gave each patron a clean white plate, and set another basket of hot garlic bread onto the table.

"That is a pile of food!" exclaimed a hungry Tyler.

"Since I didn't know what you liked, I ordered three things that I happen to like, and I hope you do." He began pointing as the three dishes explaining what they were. "Okay, take those two large spoons and serve yourself some of each, and then tell me which one you like the most."

Eric took several bites and began asking more questions. "Are you an only child?"

Tyler gulped down another wonderful bite of the lasagna. "I can't remember tasting lasagna this good."

"Try the fresco."

Tyler took a bite of the tender chicken and grinned. "Oh my, this is so good. To answer your question, how did you know?"

"Know what?"

"That I was an only child." Tyler took a bite of the chicken Parmesan.

"Boys with green eyes, cute dimples, and blond hair are always an only child." Eric made his statement with great stoic seriousness. He quickly took a bite of his dinner.

Tyler suddenly stopped chewing. "Is that true?"

Eric put his hand up indicating for Tyler to hold on while he chewed, and chewed, and chewed. Tyler sat there mesmerized and anxious for the answer. Finally, Eric swallowed and started to talk, but stopped and took a sip of the wine.

Tyler said, "Any week now will be fine."

Eric smiled. "No, it is not true."

Tyler laughed loudly, with a great smile. "Then how in the heck did you know?"

"I had a fifty-fifty shot at it. You were either an only child or not. I take it you don't gamble?"

"Hell no, I can't keep a secret. My face always shows what kind of cards I have. I am horrible at poker, but pretty good at playing blackjack. When I was little, I would camp out with the boys in the neighborhood. They would play strip poker and cheat on me, and I would be naked in four hands. Then the next time I lost, I had to do stuff to the winner. That was the beginning of my sex education. They thought it was punishment. I thought the sex was fun."

"How's the dinner? Have some more wine?"

"The meal is great. Thank you so much. I can't pick a winner, but I think if I did, it would be the lasagna. It just melts in your mouth."

"I like it, too. I come to Miami several times a year on business and one time I accidentally discovered this restaurant. Since then I make a point to find time to eat here each trip. Did you notice the staff?"'

Tyler gave him a puzzled look while stuffing his mouth with a bite of chicken. He began looking around the room. "I don't see anything unusual. There are quite a few good-looking waiters here."

"The restaurant is owned by a gay couple and all the staff including the dishwashers are gay men. There was a rainbow decal in the door, but I guess that in Miami there are many establishments that are gay friendly. I just thought it was cool they were gay owned and excelled so wonderfully. I always tip very well. So let's see, you're an only child, how did your parents handle you were gay?"

"They knew I was different early on. My friends considered me a sissy, and I came home with my shirt torn and a black eye more than once. I found out what gay was when I was about twelve, but at thirteen, I told mom and dad I was gay. Mom cried but dad didn't say a word. He got up, went down the hall, threw some of my clothes in a brown grocery bag, came back to the living room and tossed the bag to me. He grabbed my arm, and flung me out the front door. I never saw them again."

Eric felt great sadness at how horrible his father had treated him. "I'm sorry. I shouldn't have asked."

Tyler smiled slightly. "You asked because you are interested in me, and not just my fabulous body, right?"

Eric grinned. "Yes, that's true. I find myself strangely attracted to you, and I don't just mean sexually. You're just so much fun to talk with and be with, and well, I feel so comfortable with you."

"So how was your coming out party?"

Eric knew Tyler was changing the subject and he was glad he did. He felt bad for stirring up a bad memory for Tyler. "I have three brothers and one younger sister. I was as macho as could be growing up, playing high school

29

football and baseball, and went to college on a football scholarship. However, once in college, I began to notice other gay people, and one night I discovered the college town had a gay bar. I about shit in my pants, but I got up the nerve to go in and the rest his history. My folks are very religious, so they said they were glad I told them, but they said if I did gay sex, I would go to hell. My parents and I are still friends, but they live in Vermont, and I don't get up there often. When I date, I usually go out in Baltimore and sometimes in Washington."

Tyler said, "I like going out in Washington, but I only get there about once a year."

Eric thought he was probably telling the truth, as they would play it safe and wait a year before returning to scene of the crime. The waiter began clearing away the extra food, after he poured the last of the wine in their glasses, he soon returned in a few minutes with dessert and coffee.

After the waiter left, Tyler asked, "What kind of cake is that?"

"Carrot cake. It is not only the best carrot cake in the country, it is somewhat healthy because it has carrots in it."

With a bit of apprehension Tyler took a small bite. Eric waited and watched the young man's eyes light up.

"Oh my! This is delicious." He quickly forked bite after bite. Eric began eating his after nodding at the waiter, and ordering a second slice for Tyler, who gleefully gobbled it down as well.

Eric signed the credit card receipt, and laughed at Tyler. "Are you full?"

Tyler wiped his mouth with the cloth napkin. "I have never eaten or enjoyed such a wonderful meal as this. It was stupendous. I can't thank you enough."

"I'm glad you enjoyed it as much as I did. Why don't we take a walk and shake down a little of the food?"

They left the restaurant with Tyler telling all the staff how much he enjoyed the meal. He gave the waiter a hug. This act touched Eric. He began to feel that the young man was starving for affection and love. They walked a block, took a left, and soon they were walking along the boardwalk with the moon rising over the ocean. They were never at a loss for words.

Tyler reached over and took Eric's hand in his, look up into his eyes, and standing on tiptoes, he kissed him on the mouth. They kissed several more times before Tyler said, "Let's go to your hotel."

Eric replied quickly, "No, I'm sorry. I don't believe in having sex on the first date with someone I am falling for."

Tyler's mouth fell open. He had never been turned down in his entire life. "What?"

Eric laughed. "Gotcha!"

Tyler hit him in the shoulder playfully and laughed.

"I think we should go to my room so we can avoid the chance of getting beat up on the street. But you don't have to feel like having sex with me just because I paid for dinner."

"Would you stop talking and just take me there?"

Eric replied, "My car is at the restaurant."

"Let's go!"

Eric parked his car in the hotel's eight-story garage so they could avoid the lobby when entering the hotel. On the elevator ride, Tyler grabbed Eric's crotch and giggled like a schoolgirl when Eric blushed. Eric opened the door to his second room, allowing the grinning Tyler to enter first. Eric followed, turned around and put the 'do not disturb' sign on the door, and made sure he locked the deadbolt. When he turned around, he discovered a completely naked Tyler with a growing hard-on in front of him.

"How in the hell did you get out of your clothes so fast?"

Tyler laughed. "Just like 'how do you get to Carnegie Hall.' You know, practice, practice, and practice!"

Eric smiled. "You look amazing." With each answer, he took another step towards Tyler.

Tyler replied slyly, "You were talking about my eyes, no?"

"Of course."

"Or was it my nose?"

"Yes, it is beautiful, too."

"My face?"

"Outstanding."

"My chest?"

"Worth devouring."

"My legs?"

"Lick-able."

"Is that a word?"

"I don't know, but the results are the same."

Tyler laughed. "And my dick?"

It had grown steadily with each passing second of their repartee. With a steady poker face, Eric replied, "What dick?"

Tyler, taken aback, anticipated the best compliment reserved for his special appendage. "What?"

"I can't see your dick due the radiance of your entirely beautiful, gorgeous body, and the amazing smile creeping slowly across your magnificent face."

"You're full of shit!" laughed Tyler. "Come here."

Eric walked the final steps to him and Tyler almost leaped into his arms. He placed Eric's hands on this bare backside, leaving Tyler's hands free to begin removing Eric's clothes. Tyler's tongue went deep inside Eric's mouth. Eric could feel the boy's large penis bumping against his stomach.

Twenty seconds later, with nudity finally accomplished, Tyler led him to the bed.

They said little, allowing their desires to seek maximum anticipation. After a while, Tyler spun around so they could begin sucking each other at the same time. Tyler expertly pulled off his penis, and squeezed hard as the base to prevent Eric from coming too soon, yet he possessed an amazing self-control over his own sexual functions. He was as hard as possible, but mentally he controlled his climax. Tyler waited a while before going down on Eric once more, and eight minutes later, he again pulled off and squeezed.

Eric thought his eyes were going to pop out, and his penis felt like it could not possibly get any harder. It almost ached with ecstasy. He suspected that though he was in fantastic physical shape with what his doctor called the heart of a lion, he knew if Tyler did this a few more times, Eric would most likely have a heart attack.

Tyler continued sucking and stopping for two more times before grabbing a condom from the stack he placed on the bed from his pocket before stripping, and quickly placed it on Eric's tool. He then straddled Eric and slowly slid the enlarged latex covered penis into his anus, bent over and began kissing Eric deeply while rotating his buttocks up and down slowly, and deeply.

From time to time, he would break the kiss, and tenderly bite Eric's nipples or his ear lobes, and then swirl his wet tongue deep into his ear. Eric was sure he was stroking his brain and the feeling was electrifying. The wet tongue soon rolled across his cheek slowly and back to his waiting warm mouth. In time, Tyler picked up his thrusting rhythm and Eric began to moan with great delight. Sensing near ejaculation, Tyler went into hyperactive mode, plunging his body downward where Eric's penis slammed playfully and with great delight into Tyler's prostate gland, sending great shock waves of energy throughout his body. He repeated the thrusts until Eric sighed loudly as his blew the largest load of his life into the condom. Meanwhile, Tyler pushed the swollen balloon as far into him as possible.

He then froze and let Eric catch his breath, kissed him several times while pulling out, and then without looking, he opened another condom and rolled it on his tenacious looking tool. Eric had not been a bottom in a long time, wondering if his body could handle Tyler's huge member, but Tyler never doubted it. He continued his swirling tongue kiss after stopping to wet his two longest fingers and gently began probing Eric's butt. Eric knew how to tighten and loosen, and Tyler let him do so as he carefully pushed deeper into Eric's anus until he could feel his prostate like a medical physician.

Once satisfied, with Eric still on his back, Tyler spread Eric's legs, knelt between them, and then smiled at Eric wickedly. Slowly, carefully, and cautiously, he began sliding his member in until the couple became one. Tyler could feel Eric's heartbeat as the end of his penis bumped gently against Eric's pulsating prostate gland. With his soft tender beautiful hands on Eric's hips, Tyler began pulling outward until the lip of penis almost came out, and then he quickly reversed motion, pushing in until he felt the gland once more. He repeated this love making maneuver over and over, sending Eric into a plateau of delirious wonderment.

Tyler took his time, enjoying the ride for over thirty minutes until finally, he picked up a rapid pace and plunged deeper and deeper into Eric, going on pass the prostate gland and sending the handsome man into a mild shaking shock like the result of a defibrillator bringing a heart back to life.

When Tyler let loose of his juice, he physically groaned as if someone had twisted one of his toes off, and then he fell into Eric's arms. It was another twenty minutes before they could remove themselves from the sweat soaked bed and head to the shower, while throwing the sausage-like condoms into the trashcan.

They gently washed each other from head to toe, patted each other softly with the towels, and then thru the covers back on the bed, and fell into the sheets to kiss and intertwine their bodies until they were fast asleep.

About three in the morning, Eric gently removed himself from Tyler's spooning embrace, and made his way to the bathroom to pee. In the flash of two seconds, he pocketed Tyler's cell phone. In the bathroom, he removed a hidden electronic device, popped the memory chip out of the phone, and placed it in the device where he rapidly copied the information. He then put the chip back in and began peeing. He flushed the toilet with the door closed, and replaced Tyler's battery with one of Oscar's that included a GPS chip. He tested the phone by turning it on, then he cut off the light, and as he made his way to the bed, he returned the phone to Tyler's clothes.

Eric assumed that sometime during the night Tyler would also arise, rob him of his money and any other valuables, and make a quiet exit, hoping to never see Eric again.

However, when Eric awoke at fifteen past nine, late for his usual early start for the day, he found Tyler still sleeping in his arms. He kissed his forehead and his nose. Tyler opened his eyes, and Eric kissed him deeply. To his surprise, Tyler was already hard, and he pulled Eric's warm hand to his penis. Tyler reached for Eric's penis and found it a bit softer but growing quickly. They played and kissed for a while before Tyler finally said he was starving.

They ordered a huge breakfast via room service, dressed and chatted away. Tyler ate everything on the cart except what Eric managed to quickly eat himself. How the boy stayed so physically fit, while devouring food like a horse, well, it amazed and perplexed him?

"What are you doing tonight?" asked Tyler after finishing the last of the apple crepes.

"I have some work to do today, but I could be free by six. How about you?"

Tyler smiled. "I am already late for work, but they are used to it. I'd like to see you tonight."

"And I you. Shall I pick you up at six as your house?" Eric was testing him.

"No, it is hard to find, I'll just meet you here."

"Excellent. I will look forward to it. Do you want a ride home?"

"No, I'll just take a cab. No problem."

They kissed many times, and said goodbye about six times until finally, the door closed and Eric was alone at the edge of the bed.

Eric counted to five, then walked quickly to the door, and listened to see if Tyler was still there. Hearing nothing, he dropped to his feet and tried to look under the door, but it had a good floor sweep. Though Tyler had dressed, Eric remained in his boxer shorts. He checked his pants and to his amazement, all his money was there, including the fifty-one cents in coins he left on the corner of the dresser. Tyler hadn't stolen anything but his heart.

FOUR

Eric dressed, rushed out the door, ran down the stairs to the parking garage, retrieved an electronic device from the trunk of his car, placed it in the seat beside him, and quickly drove down and around the parking deck floors and onto the street. He checked to be sure Tyler wasn't in front of the hotel. He pulled over to the curb and opened the device that was like a small laptop. He hit the power button and instantly it began to beep and purr, and then produced a full color street map, showing a red dot moving away.

He drove two blocks and pulled into another hotel parking lot. He locked his car and with the device in his hands, he opened a second rental car from another company that delivered it to this hotel. He had picked up the keys from the front desk earlier. He thought it was an ugly car with a bright red color and dark tinted windows. He thought it looked like a pimp mobile, and set off again following Tyler's tracking blinking beacon on the small computer.

The tiny dot in the cell phone had an amazing range and in minutes, he was just two blocks behind Tyler as he sat in the cab taking him to his home with the other two grifters.

Eric had been following Tyler for almost thirty minutes when the cab finally exited the freeway, turned back east, and within about twelve blocks, the quality of the housing immediately turned rich. The properties became much larger, the manicured lawns a dark green, and soon fences began surrounding the compounds, including big wrought iron electric gates.

Two blocks later, they went over a canal bridge, putting this upscale neighborhood directly on the eastern shore, and probably only a few miles south of Fort Lauderdale. Eric slowed down when he saw the brakes light come on at the next intersection. The driver made a right turn and pulled to the curb. Eric immediately pulled off the road behind a parked car.

Tyler got out of the cab, and paid the driver. As the cab sped away, Tyler crossed the street, walked a block south and turned left. Eric had to be extremely cautious, as there was very little traffic along the route to hide his location. As soon as Tyler turned left, Eric made the last right turn, did a quick U-turn, and carefully pulled to a stop so he could see down the street Tyler had just taken. The boy crossed this street diagonally and walked almost to the end of the next block, retrieved a key chain from his pocket with a small beeper device. He held it up and hit the button, and the gate to the property on his right began opening. He walked in as Eric moved down the same street, but slowed in front of the house before moving on to the next block to avoid suspicion. He made a mental note of the house number and the street name, as well as the GPS coordinates.

He turned right and went a full block to get to the end of Tyler's compound and took another right. He found a rear entrance, but he spotted the security gate and didn't slow down as he passed it. He drove on to the end of the block, and the only consistent thing he found was the ten-foot fence surrounding the entire lot, but partially hidden with numerous trees, landscaping plants, and big bushes.

He parked far up the street leading to the front entrance in a spot where he could see the front gate, and decided to watch it for a while just in case he got lucky and spotted the other two men. He wanted to find out where they took the stolen loot, but while sitting there he began to surmise the situation. He initially pursued Tyler thinking he would find the thieves and turn them in, but the crime was several states away, and he had no identity of the victim, and even if he did, maybe not a willingness to prosecute. So he asked himself, why was he here?

It took a few minutes for him to accept the simple fact that he was deeply attracted to Tyler. He thought Tyler was a great guy, with a beautiful body, a childlike sense of humor, and a sexual giant, but he wondered if Tyler was worth going after?

He wasn't sure of the relationship that Tyler had with the two older thieves, and what power they might have over him. Apparently he could come and go as he pleased, but it was obvious he was not allowed to tell anyone where he lived or bring a stranger home. He thought about their lives and what it must be like to pull con jobs on unsuspecting victims. Looking at the neighborhood and upscale automobiles, he assumed they must be highly successful. He calculated they may have collected a thousand dollars at the bar, but if their mark took Tyler home, they might have robbed his house of all the valuables. He knew that for them to live in this super rich neighborhood they were stealing more than the cash and rings off a victim. Perhaps, they were blackmailing the victims as well, he thought.

Suddenly, a deep dark thought crossed his mind, so he popped out his cell phone and called his secretary. "Hey, Marti, how are you?"

"Hey, boss, How's Miami?"

"Not too hot, clear skies, and palm trees swaying."

"Life is tough, huh?" she said.

"Yeah, real tough. I need a favor. I want you to get our research team busy, and see if there are burglaries involving murder in Washington..." he gave the date he had first spotted Tyler. She relayed a few messages to him and hung up.

He didn't think Tyler was capable of murder, but he had no idea about the other guys. He set his mobile phone on the seat and looked up just in time to see a pale yellow Bentley automobile pull out of the gate and turned directly towards Eric.

Eric quickly slouched down in the seat, retrieved a hat from the passenger seat, and pulled the brim almost down to his dark sunglasses. There were two passengers, and when they reached the intersection he confirmed it was the two other men. He decided to follow them. He let them go two blocks before pulling out in traffic to trail them.

Eric turned right somewhere in southeastern side of Fort Lauderdale and glanced at the clock on the dash. Tailing the two men had taken forty-eight minutes so far, while giving him the impression they weren't out shopping and picking up some groceries. He once again chided himself for getting involved as he made yet another turn on to a six-lane main road leading him pass an upscale shopping center and into an older part of the city. He saw the men slow in front of the largest pawnshop Eric had ever seen, guessing it to be about the size of a major drug store.

However the men didn't slow down and park in front as expected, but drove on to the next intersection and turned right. Eric cautiously made his way to the turn, but the moment he saw the car pull alongside the back of the building, he continued straight while avoiding the last turn and revealing the tail. He moved up a block and made a left u-turn and pulled over across the street so he could see down the side of the building. He immediately spotted one of the men carrying a sample case through the back door followed by the second man closing the trunk of the car and carrying a similar case towards the door.

He knew the men were not the type to shop at a Pawn store. Selling their loot through the front door would require red tape, information, and identification, something successful thieves like these would avoid. He thought about it a while running scenarios through his brain until he had an idea.

He picked his cell phone and dialed his office. "Marti? Eric again. How are you?"

She wondered how he knew she was eating a donut at her desk and blushed. "Oh, I'm fine. What's up?"

"I want a report on AAA Pawn Shop at 312 Rivers Avenue in Fort Lauderdale. Phone number..." he was reading their big yellow sign on the street in front of the store. "Find out the name of the owner and if he has ever done time, or any other arrest info. I want to know everything about him. Also, find out who owns the house at 16 Watkins Boulevard, Miami. There could be two men who own it and if so, run a similar check on them. Let me know how many cars they own and details: make, model, year, color, and license tag. Got it?"

"Yes, sir. No problem," she replied as jotted the last of her notes down.

"Got to run. Call me when you get the info, and Marti?"

"Yes, boss."

"Put that donut in the trash. You're on a diet, remember?"

She rolled her eyes. "Yes, boss. You're right. Bye."

Eric grinned. "There were many things he liked about Marti as his secretary, especially her consistency. She was always on a diet and always eating a treat like a donut. He had guessed correctly."

He looked back at the car to see the two men exiting the building without the sample cases followed by a man that looked right out of central casting for a mob figure. He had a big neck underneath a shaved or bald head, a big cigar that looked permanently stuck in the corner of his mouth, and he was yelling at the two men as they climbed in their car. Behind him trailed two large bodyguards of Spanish or most likely Cuban descent.

The men in the car laughed at the man and simultaneously shot him the bird finger as they drove out of his lot, making a turn and heading straight towards Eric.

"What was that all about?" asked Eric aloud as he quickly ducked down in the seat. They turned left onto the main highway so Eric pulled out behind them, but once again, he remained back a block or two. He chewed his lower lip while thinking. He suddenly said aloud, "I think I just found their fence, or least one of them." He pondered this, while realizing these guys probably have been thieving all their lives, and appeared to be not only smart, but also successful and if so, they probably have a series of fences they use. He knew a smart con artist like them would not carry any of their loot to their personal home, so what were they taking to this guy at the pawnshop?

It surprised him when the men pulled into a well-known gay shopping district, and after parking their car, they walked into a large restaurant. He saw a waiter usher them to a table by the front window, so they could watch the beach crowd walk up and down the sidewalk. They ordered drinks and lunch without consulting a menu, so they obviously came to this establishment often, thought Eric, as he sat in the parking lot between two cars and behind two more, but still maintaining visual surveillance.

After lunch they went shopping and two hours later, they returned to their house in Miami. He drove on past their house and just as he turned to drive to his hotel, his cell phone rang.

"Marti here, are you ready?"

"Just a second," he replied as he pulled over and retrieved a memo tape recorder from his pocket and put the cell on speakerphone. "Okay, shoot. What did you find?"

"The pawn shop is owned by Al Libowski, better known as Big Al. His family is connected to the mob, and he was suspected of wiping out a Larry Tibble, a member of another crime family, but beat the rap. However, he served five years for tax evasion and other various crimes as a kid. He's built the pawnshop just over ten years ago. The FBI suspects him of numerous drug activities as well as the selling of high-powered automatic weapons. I'll email you his social security number, home address, phone numbers, picture, etc.

"As to the house in Miami, it is owned by Stephen Einstein. He is thirty-two years old, bought the house in 2004, and get this...he paid cash for it at 1.2 million. It is six thousand square feet, 8 bedrooms, pool and tennis court, and he obtained building permits to remodel the entire property. Somebody has a pile of cash. He has several checking accounts, and stock purchases for about a quarter million or so. I could find no occupation anywhere. He is not from Miami, but rather Akron, Ohio. There the trail goes cold finding no relatives, no criminal or driver license history, and not even any tag records. I guess he was born about twenty-five years old." Marti laughed at herself.

"Funny. So Stephen Einstein is obviously an alias he is using. I don't know the other guy's name."

Marti grinned. "I do. Apparently the second man likes to drive fast because I did a comparison with that street address with all known criminal records and came up empty. No one is that clean, so I ran it again including traffic tickets and fines. Bingo. He has an average of seven speeding tickets a year, but all paid promptly. His name is Jim Demos and he is thirty-five years old. I can't find out where he is from, at least not yet, but I'm working on it."

"It's probably an alias, too, but find out just in case he made a mistake."

"Yes, boss. I will send you their car details. They own six cars, one of which is a Hummer, and my favorite car, a black Porsche. These guys are leaving a dream life. Anything else?"

Eric asked, "Messages?"

"Nothing too important but Bill Montross called. He wants you to plan the security arrangements for the Governor of Virginia. He is going to Argentina on a trade mission, and his crew doesn't have experience in providing out of the country security. Bill said to tell you he is taking twenty men and two vehicles and they leave on the 20th."

"What city are they going to?"

Marti blushed. "Whoops, I'm sorry. Buenos Aires."

Eric smiled remembering the last time he was there. "Okay, email me the details. If they haven't picked a hotel I'll do it for them. Call Bill back and ask him if they are taking the governor's bulletproof limousine. Thanks for the help. I will call you later. Thanks."

Eric spent the rest of the day in his regular hotel room, which was still next door to the room he used for Tyler's visit. He made arrangements to keep the second room another night. He made about twenty-five calls following up on his associates at the office, and the four teams currently on assignment around the country. They were covering three rich businessmen and a female senator, and he was pleased with the reports received. He also spent some time gathering the information for the arrangements for the Buenos Aires trip. All of this left him no time to wonder about Tyler and his friends. He did make a call and make arrangements for dinner.

With Tyler due to arrive at six, he moved into his second hotel room, jumped in the shower, and made sure he made the room look like he had spent some time there. He wrinkled the bed, turn the television on to make it warm to the touch, wrote some notes on a pad, tore them up and put them in the trash, and opened the drapes to let the sunlight in.

He had just finished dressing when there was a knock at the door. He glanced at his watch, noting Tyler arrived at exactly six. He made a mental note of that, as most young guys could care less about being punctual.

He glanced out the peephole, and opened the door. Tyler nearly ran over him as he leaped into his arms and gave him a deep wet kiss. Eric blushed as he shut the door. "Well, you sure know how to make an entrance."

Tyler laughed. "I missed you. All day at work I kept thinking about you."

"Same here. Are you hungry?"

"I'm starved. I worked through lunch since I was late."

"Oh you poor boy," said Eric slyly. "Come on, let's go. I have a surprise for you."

Tyler's eyes lit up with anticipation like a child on Christmas morning. "Where are we going?"

"That would spoil the surprise. Let's go."

They drove about eight miles winding their way east until they ran out of road in the parking lot of a pier. Tyler thought they were going to a seafood restaurant, so he started walking towards the line of shops and restaurant to his right.

Eric asked, "Hey, are you eating alone, or would like to join me?"

"What?" responded Tyler as he turned around to see Eric heading in the opposite direction towards the pier?

"I thought we were eating in a restaurant." Tyler quickly turned around.

"That's for normal folks, and believe me, you're definitely not normal!" Eric laughed.

Tyler laughed and ran to him. "Okay, I'll follow you anywhere."

They walked up the steps and down the pier, then down a tide ramp to a long row of boats, some of which were well over ten million dollars in value. They stopped in front a sixty-foot beautiful sailboat with two masts, and polished teak wood.

"Jimmy? Are you ready?" asked Eric as he stepped aboard with Tyler right behind him.

"Yes sir. Just have a seat. Lenny will bring you some drinks and finger food, and I'll cast off."

Tyler's mouth remained wide open as they left the dock and motored out to the sea. Eric's plans had shocked him. Lenny expertly raised the sails, killed the engine, and instantly, they went from the putt-putt hum of the motor to the silent sound of the sea, as they cut through a wave. The top of the next wave splashed gently against the white side of the boat.

"This is amazing. It has been a long time since I have been on a cruise."

"Jimmy and Lenny offer a great sunset cruise with dinner. I hope you like it."

Lenny suddenly appeared with giant tropical drinks, and a tray of cut fruit and vegetables, as well as an assortment of crackers. Tyler took a sip of his rum drink and smiled, and began eating the finger food.

"This is so exciting and so unexpected. I'd eat at McDonalds with you, but this is heaven. Thank you very much," added Tyler between bites of food and more sips of the rum.

"You're welcome. I have to go back to Baltimore tomorrow for business, so I wanted tonight to be something you might remember, and thus, remember me."

"I'm sad you have to leave, but we must get together again soon. The timing is good, because I have to travel for business, too."

Eric baited him to see if he would tell the truth. "Do have a conference to go to?"

"No, the doctor is on a committee that is hosting a seminar, and I'm going along to help. I'm in charge of issuing name badges and such."

"That sounds like lots of fun," deadpanned Eric.

Tyler laughed and replied sarcastically, "Loads of fun."

There was a long second of silence before they both started laughing.

Tyler asked, "When will you be back in Miami?"

"The nineteenth. I will come in and spend the night and fly out the next morning. Will you be back by then?"

"I think so, but I'll call you a few days ahead of time. I will look forward to spending the night with you. I'm getting hard just thinking about it."

Eric laughed. "You forgot about tonight."

"Will we have time for sex after the cruise?"

"Oh yes, we'll have plenty of time."

Suddenly they heard the ringing of a small bell. "Dinner is served," called Lenny from below. Tyler and Eric went down the steps into the galley and found a beautifully set table including fresh flowers, cloth napkins, fine china and silverware, and a wine pedestal with an expensive bottle of wine waiting on ice.

They devoured their salads while Lenny brought the main course of surf and turf to the table featuring grilled dolphin, lobster tails, prime rib, baked potatoes rolled in sea salt, and hot crescent rolls basted with garlic butter.

Tyler's eyes lit up and together, they began sampling the food and spooning larger portions to their plates while Lenny refilled their wine glasses. Forty-five minutes later, Tyler announced he was filled to the brim. Eric laughed. "You forgot about dessert? Are you sure you're full?"

Tyler produced a sly smile, "Well, maybe I could eat some dessert—if you force me."

Lenny brought slices of key lime pie to the table. He set the dessert plates down on the table, produced a small stainless steel pot with hot melted chocolate, and with great flair he poured a thin line back and forth across the top of their pie. They applauded his efforts and began tasting the scrumptious dessert.

At the conclusion, Tyler gave Lenny a hug, while thanking him over and over again for such a fantastic meal. They made their way back to the long cushion bench on the deck.

Jimmy asked, "How was dinner?"

Tyler answered, "Heavenly. It was the most amazing and divine meal I have ever enjoyed."

Eric laughed. "He's right. It could not have been better."

Jimmy said, "Very good, I've been taking us on a northeastern course, but with the sun almost ready to set, I'm ready to swing around and head due south so duck your heads." He added loudly so Lenny could hear, "We're coming about!"

He spun the wheel and a few seconds later as the boat began to turn, the boom flew across their heads, filling Tyler with excitement as Jimmy expertly brought the boat about, and began taking advantage of the wind as they picked up speed. Once the boat settled on course, Tyler and Eric crossed over to the cushions on the other side so they could watch the sun set over the eastern shore.

At first the sun with still lighter in color and bright, but like time-lapse photography, it began to morph into a rich, deep golden color that gradually became less bright, and a beautiful, darken shade of orange. The glow turned the white sails above their heads a beautiful shade of peach, and Eric thought it was a wonderful color for Tyler's beautiful face.

They kissed several times before turning back to watch the last of the rays of sun disappear beyond the skyline. As they reached the harbor, the stars were shinning bright and their dinner sail was over.

Eric tipped Jimmy and Lenny lavishly, and gave each man a hug, but Tyler gave them a hug and quick kiss to their cheeks to show how happy they made them. They waved goodbye and made their way to the hotel.

Eric turned to close the door to his hotel room and then turned slowly around, expecting find Tyler standing there in the nude again, and anxious to take in the view. However, he found the room empty, but heard a moan to his right, and then the sound of a fire hose letting loose a long overdue pee into the toilet.

"Oh my, that felt good—second only to sex," laughed Tyler as he continued to let his stream flow.

Eric laughed. "Boy, you are romantic!"

Tyler washed up and stepped through the open bathroom door. "Sit down on the bed," ordered the gorgeous boy.

Eric did as commanded. Tyler began taking slow steps toward him while removing his clothes, and flamboyantly flinging his garments across the room. He arrived in Eric's arms completely nude with an arousing penis. They kissed deeply.

Tyler broke the embrace and stood up. "Stand up. I'm going to strip you."

Eric couldn't resist and allowed the boy to take his clothes off before pushing him back to the bed where they made love for almost two hours before drifting off to sleep.

Saying goodbye the next morning took thirty minutes with lots of kissing and groping until finally Tyler reluctantly left. Eric walked out to the balcony and watched until he saw Tyler get in a cab and drive away. Quickly, he packed up his clothes, returned to his main room, and packed the rest of his stuff, and made his way to the lobby to check out, and drive to the airport.

He wasn't sure what he was going to do with the information acquired in Miami, and already he was feeling he might be in love with Tyler, but afraid to believe he was hearing any truth from the grifter. He doubted that Tyler lied about everything about in his life, but Eric knew it would take time to discover what the truth was.

FIVE

Eric arrived in Annapolis with a long list of things he needed to do to catch up on the work he missed while dating Tyler in Florida. He maintained mixed thoughts about his new acquaintance, ideas that perhaps he should never see him again, but try as he may, Tyler continually crept back into his head. He drove straight to his office where his private secretary, Marti, followed him into his office with a thick stack of prepared folders of mail for him to go through, sort, and make decisions.

"Jeez, that pile is depressing," he said with a grin as he stared at the nearly foot tall pile of work she casually set on his desk.

"Well, you know what they say," she replied. "All play and no work makes the piles grow higher."

Eric laughed, as he picked up the first folder and set it to his far right. "I will deal with the Argentina project last and in more detail, let's get the business stuff done first."

She handed him the stack of assorted mail. I have pulled the bills and paid the usual ones, leaving new bills for you to approve. After the bills, there are about twenty requests for our security services, and about thirty-two résumés."

"Thank you for the excellent preparation work. Let's see." He began reading each bill, making notes on each page as to which customer or account they belonged to for entry into their accounting software, and commenting accordingly. Marti was an old school secretary who could write in shorthand and quickly made her own notes as Eric made decisions. Her husband was a career navy man that died a few years ago. A friend of Eric's had known her husband and setup an interview. Her grip was almost as strong as his, and her humor remained sharp and true. She kept her brown hair pulled back, and looked ten years younger than the truth. In the past three years she had never missed a day of work. Organization was a religion to her, and she made Eric a believer. He paid her well for her excellent work, and considered her an important asset in her company. Like everyone in his company, she maintained excellent shooting skills, worked out three days a week, excelled at learning martial arts, and carried a small pistol in her purse, and 9 MM in a wall holster under her desk just in case a nut job walked in the door.

He asked, "What is the status of our accounts?"

"I prepared a statement for you and it under the last bill."

He looked up and smiled at her smart anticipation of his requests, "Remind me to buy you lunch today."

"Shall I order takeout for both of us?"

"Yes, Chinese for me."

He studied the statement. "Three hundred thousand and change in our checking account, a million plus in savings, and 7.2 million in investment accounts. That's very good. Please continue the practice of transferring anything over four hundred thousand in checking to our investment accounts. We'll keep the savings nest egg the same. I hope to never touch it, but if we need immediate cash for an operation, I may not have time for our investment broker to make arrangements."

He paused for a moment and then handed her the pile of bills, "Go ahead and process this stuff while I study the rest of the folders. "Thank you for another great job. Give me a shout when lunch arrives."

"You're welcome." Marti left in full confidence that she loved her job, and Eric was a great boss. She told know one about the company other than they invest in securities. None of her friends possessed the benefit package Eric provided, including profit sharing. She loved her job and the team of workers in the company.

Eric read each request for his firm's service, while marking a grade in the upper right hand corner like a professor grading term papers. He placed each folder in one of three piles. After completion of the last request, he kept only the stack with the highest grades, and put the other piles on the front of his desk for Marti to send a thank you note to, but declining services at this time. It was a standard letter indicating they remained a top firm by not taking on too many clients, and referring each to three of his favorite security firms. His company was far above standard, only they never talked about it.

He picked up his phone and pressed an intercom button. "James? Eric here. Please grab Lionel and come to my office. I need your help on a few future jobs. Bring a pad. I'll see you shortly."

While waiting, he divided the top grade jobs into two piles. His researchers arrived and sat down. James had been with Eric longer Lionel. He was a graduate of MIT at the top of his class. He worked for a few years with the CIA as a computer analysis before meeting Eric by chance on a flight to the west coast. They just happen to sit beside each other. Eric found him to be a bright, extremely intelligent, happy-go-lucky guy, bordering on the geek side in his personality, but a genius at research. Eric also suspected he was gay and confronted him boldly by saying, "James, I should be upfront with you. I'm gay, and I own a prospering security firm in Annapolis. I'm a former Marine with a staff of sixty providing security details for high profile individuals, and setting up business and home security for the same. I'm very impressed by your knowledge and skills, and I could certainly use a man like you on our team. I wouldn't be any good at my job if I also didn't pick up on the fact that you, too, are gay."

Eric paused for a long second, as he watched the blood drain from the face of his fellow passenger. Eric smiled. "That's why the first thing I told you was that I am gay. I can't imagine how tough it is to keep your private life a secret with the CIA. You must be afraid all the time as to how they will react when they find out. That's not good for your physical or mental health. I know, because I felt the same as a Navy seal. That's why I own this company, and everyone knows I'm gay. In fact, many of our staff our gay, and they are a proud lot. You'll feel not only right at home, but safe in the fact that you never have to worry about who knows you're gay again."

James knew they were gay people in the CIA, some were known and others were not, and he quickly surmised that none of the known ones were ever moved up the ladder of success.

Eric continued, "I want you to send me your résumé right away, my team will check you out, and I'm confident you are the guy we're after. What is your pay grade at the company?"

James replied as if ashamed to admit, "Forty-two thousand and benefits."

Eric laughed. "I'm sorry to laugh, but I can't believe they get away with paying a top graduate of MIT such a low salary. I bet they gave you the 'you'll be serving your country' speech." Eric didn't wait for the reply, "Listen, I served my country and if needed, I'm always available to serve and help the good old USA, but business is business. I'll start you at seventy-five thousand plus better benefits, three weeks' vacation a year, and all major holidays, etc. You'll manage my new research department and immediately hire an associate to assist. You'll work a normal forty-hour workweek, but to be fair and completely honest, there will be times when an emergency arises, when I may need you far longer than normal hours, but you'll be well compensated. That's why you'll also enjoy the benefits of profit sharing.

"I also want you think ahead on how we can improve our research tools by technology and sources. I have an amazing computer geek that handles all of our computer, telephone, and alarm systems, and I think the two of you speak the same language. He is an excellent digital researcher. I want you to keep him busy by staying on top of the latest technology so that our firm always has the best gear and sources. I am willing to expand our geek department so that we have good tech agents in the field as well.

"I know the CIA probably checked you out very well so my team's research on you will be fast. About half my employees are gay and the rest get along with gay people just fine. However, due to some of our backwards-thinking top clients, we do keep our gay life private. I would like for you to visit my office as soon as you can. I think you'll like your new office, your new office friends, and your new life. How's that for an offer?" Eric laughed at himself.

James, somewhat in shock for such an outstanding offer, closed is dropped jaw and smiled. "I have Friday off. May I visit then?"

"Of course, and that is perfect for me. Come about ten, and we'll get lunch afterwards, and before you ask or even wonder, I don't want to know anything about your job at the CIA. It is of no interest to my clients or me. I'm a red-blooded, patriotic American and would never ask you to compromise your previous work or friends at the company. I will warn you, when you turn in your resignation, they are going to give you a speech on how things are really hot right now, and they need for you stay on at least six more months. That's bullshit. You haven't been there long enough to worry about a pension and with what I am paying you, and our top rated 401K-retirement program, you could walk out the door tomorrow if you decide to. Check out our website."

Eric gave him his card as the plane landed. They shook hands, said their goodbyes, and Eric walked down the airport hallway knowing he had just found his new researcher.

"Come in guys. How are you?" Eric gestured for them to sit down.

James spoke up first. "Welcome back. I take it the mission was a success?"

"A big success so I took a few days off. How are you doing?"

James had been with the firm just over a year since his meeting of Eric on the plane, and still adjusting to how different things were in this office. He smiled because none of his bosses at the CIA ever asked how he was doing. "I'm great. Jimmy and I went to Rehoboth Beach this weekend. We had a great time."

Eric turned to Lionel and asked, "And how are you, my old friend?"

Lionel laughed. "I have a new girlfriend."

Eric replied, "Hey, that's great. Does she have all her teeth this time?"

James laughed as Lionel replied, "Of course she does. She's beautiful."

"Great and I'll look forward to meeting her. Set up a dinner meeting soon. Okay, here's what I need. You each have a stack of possible new jobs for our firm. I want you to research the feasibility and viability of each job, and using the training from our seminar last month, please tell me how many men it will take for each assignment, and how many days in the field for each one. Make spreadsheets of the equipment required, and anything else you feel is relevant. I also want a cost analysis as to actual cost and billable profit. Do you have any questions?"

James asked, "How long do we have?"

"How long do you need?"

"About three days if possible—faster if required."

"Three days will be perfect. On your way out, ask Marti to order lunch for you as well. I'm buying. Thank you and I'll see you later."

Eric spent the next two hours returning phone calls and checking with his teams in the field that were currently on assignments. He walked down the hall to his version of a situation room. On a global map, he could see green lights, indicating the location of his teams, and just to the right of the marker he saw a digital clock as to their hours and days in the field. He also laughed at those clocks, as they were like the meters on a taxicab. The longer they ran upward the more money he was making, but he made sure no one wasted time in the field.

At the back of the room was a line of enclosed glass offices for his team managers. He met first with the supervisor in charge of all the teams, Bob Smalls, as well as his second in command at the firm, and received a briefing on the status of jobs in progress. He noted their lights on the board were green, meaning ongoing. Red would indicate completion. Satisfied, he went next door to talk to his new job manager, Chip Orlanda, who worked on putting together all the details of new assignments. Eric looked at the board and saw six yellow lights representing the location of each new job and a digital start date. He had a few questions for his manager before exiting the room and walking down the hallway to visit his favorite technology geek.

Eric stepped into his computer and technology lab. He spotted three assistants and then finally noted his manager bent over workbench with a hot soldering iron in his hand. "Oscar, how are you?"

"I am feeling a lot like that guy in the James Bond movies that creates all these amazing gadgets. Of course, he worked with make-believe gadgets while mine are unbelievable." He smiled, and spoke to his boss. "Hold your hand out."

Eric did as requested palm up. Using a pair of tweezers Oscar placed a small tiny black dot in his hand.

Oscar asked, "What do you think that is?"

Eric squinted as he moved the dot closer to his eyes. "A bug?" Eric looked across the dot at the sly smiling face of Oscar who was forty-seven years old with a certified genius brain, and very absentminded. He often forgot where he parked his car, but he could use computers to do just about anything, including creating many of the surveillance and communication tools the firm used. His premature gray hair remained permanently disheveled, and he possessed big bushy eyebrows known to house crumbs and small electronic parts, and his glasses were very thick. Eric couldn't imagine how he could see through them.

"You're right but not organic. It is a tiny microscopic camera. Walk around my desk and look at this monitor."

Eric slowly moved around the desk and it took him a second before he realized the picture on the monitor was a picture of Eric's shirt up close. Carefully, he lifted his hand until he could see his face. He smiled just to be sure it was live shot. "That is smallest camera I have ever seen. Where does it get its power?"

"It comes from a very tiny fuel cell that actually pulls energy from the air by seeking out any light source to recharge the batteries. Use these tweezers and slowly turn the camera away from you."

Eric took the plastic tweezers and turned the dot around. "Now move your hand to the right and upward a little, and look at the monitor."

Eric did as instructed and immediately he could see all the way across the room and into the hallway.

"Hold still and watch this," said Oscar. Touching a few keystrokes on his computer, the picture began to enlarge as the camera zoomed in.

Eric found himself astonished, especially when the microscopic camera continued to zoom in pass the room, through the hall door and then focused on the temperature on the thermostat on the wall.

"Good grief, the quality is exceptional. How long will it stay online?"

"Almost indefinitely, because when a source of light goes dark, the camera goes to sleep. When the light source returns, it immediately starts charging itself. It also has a motion sensor on it, and if something moves in the dark, it goes infrared and can broadcast the pictures it finds for about an hour before having to shut down until a light source returns."

Eric asked, "How far can it broadcast?"

Oscar smiled. "You're clever, my friend. There are actually two parts to this technology that is sort of like Wi-Fi. It broadcasts fifty to hundred yards through walls so hold out your hand." Oscar used the tweezers to hand Eric another tiny piece of equipment. "This is the router or transmitter it links to automatically. The signal goes from the camera to the transmitter, where it is enhanced, amplified, scrambled, and broadcasted to a recorder or to an uplink unit. In a perfect world, this transmitter should be where there is at least eight hours of daylight to recharge its batteries. If we can do that, the transmitter can actually send power to the camera."

"Amazing. I'm impressed. How close does the uplink have to be?"

"A mile is fine," replied Oscar as he picked up a small tiny satellite unit about the size of a flatten pint of milk. "Watch this."

Oscar hit some keystrokes and the device began to hum and whir as it began unpacking itself like a mobile transport device the astronauts used on the moon to get around. In just twenty seconds, it became the full size of a pint of milk in a carton. It began moving its tiny dish attempting to find the correct satellite. Oscar hit a few buttons to shut it down.

"Obviously it can't find a satellite in our office. This unit could be placed on a power pole, a roof, the top of a tree, or just about anywhere, and if it has a clear line of sight, it can find the satellite to relay the signals to our office on our secure satellite uplink."

As Eric gave him the tiny parts back, Oscar added, "Watch this." He quickly typed in keystrokes, and a new picture came on the screen. "I'm testing a second unit. Do you recognize that white tall column?"

Eric studied the picture, and replied, "I have no idea."

"Okay, let me zoom out a little. Stop me when you have it." Oscar held down the minus key on his keyboard, and the camera began zooming out. At fifteen seconds, Eric said stop.

He studied the monitor carefully and spotted the glossy shoe of a full dressed Marine soldier. He thought a moment and grinned. "That's the White House."

"Right boss," replied Oscar, as he again held the key down until the entire White House could be seen.

"Where is the camera placed?"

"I put it on the top of a portable toilet at a construction site about five hundred yards away. The router is on the roof of a parking garage where it gets plenty of sunlight, and the sat unit is a half-mile away on top of another garage. They have been there about a week. I plan to get them later today. The tests have been perfect."

"If you're caught, you're going to get us in trouble," warned Eric.

"The pictures are totally encrypted so all the Secret Service would see is scrambled matter, but I felt that if it could make it work with all the security they have on the President, it would be perfect for our missions."

"How much did this tool cost me?"

Oscar got a sheepish look on his face. "Well, one complete set was forty thousand so I bought two at sixty thousand."

"Ouch, well, make sure no one sits on them."

Oscar smiled. "The good news is that my team has been studying them very carefully, and I think in about a month we can produce our own version for about ten thousand a piece."

Now it was Eric's turn to smile. "That's what I like to hear. Great job. I'll give you a budget of two hundred thousand to create a supply for future jobs. I want to take one of the units to Argentina with me. Oscar, you did an awesome job on this project. Way to go."

Oscar enjoyed being praised for his work, especially from Eric, because he knew that Eric didn't bullshit, and he also kept up on technology as best he could and appreciated his team's work.

Eric returned to his office to find his lunch on his desk. He moved over to a side table where he could eat and work. He began reading through the résumé pile while devouring his food. He once again began grading each one, creating three new piles on his desk.

Tyler awoke with a huge hard on, so he began masturbating while thinking of Eric. He had just finished exploding his jizz onto his bare chest when Jim entered his room and smiled at the sight, "Thinking of me, huh?"

"You wish," teased Tyler.

Jim walked over to the bed, leaned down and gave Tyler a wet kiss, and then licked up the pile of the hot sperm. "Hmm, just a bit salty." They both laughed.

He stood up and moved to the window. "Time to get your ass up. We fly out in ninety minutes."

Tyler crawled out of bed and walked naked to the shower. Jim turned to watch his cute ass. "Pack for three days and the climate will be warm, and yes, that's all I'm going to tell you. Let's just say we have an opportunity. I'll see you downstairs in twenty minutes. Breakfast is ready for you," he added.

Tyler was ready to go back to work, but as usual, he found himself curious about where they were going. He arrived downstairs with a carry-on bag and walked to the kitchen where Marvin prepared an omelet with fruit on the side for him. Tyler devoured it quickly as Stephen drove a car up to the kitchen door and blew the horn. "I'm coming. I'm coming," yelled Tyler as he hustled to swallow the delicious breakfast.

Jim came through the kitchen and added, "How am I not surprise? You're always coming. Now get your ass in the car." He and Marvin laughed.

Tyler shot him a bird finger as he swallowed another bite, gave Marvin a hug, and out the door they went.

They drove quickly to the airport, parked the car in the long-term lot, and caught the tram to the terminal. It was only when they arrived at the gate that Tyler realized they were going to Las Vegas. He said nothing because he knew it could be diversion with a quick stopover, and another flight to the north or even out of the country. Stephen and Jim always said they trusted him, but he knew they didn't, and not knowing a destination was a reminder. Tyler didn't trust their fake hugs either. Marvin's hugs were the only ones he respected. A few hours later, they landed in Las Vegas, and made their way to the rental car agency to pick up their car. He wondered what or who the mark was, but on the flight to the west, he also wondered what Eric was doing. It made him stiff just to think about him.

Eric completed the pile of résumés and gave the top stack to Marti to set up interviews. The rest she put in a file drawer in case they needed someone in the future. Eric then assembled his Argentina team in the operation room at two o'clock. Eric was especially proud of this room. There were eight super large forty-two inch LCD television monitors on the wall, and bank of dozen monitors in a row underneath. To his right was a team of technicians who managed the room's equipment and presentations with an office that looked like the studio control room for a television network show. In the old days, he used a chalkboard and sometimes an overhead projector, but now he had the latest tools at his disposal. The managers sat up front at their workstations, and each member of their team filled in the seats on the second and third row in front of their monitors. The lights in the room gradually darkened just enough so they could see each other, but it made it easier to read the details on the monitors.

"Gentlemen, it is good to be back and welcome to the Argentina team. The governor of Virginia has personally selected us to handle his security for his trip to Buenos Aires. We should not take his safety lightly.

Any numbers of things could happen, for example, kidnapping for ransom, killing for notoriety, or just killing because they hate Americans. We have to worry about assassination attempts, bombs, and cars loaded with dynamite. I am aware you already know the following, but I just want to reiterate, this is not just another governor, this is OUR client, and no one dies on our watch."

Eric paused as his eyes scanned every man in the room to let them know he held each of them responsible for the governor's safety. "Chip, how many men are on this team?"

Chip Orlanda replied quickly, "Nineteen."

"Nineteen? Why not eighteen or twenty?"

"Well, the job specs out for only eighteen, but we counted you as the ninetieth warrior." The room laughed.

"Roger that," replied Eric with a smile. "How many vehicles?"

"Two from the states, the governor's limo and a backup vehicle that one of his security details will use. Both transports have armor and bulletproof glass, and excellent communication gear. Oscar's team added more powerful amps and antennas, and automatic channel switching with full scrambling to make it extremely unlikely the bad guys or even the local cops can hear our communications. I have rented six Land Rovers for our use—all black. We'll inspect the vehicles for bugs or bombs after our arrival."

"Tim, please tell me how many days we'll be on the ground, as well as any Intel on housing and facilities."

Tim, one of his field leaders, replied, "The governor is staying at the Green Garden hotel. It is twenty stories and we have the entire top floor of twenty rooms. It has an underground parking garage. All our meals except for the banquet will be in the hotel. We'll be there three nights and four days. We fly out of Richmond. We'll leave the office at six in the morning and fly out at nine. We arrive at four or so that afternoon. The governor has a welcome dinner with the President's key staff at eight. The meetings begin the next morning."

"How are we guarding him in a mobile situations?" Eric knew the answers, but he went through each procedure to make sure everyone was on the same page, and to discover any last minute changes or suggestions from the group as a whole.

Chip replied, "One in front and one in the rear. The other Land Rovers will transport equipment and personnel, set up the command center, move our sniper into position, and are at our disposal as needed.

Eric stated, "The governor is going to want some photo opportunities to help with his re-election campaign."

Tim replied, "We agree and arranged a banquet room in the hotel for a press conference. He'll also have photo opportunities for him and the President at his headquarters. I have cleared both of these with the governor's staff."

"Very good," began Eric, "now bring up the floor plans of the hotel starting with the garage entry. Are we going to an elevator?"

A technician in the back placed the floor plan of the parking garage on the first LCD monitor, added the hotel lobby floor plan to the second, and then the top floor on the third.

Chip spoke up while using a digital sketch pin on a drawing pad by his keyboard. "There will be half of the arrival team at the elevator with one man posted inside and two waiting for arrival. The elevator will be prepped for bugs and bombs, and closed after our tests are completed. The other half of the team will monitor the parking garage and will close it two hours before arrival. Every car will be scanned for bombs in the garage. We'll have cameras setup that can monitor the garage from our command center. Our electronics field leader will scramble all civilian cell phones minutes before the governor arrives, just in case someone attempts to fire off something detonated by the usual cell call.

"Two of mobile teams will go up the elevator first to prepare for elevator departure. We will close the adjacent elevator during his movement. Two men will make a final sweep of the governor's suite for humans and our techie will check for bugs and bombs. We will pretty much do everything in reverse for departures. We will lock all hallway and stairwell exits during arrivals or departures with some of our staff monitoring as needed. We'll put wireless sensors on every door."

Eric asked, "What about the limo storage?"

Tim spoke up, "We got lucky as there is an enclosed room for paper storage with a steel garage door. They are removing all the storage stuff and the limo will just fit in the door. One of the governor's men will guard it at all times."

"Very good, how about food safety. Arnold?"

"Got it done, boss. I'll supervise two of the governor's staff that will prepare his food. They are bringing their own liquids mostly wine, water, and coffee. I have a travel freezer filled with frozen food if we become suspicious. I have lab equipment loaded and ready to test all his food and ours."

"Excellent. I guess we would look pretty stupid if the bad guys managed to take out security with a bad burrito. Maybe we won't get Montezuma's revenge and a bad case of diarrhea this time." Eric smiled as his men laughed.

"Communications and command center?"

Larry, a former electronic whiz kid for the Marines and one Oscar's best men, spoke up, "Boss, we'll be in a room just down the hall from the governor's. Our men will also be sleeping on each side of the governor's room, and the same for our headquarters. I am taking four trunks of surveillance gear, and my team will install our own antennas on the roof of the hotel, as well as satellite links. I'm taking two battery banks in case someone cuts off our electricity, or the local power source is found to be inferior for our electronics. Each man will wear the usual earpiece and sleeve microphone. The governor won't like it, but he will do the same, just in case he needs us behind a closed door with the Argentina government officials. We will give him a card of code words to memorize should he suspect he is in a harmful situation. If any team hears the code words, they should immediately act on operation baby bird. The governor will have a translator, a personal assistant from his staff, and pretend personal assistant from our team. Melody will handle the duty for us."

Eric smiled at Melody. "I'm glad you're aboard. How's your Spanish?"

She smiled back. "As you know I am proficient in seven languages, but I think I will keep it a secret that I understand their language. He already has a translator so he doesn't need my help for that duty, but perhaps I might overhear other communications."

"Very good. Are you still kicking Bill's butt in the judo gym?"

She laughed, as Bill was also her husband. "Let's just say he does exactly what I ask of him!"

Everyone laughed, and Bill blushed. Bill added, "My momma didn't raise a fool."

Eric laughed and then asked, "Weapons?"

Harry spoke up," We have received permission to wear all the usual personal weapons on the flights down and back. I'm taking six trunks of additional gear including outfitting a marksman with a high-powered scope that will work from the rooftops. Unfortunately, there will be a government goon with him at all times."

"Six trunks of weapons! That's enough for a small army," said Eric.

Harry smiled. "Sir, with all due respect, we are a small army, and a very good one."

They all laughed again.

"And one of the most important aspects of the trip...finances."

Edward spoke up, "We received a deposit of a hundred and fifty thousand from the governor's staff, and we'll invoice for the balance after the trip. I've made all the reservations and rentals required, and I'm taking twenty thousand in Argentina currency just in case we need local cash fast. Each man will be issued $314 pesos are about hundred dollars American for incidentals."

Melody spoke up quickly, "Man?"

Edward chuckled. "Sorry ma'am. I'm old school. I meant no disrespect, especially towards any lady that can kick her husband's butt. I meant team member. I apologize."

The group laughed again as Eric spoke up, "You handled that mistake very cleverly Edward. Finally, tell me about our itinerary and timetable."

Chip spoke up, "We leave at six Friday morning and travel to Richmond. Everyone has a print out on your desk for the rest of the journey. If all goes well, we'll back late Monday."

Eric said, "Very good. I have one last minute change for you. I'm flying to Miami tomorrow morning, and will meet your connection flight on Friday morning in Miami."

Chip spoke, "I will change your flight stuff. What time do you want to leave tomorrow morning?"

"Early," replied Eric. Anything you can get on short notice will be fine, but if you will, call Johnny Broome at US Air, he'll get me onboard. Do you still have his number?"

Chip replied, "Yes sir, I'll take care of the change."

"Okay, it sounds like we're as ready as can be. My biggest fear is that we don't know who are enemy is. It could be bad guys from the opposition party, it could be someone treated badly by the President's goons, it could be someone that hates all Americans, or just some political group looking for media exposure, and a chance to embarrass the government. Everyone should read the reports on the status of politics and groups there. I could ask questions, you know. You're probably aware that two of our team has been down there for about a week, and you'll have their field reports on your desks in the morning. So far, their analysis is good, but they said we could not trust the police, as corruption is as bad as any Latin country with short-term loyalties."

He paused to let them think for a moment before adding, "Thank you for a great job. I'll see you in Miami. Meeting adjourned."

SIX

Once they were in their suites at the beautiful Mirage Hotel, Stephen called a meeting, so they all sat down in the sitting area. Tyler knew the routine, so he made no jokes and waited for Stephen to explain. Looking at Jim he asked, "Did you sweep the room?"

Jim replied, "Yes, I found nothing. We're clear, but I would be damn careful what you say on the hotel phone or cell phones. Here are your phones for Las Vegas." Jim tossed them new throwaway phones he bought in a store downstairs with a thousand minutes pre-paid. These phones would end up in a dumpster before they left town. Jim had already stored their temporary speed dial numbers in the phone so they could reach each other by pressing one key.

Stephen began the meeting as he handed a picture and fake drivers licenses to Jim and Tyler. "Okay, we have three marks and all three are rich gay men. They are in town for an AIDS charity auction with celebrities. Here's the fun part. They are also heavy gamblers. Tyler, you'll take Toby Embler. He's worth about three hundred million dollars, and has mansions in Los Angeles, Cancun, and New York. Unbelievably, he made his money in fast-food franchises covering a number of brands. He was arrested several years ago, and accused of beating a young man he was dating. He bought his way out of it and the charges were dropped. He has been suspected of numerous other petty crimes, so be careful. Let's just hope you look young enough to gain his attention. You know how you need to fix your hair, and dress. I'm counting on you to rob him of at least fifty thousand, but if he wants to take you home to say Los Angeles, go with him, and we'll follow while making plans to rob his house as well.

"Jim, this is your guy. His name is Ricky Farrow. He just broke up with a long time younger partner. He is forty-five, in good shape, wears a toupee, and fifthly rich. He inherited his money from his mom who owns a hotel chain. He has never worked a single job in his entire life. He is a gay playboy. He lives in Detroit and owns an island in the Caribbean. You, too, have a goal of at least fifty thousand. He drinks a lot, so you might be able to make money disappear while he is making his bets at the table. Just be aware there are cameras everywhere in Las Vegas, especially in the casinos.

"I'm taking Rob Ensley."

Tyler interrupted, "The video game guy?"

"That's right. His company develops video games and they are one of the top one hundred companies in America. He is worth billions, but doesn't have a boyfriend, at least not for a few more hours."

They all laughed. "I am hoping to bring home a ton of cash. You can steal jewelry if you want, and I have setup the usual courier boxes just in case, but it is the money we're after as it is hard to trace, and perhaps they'll be too embarrassed to file a police complaint. You are to strip and do embarrassing things to your mark when you're done. Our plane leaves Las Vegas in three days with an early morning flight. If you're still working your mark until late the night before, be sure and drug him so we're gone before he wakes up. Any questions?"

Tyler asked, "Yeah, where are they now?"

"They are having cocktails with the rest of the auction invitees. Shall we join them? I have our invitations right here."

Tyler got up, handed the picture back to Stephen, and took his invitation ticket. You go ahead, as I need to change clothes and get younger looking."

"Right, perhaps you shouldn't be rich yourself, but rather your mom is. She got sick and sent you to the auction for her."

"Okay, got it. See you later."

Tyler went to his room, closed the door, and instantly knelt down on the floor so he could see under the door. He watched as Jim and Stephen changed clothes, and then left the room. Once he was sure they were gone, he went to his carry-on bag, and removed his cell phone from Miami and turned it on. He had just violated one of Stephen's numerous rules, and he knew that if he were caught, he would get a beating. He walked to the window and dialed Eric's cell phone. The dialed number began to ring.

Unfortunately, Tyler called while Eric was in the briefing room going over the details of the trip to Buenos Aires. He had left his cell phone on his desk. After four rings his voice mail kicked in. Tyler smiled at the sound of Eric's voice.

After the beep he spoke. "Hi Eric, It's me Tyler. I'm sorry, but I was called out-of-town suddenly, and will be gone for a few days. I don't think my cell will work there, so I'll call you when I get back. I miss you. Have a good week. See you later."

Tyler was sad that he missed him. He turned his personal phone off and hid it in his bag while removing his clothes. He combed his hair down over his forehead and spiked some of the hair on top of his head. He used a lip-gloss for his lips that made them look wet and inviting. He removed his tee shirt and put on an oxford-striped shirt leaving the top two buttons undone as if he had cleavage. He laughed at the thought. He put on a pair of bun briefs he got from a magazine that were tight in the back showing off his ass. The front was tight as well, so he pushed his big dick sideways to make it more visible.

He undid the zipper of his pants and lowered it about an inch so that it appeared as if he accidentally left it down, but opened just enough to create a hint of invitation, and most likely get some attention. He added a touch of his favorite cologne to his crotch, navel, chest, and behind his ears. He pulled on an expensive pair of tight slacks and laughed at the sight of his package and ass. He put on penny loafers with no socks and thankfully, he shaved his legs, crotch, and ass before his date with Eric. He put on a fake expensive watch, a few fancy gold rings, and a wad of pocket cash that Stephen left for him. He had to appear very rich and thus gain his mark's total confidence. He snatched up his invitation and made his way to the elevator. He adjusted his dick one last time before the door opened on the floor of the party.

Tyler checked in at the registration table after showing his invitation as well as his fake drivers license. They placed a green wristband on his right arm indicating he was old enough to drink. He was admitted to the large conference room where a band was playing on a stage to his left, and along the right wall was a large open bar. He went directly to the bar and ordered a Sex-On-The-Beach drink. The bartender fixed it with fruit slices and an umbrella. Tyler took the drink, pulled out the umbrella and fruit slices, and rudely dropped them on the bar and downed the drink in one long swig. He left the glass on the bar, and began scanning the room for his victim. Finding his mark, he began casually making his way through the crowd. He recognized several gay celebrities, but paid no attention to anyone as he pushed his way forward until he was about six feet from Toby Embler.

Tyler sighed. The mark wasn't great looking, but thankfully not butt ugly. He was talking with two men and a lady, while standing sideways to Tyler. Tyler moved a few steps to his right so he would be standing directly in front of Toby. To his dismay, suddenly some other man came up and tried to start talking to him. Tyler said very little in reply, but the man was several drinks ahead of him and just kept rambling on. Finally Tyler said, "Excuse me, sir. My boyfriend is due back any minute from the bar, and he gets pissed if anyone is seen talking to me, so unless you want your nose broke, I suggest you move along. It was nice to meet you," he added politely.

The astonished man quickly left Tyler and rushed back to the bar, so Tyler turned back around looking directly towards the people Toby was talking to, not wanting to make obvious eye contact with the mark. Tyler muttered to himself, "Come on, honey, quit talking and pay attention to the hottest guy in the room who is standing here with velvet young skin and underwear creasing his ass." Then it happened.

Toby laughed heartily at something someone in his group said, and in so doing, his eyes caught sight of Tyler. He glanced left and right to see if Tyler was with someone, and each time his eyes came back to Tyler's body. "I'm reeling this fish in," whispered Tyler to no one, as he allowed himself to turn his head and suddenly, meet Toby's eyes. He smiled sweetly, and then looked down at his feet as if embarrassed, and tried to force himself to blush a bit by holding his breath. He managed to catch sight of Toby's eyes once again. A few minutes later, Toby broke away from his acquaintances and walked over to Tyler.

Toby said, "Hi, my name is Toby. What's yours?"

"Stone."

Toby smiled. "Stone. That's an unusual name."

"Yeah, I know," he replied sounding like a kid. "My mother is a big history buff, and named me after Stonewall Jackson. He was my great, great, great, uncle. My name is Stone Jackson. What's yours?'

"Toby Embler. Aren't you a little young to be stuck at one of these charity auctions?"

"I'm sixteen, thank you very much. My mom sent me. She got one of her migraine headaches this morning, and the next thing I know I'm on our private jet headed to Las Vegas. I told her I would go if I could see several of the Cirque de Soleil shows. She gave me a half million to spend at the auction. She said I could keep anything I bought. I hope they have some good stuff. I like video games and stereos."

Toby laughed as he found himself impressed that the good-looking boy was in charge of so much money. Tyler saw him take a look at his penis package. Tyler held still for a long moment giving his mark plenty of time to stare at it, and then he pretended to drop his napkin off to his right, and turned and bent over to pick it up, giving Toby a fine close-up of his butt. Toby licked his lips when he saw the boy's cute tight ass.

Toby asked, "Are you comfortable being around gay people?"

"I better be. I have been one all my life."

Toby smiled, as his blood began making its way to his penis veins creating a stir. "Well, I think we should see the Mystère Cirque de Soleil show first. Give me a moment," he said as he snapped out his phone. "Bobby? This is Toby Embler. I need two tickets for the Mystère show tonight, and I don't care what they cost. If they are great seats, your tip will be five hundred dollars. Can you do that?" He paused and then added, "Very good, one more thing. Book me a table for two a Ramones for six. Thanks."

He turned back to Tyler. "It's all set. You're going to the circus tonight, so why don't we get out of here and walk through the casino.

"Oh my goodness," feigned a surprised Tyler. You're amazing. How did you get the tickets so fast?"

"Money talks and cute guys walk. Come on, let's go."

Toby led Tyler through the crowd, as Tyler caught sight of Jim talking to his mark, and Stephen doing the same with his. He winked at them, as if to say his mark was a piece of cake, and don't I look cute. They winked back at him, as they continued talking with their new friends.

Tyler and Toby made their way into the big casino, which is easy because you have to go through the casino to get to anything in the hotel. When they reached the blackjack tables Tyler spoke up. Do you mind if I play for a little while?"

Toby gave him a surprised stare. "I think you have to be eighteen to play."

"You're right. I used a fake ID when I checked in. See my green wristband. That makes me legal. Come on."

Tyler didn't wait for an answer, but grabbed Toby's hand, pulling him to the nearest table. Tyler sat down, showed the dealer his wrist, and then bought five thousand in chips after pulling out his huge wad of cash. Toby bought a thousand in chips, sat down beside Tyler on a stool, and put his hand on Tyler's thigh.

Tyler was good at blackjack, but deliberately, he lost about six hands before winning one, but in doing so, he gained back all of his money. They played for about an hour, but about every five minutes or so, Toby managed to work his hand higher up Tyler's thigh until he could feel his penis. Tyler just looked over at him with soft warm eyes and smiled, indicating Toby could do whatever he wanted.

They left for dinner with Tyler up a thousand. He would pocket that money, hiding it from Stephen and Jim, and put it in his safe deposit box when they got back home. Tyler said he had to pee before dinner, so they walked into one of the large bathrooms at the Mirage. They stood side by side while Tyler gave Toby his first look at Tyler's huge penis. The mark couldn't wait to go down on that thing, but he would have to wait a little longer.

They ate prime rib for dinner and Toby did most of the talking about his work and life. He bragged about being rich, his houses, yachts, planes, and more. Tyler pretended to be fascinated when he was actually bored out of his mind.

Toby picked up the show tickets from the concierge and gave him the promised five hundred dollar tip. He returned to Tyler with a smile, and they began making their way into the huge theater for the show. Tyler didn't have to act while watching the Cirque de Soleil troupe as they were beyond fantastic. After the show, as they were exiting the theater, Toby began making a phone call.

He hung up and smiled at Tyler. "I've ordered champagne, so let's go up to my room for a drink or two."

Tyler pretended to be wary. "I'm not sure I should do that. I just met you."

Toby went to work. "It's nothing, just a few drinks, and then we'll come back down and play some blackjack."

Tyler answered innocently. "Okay, if it just for a few drinks."

"Very good," replied Toby as he led him to the elevators. The car went to the top floor where Toby enjoyed a large suite reserved for big spenders. He showed Tyler around the room while the boy pretended to be impressed, but he was really trying to spot anything he could steal, and especially if the room contained a safe. He suspected it did when he walked over to a painting in the bedroom, and easily spotted a piano hinge on the right side while pretending to be interested in the painting to the right of the one covering the safe.

He returned to the bar in the suite where Toby poured two flutes with expensive champagne. Tyler playfully sipped at the golden drink before downing it quickly. "Do you have anything a little stronger, like perhaps a Sex-On-The-Beach?"

Toby laughed. "Coming right up. I think I can make one."

Tyler replied quickly as he came around the bar, "Aw, you go sit down. I'll do it. Do you want one?"

Tyler leaned into Toby while gently pushing him out-of-the-way. He quickly made the drinks and brought them to Toby. "These are much better, but they have a little kick to them. Tyler made several more before Toby said he had to pee. He made his way through the bedroom and into the bathroom. Tyler glanced around the room, looking for other things to steal, and began stripping out of his clothes. He played with himself to get aroused, as Toby's body was not going to make anything happen. He wasn't ugly, just not as cute as Eric.

Toby stepped out of the bathroom to find a naked gorgeous boy lying across his bed. "You're naked!"

"And you're not. The drinks made me hot, you know, like lying on a hot summer beach. The only thing missing is sex on the beach. Are you going to get naked or what?"

Toby began rapidly peeling out of his clothes. In the bathroom, he had tried to think of all kind of ways to get the boy naked, but Tyler was way ahead of him. Toby moved over to the bed and began licking his tongue slowly up Tyler's well shaven smooth legs. When he got to his crotch, he began licking his balls. Tyler closed his eyes and thought of Eric, and his tool began to grow accordingly. Toby went down on it expertly and that helped Tyler a bunch, as the mark sucked tighter and tighter, and then began biting it roughly.

"Ow! You're biting me, dude," he complained.

Toby didn't reply, but just looked up and winked at him, as he continued sucking hard and a few minutes later began biting once more.

"Ow! Come here, you're killing me."

He pulled Toby up so he was lying across his bare body and began kissing him. Toby's hands wondered to Tyler's tits, and began pinching his left one very hard. "Ow! That hurts."

Toby responded by roughly pushing his large tongue way down Tyler's throat. Tyler thought this was about as far from being romantic as a person could get. He began to think the man was searching for food in Tyler's stomach. After he gagged a time or two, he tried to talk, but managed nothing more than grunt, which Toby ignored as he slipped a finger on his left hand into Tyler's anus, while continuing to pinch the tar out of the boy's tit with his right hand. Not wanting to gag, Tyler reluctantly bit Toby's tongue.

"Damn!" Toby exclaimed, as he yanked his tongue out of Tyler's mouth. "That hurt."

"That's what I was trying to tell you. You're hurting me."

Toby scoffed. "You're just not used to good, hard, rough sex, but I'll teach you." Suddenly, he punched Tyler hard into the stomach, knocking the breath out of him. While Tyler gasped, Toby quickly opened the nightstand drawer and removed four large rubber devices that looked like one-inch rubber bands. He expertly slipped one over each wrist and looped them over the upper bedposts. He grabbed the boy's feet and banded them as well. He reached back in the drawer and removed several other items.

Tyler had weakened while trying to catch his breath, but once accomplished, he discovered Toby had quickly tied him up. It scared him. "Hey, let me go. I'll have all the sex with you want, but not like this. Let me go."

Toby laughed at him. That made Tyler mad. He yelled at him. "I said let me go, you pervert!"

Toby grabbed Tyler's penis and squeezed it harshly.

Tyler exclaimed, "Ow! Stop it! That hurts."

Toby laughed again. Tyler was pissed and spit at him. Toby hit him in the stomach again, and Tyler nearly blacked out at the pain. Toby rolled up a washcloth from the bathroom and pushed it into Tyler's mouth. Tyler could hear the air rushing to and from his lungs as it whistled through his nose. He knew he was now in big trouble, and there was little he could do. He was very angry, but Tyler felt anger might be something Toby enjoyed, and it could lead to more punches. He decided not to react at all, and just get it over with. He had experienced bigger dicks than Toby's so he wasn't worried about being raped. He was worried about getting AIDS or beaten to death.

Toby left the room briefly and returned with his version of the Sex-On-The-Beach drinks. He had a straw and forced the straw into the corner of Tyler's mouth. "Drink it all." Tyler did as commanded, hoping to dull the pain, though the drink had at least five shots of something in it. It burned his throat, but he could feel a buzz forming, and he was thankful for it.

Toby leaned down and began sucking him once more while using his left hand to squeeze one of Tyler's tits, and the right fist wrapped tightly around his balls and was squeezing them hard and releasing, as Toby went up and down on him. The pain when he squeezed forced Tyler's jizz back down, but he was trying to shoot, hoping that if he did, perhaps things would soon end. However, Toby knew exactly what he was doing.

Once satisfied, he returned to the drawer, retrieving a large sharp hunting knife. He put it up to Tyler's eyes, which went wide with fear. Toby liked the fear that he saw. "Okay, Tyler. This is what you're going to do. I'm going to remove the washcloth from your mouth. If you make a noise, I'm going to poke the tip of the knife into your testicles. You are going to suck the tar out of my dick and if you bite me, I'll cut your dick off and feed it to you, and leave you here to bleed to death. Do you understand me?"

Terrified, Tyler nodded yes slowly. As the blood drained from his face, he began shaking with fear. He sucked in fresh air as the rolled rag came out of his mouth, but seconds later Toby's slammed his enlarged penis down Tyler's throat. With Tyler on his back and Toby on top of him, there was little sucking he could do. He just kept his lips tight, as Toby slammed in and out of his throat, basically raping his mouth. Each time that Toby came close to ejaculating, he would pull out, and harshly thump his penis like a farmer thumping a watermelon to see if it was ripe. Tyler assumed that sent the sperm way back inside trying to hide.

Finally satisfied, he told Tyler to suck his balls, which he did while doing what he thought was his best work for the beast. After a while, Toby laughed at Tyler, and told the boy he wanted Tyler to rim him. Tyler shook his head no, but Toby brought the knife up, allowing the point to touch the tender skin under Tyler's left arm.

Toby said, "This blade is very sharp. If I just push it just a little, it will jump through your skin and into your heart in less than second. Your heart is just inches from the point. So do you want to rim me or die?"

Tyler sighed as Toby laughed. "That's what I thought. Do it good." He turned around and put his ass right in Tyler face. Reluctantly, Tyler did something he had never done before, and fought back the gag reflex. After a few minutes, Toby climbed off of him. He went to the bathroom and got a wet washcloth and washed Tyler's face and tongue.

He slipped on a condom and made his way between Tyler's legs while smiling slyly at his captive. He brought his body forward and pushed his swollen member hard and deep into Tyler. Toby thought Tyler would scream, but a dick up his butt was something Tyler had been doing since he was a little boy. He even once handled two dicks at the same time.

Toby began pumping him and after a while, Tyler's penis ejaculated from all the bumping against his prostrate. For the first time in his life, the moment of ejaculation felt awful to him. Toby would stop now and then, holding back his jizz, and start all over again. Tyler closed his eyes and hoped it would end soon.

He had no idea how long the rape continued, but finally he heard Toby groan loudly. Minutes later, he pulled out of Tyler and began cleaning himself up. He brought warm washcloths to the bed and began cleaning Tyler up. "You did good, kid. You're a natural. I think you could learn to be a good slave and if so, I'll reward you with so much money you won't know what to do with it all. Of course, you can't tell because of two reasons: one, I would tell your sweet mom how you licked my ass with glee and two, either me or a friend of mine will gut you with this knife. Do I make myself clear? "

Tyler nodded yes. Toby untied him. Tyler quickly dressed and made his way out of the room, across the suite, and out the door. He made it to his room, stripped, and rushed into the shower, before sliding down to the shower floor and crying his heart out as the water splashed down on him. He scrubbed every square inch of his body numerous times, and ran a soapy finger in and out of his butt. After a while, he got out of the shower, brushed his teeth and gargled several times. He dried off and went to bed. Jim and Stephen had not returned, so he assumed they must be with their marks. He wanted revenge, but Stephen would tell him the best revenge would be to rob him, but to do that he would have to continue to be friends with Toby, and Tyler swore that was not going to happen.

However, if he refused, Stephen and Jim would beat him and force him to go back, so slowly an idea crept through his brain. He got up and dressed, put on clean clothes, and put the rest of his stuff in his bag. He went back to the bathroom and made it look like he hadn't been there. He hid the towels behind a chair. He made the bed. He took his phone, the seed money Stephen gave him, plus the thousand he had won. He left everything else behind, made his way out of the room, and went to the far end of the hall where he saw a cute bellboy pushing an empty cart into an elevator.

"Can I ride down with you?"

"Hmm, this is supposed to be for staff. You're supposed to use the fancy elevators up front."

"I know but this girl keeps chasing me, and she is so ugly that I have to find a back way out of this hotel." Tyler took a fifty from his wad. "I'll give you this to help me escape."

The boy nodded yes, and Tyler said, "Please don't tell anyone you helped me or even saw me, or she'll find me. Okay?"

"Sure, what happens in Vegas stays in Vegas."

Tyler smiled for the first time in the last few hours. The boy took him to the parking garage and showed him how to make his way towards the back of the hotel where the staff comes in. Tyler didn't see any cameras in the hallway and made his way out to the street. He flagged a taxi and caught a ride to the airport. By dawn, he was on a flight to Baltimore. He was sore all over, but he slept the entire trip, dreaming of Eric.

SEVEN

Tyler arrived in Baltimore just a few hours after Eric flew out to Miami from Dulles. They were just a hundred miles and two hours apart, but the difference might as well have been a world away.

Tyler was excited and naively thought he was going to surprise Eric with his unexpected visit. Tyler pushed his way through the crowd exiting the plane and found a phone booth. He lifted the heavy phone book and looked up insurance adjusters in the yellow pages. He quickly scrolled down the names looking for Eric Hanson. There were several big ads that he skimmed through until finally he found a small listing for Hanson Adjusters. He looked left and right to see if anyone was watching him and yanked the page out of the book. With no luggage to wait on, he bounded down the escalator steps to the street in front of the airport. He quickly hailed a cab, and gave him the address to Eric's Baltimore office.

In the back of the cab, he suddenly panicked. He wondered what he looked like, as he had left the hotel in a hurry with his hair still wet and slept on the plane. He tried to find a mirror where he could see his face, but found nothing that would work. He attempted to smell his own breath, and wondered if he had morning dragon breath as he called it.

The ride in from the airport was beautiful in the early morning as Baltimore came alive, and about forty minutes later he paid the driver and stepped out of the cab and onto the curb. He gave the driver the fare and a tip, and watched him drive away. He walked briskly, and climbed the steps to the old brick building and to the front door for Eric's office. He read the stencil name on the door for Hanson Insurance Adjusters, and the instruction below: Please push black button on the right.

Excited, Tyler quickly pushed the button and waited.

In Marti's office area in the Annapolis office for Eric's security firm, a special line suddenly lit up on her phone with a distinctive ring. She knew that the call was from the door intercom at the false adjuster business in Baltimore. "Good Morning, welcome to Hanson Insurance Adjusters. This is Marti, how may I help you?"

Tyler's eyes lit up. "This is Tyler Savage. I'm a friend of Eric's and just arrived in town, and thought I would drop in to say hi."

Marti's brow wrinkled as to why a friend of Eric's would show up at the fake office, but Eric's training made it easy for to her reply. "I'm sorry, Mister Hanson is out-of-town. I'd be happy to give him a message. "

Tyler frowned. "Do you know when he'll be back?"

"I suspect in about five to six days. I'm sure he'll call in for his messages. Would you like to leave one?"

Tyler's shoulders sagged and dejectedly answered, "Yes ma'am. My name is Tyler Savage. He can reach me on my cell phone at 305.231.6696.

Please tell him I'm in Baltimore, and to call me as soon as he can. I'll stay in a local hotel, but I don't know which one yet. Thank you."

"I've got it. Thank you for calling. Have a great day," she added.

Tyler turned and went back down the steps, wishing the cab were still there. Knowing that his plan A had just failed, he decided it was okay and he would get a room, clean up, and wait for Eric to call. He looked in all directions for a hotel and found none. He pulled out his cell phone, dialed 411 for information, and called another cab company. He gave them Eric's address and ordered a cab. After he hung up, he went back to the brick steps and sat down to wait for his ride.

Marti checked Eric's flight schedule and realized he was still in the air on the way to Miami. She sent him a text message with the Tyler info attached. She assumed he would get the message as soon as he landed.

An hour later, Eric's plane touched down and as it taxied to the terminal, he turned on his cell phone. Seconds later, he looked down at the screen, and quickly realizing he missed six calls and one text message. He scrolled through the calls, recognizing each person, and then opened the text message. As he read the note his heart sank. He had come to Miami to see Tyler, and Tyler was in Baltimore trying to see him.

He was tempted to get back on another flight to Baltimore, but the long ride on the tarmac gave him time to think. He could only assume that Tyler was on a job with his buddies, and so they were all out-of-town. He had to be ready to catch up with the team's flight in the morning, so there was no point in flying home and back down again. He thought he might be able to put the opportunity to good use.

After exiting the plane, he walked to a quiet corner of the terminal and returned Tyler's call.

Tyler checked into a nearby Sheraton hotel by paying cash for one night. He knew that Stephen, who gave him the plastic card he carried, could easily trace a credit card transaction. Feeling hungry and grungy when he arrived in his room, he made two quick decisions. He ordered a large breakfast via room service, and stripped and went to the shower to scrub his body all over once again. He felt he would never get the smell of Tony off his still sore body. He left his cell phone in his pants pocket as he dropped them to the floor by the bed. He turned on the television and headed to the hot water. He never heard the ring of Eric's phone call.

Eric let it ring through to voice mail and left a message, "Tyler? How are you? What are doing in Baltimore? I wish I had known you were coming. I'm sorry, but I'm on the way to Los Angeles for a meeting, but I'll be back on Wednesday. Call me on my cell at 410.671.3393. It was good to hear from you. Call me."

Eric hung up and made his way to the luggage spindles to pick up his bags. He found his rental car as soon as possible and drove to the same hotel he stayed in before, so he knew the parking garage and the floor plan. He had just made it to his room when his cell phone rang.

"Hello?"

"Eric! It's Tyler. I'm fine. How are you and where are you?" Tyler fell on the bed in the nude having just dried off from his shower when he saw his pants moving from the cell phone vibrating. He immediately started playing with himself.

"I'm in Dallas," he lied, "and on the way to Los Angeles for a meeting. I'm so sorry I missed you. You should have told me you were coming. I hope you didn't make the trip just to see me."

"No, my friends and I were also at a meeting, and I got bored and they said I could fly home early," he lied. "So I fixed my ticket so I could fly through Baltimore. Unfortunately, my luggage got lost, and so I'm in the Sheraton near your office with just the clothes on my back. Well, actually I'm naked, because I just got out of the shower. Boy, I am horny and wishing you were here."

Eric smiled as he felt his groin stir. "Me, too. Dang it. If you had been one day earlier your legs would have been sore by now."

Tyler laughed. "And so would your dick."

"How long can you stay? I'll be home Wednesday."

Tyler thought for a second and replied, "Well, I ain't leaving until you get here. I'll just go shopping and buy some clothes, go see a few movies, and count the minutes until you get here."

"Very good. Listen, I have to get to my next flight. I'll call you later tonight. Give me the hotel room and phone number just in case your cell runs down."

"Shit. I forgot my phone charger. Okay, here's the number." After they said their goodbyes and hung up, Tyler got a note pad out and began making a shopping list that included not only clothes, but also a new pre-paid phone. There was a knock at the door so he walked to the door, and opened it while hiding his naked body behind it.

"Hi," said the cute boy.

Tyler asked, "Do you embarrass easily?"

"I have been doing this job for twenty months, so no, I have just about seen it all."

"Very well, roll it on in." Tyler grinned.

Tyler held the door as the boy pushed a table cart into the room and then he let the door close. He walked over to the bed to get his cash as the boy turned around, realizing his customer was gorgeous and totally naked.

"Hmm..." he stuttered, "I have your big breakfast ready for you and three pints of chocolate milk as requested. The silverware is on the side. Is there anything else I can do for you?"

Tyler couldn't help himself, "Well, as a matter of fact there is. I just took a shower, and I have an itch right here in the middle of my back." He turned around so the boy could see his ass and used his left hand to point to the middle of his back where he couldn't reach. "Would you mind scratching it for me?"

The boy was twenty and going to the local community college, and his job training taught him he should most politely decline, saying it was against company policy, but having recently come out of the closest, his mind raced for proper answers until all that fell out of his mouth was, "Sure."

The boy walked over and began using his right hand to scratch Tyler's back. Tyler reached around and with his left hand and pulled the boy's open nervous left palm to his buttocks and helped him squeeze, which the boy gladly did. Confident the boy was as gay as he was, he pulled his left hand around to his front and placed his fist around Tyler's arousing penis. Tyler then allowed his own right hand to reach around and squeeze the boy's swelling lumpy crotch.

After the horrible experience with Tony, Tyler would have preferred to be in Eric's arms, but he wanted to be in the arms of someone clean and nice, and in this case innocent. Tyler turned around and kissed the room service waiter on the lips lightly several times before pushing his tongue inside.

He broke the wet kiss to ask, "How long do we have before you'll be missed?"

The boy gulped. "Ten minutes, no wait a minute, I'll tell them I had to take a dump. Uh, fifteen minutes."

Tyler smiled. "Then get your clothes off fast!"

Not wanting to get him fired, Tyler shot into the boy's mouth at fourteen minutes, got him dressed, brushed his hair with his fingers, and walked him to the door while putting a fifty dollar tip in his hand.

Tyler asked, "What time do you get off from work?"

The boy replied, "At five."

"Would you like to meet me for dinner?"

The boy said sure, so the boy picked the place and told Tyler how to get there. Tyler gave him yet another deep wet kiss and pushed him out the door. After the door closed, Tyler laughed at his boldness, turned up the television and sat down at the cart to eat his breakfast.

Eric returned all his calls, and made some notes, changed clothes and drove his rental car in the direction of Tyler's house in Miami. He wasn't sure why he was going there because he wanted to trust Tyler, but to trust a thief is asking for trouble, he thought. He had a nagging feeling that the older couple made a life of crime easy for the young man, but he hoped he had not been a thief too long to quit.

He pulled around to the back of the house and parked his car about a block away with nose of the car pointing at the house so no one from that direction could see his tag. He slipped a small backpack over his shoulder and pretended to be enjoying a walk as he crossed the mostly deserted street. He noticed the rear motorized gate and walked on past it until he found a tree with a limb hanging over the fence. He checked his surroundings for witnesses, found none, and scurried up the tree quickly thanks to his upper body workouts. He worked his way out the limb until he was on the other side of the fence, then swung his body down while holding on with his hands, and then dropped to the ground and rolled to break his fall. He stood up and checked the ground for deep footprints but found none. Before moving, he retrieved small pair binoculars from his bag, and began searching the grounds and house for surveillance cameras. Finding none, he proceeded quickly to the house, and listened for any movement. He expected to find perhaps a chef and cleaning staff, but he heard nothing. He wondered if perhaps they had time off while the gang was out-of-town.

He checked a few doors, but they were locked. He noted the alarm system and went around back until he found the phone utility box and just above it the alarm connection box. He removed a small tool case from his bag, popped out the right tools, and easily removed a wire from each of the phone lines and patched around the alarm system using a red jumper wire with alligator clips. He went to the kitchen door and using small tools from his lock pick set, he opened the door in twenty seconds.

He was about to leave the kitchen area when a flashing red light in the corner caught his eye. It was the alarm system and it was armed. Working rapidly and with great skill, he picked the lock on the keypad metal box, attached a small device about the size of a pack of cigarettes, clipped two alligator clips at the end of a strand of wire protruding from the electronic device, attached it to the circuit board access port, and hit a green button. Instantly, it rapidly scanned through combinations and details about the unit, and ten seconds later, the alarm suddenly turned off. He then programmed a simple code into their system that would allow him in the future to turn the alarm on and off as easily as the house owners did. He turned it off for now, so that when he re-armed it, it would no longer show that the system had faulted. He returned the tools to his bag after closing the cover to the alarm's keypad.

Cautiously, he walked to the kitchen sink and noted the base near the drain was completely dry. He knew no one had worked in the kitchen for at least twenty-four hours. He made his way through the dining room and stepped into a hall bath. He again checked the sink and it was dry. He felt the tank behind the toilet and it felt like the room temperature, indicating it had not been flushed in a day or more. He went into a large study with long walls filled with books, expensive books with leather bindings. He studied the shelving section by section until he found what he was looking for. He spotted a sweep pattern in the plush carpet in front of shelf, beginning from the right corner. Using his tiny LED flashlight, he went down the left side until he found the hidden hinge. He went back to the right side and pulled. Nothing happen.

He was sure he was right so he tugged again. He couldn't budge it. He began studying each of the shelves, looking for a trigger or latch. They were all filled with books right to the edge, except the fourth one, which was just above his eye level. He noted there was a small globe sitting on that corner. It puzzled him because most globes are sitting on some wooden or brass rack. He reached up to pull it down and it wouldn't move.

He smiled as the realization reached his brain, and gave the globe a slight twist. Instantly, the entire wall of shelves started moving towards him with the whirr of a hidden motor. Behind the shelf, he discovered a locked door. He did that lock in thirty seconds. He checked the door for additional alarms, fearful of an instant alert, but finding none, he flipped on a light switch and entered a secret room. Inside, he found the three walls from floor to ceiling completely filled with what appeared to be the same metal boxes that a bank used in a vault for safe deposit boxes. At one end, he found an expensive large safe with an electronic mechanism as well as a key cylinder and polished steel turn handle. To crack the safe, you'd have the key and excellent safe cracking skills.

He didn't have the tools with him to break the safe, but with a bit of luck and skill, he did manage to pick the lock on one of the boxes. Inside, he found bags of diamonds. He turned around and began counting the boxes and found twenty-four of them. The safe was about five feet tall and three feet wide by three feet deep. He thought about his discovery and realized like most professional thieves, they were always planning for the day they would quit and retire. They couldn't trust a bank, so they created their own bank, and stockpiled their future wealth here.

He wasn't sure what he was going to do with knowledge he had learned, but he retrieved a very expensive tiny camera, took some quick pictures, and put everything back in it's place. Although he had been wearing thin latex gloves, he made sure there wasn't a smudge of anything anywhere before putting out the lights.

He began exploring from room to room in the house until he had seen everything including Tyler's room. The other two men kept most of their clothes in the same room, but Tyler's kept all his clothes in his own room. He suspected that from time to time, the two older men enjoyed sex with Tyler, but in reality it was an older couple in charge, and Tyler was at some point going to be odd man out.

From his previous tailing of the two men, he suspected they were fencing their stolen items quickly, but the thieves were retaining untraceable items like diamonds, as well as gold and cash. Tyler was young, inexperienced, and none the wiser, and probably cut out of those items.

He returned to the study and sat down at one of the two desks and turned on the computer monitor. It was password protected. He smiled as he took another small device from a zipper compartment on his bag and inserted one end of the device into an USB port. He pushed a button on it and the computer immediately rebooted, and a second later, it came up with a display of the root directory of the entire hard drive, bypassing all security controls. He plugged a portable five hundred gigabytes all digital hard drive into another USB port and tapped a button on the device, and instantly it began downloading the entire drive to the portable drive. He knew the two devices would not leave any footprint on the computer, preventing detection of infiltration.

While it was working, he went to the other desk, and repeated the same procedure until he had all the information on both computers. He searched the desks carefully, while looking and making pictures of anything of interest with his small camera. He found some banking account numbers, but these appeared to be used strictly for household utilities and employees.

He sat back in the office chair and studied the room. He smiled as he stood up and placed the tiny camera he picked up from Oscar before leaving town. He placed it high on the bookshelf behind the desk looking downward so he could see the computer monitor and keyboard strokes.

He returned to the kitchen and reset the alarm allowing him time to get out the door and lock it. He undid his work on the outside alarm and phone system, and made his way towards the fence. He searched the area until satisfied the top of the pool utility shed was the right place for the router. He climbed up and placed it on the backside of the roof and out of view from the house, and checked to be sure it would always get sunlight. He flipped on the switch and watched as a red light flashed red about six times before going green. The camera was now reaching the router. This made him smile.

His next problem was how to reach the limb so he could get over the fence. He took a roll of nylon cord from the bag and put on a pair of black workout gloves. He tied a stick to one end of the rope and threw it over the limb, and then let out the loose line so it encircled the limb and fell to the ground. He untied the stick, but used it to wind up the cord until it was just over his head. Holding on tight he lifted his legs allowing his body weight to bend the limb downward. He began twisting the limb to roll up more cord as the limb bent even farther down. Once he was within reach, he shifted his weight up and down causing the limb to sway. As the limb arc downward he reached up and grabbed the limb and rode it upward until he had his arms and legs over the limb. Holding the cord in his teeth he worked his way over the wall and dropped down. He untied the cord, threw the stick away, and made his way across the street and into the park.

He searched around until he found a telephone pole in the sun and away from tall limbs. He again scanned the area and was amazed that he could not see another human being anywhere. He removed the nylon cord from his backpack once again, tied a stick to the end and threw it over the third step rod sticking out of the pole. The phone company never put the rods all the way to ground fearing a kid might climb the pole. They normally used a ladder for the first twelve feet, and then used the rods the rest of the way. Using his muscles, he pulled himself upward until he got a hand on the first rung and worked his way upwards, hand over hand, until he could put his feet on the first run. Then he simply climbed the rods as easily as using a ladder for the rest of the way.

At top of the pole he fastened the satellite relay link exactly in the center using a Velcro strap, while making sure it was completely out of sight from the ground below. He again turned on the button and the red light flashed for about ten seconds and went green. It began to whirr as it began unfolding until a tiny satellite dish was formed, turned and twisted until it soon locked on to a satellite some twenty-two thousand miles in space. It made Eric shake his head in disbelief at the technology. He was in business.

He climbed down and made his way back to his car, drove a few miles before stopping and buying some lunch, and then returned to his hotel. He had just entered the room when his cell phone rang. He had to stop himself from answering until he could see the caller ID. It was Tyler. He looked at his watch and realized he was not yet arriving in Los Angeles, at least time wise, so he ignored the call for now.

Tyler wasn't expecting to catch Eric, as he knew the flight would take about three hours, but he wanted to leave him a message. "Hi Eric. I know you're flying, but I wanted to call and give you my new cell phone number as the battery is quickly dying on this old one. My new number is 410.313.7821. Call me when you get in. I'm throwing this old phone in the trash. Bye."

Tyler hung up and just as he was about to throw it in the trash as planned, it suddenly rang and he nearly jumped out of his shoes. He quickly looked at the caller ID, and realized it was Stephen calling him. What to do?

He took a deep breath, chewed his lip, and then threw the phone in the trash.

He decided talking to Stephen or Jim would let them know he was alive, and they would want to know where he was. He wanted nothing more to do with them, and he was afraid of them. Stephen hit him from time to time, and sometimes threatened to kill him because Tyler made a mistake on a job. Tyler knew they kept secret information from him. He also knew they were lying to him about how much they obtained for the fenced merchandise, leaving his one third cut shorter than it should have been. He knew he was a witness to their crimes, and Stephen didn't like loose ends. He suspected Stephen would kill him when they tired of him.

Stephen left a voicemail message and hung up. Turning to Jim he said, "He's not answering."

Jim came out of the bathroom in their hotel room. "Where in the hell is he. We haven't seen him in almost twenty-four hours."

Stephen thought for a few seconds. "Something is wrong. That boy can't be still except when he is asleep. He would have called and given us an update on his progress or something. This isn't like him."

"I'm going to see if Toby Embler is still here." Jim picked up the phone and asked to be connected to Toby's room. It rang three times and Toby picked up. Jim said, "Oh, I'm sorry. They've connected me to the wrong room." He hung up. "Well, he's still here. Were you successful with your mark?"

"Yes, I'll clean him out tonight. And you?"

"Same here. It will be like taking candy from a baby. He is such a stupid jerk. If I have to kiss him one more time I'm going to throw up."

"I know what you mean. What should we do about Tyler?"

"You don't think that guy kidnapped him, do you?"

Stephen replied, "I want to see inside his room. What time is the auction?"

Jim checked his watch. "In about an hour, why?"

"You go to the auction early and watch for Toby. When you see him, buzz me, and I'll go check out his room before coming down."

"Okay, we'd better get ready. We have to wear black tie tonight."

"Don't forget to bid early, and then drop out so we don't waste any money, but appear active."

"Our plane leaves at four in the morning, so we'll have to do our business, drug them, and get the hell out-of-town."

"Believe me, I'll be ready to get rid of my mark."

Eric set up his laptop and began uploading the data on both drives to the firm's secured FTP site. He called James at his office. "James, how are you? That's good. Listen, I'm uploading the contents of two computers to our FTP site, code number 06237 and 06238 and 'marvel' is the password. You and Lionel take a look and give me a report on everything you find. I'm looking for hidden bank accounts, offshore accounts, stocks and bonds, passwords, etc. I'm also looking for the combination to a H.L. Security Enterprise Bank Safe, model 634932, and serial number 845F29E452. It will be disguised by any number of ways. Let me know when you have it all sorted out. Get me details on that safe. Thanks. Bye."

Eric typed in the link to the camera to test it out. The sat dish was broadcasting up to space, down to his office, and then it went out on his secure website in a hidden area. He punched in the codes and presto; he was looking at the office with full color quality. He zoomed in and out with the on-screen controls and smiled. He opened his notepad and dialed one of the house phone lines. Suddenly, he could hear the phone ringing and see the light blinking on the line one of the desk phone. He laughed out loud.

He called his office and dialed Oscar's extension. "Oscar, this is Eric. I set up the camera as instructed, and the picture and audio is amazing. Take a look."

Oscar back peddled his rolling office chair to another workstation and typed in the code. Two seconds later, he was looking at exactly the same thing that Eric was.

Eric grinned. "Now watch this." Eric hit redial on his phone. When the phone in the house rang, he laughed. "Do you hear that? Crystal clear. You're a genius. Make some more of these units as soon as possible. About the only thing to worry about is how to recover our equipment? I will think about that. Keep up the good work and thanks. Start digitally recording this camera along with the audio. Create a case number. Thanks again."

Eric went out and ate dinner at a nearby restaurant. He returned to his room, checked his watch, and called Tyler on the new phone. "Hey, buddy. How are you?"

"I'm on the way to dinner. I'm starved."

He lied, "Me, too. What a long boring flight."

"I see you got my new number. I'm so glad you called. I can't wait for you to get back home. Listen, is it okay that I came to see you. I mean if I was just a two night stand I'll understand, but I think of you as way more than that."

Eric smiled. He hoped Tyler was telling the truth. "Yes, it is fine. We'll have a good time, and I'll show you all of Baltimore when I get there. Well, you go eat. I'm going to take a nap and then go to bed. I'm whooped."

Tyler laughed. "A nap before bed. That makes no sense. I miss you. Call me when you can, and I promise not to bother you while you're on your business trip. See you soon. Bye."

Tyler met the room service guy at the restaurant for dinner and things went well. They decided to go to a movie and then the guy asked Tyler to come home with him, as he was afraid to be seen at the hotel. Tyler did and they enjoyed sex together for a few hours before Tyler caught a cab back to the hotel. It wasn't love, he thought, but it was fun. He had the boy's phone number in his pocket just in case he needed it.

Jim buzzed Stephen as soon as he saw Toby appear in the reception area where the rich were drinking cocktails waiting on the auction to start. The host felt if they were drunk enough they would bid higher, so the alcohol flowed freely. He spotted Stephen's man and his own mark, and sighed. He hung up and reluctantly went over to him. The old man gave him a kiss, a hug, and squeezed his butt. Well, at least the old man's motor was still running, he thought.

Stephen made his way down a flight of stairs and searched the hallway for the cameras. Thankfully, there was only one in the direction he needed to go, but he had not yet got to it. It took out a small spray can and reached up and sprayed white foam over the lens blinding the camera. He then ran to the door, slid a credit card device into the door magnetic reader of the door, and pushed a button. The device ran through thousands of combination in three seconds, and the door lock clicked green. He pocketed the device, pushed in, and closed the door.

He went from room to room, but Tyler was nowhere to be found. He began to search for any of Tyler's clothes, but he found nothing. He started going through the drawers, and it startled him when he opened the drawer by the bed with the sex tools and big knife inside. He studied them a second, and finally he saw several long strands of blond hair. It had to be Tyler's. What had this guy done to him? Was he alive, he wondered?

He closed the drawer, and exited the room while being careful not to leave any fingerprints. He checked the hall and walked out towards the camera. He retrieved a chrome telescoping wand like the kind a professor might stretch out to point to something on a wall board, placed a small tissue on the end, and from out of view, he used it to wipe the lens clear of the foam, compacted the device, and tossed the tissue in a nearby trash can.

He made his way to the reception and upon entering he spotted Jim and gave him a signal by pulling his right ear lobe. Stephen then went out in the hallway and waited. Jim excused himself from his soon to be victim and went out in the hall. Together, they walked away from the room.

Jim couldn't wait. "What did you find?"

I didn't find Tyler or any of his clothes, but I did find something puzzling. In a drawer by the bed, I found quite a few sex toys designed for rough sex. I saw the bands for tying hands and feet of the person on the receiving in, tit clamps, a rolled washcloth to muffled screams, a big knife, a huge dildo, a lot of lubricant, and several arm condoms."

"Jeez Louise," exclaimed Jim alarmed at the news. "You don't think he did something to Tyler do you?"

"I found several long blond hairs on one of the bands used to tie off the hands and feet."

"Oh no. That poor boy, but where is he?"

"I don't know but we have to find out."

"What if he killed Tyler?"

"Then we have to be careful he doesn't do the same to us, and if he did kill the boy, we may have to kill him to keep Tyler's body from being traced back to us. I'm sure the cameras in the hotel have recorded the three of us with him at some point."

"And I was hoping we wouldn't have to kill again. How long as it been since the last one—eighteen months or so?"

"About that. Okay, I'll speed up the handling of my mark. I will fake being sick, ask him to take me to his room, and make my move. Once I'm done, I'll go back to our room and pack, and wait for you. Then we'll go to Toby's room, and find out about Tyler. Is that okay with you?" Stephen always asked a question, but Jim knew the answer had already been decided.

"Sure, whatever. Let's get this done and get the hell out of here. I'm going to need disinfectant after I finished with my mark."

Tyler was tired from his long day, beginning the night before, and went to bed early feeling very safe in his Sheraton room and far from Stephen and Jim.

Eric studied his Argentina security plans for about two hours before going to bed, as tomorrow would be a long day as they flew to and settled into their hotel in Buenos Aires. He hoped everything went well.

EIGHT

Stephen nonchalantly slipped some drug powder in Rob's cocktail while feigning sick in the bathroom in Rob's room. After several stupid toasts, Rob suddenly fell asleep. Stephen quickly went through his luggage and took anything of value. He took the man's wallet and removed the cash and credit cards, and a stack of traveler's checks. He found the wall safe and went over to Rob and searched his pockets until he found the key. He opened the safe and removed about fifty thousand in cash, but left several thousand more in casino chips. He went back to the bathroom and picked up the man's electric shaver. Using the trimmer, he cut a path straight down the center of the man's head from front to rear. Once he got it short enough, he shaved the stripe. It gave him the look of a reverse Mohawk. He did this to shame him into leaving the hotel and town as soon as possible. He hoped he wouldn't report the crime, but Jim and Stephen used fictitious names and identification so it wouldn't matter if he did. No one would be able to track them.

Jim experienced a little more trouble as his mark wanted sex. They started getting undressed, but the man wouldn't drink his spiked champagne. Desperate, Jim got on his knees as if ready to suck his new friend, when suddenly he said, "What is this?" he said as he pointed at the man's genitals. "Is that a growth?"

Alarmed the man bent over to look just as Jim swung his head upward hard and fast, hitting the man's jaw with his head, knocking him out cold. "Ow, that hurt," complained Jim, as he quickly dressed. He poured the bad drink down the toilet and flushed it. He robbed the mark of all his cash and credit cards, and took the money pouch he had felt under the man's shirt the night before. He found a nice gold watch in the safe and more cash. He then hurried to the room.

They packed all their stuff and put the loot in UPS Air Boxes with their pre-done labels affixed. Then they made their way down to Toby's room hoping he was alone. Stephen took care of the camera again, and using his keycard tool on the door, they burst into the room. Toby was in the shower and thankfully alone. When he came out of the bathroom, Stephen hit him in the back of the neck with a hard judo chop that sent the man to the floor. Jim quickly tied his hands behind his back with the bands they found in the drawer and stepped on his balls to wake him up. They left him lying on his stomach making it difficult for him to see their faces.

Toby started to scream at the pain. Stephen leaned down with the knife in his hand and put the tip in front of Toby's eyes. "If you make another sound I'm going to cut your balls off. Do you understand?"

Toby shut up and nodded his head.

"Good. You left the auction last night with a friend of ours, and he hasn't been seen since. Where is he?"

"I don't know. He wanted sex, and I told him I don't have sex with strangers."

Stephen slapped the back of Toby's head with the flat of the blade.

"Ow," complained Toby again.

"Obviously, we have already been in your drawer, and it looks like you were ready for sex with strangers since you arrived by yourself. Now what happen to Bobby?" He'd almost said Tyler's name, but quickly recalled Tyler's faked identity name.

"Nothing, we had a good time and made out a little..."

Stephen took the tip of the blade and stabbed Toby's scrotum sack lightly.

"Ow!"

"If you lie one more time I'm going to cut those balls off and you're going to eat them."

Toby sighed hard. "Okay, okay. We had sex."

"Rough sex?"

"Not for me. I thought it was fun."

Stephen sliced a thin line across Toby's butt with the knife.

"Ow!"

"You sick bastard. What did you do to him?"

"I tied him up and fucked the tar out of him. I didn't hurt him. Afterwards, I washed him up, let him go, and he left."

"About what time?"

"It was about two this morning."

"So you raped him"

"I wouldn't call it that. He got naked on his own."

"Did he have a choice on being tied while you were fucking him?"

Toby went silent.

Stephen said, "I didn't think so." He turned to Jim. "Get his wallet, empty the safe, pack all his clothes, and leave nothing for him."

"You're robbing me for having sex with your friend?"

Stephen hit him with the blade again, "We're robbing you because you raped our friend, and if we don't find him safe and sound, we're going to come back and kill you."

"Hell, it's my word against his."

Stephen smiled and slowly reached around the man's head, so Toby could see the small tape recorder he held in his hand. "We have your confession on tape."

Toby sighed heavily.

Once Jim packed everything, Stephen took the rolled up washcloth he found in the drawer and pushed it deep into Toby's mouth. He grabbed the huge dildo and without lubricant, he rammed him as harshly as he could into Toby's butt. The man screamed through the sock.

Jim laughed wickedly. "Ooo, that had to hurt."

"I bet it felt good to a bastard like this. Get his shaver and stripe him."

Jim went to work making the same reverse Mohawk down the center of the man's long black hair. Feeling sadistic, he shaved off one of the man's eyebrows. However, even Jim flinched when Stephen took his heel and slammed it down as hard as he good onto Toby's testicles.

He laughed. "I doubt those things make any more sperm. Did you hear them crack?"

Toby was agonizing in pain, but Stephen didn't let up. He took the knife and cut stripes across the toes of the man's feet and his heels, making it difficult and painful for him to walk. He took the knife to the man's forehead cutting several stripes, and did the same to both cheeks; he then broke his nose with a quick punch. "I hope this will keep a good looking guy like Bobby from ever hanging out with you again."

He turned Toby over throwing a sheet over his head so he couldn't see their faces. He took the knife and sliced the man's penis. He kicked Toby numerous times in the face and the ribs. After the man blacked out at the pain, Stephen took the knife and sliced open the bands and they left.

An hour later, they boarded their flight after dropping the UPS boxes at the airport's shipping station.

Toby woke a half hour later and managed to stop the bleeding to his face and feet, but as he dressed and put his socks and shoes on, he screamed at the pain. He wrapped his bleeding penis in another washcloth, and made it to his rental car. He drove to an all night walk-in clinic, and gave them his BlueCross BlueShield card so they would stitch him up. He gave them no stories or excuses, and so they did the work. He went back to his room, took some of the drugs they gave him and passed out. It would take a few days before money could be wired to him, a private jet secured, and finally the courage to sneak out of the hotel in the middle of the night and fly home.

Jim whispered to Stephen on the flight. "You were brutal tonight. I like that. It turns me on."

"Oh, you want me to tie you up tonight?"

"Hell, no. I'd kick your ass."

They both laughed. Stephen said, "We're not done with Toby. We have all his credit card info. We'll search it out and start stealing from him electronically. If Tyler is hurt, we'll go to Toby's house and rob, torture, and kill him."

"Amen, but I wonder what happen to Tyler."

TJ Johnson

"I'm hoping he is home waiting for us. That's what I would have done. He probably ran as far away from Toby as possible."

"Well, old Toby ain't going to be running anywhere for a long, long time."

They both laughed again.

"Good morning, gentlemen, and I use that word loosely," said Eric as he stepped aboard the plane to join his men and the governor.

"Good morning boss. I'm glad you could join us after working on your tan in Miami." The guys laughed.

Eric put his carry-on stuff in the overhead compartment across from his seat. "I wish. I had to climb a tree, use my skills to open a few doors, climb onto a roof, and finish with a climb to the top of a telephone pole. Not a fun day for me. How's it going so far?"

Bob, his team leader, was in the seat next to his, "Everything is set, and although we don't officially go on duty until we get there, here's the passenger list and information James and Lionel researched for us. I don't see any problems, but I thought you might want to scan through it." Bob was also an ex-marine and a good leader in the field. He made quick, precise decisions, and willing to back everything he said and did. He had five kids and two wives. The ex-wife had the kids, and to keep her happy and the kids well taken care of, he needed the excellent money Eric paid for his service.

Bob added, "It took a little work but the flight crew checks out."

Eric replied, "I assume there were no last minute substitutions." Eric took the research list and began reading through it.

"I checked each person myself, and Jimmy is still at the door waiting for it to close, so that no one suddenly runs up late and jumps onboard."

"Good."

"Eric, how are you?" Eric turned to see Bill Montross with his hand out and smile on his face. Bill was six feet six inches tall, and made a stoic impression as the head of the governor's security team. He was ex-army, which Eric often ribbed him for, and called him the jolly green giant.

Eric took his big hand in his. "I'm great and it's good to see you."

Bill said, "I'll introduce you to the governor when we get there. He's safe in first class."

"Good. Any changes since we talked the other day?"

Bill smiled. "Not yet, but he is a man that goes with the flow. This trip is important to Virginia's economy. Our paper mills want to triple their production to Argentina."

Eric laughed. "Okay, I'll play along, but the word on the street is your governor plans to run for a higher office next year, and this trip is about building up his foreign policy experience and photo ops."

Bill slightly blushed. "I'm not sure what you heard but no decisions have been made…"

Eric interrupted, "Yet."

Bill laughed. "You're tough today. What's a matter? No mint on your pillow in Miami?"

Eric laughed. "Yeah, that's it. We have everything set for you." He turned to Bob, "Bob, do you have one of our radios for Bill?"

"I gave it to him this morning."

Eric continued, "Bill, just remember, this country used to be filled with violence, and though things have quieted in the last few years, there is still a lot of cops and politicians on the take, so don't trust anyone. If you're suspicious of anything, then get on that radio."

The plane started taxing to the runway. "No problem, well, I had better sit down and strap in. Talk at you on the ground."

"I will see you soon."

Stephen and Jim arrived at the house at dawn, having slept most of the way home, but they called ahead so Marvin prepared breakfast for them. They sat down to eat and asked Marvin, "Have you seen Tyler?"

"He's not with you?"

"No, he disappeared in Las Vegas after a bad situation with a mark. Has he called?"

Marvin frowned, as he liked Tyler. "No, no one has called."

"Well, let me know if you hear from him." Jim lied, "I'm worried about him."

"Okay, who wants more coffee?" Marvin brought the coffee to the table and warmed their cups with a bit more.

Jim said to Stephen, "What do you have planned today?"

"Once the UPS boxes arrive I think you should make a trip to Fort Lauderdale."

"Okay, you aren't coming?"

"No, I want to do a little fishing with the credit and bank cards from the three marks. If they were stupid enough not to call the cops, and I suspect they might be too embarrassed to do so with those bare stripes on their heads, then I'll move a little of their money offshore for safe keeping."

"I know you said we might pay Toby a visit one day, are you thinking the others might be worth a future trip, too?"

Stephen smiled. "You read my mind."

"What about Tyler? Do you think that guy killed him?"

Stephen sighed. "It's a possibility, and that might be safer for us."

"Safer? How so?"

"Well, if he was so upset at what Toby did to him that he went to the police, well, he might accidentally spill the beans on us?"

"Shit! He'd better not."

"That's why if the mark killed him, then there wouldn't be a link to us." He paused while they thought about Tyler for a second. Stephen added,

"I'm going to do a little online research and see if he went to the police. I may hire a private dick out there to look for him since we can't do it ourselves."

"Okay, I'm going to take a shower and get a nap while we wait for the shipment. See you later."

Tyler yawned like an African lion sunning in the morning sun. It was the best night of sleep he had experienced in a while. He felt his harden penis, but rolled over hoping for another hour or two of sleep, but for some reason he couldn't go back to sleep. He walked naked to the shower, and let the hot water wake his tired bones up. As the water ran over his head, he thought about what happen to him in Las Vegas with that creep Toby. In his young life, he had been beaten before by a mark, but never as cruel as Toby did. He knew he never wanted to put himself in that situation again. Toby made him feel like a whore. Tyler felt he used sex as a tool for stealing, bur rarely a real whore. This time though, with no reward, he got himself violated in the most awful way. He vowed not to go back to Miami, and to never see Stephen and Jim again.

After he dried off, he brushed his hair while standing in front of the mirror naked. He still had some purple bruises on his skin, and it pissed him off. He suspected Stephen and Jim would think he would turn them in, and thus, turn on him. He knew they dealt with bigger crime bosses to fence their winnings, as he called it, and he wouldn't put it past them to put a hit out on him. He wondered if they thought he was dead. He smiled because if they did, he would be free to start his life over.

He knew overall they had been good to him with a place to live, clothes to wear, food to eat, but he also knew they were using him in many ways, including sex for themselves, as well as using his body to rob rich marks. The only thing he learned from them was how to be a better thief. He knew it has been fun for a while, but while they were building up their wealth, he wasn't quickly improving his bank account, or his ability to become independent like having his own car and house. He knew they cheated him on the split, but because he had seen Stephen's violent temper, he said little about his diminished share. Tyler never acted like it before, but he had always been afraid of Stephen, and perhaps Jim, too.

He recalled one time in San Francisco when an innocent drunk accidentally walked into the middle of Stephen setting up a con job, and just as the mark was about to fall for it, he ran away, leaving Stephen empty handed after three days of work. Tyler saw him beat the poor drunk man to a pulp, and only Jim prevented Stephen from running over the fallen bleeding man with the rental car.

"No," he said aloud. He would not go back to them, and although he could be naïve at times, he knew that if Eric didn't want him as an equal partner, he would leave Baltimore and go somewhere else. He would get a job and try to work on his education and skills. The only thing he was really good at was operating computers, but he didn't know how that could make him money. He would also have to return to Miami to empty his secret safe deposit box, but for now he had plenty of cash, and he would not use any of Stephen's credit cards, as they would track him. He threw the cards away preventing any temptation to do so.

He put on the hotel's guest terry cloth bathrobe, ordered room service and waited for his favorite hotel employee to bring it to him. He turned on the television and began flipping through the channels.

Eric walked ahead of the governor through the airport terminal, with his men flanking left and right, and behind. They immediately took a back hallway, anxious to remove the governor from public eye. His advance team had done a good job. All the vehicles were ready and idling at the edge of the sidewalk. He spoke into his radio sleeve microphone, received an all-clear code word, and pushed through the door into the sunshine. The governor's limo door was open with two of his agents on each side of the door with their eyes scanning the crowd for threats. They walked him briskly, placed him and his press secretary inside, and shut the door. Eric's team loaded up in the Land Rovers and split into teams with some leading the convoy and the others following. Their destination was a hotel about a twenty-minutes away. For the moment, they were safe from snipers in the bulletproof limo with armor plating and protective glass.

Eric was in the lead vehicle with John driving. Bob, the team leader, was in the front passenger seat. Eric instantly began scanning the area for possible targets or problems as they drove across the airport property towards the exit. Just as they rounded the last building and minutes from the expressway, they found themselves suddenly surrounded by a line of army jeeps and trucks filled with soldiers with weapons drawn.

Eric barked immediate orders into his radio. "Team two, veer right and halt! John, go left. Halt. All but John stepped out with weapons drawn."

In a precise manner that only took three seconds, Eric's agents effectively surrounded the governor's limo like the wagon trains of the western days, preparing to defend themselves against the hostiles.

"Hold your fire," commanded Eric, as he began walking towards the lead jeep.

A colonel stepped out of the jeep. "Put down your weapons," the man commanded.

"You put down yours. We have a governor to protect," stated Eric forcefully.

"I'm here to protect you."

Eric smiled. "Sir, my men have been in contact with your government for weeks planning this visit. We don't even know who you are. You obviously know who we are."

"I'm Colonel Goldez, and I was sent to lead you into town safely."

TJ Johnson

"Okay, you lead and we'll follow."

The colonel sighed, as he knew he would not gain any favor unless he was actually escorting the governor, but as he studied the gringo's eyes, he didn't feel that Eric would back down. He knew they were the eyes of soldier much like himself, but better trained and well armed.

Eric knew that as well so he made a call into his radio "Alberto, get me General Fredrico on the horn. Tell him there is a troop of his men interfering with the plans that he personally approved. Tell him that a Colonel Goldez has stopped us. Over."

Goldez became alarmed. "Okay, we'll back off. We were just trying to help you."

Eric wisely said, "I know and we appreciate it, but we need to move quick and fast, and that is not so easily accomplished with fifteen army vehicles. Thank you for your efforts."

"Yeah, yeah," grumbled the colonel, as he walked to his jeep, waved to his men, and then led his soldiers away.

The governor spoke to Bill, "Your man is pretty clever. I assume there was no one on the other end of the radio."

Bill smiled. "Well, actually there was, one of Eric's advance men in his command center who was completely confused at Eric's statement, but smart enough not to say anything. We don't have an Alberto on our team. That's a control word indicating do not follow the orders following the use of Alberto's name." The governor grinned.

They once again formed up their convoy and made their way to town. Eric shoulders didn't relax until the governor was safe in his room and the floor secured with his extra men. He went to the command center, checked out the details and reminded his agents of the luncheon in a few hours. Melody was already in place with the rest of the governor's staff. He then went to his room, opened his laptop, and picked up his firm's private secured Wi-Fi that bounced him to his home office, thanks to an antenna on the balcony outside the command center.

He checked his email and then called Marti on their secure and very private cell service, managed and scrambled by the command center down the hall. "Hey, Eric here. How's it going on the home front?"

"Hey, boss, how are you?"

"We're good with just a little hitch at the airport. I've already checked email, any messages?"

She related a few and then said, "Oscar wants to talk with you. He said the bug is hot. What the hell does that mean?"

Eric laughed. "You know Oscar. He reads too many spy novels. Transfer me to him and thanks for the help. I'll talk at you later."

After a few seconds, Eric heard a click. "Hey boss," said Oscar. "Did you get my message?"

"Yeah, very clever. How's the signal?"

84

"Good, very good. Are you online?"

Eric quickly tapped the keystrokes on his keyboard, and then suddenly, he saw a picture of Stephen's office in the Miami mansion online. "When did they get back?"

"Early this morning. I've seen two men so far, but I heard a third male voice that said something from the hallway and just out of sight. He just wanted to know what they wanted for lunch, so it must have been the cook. He sounded older. What are we looking for?"

Eric knew it was time tell Oscar a few things "You're looking at the office of two very experienced thieves and con men. They prey on folks, gain their confidence, and rob them blind. I suspect they are also not afraid to bash a few heads in the process. They are working with a known crime boss in the area that runs a series of pawnshops. I think they are related to the mob in some way. The shops fence the stolen goods out the back door. Our job is to build a case against them, but they are very good at what they do. That room has a secret vault behind the bookshelf to the right of the camera. Let me know if they go in there, but I am hoping you'll be able to see what they are doing on their computers, so we can learn where they're hiding their cash. It'll be offshore like in Cayman. They may also be using the computers to plan their next crime, so watch for plane tickets, hotel reservations, etc. Let me know if they talk about leaving town in any way."

"Okay, I got it, but I wish I had known we were so interested in their computer stuff, I could have given you a couple of sniffers."

"A couple of what?"

Oscar laughed. "You didn't read my memo? You approved their purchase. A sniffer is a device that records every single keystroke on a computer. With that tool you can learn their accounts, passwords, and secret sites."

"Oh, sorry."

"Oh, don't worry. I still have my tricks. While I watch them for a while, I will figure out their IP addresses, and I think I can get what we want electronically."

"They can't know we're watching," warned Eric.

"They won't have a clue."

Eric smiled. "Very good. Keep me posted. Oh, one more thing. These guys are major crooks, and they do most of their work by setting up a mark and robbing him of everything. So watch for any orders they make for any kind of burglar equipment, or any communication with possible other thieves or marks."

"Roger, got it. Once I learn their email addresses, I can set up a parasite mailbox."

Eric sighed. "I am afraid to ask, but what is a parasite mailbox?"

"Whenever they receive an email, I will get a duplicate in the parasite box. Whenever they send, I automatically get a copy in the parasite box send folder, and they won't have a hint I'm doing it."

"How'd you learn to do all this?"

"Well, I was a geek all my life and surfed the net all the time, and made friends with other geeks. I had to quit that stuff when my dad caught me snooping into the Pentagon computer system. I wasn't trying to steal anything, or cause any havoc, it was just a thrill that I could actually do it. The next thing I know he signed me up for the Marines. After they discovered my computer talents, they quit making me shoot a rifle, and sat me down with a bank of computers to try and snoop on their enemies. I was very good, but as you know, the pay is lousy, and I like buying big boy toys."

"Okay, good enough for me. Send me a daily synopsis if you find any action in Miami. Thanks. Bye."

Tyler decided to go exploring so he dressed and headed out the door with a smile on his face, and happy-go-lucky gait in his walk. Perhaps because he was always with Stephen and Jim, he never realized the stress that his life with them placed on him. He actually felt lighter as walked. He also felt confident he would no longer bare the burden of possible arrest if they were caught, or death if Stephen tired of him. He assumed he must have gotten used to it, but he was always afraid, though he pretended not to be. He felt it was a good thing they loved his body, and that Jim loved to suck the jizz out of him. He never left a wasted drop, while Stephen liked to fuck him, sometimes harder than he wanted, but he never complained. They tried to get him to use a little coke or other drugs, including ecstasy, but he never used drugs because he feared drugs would make it easy for them to kill him. All addictions scared him. He drank but not too much. He loved ice cream with a passion, but always held his order to just two scoops. His real weakness was Famous Amos oatmeal raison, chocolate chip cookies. He had to be on guard with those delights, or he would eat the entire new box while watching a movie on the big screen.

He waved to his hotel friend, as he went through the lobby, and sucked in a deep breath of fresh air. He began walking down the street. He hadn't gone far until his spotted an IHOP restaurant. He suddenly decided he was ready for lunch and ordered a club sandwich and a diet Pepsi. He checked out the men coming in and out of the restaurant, but since they were in a business district, most of the men were wearing ties and suits, so he couldn't see their ass very well, but he liked seeing dressed up men. He wondered if he would look a bit older in a suit. Maybe Eric would like that he looked like an adult, he thought.

He tipped well and left the restaurant, caught a cab, and asked about the nearest mall. He selected Harbor Place with over two hundred stores and tipped the driver for his choice. He went in the mall and found the directory of stores. Tyler possessed a good memory, and quickly committed to his brain the locations for several of his favorite stores. He decided he needed to buy some clothes, since he had left everything in Las Vegas. He bought three shirts and two pairs of slacks from the Tommy Hilfiger store. He also bought a few more shirts in a Calvin store plus two pairs of jeans, six white t-shirts, and his favorite Calvin underwear mixing tight briefs and boxer briefs.

He strolled into an L.L. Bean store and bought a new belt, four pairs of flannel boxers, his favorite to lounge around in, and a new medium temperature jacket. He also bought a new pair of deck shoes. The guy checking out his purchases also managed to check out Tyler when he was looking at the new jacket in the mirror. He also bought a new athletic duffle bag and a new backpack, both of which he usually carried on the plane with him when he traveled. Tyler asked the salesman to help him repack his purchases, so he could carry them through the mall.

As he walked on down the mall, he spotted some of those rental carts, put fifty cents in the machine, and was soon pushing his packages down the mall, filling pretty happy with himself. He found a men's clothing store and decided he wanted to try on some suits. He found a good-looking younger salesman to help him, after turning down two ugly old guys. He picked out a banker's suit that was dark blue with a faint gray pinstripe. He went into the fitting room and came out with suit not fitting very well.

"Come to the fitting mirror and let's see what we need to do," said the salesman.

Tyler was laughing, as he felt like he was wearing some big guy's clothes. He stepped onto a footstool and laughed at his image in the mirror. "Either the suit is too big or I'm too small."

The salesman felt his shoulders, checked his sleeves, and said, "I'll be right back. In a flash, he had the same suit in a smaller, regular size. He removed Tyler's big coat and helped him into one that was closer to fitting him.

"Now we're on track," grinned Tyler, as he turned left and right admiring the jacket.

"Hold still a second. I want to pin it and let you look at it again." The man took straight pins and took in the back a little, contouring his shape, pinned some extra fabric under the arms, marked the sleeves with chalk and drew a slanted line from the back of his shoulders and downward. "How's that feel?"

"It's amazing. I like it."

"Good, but you can't wear it with it all pinned and chalked, so we'll have a tailor work on it for you. Let's see those pants," said the salesman as Tyler slid out of the coat.

He had let go of the too large pants as he took off the jacket, and the pants suddenly fell to his knees. "Whoops," blushed Tyler but happy to show the cute guy his body.

"Here's take these and try them on," said the guy without blushing, and handing him a smaller pair of pants.

"No problem," said Tyler as he stepped out of big pants and slid on the others on right there in the mirror.

"Stand on the stool again, and hold still, so I don't stick you with a pin. This pair already fits better, but I'll can still take them in so they look custom made." The guy pinned the back, the length for the cuffs, and checked the crotch. Without a hint of being gay he said, "I take it you like to show off your package, so I can tighten up your crotch some so it doesn't look like an old man. With a body like yours, it would be a shame not to show a bit more. Is that okay?"

"Perfect. I'm Tyler, and yes, I'm gay."

The salesman grinned. "I'm Larry and so am I. Okay, go take those off. I can have these ready for you tomorrow if that is okay with you." Larry began folding the clothes and Tyler got out of the pants and began dressing.

"That's perfect. I've never owned a suit. Would you mind helping me pick out a shirt or two to go with it and some ties?"

"I'd be happy to. Go ahead and finish dressing, while I turn these into the tailor, and I'll be right back."

After tying his shoes, Tyler met him at the dress shirt counter. Larry snatched another suit identical to the one Tyler was buying from the rack, and used it to show him shirts and ties. Tyler picked out two shirts and ties. "Larry? May I ask you a question?"

"Sure, anything." He thought he might ask if he was single.

"Well, as I said I have never owned a suit so I don't know how to tie a tie. Would you teach me?"

Larry smiled, and felt a little sorry for him, but then again, Tyler was so cute, it just made him more innocent looking. "Of course I will. Come back to the mirror." Putting his arms around Tyler from behind, he tied the tie several times.

It took about twenty minutes, but soon Tyler was tying a Windsor knot like a pro. As he paid for everything, he kept thanking Larry for his help. Larry gave him his personal number, and Tyler smiled and gave him a twenty-dollar bill for a tip.

He added the shirts and ties to his cart and headed for the door. He had stored the cab company's phone number in his cell phone, so he called for a cab. It shocked him when the car drove right up. "That was fast."

"I was just turning into the mall when I heard the radio. Let me help you."

The driver and Tyler got all his stuff in the car, and then drove him to the Sheraton. A bell captain helped him load up a cart. Tyler tipped the cab driver and bellman for carrying his new purchases to his room. The bellman told him the hotel had a dry cleaning service, and suggested Tyler sort his clothes, and then dial extension 7633 for service. Tyler made a pile of the clothes for the cleaners, including some of his dirty clothes, and then made the call. He hung up and put away the rest of the clothes. Exhausted from his shopping trip, he fell on the bed to take a nap.

NINE

In Buenos Aires, Eric methodically confirmed the location of his teams as they made their way down to the banquet room in the hotel for an informal dinner with Argentina's second in command, about ten of his advisors, the United States ambassador and his staff, and the governor and his advisors from Virginia. Food had been checked, waiters frisked, exits protected, and though they were meeting in the governor's hotel, Eric still had the limo and Land Rovers standing by in case they were required to make a quick exit in case of a bomb threat or an assassination attempt.

The governor's security detail stayed close to the governor, as he met the various guests, while Eric's men handled the perimeter, except for a one of his men that Eric called Big Ralph. Simply put, Ralph could easily bench press the governor, and he was there in case someone came running with a knife. Ralph would stop the guy without using a gun. No one on Eric's team doubted anyone could get pass Ralph. However, if an attacker displayed a gun, hand grenade, or a bomb, his men would instantly shoot the assailant dead before they might do any harm to anyone. Their training for this scenario required two rapid shots to the heart from their 9mm handguns that everyone on his team carried in a custom fitted shoulder harness underneath their suits.

The event took about two and half hours before final toasts and then everyone said good night, while looking forward to tomorrow's negotiations, and an afternoon of sightseeing. Eric was not looking forward to the later, as that opened a whole realm of possibilities and opportunities for bad guys, but he knew they didn't pay him to keep the governor locked in a hotel.

After delivering the governor to the safety of his room, and making sure the current shift was good to go, Eric returned to his room, ordered room service, stripped out of his weapons, radios, and his suit, put on a comfortable warm-up suit, and fell on the bed. He picked up his cell and dialed Tyler.

Tyler's nap had been longer than he planned, but he was still recovering from Las Vegas and the stress, and so he slept long after the sun had set. When his phone rang, he was afraid it would be Stephen or Jim, but as he yawned, he remembered he had thrown that phone away. He grinned when he looked at the caller ID. "Eric? How are you?" Tyler rolled on to his back and began playing with his erection.

"I'm exhausted. It was a long day with meetings and such. I was so tired at tonight's dinner meeting that I didn't eat, so I just ordered room service."

"I guess I was so tired from shopping today that I slept through dinner. I'll probably have to get room service, too."

"What did you buy?"

"Lots of clothes," replied Tyler.

"I guess there were some important sales for you to buy so many clothes."

"No, you see, I arrived here with only the clothes on my back."

"The airline lost your luggage?"

"No, I ran away."

The sudden honest answer caught him off guard. He paused and asked, "Ran away from whom?"

"From the two men I was staying with, and from a man that, hmm..." he wasn't ready to tell Eric he had been raped, not yet at least. "Well, he threatened to kill me. I left them all in Las Vegas including my luggage. I don't plan to go back to Miami to get the rest of my stuff either, though I do need to go there to clean out my bank deposit box. My friends will not be happy that I left, but I'm so tired of them. I wasn't very happy with the way my life was going, I didn't trust them, and sometimes they threatened me as well. I mean it was fun for a while, but after meeting you, I realized I wanted a more permanent direction for my life. I'd like to get a real job, and maybe go back to school."

"I'm sorry you had the problem and very sorry you were threatened. Are you okay?" Eric's brain was rapidly analyzing all this new information, but he liked the tone of Tyler's message.

"Yes, I feel safe in Baltimore, because you are the only person on the planet that knows where I am. Buying new clothes made me feel like I was starting life all over again."

"Do you have money?"

"Yeah, I have a couple of thousand on me, so that'll take care of the hotel, food, tips, clothes and more until you get back."

"Don't use any credit cards. They could track those."

Tyler smiled while enjoying that Eric cared about him. "I threw them all away. I'll pay cash and I want to take you to dinner."

"You're on. That sounds great." Eric kept listening while letting Tyler talk as much as he wanted to, but his mind was processing what he had heard. He knew something happened in Las Vegas, and that Tyler was afraid of Stephen and Jim. Eric began his investigation of the grifters without a planned outcome, but now he knew he wanted to nail them, put them out of business, and maybe in jail, but he wasn't sure what he was going to do with Tyler.

In Buenos Aires, Pablo and three of his men were in a room two floors down from the governor's floor. He didn't really know much about the governor, other than he was divorced after a suspected affair with his much younger press secretary, but he was an American official, and his death would create an international incident, and hopefully humiliate and embarrass the current president of Argentina. There was an election coming, and he hoped to prove that the president was inept and incompetent, and couldn't even protect an American guest. Plus many in the opposing party hated Americans, preferring to side with Cuba, Columbia, and China, and their communist led governments. Anytime he could take a jab at America, he welcomed the opportunity.

Pablo grew up an orphan on the streets of Buenos Aires, surviving by stealing, but about the age of fifteen, he killed his first man over a loaf of bread he stole from a cart. The man chased and cornered him in an alley. With no escape, he pulled a knife, stabbed the man in the chest, and ran away still clutching the loaf of bread.

He had two scars on his face, the result of fights, but in his early twenties, he met a man that brought him into their crime gang. This led to an affiliation with a group of individuals that wanted to return the communist party to power on the promise the individuals that did the dirty work for the politicians, once in power they would receive high authority and wealth in the new regime.

His dark black eyes could burn a hole through a victim. His pulled back his long black hair into a ponytail. He was short at five feet eight inches, but never afraid of anyone. He had lost count as to how many people he had killed for this group. Killing never bothered him, and he knew he would keep on killing until they won.

He and his men went over the plans for three separate assaults, assuming at least one attack would result in the bloody death of the governor. They were organized and well backed with plenty of cash and weapons. The first attack would be in the hall just a turn away from the elevator. The second attack was the firing of a rocket-propelled grenade from a block south of the governor's route to visit the president. The last attack involved four vehicles: a garbage truck, a semi truck, a van, and a small car towing a street vender's food cart. The timing of this final attack had to be precisely perfect. They purchased or stole the vehicles, and prepped and stored them in an old warehouse just four blocks away. They would be moved into position at the last possible moment. He had three more of his men flying in tomorrow to assist. He also hired a pilot to keep a plane ready to fly so he and his men could escape out of the country as soon as the governor was dead.

After his men returned to their rooms, he privately worked on the script for the audio tape he would drop in a postal box before they left town, claiming victory over the president and the Americans.

Jim sighed as he walked into the office and spotted Stephen behind his desk typing away on his computer. "Honey, it's time to go to bed. I'm still jet lagged from our trip home from Las Vegas. What are you doing?"

Stephen looked up and smiled slyly at his partner. "I was successful in moving about two hundred grand from that bastard's bank accounts. He didn't stop a single credit card or bank debit card. He is so stupid. I used his credit cards to buy expensive items from our Internet web store, then transferred the cash to our bank accounts overseas."

"What? We don't have a web store. What store?" Jim moved around the desk and began massaging Stephen's shoulders while looking at the computer.

Stephen clicked a few mouse strokes and brought up a website called "Sexy Discounts". Jim immediately saw this gorgeous naked guy sitting on the hood of brand new Porsche. The car price was about half what it would cost at a dealership."

"How can you sell it so cheap?"

Stephen laughed. "Simple, I never get around to delivering it!"

Jim chuckled. "So how do you get them to pay for it?"

"I ask for a twenty percent deposit to arrange shipping from Europe to their door. I provide them with a bill of sale, shipping manifestoes, warranty documents, and more. It all looks very legitimate, but it's a scam. I sold this bozo a car using his credit card. I will also sell a few more cars and then pull the plug. One day the site is up, displaying the status of their orders, and the next day it is all gone. Once the cash is in our Italian bank account, I'll immediately transfer it to our Cayman accounts and close the Italian one. It is only an Internet transaction, and there is no way to trace it back to here. I'm actually accessing the Internet store remotely through a web host company in Italy so they can't find us. I paid them a thousand dollars to keep their mouths shut. I transferred all but about five thousand of the man's money from his checking accounts. It took some work to get into his account, but I did it."

"This is amazing. I thought you were watching porn on the Internet. Why didn't you take all of his money?"

"Because I wanted to put as much time as possible between the act of stealing his money, and the discovery of the crime. If I took it all, he would immediately know something is wrong."

"Excellent, well, come to bed. I'm horny."

Stephen laughed. "You're always horny. I'll be there in just a minute. I'm waiting on a transfer to complete in Cayman."

"I'll be naked, warm, and waiting," replied Jim as he kissed the top of Stephen's head and exited the room.

That afternoon, Stephen had collected the UPS boxes they shipped from Las Vegas, and then made his way to the Fort Lauderdale pawnshop. He returned with a few items he didn't sell, and put them in the hidden safe room in their office. Each time he went in the secret room, he marveled at how much they had achieved. The big safe held over two million in cash, and the secured metal drawers around the room held about five million in diamonds and gold. They assumed that one day they would have to leave in a hurry, so in the far corner was a stack of empty black duffle bags. The top right box near the duffle bags appeared locked like the rest, but it wasn't. Inside were the master key to the boxes, the key for the safe, as well as the combination to the safe, a stack of traveler's checks, numerous fake credit cards, and two stacks of passports, half for Stephen and the other half for Jim. They never made extra passports for Tyler, believing he was expendable. If they had to leave in a hurry, they would have shot Tyler to keep his mouth shut forever.

Last year they purchase an island off the coast of Costa Rica that was the former home of a murdered Columbian drug lord. It was an extravagant six thousand square foot home with marbled floors near a view overlooking the ocean. The purchase came with everything including a huge yacht, two sailboats, personal watercraft, and their own airport with a runway across the top of the island that took three years to build. The island was also completely self-contained with a combination of water and diesel power plant, and several deep, freshwater wells. There were several waterfalls on the island and they used the largest one to turn a waterwheel to also generate electricity. A staff of twelve kept the island in peak condition at all times. Stephen felt they would retire to the island by the end of the year. He liked pulling off their con jobs, the excitement it brought, and the fun at humiliating their victims. It became a game for him, and he always won. It did not bother him in the least to take advantage of fellow gay men all around the country. However, he knew if they kept at it for much longer, their luck would finally run out. He didn't plan to wait for that to happen.

TEN

Eric was up at six, preparing for a briefing with his staff at seven. The governor completed his in room breakfast after the testing of the food by Arnold, one of Eric's men, and then dressed for his upcoming trip to visit the president. Eric reminded his men to stay alert and assume nothing. He read an embassy brief on various anti-American groups in Argentina. He also read a report from the State Department in Washington, warning of recent activity in Buenos Aires. They went through the procedures for the trip and then broke up the meeting in time to get ready for their escort duties.

Each of Eric's security detail was at high alert as they exited the governor's room and made their way down the hall, around the turn, and over to the elevator. Just a few minutes prior to this, one of Eric's men had ridden the elevator down and back up to be sure there were no other passengers onboard when the door open.

They made their way to the parking garage, assembled the motorcade, and left the building under a police escort. About half way there, a policeman on his motorcycle pulled alongside the governor's limo. The hair suddenly stood up on Eric's neck as he barked commands into his radio. The Land Rover in the rear of the motorcade suddenly pulled out of line and stepped on it and pulled right behind the motorcycle and began blowing the horn. The cop looked in his rear mirror at the flashing lights on the black SUV right on his tail. He turned to see that it was the Americans in the front seat. He turned back around without moving away from the limo. The Land Rover reluctantly moved close and finally gave the cop's bumper a slight tap.

It rattled the cop, forcing him to adjust his balance to keep control of his bike, and pulled off to the left while giving the driver of the Land Rover a hand gesture. The guys in the Land Rover laughed as they dropped back into line once more. Eric smiled as he looked over at the governor who was silently rehearsing his speech without noticing the possible problem.

After the governor was secured in the meeting room with the President, Eric left the personal detail behind and went down the hall to meet with the American ambassador's security officer. He reported the incident with the cop. The officer made a call. The conversation was polite, and then the officer hung up while promising Eric there would be no other problems with the local police.

The governor enjoyed a private lunch with the president before returning to additional meetings that afternoon. Later they returned to the hotel to prepare for a formal dinner at the presidents' house with a guest list of about hundred people in the huge ballroom. Two of Eric's men carefully watched the president's security team as they frisked each attendee and saw nothing to alarm anyone. Arnold stayed with the food staff as they prepared the governor's meal.

An hour later, Eric and his men followed the same routine to the parking garage via the elevator, but deliberately took a new route to the governor's palace. They experienced no problems with motorcycle cops as promised.

After dinner, the boring speeches began, so Eric walked out of the palace door's to get some fresh air. He dialed a number on his cell phone and paused for it to ring. He waited while his cell phone signal made its way to the command center antenna, and then off into space to bounce off the satellite and back to Annapolis before rejoining a cell network nearby. It took less than a second for the connection.

"Hey good-looking," said Tyler as he answered his cell phone noting the caller ID. "How are you?"

"I'm bored to death with all the meetings and just stepped out of a dinner meeting to get some fresh air and see how you were doing in Baltimore."

Tyler slipped his free hand into his underwear and began playing with his arousing penis. "I went to a movie this afternoon, and walked along the wharf taking in the sea air and marveling at the all the big boats. I saw a sailboat that was at least seventy feet long. Boy, I'd like to learn how to sail one of those."

Eric laughed at how easily Tyler could chat and entertain himself, and he already longed to spend more time with him. He hated lying about his day to Tyler, but he was far from clearing Tyler for his real life. They talked for a half hour until Eric finally had to say goodnight. Tyler hit the off button, yanked his shorts down, and finished the ejaculation he had been working on. He felt so good after talking with Eric, and felt Eric's life was the kind of world he was hoping to slide into.

Eric went through the final details for tomorrow morning's departure from Buenos Aries with his field agents. He studied yet another route to the airport and the checklist for a successful day including his men at the airport, parking garage, and floor crew.

He was up at six, dressed, and fully packed within thirty minutes. His men ate their breakfast in the living room of his suite. They all checked their weapons and prepared for the protection required. Eric spoke briefly with Jimmy, a short blond guy with a rock solid body, and the most accurate shot in Eric's company. He was assigned to the roof opposite the hotel and carried a special made sniper rifle with an amazing scope. They shook hands as Jimmy quickly departed. Fifteen minutes later, he radioed to Eric he was ready.

Eric made his way to the governor's door where Bill Montross informed him they would be just five more minutes, as the governor's wife was feeling a bit woozy this morning.

Eric smiled. "Too many toasts last night, huh?"

Bill grinned. "You got it."

Eric began making the walk to the elevator while counting the steps. Before he got to the turn, he thought he heard something above the ceiling so he stopped for a second.

One of Pablo's men was using a window washer's extension pole to push a tightly wrapped bomb of six dynamite sticks down the heat and air duct system. He had already pushed the bomb as far the stick could reach so he began sliding his body forward creating the slight sound that Eric heard. Just as the man inched forward once more, his belt buckle caught on an exposed metal screw. When he tried to push forward, he came to a sudden halt, and accidentally dropped the pole. It echoed inside the sheet metal cavern. The man froze hoping no one heard.

Eric quickly moved his back to the wall and waved at his men down the hall, while pointing at the ductwork. Bill stepped inside the governor's room and quickly moved everyone into the adjoining bedroom and waited. Silently, Eric drew his gun as did his men and they waited.

The man in the shaft waited two full minutes before trying to dislodge his belt from the screw. As he did so, the buckled popped the bottom of the shaft.

Eric heard the unmistakable sound of the metal on metal and knew there was someone in the shaft. He brought his pistol up and took aim at the spot where he thought the clink sound originated and fired three shots, while moving his gun down the hall about twelve inches apart. He returned his aim and fired four more shots, each one a foot forward of the previous one.

Pablo's man was shot in the stomach, testicles, and right knee. The second barrage caught him in the chest and face. Two shots missed his already dead torso.

Eric froze and listened. He heard nothing. He swapped out his gun clip. He glanced along the black holes his bullets created. Suddenly, they began turning red and blood began dripping down to the carpet. He waived to the nearest man to him and got him to boost him up to the vent. He yanked off the nearest cover and peered inside. To his left he saw the dead man's body, and just to his right he saw the dynamite. He carefully retrieved it with the man's pole, and pulled it out of the shaft. His men became alarmed when they saw the bomb. Eric holstered his weapon, took out his knife and cut the wires away from blasting caps, effectively disarming the bomb.

"Put this in a room and lock the door." He handed the bomb to the agent standing next to him.

Eric ran down the hall to the governor's door and stepped inside. "Bill, it is all clear. There was a bomb in the overhead air shaft. I have diffused the bomb and killed the assassin. We need to leave now."

Bill nodded as he pushed the frightened governor and his associates towards the door. The security detail surrounded them as they made their way to the hallway. Eric made a quick decision and turned away from the usual elevator, and made his way down the hall to his backup plan. They descended on the service elevator, made their way through the kitchen and into the garage area.

As they boarded, Eric spoke quickly into his radio to alert the rest of the men about the attempt. "Stay alert," he said. He turned to a police captain and told him there was a bomb in room 733. He climbed into the limo and sped off with the motorcade in front and behind as usual.

Jimmy was on the roof scouting left and right. He thought he saw movement two buildings over so he turned his gun and scope in that direction.

Pablo had been in an office window across from the parking garage. He radioed his man on the roof that the limo was coming.

Jimmy found movement nearby, but it was two window washers setting up their scaffolding for today's job. He rapidly began scanning roofs and windows along the way back to the hotel.

The limo reached the street and made a turn and was in full view.

"Now!" screamed Pablo.

One of his men sprang up from his hiding position on the roof, brought the RPG launcher up to his shoulder, and took aim.

Eric spotted him and screamed at the limo driver to hang a hard left fast. Jimmy caught sight of the shooter as he heard Eric's voice in his earpiece. He aimed and fired in less than a half second.

The man pulled the trigger just as Jimmy's shot entered his brain through his right eye. Instantly, the dead man moved the butt of the rifle as he fired, deflecting his aim of the RPG just slightly. It missed the rear of the limo and sailed in front of the following Land Rover, skipped on the pavement and slammed into an office building before exploding.

Although debris from the explosion was instantly flying through the air, his men made it safely through the area. Eric urged the governor to the floor. He gave orders from the lead Land Rover to pick a way back to the route and rush them to the airport.

Pablo cursed as he ran out the back of the building and climbed into the car towing the stainless steel food cart. He spoke rapid Spanish into his radio.

Unknowingly, Eric men's took the logical shorter route to the airport as Pablo predicted. They sped through two intersections, but in the confusion after the grenade attack, they lost their police escort.

The front two Land Rovers made it through the next intersection just fine, but as the Limo approached, the driver suddenly slammed on brakes as an unseen, big semi truck pulled across the street and crashed into a power pole.

"Back up quick!" yelled Eric to the driver and into his radio.

While they waited for the rear Land Rover to back up, Eric turned just in time to see a garbage truck racing towards them from an alley across the street.

"Move to the other side NOW!" Eric downed the window about five inches, but only had time to fire to a burst of shots through the window killing the driver. The limo took the impact as the truck slammed into it, pushing the car across the street and tightly packing it against the parked cars lining the roadway.

"Is everybody all right?" He waited a brief moment as he went from face to face. "Driver, will the vehicle move?"

The driver put the shift into rear and hit the gas pedal and heard a loud grinding noise.

"Forget it, the collision broke the transmission or the drive shaft."

Eric quickly turned and looked out the back window at the remaining Land Rovers. He spoke rapid new orders into his microphone. "Make room. We're running to the lead vehicle." The limo's rear doors were pinned on one side by the truck and the other by the parked cars.

"Shield your eyes!" He kicked open the rear window with a judo move, slamming his heel through the glass, and then jumped through it. He reached back to help the governor, his aide, one of his agents, and the driver out. Three of the men from the Land Rover surrounded them as they made their way to the lead vehicle. Eric and his team scanned all directions carefully. People were confused at the crash of the big truck and now the garbage truck.

Just as he reached the Land Rover and climbed aboard, he saw a car pulling a food cart coming towards them.

Once inside in the car, Eric quickly exclaimed, "Let's go! Get us to the airport." He turned to check on the governor. "Sir, are you okay?"

"Yes, what happen?"

"I'll go over it in a moment. Hang on tight." He turned back to the driver. "Step on it."

The car pulling the cart drove right in front of them, forcing Eric's driver to slam on his brakes. Pablo pulled hard on the metal ring in his right hand. The ring was attached to a wire that pulled a pin on the hitch of the cart, releasing the trailer. Pablo's car began pulling away without the cart. Eric thought it was odd, but then his eye caught sight of a small, thin wire sparkling in the morning sun, and it was tied to Pablo's bumper and leading inside the food cart. The realization hit him like a zap of electricity.

"Back up now!" He gave the command while also yelling into his radio. Both Land Rovers began to rapidly speed backwards. They traveled only fifteen yards when the food cart suddenly blew up, blowing out the glass of the Land Rover, and blinding his driver temporarily as blood poured down his face. Thankfully, the driver managed to put his foot on the brake.

"Bill, get Roy in the other car, and take over driving."

Eric exited the Land Rover car and began running toward the car that had been pulling the cart. Pablo was trying to make his way through traffic. Catching a glimpse of Eric running towards him he leaped from the vehicle, took a wild shot at Eric, and turned to run down an alley.

Eric rounded the corner and ducked a second shot, then leaped over a trash can, ran across an alley and caught a glimpse of Pablo as he lined up a steadier shot. Eric dove to the ground as Pablo fired, spun over and came up with his pistol and held the trigger down. The 9mm fired rapid shots as Eric instantly adjusted his aim. The first shot missed, the second caught Pablo in the knee, the third in the stomach, the fourth in the heart, and the fifth in the face. Pablo flew back and into a plate glass window of a bakery.

Eric ran up and checked to see that he was dead and then sprinted back to his men. It took a few minutes to retrieve the bleeding Roy from the driver's seat and place him in the passenger seat of the second Land Rover. Bill had just gotten behind the wheel. Eric climbed in, "Let's go!"

Twelve seemingly long minutes later, they reached the plane safely and quickly departed leaving their vehicles on the tarmac. While his press secretary remained petrified and shaking, except for a few scrapes and bruises, the group escaped unharmed.

Eric checked to make sure all his motorcade men made the flight, and the governor's doctor was painstakingly removing the shards of glass from Roy's face and eyes. Eric called ahead to have an eye surgeon standing by in Annapolis. He got on the radio to their command center in the hotel in Buenos Aires and told them the governor was safe in the air. He gave the order to dismantle, pack, and get the heck out-of-town as quickly as possible. The firm's transport plane was readied, and they would be in the air in two hours.

Although they expected no other problems, all his men reloaded their weapons and settled down in their seats. Eric sat opposite Bill Montross as Bill spoke, "Well, that was interesting."

"Too interesting. I killed the guy in the air shaft, the garbage truck driver, and the guy pulling the cart. Jimmy got their guy on the roof."

"Excellent. I'm sure they'll be an investigation, but way to go, you saved the governor."

"I didn't get the guy in the big truck and that worries me."

"I'm sure the police have caught up with him. I'll make some calls and see what I can find out."

Eric finally relaxed and felt sleepy as the surge of adrenalin suddenly went away. He was asleep in a few minutes.

Stephen was up early researching private detectives in Las Vegas. After an hour, he selected three and began phone interviews. He used one of his aliases. Using a pre-paid throw away phone, he waited on the phone to ring and answer. "Hello, this is Bobby Jones. Is Mister Lester available?"

"One moment please."

A brief pause of nauseating elevator music turned up too loud, and then a man in a low voice answered, "Hello, this is Tommy Lester. How can I help you?"

Stephen began his story "My name is Bobby Jones. My stepbrother, Tyler Savage, went out to Las Vegas last weekend and was supposed to come home on Sunday, but didn't make his flight. He called me on Saturday telling me he had met the most marvelous man by the name of Toby Embler. They were going to a charity function for AIDS or something. He calls me almost every day, usually to brag about something he has done, and called at least three times a day from Las Vegas until Saturday night. I haven't heard a word since. Mom is really upset, as she didn't want him to go in the first place, but I assured her all would be fine. Can you help us find him?"

"Did you call the police?"

Stephen had been ready for this question. "No and I will be blunt to save time. Tyler has a record and has been out of jail for about a year. Mom thinks he had been the perfect kid since then, but I know better. I thought we would try a private detective because I think the cops would say he is a criminal and do nothing to find him."

"I see, well, okay. I need the facts and pictures."

"Do you have an email address?"

"Yes, of course." He gave Stephen the email address.

"I've prepared several pictures and timeline of his weekend in Las Vegas. I also have included a copy of his drivers license. I will include the hotel information, his flight, and even his cell phone number, as well as my information. How much do you charge?"

Tommy gave him his fee schedule.

"That's no problem, do you accept credit cards? Great, I'll send you my credit card info. Go ahead and charge twenty-five hundred to get you started. Bye for now and you'll have the info in just a few minutes."

Stephen hung-up laughing and began emailing all the details as promised.

Jim entered the room with a yawn while stretching his arms and said, "What have you been up to so early?"

Stephen got up and said, "I hired a detective to find Tyler. I'm starved. Let's eat." They walked to the kitchen.

Stephen devoured an awesome ham, sausage, and cheese omelet Marvin made for him. Jim finished the rest of his southwestern version with hot peppers.

Jim set his fork down, took another sip of his coffee and asked, "Why don't we fly down to Costa Rica for a couple of weeks and rest a spell?"

Stephen wiped his mouth with the linen napkin and smiled. "Boy, I would love that, but I think we have a few loose ends to tie up, and I'm hoping we find Tyler. Let's give it a few days and see what happens with the private detective. "I was thinking about my mark on the last job. He said he has a gorgeous ten thousand square foot home, a dozen cars, and major art collection. I bet he keeps a lot of pretty things around that house and perhaps some cash, too."

"What was his name?"

"Rob Ensley. He's from San Diego."

"Well, at least it would be warmer," replied Jim after another sip of coffee. "What do you have in mind?"

"I was thinking of flying out in a few days, scoping his place out, and see if there's a score to bring home."

"I guess I had better go to the gym and work on my back muscles so I can carry all the loot out," said Jim sarcastically.

Stephen laughed. "You'd better head there right away so you get all the help you can get."

Jim playfully flung his napkin at him, "That's funny. Last night you said my back was wonderful."

Stephen stood up laughing. "Honey, I said your butt was wonderful!"

ELEVEN

Tyler smiled when his favorite room server showed up at the door with his breakfast. Tyler made him sit down and eat some with him as they talked a while. Afterwards, the waiter went back to work and Tyler took a long shower while guessing what time Eric would arrive. He went through his clothes trying to figure out what to wear, while constantly checking the clock.

Eric and the team arrived at the office just after two that afternoon. They dropped their weapons gear in the armory for safe storage and cleaning, then placed their radios on a wheeled cart for tech support, and finally personal stuff and paperwork to their offices. After a short break, they all moved to the conference room. Following Eric's instructions, Marti arranged a scrumptious buffet for the team, so they filed thru the line stuffing their plates with the hot food. Eric finished eating his meal, and then moved to the podium to begin the debriefing.

"Well, that was an interesting end to our little visit to Buenos Aires. Let me quickly say the doctor has called and Bill is doing fine. They did minor surgery and removed all of the glass. I told him to go home and rest. I think there will be a little bit of red tape for our embassy staff in Buenos Aires, as the Argentineans will probably say that the cowboy Americans shot innocent civilians. I never take killing lightly, but the men we shot intended to kill the governor and us. We got lucky in the hall. That was a mistake on my part. We'll add ductwork screening to our checklist.

"I think we should practice some driving skills and tactics for motorcades. We moved too slow and reacted too late. That RPG was a wakeup call. We should have moved faster and kept going as fast as possible. We were so busy staying together in a convoy that we nearly got our butts blasted into dust particles.

"For the next few days we'll run some auto drills on the back lot. I think the moment we have the first hint of an incident we should go into hyper mode and assume that everything the enemy has is coming at us at once, because one way or the other it is.

"Our enemy had weeks to plan today's events. I give them some credit as they had not one, but several backup plans. The bomb in the hall would have done the job had I not heard the noise above. Jimmy reacted quickly to the RPG, but he can't look left and right at the same time for collisions. Next time, I want at least two or more men on sniper lookout.

"Those two trucks quickly shut down the limo. We're lucky the steel in the doors held, but it also trapped us. Do you have any ideas on the attack on the street?"

Al spoke up. "It wasn't our limo, but I think we could create a small explosive for a hidden roof hatch and perhaps, something for the doors as well."

"Interesting, but we have to protect the people inside."

Al responded, "It'll be the same as the hatch explosions they used on space capsules."

The group of men laughed.

"Very good. Okay, I want you to go to your offices and think of everything we did wrong, and I want a long list of suggestions on how we can improve. Place everything in your field reports and give them to Marti before you leave today. Good job on this trip, and I hope all of you believe we can be better. I'm proud of you. Thank you."

Eric returned to his office, signed a bunch of paperwork Marti prepared, wrote his own report, and was just about to leave when Oscar buzzed him.

"Can you come down for a visit? I have some news for you on our camera in Miami."

"I'll be right there."

Oscar had digitally edited hours of surveillance data down to about a four-minute presentation.

"Hey, Oscar. How are you?"

"Great. How was Buenos Aires?"

"Let's just say I'm glad to be home. What have you got?'

"Our little camera has done an admiral job for us. Here's a little bit of the good stuff. He rolled the video on the large LCD monitor on the opposite wall. This guy is calling himself Stephen Einstein, although on the phone he uses a variety of alias. I have compiled a list. I don't know how he remembers all of them. He is by far the brains and brawn of this outfit. You did know they were gay, didn't you?"

"Yes I did. They are also thieves who prey on rich gay people, but I suspect they have done far more serious crimes."

"I wouldn't be surprised. Here are some blowups of his keystrokes. I enhanced this and discovered he is running a scam out of Italy. He takes credit cards for big deposits, and transfers the money to his Cayman bank account. I went to work on that and though hard to break into, he has seven accounts in Cayman worth about six million, and two more accounts in Costa Rica. I did some title research work and found where he apparently bought an island there. They must be loaded.

"Anyhow, he also made calls to a pawnbroker in Fort Lauderdale who told them they sold the loot for three hundred thousand. He argued with the guy, but finally accepted it, and said Jim would pick up the cash in a few hours. Jim is his partner in crime and I guess lover, so to speak.

"Jim brought some bags of their loot and cash into the office, and took it to their safe room. That is one slick piece of cabinetry. I wish we had a camera in there, but with a little bit of luck I found a way to see part of it.

When he opens the bookcase, there is a sheet of black Plexiglas attached to the back. I'm not sure why perhaps a sounding board."

Eric cut in. "I saw it, too. I think it there because it is lighter than a huge thick piece of backboard for the cabinet. From the front, the back of the bookcase looks just like the rest of the room with a wood grain finish, but when it swung out, I realized it had to be a lighter cabinet to make it easy to swivel in and out.

"Well, once they cut the light on in the safe room, I can see a reflection of what they are doing. He puts the cash in the safe, and the wall is a line of safe deposit boxes like in a bank. He puts jewelry, diamonds and gold in those drawers. I watched him go in there several times and when I slowed it down, I realized that he immediately goes to the far right out of view, and then returns with a ring of keys in his to both the safe and the boxes. The safe takes one key and the combination. When he finishes, he disappears out of sight and leaves with no keys.

"Well, it pissed me off that I couldn't see where he was putting the keys. So I enhanced the audio. This is the sound of him putting the keys in one of those drawers." He played the metallic sound at ten times slower than normal resulting in a distinct sound. He heard the key go in the lock, the lock turned and clicked, and then they heard the scraping of the drawer opening. He then played the sound of the box out of view when he first came in the room. All Eric heard was the scraping noise.

Eric suddenly said, "He's not using a key on the first box."

Oscar smiled. "They keep the keys to the kingdom in an unlocked safety deposit box. I did some measuring, and I think there are six boxes out of view."

"They wouldn't use the bottom boxes as those might be pulled on. I bet it is in the top row," stated Eric.

"I agree, so that means it is one of two boxes to far right at the top."

"Good job. What else have you got?"

"I'm not sure, but they are concerned about a Tyler Savage. They hired a private investigator, Tommy Lester, to find him. They used a stolen credit card to pay for it. I checked the card, and it is in someone else's name. They said Tyler had been with a Tony Embler. I did some research and found a Tony Embler that stayed in the Mirage hotel during the dates they gave the detective. He listed his home as Seattle. I printed out a credit report and other bio stuff on him for you."

"They won't find Tyler in Las Vegas. He's in Baltimore."

"How'd you know that?"

Eric smiled. "Because I'm on the way to see him."

Oscar gave him a puzzled look. "Okay, I'm stumped. Well, here is the email information Stephen sent to Tommy in Vegas."

"Thanks, you are amazing. Any chance of getting the combination to the safe?"

"I'm working on it." Oscar handed him a sheet of paper. "This is a transcript of a discussion they had about Tyler and Toby."

Eric read the printout:

"I know you said we might pay Toby a visit one day, are you thinking the others might be worth a future trip, too?"

Stephen smiled. "You read my mine."

"What about Tyler? Do you think that guy killed him?"

Stephen sighed, "It's a possibility, and that might be safer for us."

"Safer? How so?"

"Well, if he was so upset at what Toby did to him, he might have gone to the police, and he just might accidentally spill the beans on us."

"Shit? He'd better not."

"I'm going to do a little online research, and see if he went to the police. I may hire a private dick out there to look for him since we can't do it ourselves."

"Okay, I'm going to go shower and take a nap while we wait for the shipment. See you later."

Eric stated the obvious. "Sounds like they wouldn't care if Tyler was killed."

"I think they are going to hit that Toby Embler guy at some point and I agree, I think they would kill Tyler. They are going after a guy in San Diego by the name of Ron Ensley, too."

Eric asked, "Can you make all their money in those offshore accounts disappear?"

"Yeah, sure, if you want."

"Not yet, just be prepared to do so at a moment's notice. Marti has a list of our own Cayman and Swiss accounts. We'll put their loot in our holdings when the time comes. I think these bastards are worst than I thought and mostly likely killers as well. Good job. Document everything you told me in a report, and save the tape, just in case there is a need for a criminal trial. Thanks."

Oscar laughed. "Boss, no one uses video tape anymore. It's a digital world out there. I saved it to a DVD."

Eric smiled as he turned to leave, and then turned back again as he thought of just one more thing. "In Buenos Aires, we were almost blown up by a bomb in the duct work attached to the hall ceiling. We need a way to make sure all ductwork is clear in halls and rooms for our clients and team members. We need something we can use quickly but efficiently. I don't know if we need an x-ray type device, sound sensors, or what. Will you work on some ideas for me?"

"Yeah, sure boss. I'm glad you are okay."

"Thanks. I had to shoot a man in the ductwork, remove the dynamite, and then make a hasty exit. If I hadn't heard the guy move, I would not be standing here now. Thanks again for all your help."

"Jeez!" exclaimed Oscar. "That was close."

Eric began the drive to Baltimore thinking about the information that Oscar had presented him. He decided to withhold his information until he heard what Tyler had to say. He soon arrived at his rarely used apartment, and set about making sure it looked okay. He kept the refrigerator stocked but only with things that wouldn't go bad like can goods, soda pop, beer, and frozen food.

He showered, dressed in clean clothes from his drawers and closet, and made a call to Tyler. "I'm home. Shall I come get you?"

Tyler laughed. "Give me twenty minutes to get cleaned up. Come on up to the room." He hung up quickly and began dressing and primping.

Soon he heard a knock at the door. He opened it quickly and found the room service guy at the door. "I just got off. Do you want to go get something to eat?"

"Sorry, Tim. My friend should arrive any minute. I'll call you, okay?" Tyler saw the immediate disappointment in his face and felt bad. He knew what that felt like. "Come here a second." He pulled the boy in the room, kissed him long and deep, while stuffing his hands in the boy's pants and massaging his package. Tyler then knelt and began using his mouth and it didn't take long until the young man exploded. Then he stood up. "Okay, that will have to hold you until next time, okay?"

Tim sighed with a big smile, hugged him tightly and left. He waited at the elevator and when the door opened out stepped a very handsome man. Tim smiled, as did Eric.

Eric knocked on the door and once again Tyler opened it after brushing his teeth. "You're here!"

Tyler flung himself in Eric's arms as Eric pushed his way into the room, closed the door, planted a kiss, and felt Tyler's tongue probing deep into his mouth. They kissed over and over, but forced themselves to break apart so they could go eat dinner.

Eric decided on the Wharf restaurant after asking Tyler if he loved seafood and he replied emphatically yes. They chatted during the serving of their salads, and soon Eric learned Tyler could eat his weight in Alaskan crab legs, and he was tenacious with the tiny probing fork as he dug deeper into the crab caverns to get the juiciest meat out. At the end of the meal, the waitresses brought him several extra napkins, followed by a steamy washcloth to clean his face and hands. He was deliriously happy. To Eric's amazement, the boy also ate a huge slice of carrot cake.

"How in the world do you eat so much and not gain a pound?"

Tyler laughed. "I guess it is a faster metabolism, and of course, I dance a lot of it off. How was your trip?

Eric tried to be bland to avoid as much detail as possible. "There were a few exciting moments, but most of the time it was boring. I wish you had been there."

"Well, next time you can take me, and it'll be anything but boring!"

Eric laughed. "Okay, you've got a deal. How did you become involved in the two men you lived with in Miami?"

Tyler sighed, took a long sip of his beer. "I want us to be good friends. I think about you all the time, and I want to start my life all over again. I believe you are a good person, and I want to learn how to be a good person, too. I want to be your boyfriend. I..."

Eric interrupted him. "I see you have been rehearsing this speech. Should I take notes," he teased.

Tyler blushed and laughed. "You're right. I did practice, because I didn't want to mess this up."

"Just tell me the truth and get it over with," urged Eric, as he reached under the table and patted Tyler's knee.

Tyler took a deep breath. "I learned to survive on the streets by doing just about everything. I bagged groceries but got fired on my eighth day for eating an apple. It was the only thing I had to eat the entire day. I tried to get another job, but I was too young. I met a street hustler, who was the same age, and we began to pal around, have some sex, and he taught me how to hustle men. I began making a lot of money, and spent most of it on food until we both had enough money to finally get a one-bedroom apartment.

"More than once I got beat up by some stupid john who refused to pay me for services rendered. I was always careful and made sure they used a condom. I learned to fight back, and insist on the money up front or no sex. I was a street hustler for two years, and quit after the brutal death of my friend by a man who wanted more from him.

"I was dancing in a club one night when Stephen approached me. I could tell he was a giant step up from the street guys I met. He was good-looking, clean, and he smelled great. We danced a while when suddenly I felt Jim dancing behind me, and soon we were dirty dancing in a tight threesome with me like the white cream in an Oreo cookie. I went back to their hotel, and they insisted I take a shower first, and then we had a wonderful all night threesome. They gave me five hundred dollars the next morning, but said they had a job for me to do, and if I did it well, I would get a thousand dollars.

"The job was easy. They bought me new clothes, had my hair done, and we went to this very upscale gay club. We danced a while, but they were not looking at me since they were scouting the room. When they found the man they wanted, my job was to make friends with him, and get him to take me home with him. Stephen and Jim would follow. After sex, the man fell asleep. I would dress and let them in the front door. Stephen immediately would go to the man and give him a shot that left him asleep no matter how much noise we made.

"I wanted to steal DVD's but they showed me how to steal only the smaller but more valuable things like gold rings and other jewelry, expensive watches, and cash. We also took his credit and debit cards. Stephen soon found a small safe in the back of a closet. It took him only fifty seconds to open it. We found about ten thousand dollars.

"After we left the house, they gave me the promised thousand dollars, put the rest of the loot in an overnight UPS box, and put it in a drop box station." Tyler paused for a few seconds, sighed, and continued, "This is where I made a stupid decision. They took me to eat at a Waffle House at three in the morning. They explained I should leave town because I would be the number one suspect. The cops would have a sketch of me, and they would search everywhere to attempt to catch me. Sometimes, they warned, the victims get mean, and might come after me and beat me up. Once they had me scared, then they offered to take me with them to Miami and live with them. I had never been on a plane, but later that morning we were on a direct flight to Miami and the warm sunshine. I couldn't believe their house, and they had a room all set up for me. It was just too easy to say yes.

"We swam nude in the pool, drank strawberry daiquiris, and always had a good time. We began having sex together, all three at the same time. They loved my body, although sometimes Stephen got rough fucking me very hard, and Jim would be a little jealous and squeeze the fire out of my tits.

"At least twice a month we would fly out to a new destination and find a mark to rob. I thought they loved me, even though they were a couple. I was sort of like their son or maybe their protégé. During my second year, I heard them arguing one day, and I heard Stephen say not to worry about Tyler because if ever turned against them or went to the cops, he would personally shoot me in the head. That scared the crap out of me. A few times while I was learning the ropes, I made a mistake, and Stephen would always hit or slap me hard in the face. Twice he sucker-punched me, and walked away laughing while I lay on the floor moaning. I made sure I was good, but I began putting money in a safe deposit box in a bank not far from the house, in case I ever had to run." Tyler stopped and Eric could tell he was nervous and breathing hard.

Eric smiled and winked at him. "Thank you for being honest with me. I'm concerned about your past, but only as to how it effects your future."

Tyler laughed. "What? That was one of those sentences like the preachers say on television. Try again for this simple boy."

Eric said, "Everybody makes mistakes growing up. I got in a lot of trouble when I was a kid, too, and had I not gone into the Marines, I might have ended up a criminal or dead. The Marines made a man out of me, and I was in the Corp for eight years. I would probably still be in the military if I had been straight, but gay and the military unfortunately are still like water and oil. So you messed up, and you stole, but the question is this: Do you want to continue your criminal life in a new locale, or..." He paused briefly, and then asked, "Are you looking for something better?"

Tyler sighed. "It was probably good what happen to me in Las Vegas because although it felt very bad, it made me decide to give up the easy money. Getting raped is no way to live. I want a boyfriend that loves me for who I am and not just my body, or my ability to trap a man and steal from him. I want to feel safe and grow old with the man I love."

Eric smiled at him. "I gather this is hard for you, but tell me what happened in Las Vegas."

Tyler suspected he would have to tell Eric, but he was afraid Eric would think less of him. He had thought a lot about this during his three days in the hotel. He sighed. "We had flown to Las Vegas for a gay AIDS charity event for rich folks. We each had a mark that we were to buddy up with, steal everything, and fly out early in the morning as usual. My mark was Tony Embler from Seattle. At first, the man was nice and made me laugh, but on the night I was to steal from him, he suddenly opened a drawer next to the bed with a variety of sex toys. He abruptly punched me and managed to tie my arms and legs to the bedposts, and then began making me do awful things. Hours later he raped me as hard as he possibly could. Thankfully, I had experienced big dicks up my ass for years, and so I just relaxed and let it happen. He assumed that my quiet nature meant I was fine with what happened, but when he untied me, I got the hell out of there. I went back to my room, and decided right then to leave. I left everything including my luggage and came here.

"I don't want to go back to Stephen and Jim because I believe at some point they are going to kill me to shut me up. I want to start over. I may be only twenty, and soon to be twenty-one, but I have learned a lot about people and life in a very short time." He paused and looked soulfully at Eric's eyes. "Are you ashamed of me? Do you hate me? Do you want me to leave?"

Eric smiled. "No, I don't, but now it is time for me to be honest with you." Tyler faced relayed a puzzled look. Eric added, "Hang on and listen. I don't live in Baltimore. I didn't go to a convention in Los Angeles. I came out of the Marines and began a security firm. I have sixty people working with me, and it is our job to protect individuals from rich executives to politicians. This weekend I was in Buenos Aires protecting the governor of Virginia on a trade mission.

"My office in Baltimore is a fake store front if you will. My apartment there is also a fake. I use it until I get to the point where I can trust someone, and then I tell the truth. I live in Annapolis near the Naval Academy and my office is nearby."

Tyler asked, "So are you like a James Bond or something?"

Eric laughed. "Definitely not. I never get the girl in the end. I wanted the boys!"

They both laughed before Eric continued, "More truth. I spotted you in a strip bar in Washington a few weeks ago. I was sitting in the dark at the back of the bar. It only took me a few minutes until I saw you lift some cash from a guy. I also noted Stephen and Jim, and soon caught on the three of you were working together. My impression was like most men as to how cute you are, but the shock of seeing you steal perplexed me. I was thinking why would a guy with so much potential stoop so low and become a thief. When I saw you leave with that guy, followed my Stephen and Jim, I suspected you were going to rob him, and I hoped you wouldn't kill him."

"I have never killed anyone. I can't believe you noticed me then, but how did you show up in Miami."

"Obviously, I didn't know you lived in Miami. I was there working with a top rich client who happens to be gay. He makes my job harder because he likes to go out to the dance clubs in the major cities. When I met you, my men and I were working to protect him. Because of that work, I also spotted you at the software convention, and watched you land another mark."

Tyler eyes went wide. "Oh my gosh. You already knew all about me, didn't you?"

"Yes, I did. I tracked you in Miami and found out where you live. I followed Jim to the pawnbroker I suspect is your fence for all the stolen property."

"You're right. You're good. What else do you know?"

"While you were in Las Vegas, I broke into the house…"

"Wait a minute, they have a security system."

Eric grinned. "Yes they do, but not strong enough for me. I planted a camera so my team could see Stephen's computer. I found the wall safe room."

"Wait a minute, the what?"

"Just to the left of Stephen's desk is a bookshelf that is actually a door. It'll pull out from the right corner, and you go through a door and into a secret room. In that room is a big bank safe and a wall of safe deposit boxes."

"You're kidding. I never knew that was there."

"They hide a lot of cash, gold, and diamonds in there. My surveillance continued, and this week we knew that you hadn't returned from Las Vegas. Yesterday, Stephen hired a private detective to find you. They discussed that perhaps Tony had killed you after he raped you. They decided that might have been a good thing. They were afraid you might go to the police and turn them in. You're right, they would kill you if they could."

Eric stopped as he watched the blood drain from Tyler's face leaving him pale and shaken. "Don't worry. I'm not going to let that happen. They are not going to get the chance to do anything to you. However, I do have a dilemma. I'm not a cop, and I'm not sure why I wanted to learn more about the three of you. I have to say that sometimes it pisses me off when I see gay men doing the world harm while so many hardworking gay folks are doing their best to show the world they are good, decent, and honest, and only want to be treated fairly. I say shame on crooks like you that give gay people such a bad rap.

"But...I saw something in you that I not only liked, I loved. I think you are smart, and I now believe you deserve a chance to start over. I wanted to help you get out of that life of crime and away from those men, but I wasn't sure if you wanted to until now."

Tears began to stream down Tyler's face. "I am ashamed of what I have done. I do what to start over. Can you really help me?"

"Yes, I can. I think I have decided your punishment for stealing, will not be to go to prison, but rather to do two things. First, you're going to help me put Stephen and Jim out of business and in jail, and secondly, when the right time comes, I want you to volunteer to speak to and help other young gay teens make it in this world so they don't have to trade their bodies for food. Are you willing to do this?"

"Yes, I will, but I don't know what to do."

"Tyler, let me blunt. In a case like yours, I can only give you one chance to a new life. If you lie to me, and go back to a life of crime, you and I are history. Is that clear?" Tyler nodded yes as Eric continued. "I'll be taking a slight risk, so please don't let me down. However, should you fall in love with someone else, all you have to do is tell me. I can handle that. I can't handle being lied to." He paused while Tyler nodded again.

Eric smiled. "Come on, let's get you checked out of your hotel and head to Annapolis."

After they collected all his new clothes, they left the hotel. On the drive south, Tyler reached over and took Eric's hand. "I am so glad you came home today. I had thought about what would happen when I ran out of cash, and my only choice would have been to return to Miami and get the cash from my safety deposit box, but I was afraid to go Miami. I also didn't know where I should go and how to learn a trade. Where would I live? Who would I love? And who would love me?"

"You're going to be fine. Now pay attention to the route to my office, so if you're ever lost, you'll know how to get back."

They took the next exit, made a couple of turns, and soon arrived at the security guard house leading to his office and grounds. He pulled into the parking garage and led Tyler through the door after pausing for an optical unit to scan his right eye for positive identification.

"That's cool. I bet no one could get in there."

Eric grinned. "It's possible, but if I told you how, I would have to kill you."

Tyler held up his hands. "Never mind. I don't want to know." They both laughed.

The office staff was gone for the day, but he gave Tyler the tour including his office, and then they went down to Oscar's office. Eric sat down and began flipping on some switches including the big LCD monitor.

Tyler quickly said, "Oh my gosh, that is Stephen's computer. Are we seeing this live?"

"Yes we are, but let me show you a montage of clips that Oscar put together for me. Let me see if I can find it..." Eric rolled the mouse down the list until he found it and clicked on it. On the big screen, Tyler began to watch the same footage Eric had seen earlier. He also froze when he heard them talk about killing him.

"Those bastards are not even sorry for my getting beat up and raped. They are not all worried that I was hurt or killed. I hate them!"

As the footage ended, Eric closed the file, and suddenly on the screen was a picture of Stephen typing at the keyboard. Tyler took a step back as if Stephen was in the room with them. They could hear another voice off camera.

"Let me see if I can maneuver the camera so we can see who that it is." Eric fumbled through the software and could not make it move.

"Get up," ordered Tyler. "Let me try."

Eric relinquished his chair so Tyler could sit down. In just a few clicks and punches of the keyboard, Tyler obtained control of the camera and moved the lens silently upward until they had a picture of Jim. He was standing with a man that Tyler didn't know.

Eric asked, "Any idea who that he is?"

"No, I've never seen him before."

"Take his picture," said Eric. "Oscar has a way of taking his picture so we can run it through the computer database to find out if he has a record."

Tyler studied the menu sections across the top of the screen until he managed to take the mouse and draw a box around the man's face, and then he clicked it, and it suddenly took over the entire screen.

"Very good. You're a natural with the computers. Save it for Oscar to investigate tomorrow."

"Computers were always easy for me. It's about the only thing I'm good at it, well, besides sex of course."

Eric laughed. "Okay, time to go home."

They drove a few blocks away to Eric's home. It, too, had an electric security gate but no guard, but the house and grounds were secured with a top-notch digital alarm system. He hit a button above his head and the garage door went up. Eric helped carry Tyler's stuff into the house, and together, they put everything in the spare bedroom.

Eric asked, "Are you tired?"

"Heck no, I slept in this morning, took a nap this afternoon, and mainly just sat around waiting for you to come home. "Are you tired?"

"Yes, I am. The job in Buenos Aires ended well, but only after we were attacked four times, and I had to kill a few bad guys."

"Jeez, I had no idea. You are like James Bond."

"I'm also a little sore, and was thinking about getting in the Jacuzzi a while. Maybe the bubbles and hot water will soothe me a bit."

"Let's do it," said Tyler as he began unbuttoning his shirt. Eric went to his room and undressed. Just as he was about to pull his boxers off, Tyler entered the room totally naked.

Eric grinned. "Well, aren't you cute?"

Tyler came to him and kissed longingly. "I'm horny, too. Come on, where's the water?" He yanked Eric's shorts down, and together, they made their way down the stairs and into a workout area with weights and treadmill, and over to the wet area. Eric pulled the lid off, hit the button for the pumps and lights, and stepped into the bubbling pool. Tyler followed him, and soon they were caressing and kissing each other and enjoying the water.

After they returned to Eric's room, the sex lasted more than an hour. There was just over a seven-year age difference, but Eric had never been more in love that he was with Tyler. Tyler felt more than love with Eric. He felt safe and secure, and for the first time in his life, he felt like he had a boyfriend, and a real future.

TWELVE

Tyler groaned when Eric woke up at six, rolled out of the covers, and walked into the shower. However, just after he finished shaving, Eric felt a cold draft as Tyler stepped in to enjoy the hot water with him. They quickly washed each other's body, kissed a dozen times or more, dried off and then dressed before going downstairs for breakfast. Eric ate with careful attention to health foods, and so he filled his refrigerator with fruit and yogurt, apples and oranges. Tyler rolled his eyes, and for the first time since leaving his life of crime, he missed Martin's omelets, but said nothing as he downed his second banana and a tall glass of fresh orange juice.

Tyler followed Eric's instructions and dressed in a pair of nice slacks and a dress shirt. He wanted him to look professional and perhaps a bit older. They arrived at the office at half past seven. Tyler sat across from Eric in his office with the door closed.

"Here's the plan I have come up with. When I finish, you tell me what you think, and what you like or don't like. Is that fair enough?" Tyler nodded affirmatively. "My teams, staff, and all the employees know that I'm gay and have no problem with it, or they wouldn't be here. However, they also do exactly as ordered as this is not a democracy, but rather a private company and I own all the stock. They do, however, enjoy profit sharing as if they were stockholders. We're not in the military, but we work and operate as if we were.

"I propose you join our company as an intern, a trial if you will, to see if you like working here. If you don't, we'll find a job for you on the outside. I also think you need to go to school, and at least get your GED or high school diploma. If you want, I'll help you go to college, but first we'll find out not only what you like to do, but also what you're willing to stick with, and learn all you can on how to do that job even better.

"Since you like computers, I think we'll start by testing that field, and spend about half of your day working with Oscar and his team, and that will be after lunch."

"What will I do in the mornings?"

"Well, you won't sleep in," laughed Eric. "I propose that you go through our new agent training program that will teach you how to protect yourself from the bad guys, and if you like working here, you could move up to working in the field as well. To do that, you need to master all levels of agent training. You would learn how to shoot correctly, how to protect yourself in a hostile environment, and how to take the offense and when to do so. You'll learn a variety of martial arts techniques. It would be sort of like going into the Marines with better food, and you get to sleep in..." he paused and smiled as continued, "my bed. You also learn to take orders and carry the commands out perfectly. Are you willing to learn?"

"You bet I am. This is cool."

"Okay, now to maintain a chain of command, I suggest for a while, you call me Mister Hanson at the office or anytime we are around co-workers. I want you to say yes sir and no sir to my men until you've earned their respect. I don't want them to think that because you sleep with the boss, that you're spoiled and lazy. So I'll tell them to work your ass off."

Tyler laughed. "Don't go doing me any favors."

"Most companies don't pay their interns, but we do. We expect a lot, so we pay well. Are you ready?"

"Yep, I'm ready."

Eric hit a button on his phone. "Marti, could you come in please?"

As she entered, Eric said, "Marti this is Tyler Savage. He's a friend of mine, and is going to start today as an intern to see if our company is right for him, and if he is right for us. Please have him fill out all the usual hiring paperwork, and then prepare an ID badge, gate and car pass. When you're done, give me a buzz, and I'll introduce him to the range master."

Tyler returned in forty minutes wearing his new ID badge and followed Eric to the rear of the building. They took an elevator down two floors and stepped off. Tyler could hear gunshots. They went through two sets of doors and the gunshots became a little louder. Eric waited for a tall man with broad shoulders, a military haircut, and a very serious look on his face to join them. To Tyler he looked like a chiseled Marine and as tough as nails.

"Bob, this is our new intern Tyler Savage. He's almost twenty-one and has zero experience with a gun. I want you to teach him how to shoot properly with a 9mm and a rifle, and how to fire under difficulty, with precise decisions, and as usual, safety, safety, and safety."

"Roger, will do. Nice to me you Savage. Let's get to work."

Eric added, "Better get him some greens and gear, and thanks for the help. Buzz me when you're done for today. He has martial arts next on his list."

"Roger, sir."

Eric left as Bob shook Tyler's hand firmly. Tyler almost flinched at the pain, but said nothing. Roger took him down the hall and into a room marked 'gear room'. He issued Tyler army green pants, shirt, belt, socks, and boots, as well as a locker, so he quickly dressed into his training clothes. Bob showed him how to tuck his shirt in and lace his boots correctly. Once satisfied, they returned to the range. Bob took his ID card and swiped it in the machine next to the door. The door lock buzzed, and they entered a secure room housing all of their weapons and ammunition, and known by the team as the armory.

Tyler stood at a skinny counter about chest high, at least for Tyler. Bob returned with a brand new 9mm pistol and three boxes of shells. Bob said in a strict serious tone, much like that of a drill sergeant at Paris Island Training Depot. "This weapon has been issued to you and the serial number is recorded in the books. You will not lose this weapon, and you will not fire this weapon unless told to do so. I will teach you in steps everything you must do, and by the end of the week, you will be hitting bull's-eyes. Is that clear?"

"Yes, sir," replied Tyler quickly.

"I want you to memorize the serial number because everyone here has the same model, but also the same responsibility for their gun. You are never to pick up anyone's gun but your own."

Bob showed him how to operate the gun, how to put the safety on and take it off, how to manage and absorb recoil and load a bullet, and they practiced this several times. He then showed him how to load several clips. He then fitted Tyler with a leather shoulder holster that he would wear while hiding his gun from public view. If he passed the gun training, he would receive a permit by the Federal Government to carry a concealed weapon, the result of a deal Eric worked out with a friend at the FBI. The harness consisted of a leather strap that went around each shoulder, under the arm, and across his back. Bob had to take the straps all the way in due to Tyler's skinny frame. "I could take this in permanently, but since you are going to be taking martial arts, you'll grow some muscles and then it will fit right."

The pistol went in the holster under his left arm so he could retrieve it with his right hand. Below his right arm was an extension clipped to his belt that held a Velcro device that held extra clips. Once satisfied with his gear, Bob gave him a pair of shooting glasses, and a headset to protect his ears. Bob protectively carried the pistol as they went through several sets of doors into the large room that looked like a tunnel but housed the gun range.

Tyler marveled at the underground bunker where Eric's men could practice with pistols and rifles, and there were several men practicing. They went to the far end, so they could practice in private. Bob showed him how to stand and hold the gun. He practiced over and over retrieving the gun from his holster, and bringing it up to fire until he could return time after time to the correct position with perfection. Tyler wanted to make Eric proud and tried as hard as he could.

Bob loaded a clip and pulled the slide to load a shell. He then dropped the clip out, ejected the shell, checked the barrel for empty, and handed the gun to Tyler. The boy smiled slightly, popped another clip in, loaded a shell, and brought the gun up to the firing position.

"Very good. It's all about following each step carefully so you never make a mistake. You're a natural. The key to good shooting is to be relaxed at all times, even in difficult situations, and especially when someone is shooting at you. If you fire due to reactionary fear, you'll miss your target. Now look down the barrel and sight it carefully on the target. Never pull the trigger. Always squeeze the trigger."

Bob knew that most kids in the current generation acted as if they always knew more than the teacher did. He was pleased this young kid was smart enough to do exactly as told.

117

Two hours later, Eric picked up Tyler, and they went up a floor and down another hall to the gym. Around the exterior of the gym, he saw several glassed in rooms with weights, treadmills, and other exercise equipment. There was also a training room like the one you might find in an NFL locker room. Tyler saw an agent getting a massage, and another sitting in a whirlpool. Eric took training and physical health very seriously and demanded it of every team member, including Marti, his secretary, who shot with a score of ninety-six on the range.

A Japanese man approached them as they walked across the room. "Tyler, this is George Harishita, your instructor."

They shook hands with Tyler once again flinching at the vise grip of a fist this small oriental man possessed.

"George, Tyler is an intern and almost twenty-one years old. He has zero experience in martial arts, and probably fitness in general. He will work with you two hours each morning after firearms training. Make him ready to defend himself, protect himself, and then start advancing him through our usual training. He might need a few muscles in the process."

George replied with a grin, "Of course, no problem."

"Very good. Tyler, come to my office when you're done."

"Yes sir," replied Tyler.

Eric left with a smile on his face. His knew his boyfriend would be sore in different places tonight.

Eric stopped at Oscar's office. "Any luck on identifying the face we froze last night?"

"You froze this face?" Oscar looked at Eric in disbelief.

"I said we. Actually, Tyler, the new intern did it for me."

"That makes sense."

"Tyler will be training with your team in the afternoons. He seems to be a natural with computers, but work with him and let me know if he is best suited here and if not, I'll move him."

"Is he the same Tyler the surveillance is all about?"

"Yes he is. Those men are hoping he is already dead, but when they find out he is not, they will come after him."

"I understand," replied Oscar. "As to the picture this morning, it all makes sense now. That man is one Alberto Romero, aka Al the enforcer. He's a killer for the mob. A very successful assassin when he wants to be. There is a long history on him, and though the cops have brought him in many times, they have yet to pin a single crime to his ass."

"Keep me posted on his whereabouts."

"One more thing, your bad guys are going to San Diego this afternoon. They are going to see Rob Ensley, and I think they intend to rob him blind."

118

"Get me Rob's phone number. I'll be in my office."

Eric returned to his office and called Gary Roberts at FBI headquarters in Washington. Eric called a private line that rang directly into Gary's office. They served together in the Navy Seals and remained good friends ever since. Eric was godfather to both of Gary's children. He knew Eric was gay and supported him heartily, saying he was glad there was less competition for him to worry about in his chase for the pretty women in this world. That was years ago. He was married to a wonderful woman that also cared for Eric, worrying about him and his missions, as she did her husband. She also kept trying to fix Eric up with the perfect guy. So far she was batting zero on that challenge.

"Eric? Gary here. How are you?"

Eric smiled as his long time friend always sounded chipper no matter the situation. "I'm great, though I almost got blown up in Buenos Aires protecting Virginia's Governor from the bad guys. I killed four."

"Hurrah!" shouted Gary as if still in the Marines. "I'm glad you're fine. What's up?"

Eric told him about Stephen and Jim, his rescue of Tyler, and the discovery of perhaps an assassin by the name of Alberto Romero, seeking to kill Tyler.

Gary sighed. "Jeez. He is definitely a bad dude. We'd love to nail the son of a bitch, but he is as slippery as a fish."

"I want to call the cops in San Diego and alert them to the possible arrival of Stephen and Jim later today. I thought that perhaps you might give me an introduction so the locals will take the news seriously. In addition, would you consider putting a bulletin of sorts on the line for Alberto? I'd like to know if he is moving, and if so where. He doesn't know where Tyler is, but there's a private detective in Las Vegas on his trail."

"Yeah, sure, but keep me in the loop on this guy, too. If there's a way we can pin a crime on him, I want to be involved. Hold on, let me conference in San Diego."

Gary stayed on the line while Eric explained the situation with Stephen and Jim, and Alberto. He gave them the address of the mark, and urged them to stake out the house carefully, as these guys were very good at their craft. The officer in charge was Larry Anderson and he promised they would. Eric gave his office phone and info to him. He would email pictures of all three to Larry after he hung up.

On his computer in Annapolis, Oscar watched Jim remove some cash out of the safe room as Stephen finished up on the computer.

Jim said as he pushed the bookshelf in place, "Come on, dear, we're going to miss our flight."

"Yes, mother harry, I'm coming." They both laughed, and Oscar shot them the bird on the monitor. Too bad they can't see it, he thought.

Eric dialed the number Oscar emailed him. He had to bluff his way through a housekeeper before finally getting Rob on the phone. He used a non-traceable phone line. "Rob, you don't know me, but I know a lot about you. For starters, you were in Las Vegas last week for an AIDS charity."

Rob laughed. "Well everybody knows that."

Eric sighed. "Does everyone know you slept with a guy there that robbed you of a lot cash and stuff?"

The phone went silent. "How did you know that?"

The man's name that marked you is Stephen Einstein, or at least that's his current name. He works with a partner named Jim Demos. It was all a setup, and they both had marks to rob and then fly out of Las Vegas."

"Who are you?"

Eric lied. "I'm a private investigator working on another group of gay men they robbed in Chicago. I want to warn you about a couple of things. If you haven't changed your credit and bankcards, you should do it now, as they are still stealing from you. They are also boarding a flight out of Miami right about now and heading to San Diego."

"They are coming here?"

"Yes, they are. They are coming to rob your house."

"Shit!" exclaimed Rob.

"My advice is to go to the cops, tell them the truth, and let them know they are coming to you. Write this name down. I just spoke to the FBI in Washington, and together, we spoke to detective Larry Anderson of the San Diego Police Department. I have already told them all about the case. They know what happen to you. They are going to stake out your house. If you call them, they could put a man inside to protect you."

"I'll have to think about this."

"Rob, the final thing I have to tell you is they are not only robbers, they are killers as well. You could end up dead if you're not careful. You decide, but if it were me, I'd call the cops. Goodbye and good luck." He hit the send key on his computer sending the email he had written before calling Rob, outlining what he knew about Stephen and Jim, along with their pictures. His information did not include anything about Tyler. After many discussions with Tyler, Eric realized that Tyler was really a victim, too. He did, however, steal and Eric was still working his head around that conundrum.

Eric hung up before Rob could say anything more. Rob immediately called his attorney, and they agreed to call the police. He looked down at his laptop and opened the email. Attached where pictures of Stephen and Jim. Rob then drove to the police department, met his attorney in foyer, and then they went to see Larry Anderson.

The cops finally decided to set up a perimeter to catch them in the act of breaking in. The lead detective took several of his men to the airport, obtained a list of the gates with traffic coming in from Miami. Each man carried the pictures of the two men. An hour later, they spotted both men as they got off the plane. He radioed his men near the house, so they could hunker down out of sight. He hung up realizing he now fully believed the story.

He arranged two cars to route a tandem tail of the suspects, swapping places from time to time, while trying to avoid discovery. The lead detective drove parallel to the suspects as they left the airport in their rental car. He was surprised when then drove into a very upscale hotel. He had never seen crooks use a fancy place as a 'hideout'.

After the thieves took the elevator to their room, he approached the manager, obtained their room number, and told him to tell no one he had asked. He bought a paper and sat down in the lobby to read and watch for them. He brought his radio up quickly to his mouth, "This is Larry. I'm in the lobby watching for the suspects. Just sit tight and let's see what they do."

George spent about an hour putting Tyler through basic judo moves to defend against an attacker. They went through each maneuver over and over with George demonstrating both tremendous patience, and an expectation of perfection. He also praised the boy for his successes, something Tyler hadn't heard in many years, perhaps his whole life. Tyler liked him a lot and thought he was a little like that Mister Miyagi character in The Karate Kid movies. He did everything George asked him to do.

The second hour was all about physical fitness. They spent twenty minutes on stretching, and George was surprised at just how limber Tyler was. He handled pushups pretty well until they got to fifty, and then his arms became weak. He could do jumping jacks as they were like a dance move, and he easily handled the basic treadmill workout. At the end of the hour, Tyler was sweating and George sent him to the showers.

Tyler arrived at Eric's office just minutes before noon. Eric looked up and laughed. "Hungry?"

"No, I'm way past hungry, I'm starved! That fruit you gave me didn't last."

Eric snatched up his car keys and stood to leave. "Follow me. We'll get you a tofu lunch to build you up."

"I hope you're kidding. I need a Big Mac or a Whopper, or both! I definitely need a large fry. My body craves some quality junk food," pleaded Tyler.

Eric laughed as they went to the car and drove over to a food area where they settle on a semi-healthy sub sandwich with whole wheat bread. Tyler also obtained two big cookies and large coke. Eric drank water and skipped the cookie by giving his to Tyler.

"Do you always eat healthy?"

Eric smiled. "No, not always, especially when I'm on the run or doing surveillance, but I try to eat healthy. Sometimes my life or the lives of my team depend on my ability to be able to have great stamina for running, fighting, or thinking. How was your training this morning?"

"I liked shooting the pistol a lot. Bob is a no-nonsense kind of guy, but he knows guns inside and out. He said that by the end of the week I would be hitting all center-blacks at fifty feet. Martial arts training was very interesting. George is so nice that you hate to let him down. I learned a few basic moves, and he said I would have those moves at full speed by the end of the week. Remind me to pack a shaving kit so that I have stuff for the showers, as well as socks and underwear."

"You did very well. This afternoon you'll begin your training with Oscar. He is a computer and technology genius. He knows you have excellent, but untrained computer skills. He reminded me that was how he started as well, and only his curiosity of what else he might learn how to do forced him to get computer tech training, so he could get even better. He can breach just about any security computer system, and knows the inside tricks for telephone and alarm systems. He is the one that developed the camera in Stephen's office and has been monitoring the surveillance. He uses a digital hard drive to compress and store the data as it comes in."

Eric checked his watch. "Are you about done?"

Tyler looked up with about a third of his second cookie gone. "Yeah, sure," he mumbled as crumbs fell from his mouth. He stuffed the rest of the big cookie in his mouth, and got up to leave.

Eric laughed at him as they entered the car. "Wait," Tyler managed to say as he chewed the last of the cookie, swallowed, took several sips of his coke and swallowed again, and then leaned over and kissed Eric. "I've been waiting to do that all day."

"Me, too, but put your seatbelt on and let's go." They drove a little with Eric taking a tight turn. "Do you know how to drive?"

"Yes, but I don't have a license. I mean I have a fake one, but not a real one. Stephen and Jim would never let me drive in Miami, as they were afraid I would wreck, and they would have to deal with the police."

"I'll make you a deal. You give me two good weeks of top training, and I'll arrange for you to get some defensive driver training. That's where you learn how to do one eighties, weaves, and more. You'll find it a blast. We'll also get you a real drivers license and a passport as well."

"All right! That sounds good to me. Listen, will you promise to tell me if I'm not doing something right?"

"Roger, will do. Hang on!" Eric expertly spun out into traffic, crossed three lanes, and took the next turn.

Oscar and Tyler hit it off well as they liked some of the same rock bands and movies. He spent part of his time showing Tyler how his department works, and what sources to use to research a suspect or operation. He then told Tyler how to set up his workstation, but let Tyler do all the connections himself. He was soon operational. Sitting side by side, he began by having Tyler begin researching a suspect by first using the man's current name, but Tyler found very little information.

"That's okay, it's probably an alias."

Tyler asked, "A what?"

"A fictitious name. Some crooks have a long list of them."

"Oh," replied Tyler with a somber guilty look.

"We have his picture. Let's run a high tech face search using the FBI's computer network."

"Is that legal?"

"Yes, we have a contract with them. The boss is good with the CIA, too. He even works with Interpol. Eric is well respected everywhere in security circles."

Oscar showed him what to type in to connect to the FBI. He gave Tyler a clearance and password. Tyler then did a cut and paste of the man's photo into an online form. After he hit search, the entire picture suddenly exploded into thousands of digital bits like a fireworks explosion and then began rebuilding the picture. He was mesmerized by the rapid activity he saw. When completed, Tyler saw numerous tiny red dots placed in several key spots on the pictures.

"What are those spots for?"

"They are unique characteristics like moles or scars, or shading of the skin that make this suspect's picture unique."

A bar graph began running across the bottom of the skin, then the screen split into two parts with the original picture in the left pane, and a rapid flash of thousands of pictures as it finally narrowed down and found the suspect.

"Ah ha!" grinned Oscar. "Our suspect's real name is Alfred Alonso." He began scrolling down and reading. "He has a long rap sheet. He did time in San Quentin. So you see, we can find just about anyone that's been convicted of a crime. Okay, let's find out where Alfred is right now."

Oscar showed him how to search all over the country for an Alfred Alonso using everything they could find in the FBI file. Soon they found out he received a traffic ticket in Saint Louis just two weeks ago. Oscar began searching all databases in Saint Louis, and soon found that Alfred had applied for electricity for a residence on 112 Green St.

"We found where he lives, but let's see if has a probation officer there and a job." Twenty minutes later they found he worked in a cafeteria.

Tyler asked, "Why is he a suspect of interest to our firm?"

Oscar replied, "Good question. In 2005, he was suspected of bombing a software company. Seems he has a thing against computer folks. They never proved it, and so he wasn't prosecuted, but the FBI agents in

123

charge were convinced he did it. They report him as being pretty clever and deadly with explosives.

"We have a client by the name of Larry Menard. He runs a big software development company. Whenever he travels, we check out the location of known suspects that might want to hurt him. Our client is going to Hollywood next week for a computer show. Thankfully, it appears Alfred is safe in Saint Louis, but we don't know that for sure. We'll do a request for location to his probation officer to see if he reported in lately. If not, we'll have an officer visit him.

"Now we write up a quick report to add to the file for the Hollywood trip. The agents assigned to this mission will see his photo in the preparation materials so they will recognize him should he show up at the computer show. Now that was just one suspect. Here's a list of the men we need to find this afternoon. You start at the top, and I'll start at the bottom, and let's see what we can dig up. If you become stuck, ask me for tips, but first try to sort it out yourself."

Tyler was fascinated with the firm's network abilities, and especially Oscar. The new intern was slow on the first one, as he recalled the steps required to track somebody down. When he was stumped, Oscar added more tricks to his arsenal. In two hours, they completed the lists and dropped the information into the report file for the mission. Oscar praised him for his attention to detail, as well as his detective insight. He didn't know Tyler felt hungry for the confidence boost he gave him.

Oscar shifted gears and showed Tyler how to test field radios for the teams. They checked the programming for each radio, as well as the charge on the batteries, and then placed each unit in a custom slot cut into a case section of foam rubber inside the metal transport briefcase. The cases were left open on a big bench; a small wire ran to a built-in trickle charger plugged into the wall circuit to keep the batteries at peak performance.

They moved to a larger lab room where they worked on a command center electronic gear case. He explained that this unit is where the radio signals came in and out again at a rapid pace, and connected the field to the home office. He showed Tyler how the team members wear a radio with the microphone in their sleeve and an earbud in their ear, and all attached to a radio on their belt under a jacket.

Oscar showed him how to setup the command center gear as if they just arrived in the field, like a hotel room. They would carry several equipment footlockers especially equipped for everything they needed in the field when it came to communications. They tested the radios, making adjustments as needed, and once completed, Oscar began showing him what to do if things went wrong. He replaced field radios, antennas, batteries, headsets and microphones. He learned how to switch to a backup master radio in the command center. They did some technical work to peak out their signals by using a digital scope, and he learned how to scramble the signals so their conversations remained secure and private. In future sessions, he would learn how to operate the field computers that managed everything in the command center.

Oscar explained that these command centers could be used anywhere in the USA or any foreign country. They could not count on excellent radio tower signals, or the bandwidth they needed, so they brought their own. They also maintained top security for all communications including audio, video, and data. To accomplish this level of protection and service, they used a hybrid of signals and technology. They always set up a small satellite receive and transmit dish that would bounce their scrambled signals for audio, video, and data into space and back down to their office in Annapolis.

The command team would also install their own antennas for radio communications, cell phone circuits, and Wi-Fi. Each signal would also be scrambled, preventing the bad guys from knowing anything about them. Eric secured permission from our government to use high-powered amplifiers not available in your local neighborhoods. They were similar to the same setup the Secret Service used. Oscar said he knew this because there were three of their former agents working for the firm. They also carried their own power grid that supplied power to the footlocker racks, converted it to twelve-volt batteries and back again from DC to AC current. This protected the gear from brownouts, surges and spikes. One small case contained a lightweight Honda generator for isolated power situations and additional fuel cells.

Before Tyler realized it, the time was five o'clock and the end of the day for most of the firm, though often there was some staff working late. Oscar and Tyler began securing their gear for the night. Oscar once again praised him for his first day's work in the tech lab before saying goodnight.

Tyler walked back to Eric's office, but waited outside while Eric discussed an upcoming project with two men. He noticed everyone leaving for the day, and smiled when Marti came over to see how his day went.

"I bet you're sore from all the training."

Tyler grinned. "Not yet but it was a fast day. There is so much to learn."

"I can imagine. Most of our new recruits are ex-whatever, you know, Marines, Rangers, Navy Seals, government agents, or they are computer geeks, or just pure geniuses walking around amongst the normal folks like me. Eric has a way of finding and recruiting the best, so hold your chin up because you were selected by the best boss in the world to join our team. He is exceptionally good at what he does. I'll see you tomorrow."

Tyler realized she didn't know the whole story, but he did feel a bit of pride that he had made it through the rough times and a life of crime, and now he was on the way up the ladder of success with a good-looking man pushing him all the way. Tyler watched the men exit Eric's office, but waited patiently for Eric.

"Are you tired?" asked Eric as he shut his door, and they began walking down the hall.

"Hell no, I'm not even sore," bragged Tyler.

"Good, I was thinking about taking on a seven-mile run when we get home. Are you up for it?"

Tyler stopped walking and looked at him. "You're kidding, right?"

Eric kept a straight face for almost two seconds before laughing. "I'm kidding. How about some Italian food? I just love fettuccine Alfredo with grilled chicken. I only allow myself to eat it once a month, but I know a place that makes it better than anyone."

"Sounds good to me."

On the west coast in San Diego, Stephen and Jim finally exited their room just as Larry was about to swap places with another detective so he could take a leak. The group of men carefully watched the suspects as they walked a block south and into a large Mexican Restaurant. Larry went inside asked for a table, and immediately went to the bathroom. He walked right past Stephen and Jim while memorizing their faces.

He reported later they drank a few beers, ate dinner, and left the restaurant forty-seven minutes later, returning to the hotel. Larry left a car with two detectives across the street while the rest of the detail returned to headquarters for the shift change. He returned a few hours later with two fresh men who took the place of the others. Just after midnight they woke Larry who had fallen asleep in the back of the sedan. He wiped his eyes free of the sandman in time to see Stephen and Jim enter their rental car and leave the hotel. Larry jumped out of their car and ran to his car. They pulled out tailing them swapping positions every few blocks.

Stephen was driving slow and safe for the first two miles, but as he entered a business district, he began making right and left turns quickly. Larry radioed to his men. "I think he made us. Just pull off the tail, drive to 211 Fox Street, and then park a block away. Try to hide your car and wait."

Larry made the next right as Stephen made a left, leaving his tail position, too. Larry also drove to Fox street, parked between two other cars on the street, put a ticket under his wiper blade like a civilian, and slumped down in the seat.

Ten minutes later, a pair of headlights came over the hill facing him. He kept his eyes barely above the dash so he could watch for the type of car. He had guessed right and just as Stephen was about pass his car Larry ducked down. Jim noted the cars on his left and saw the one with the ticket, but paid little attention. So far Larry's ploy was working.

Stephen slowed in front of 211 Fox Street, while scanning the entrance for security and especially cameras. He drove to the next block and made a right and drove around the perimeter of the property looking for ways to get over the wall that surrounded the property. When he reached the rear, he saw a gate suddenly open and what appeared to be a housekeeper making her exit, locking the gate with a key she kept around her neck. He quit looking for a way to get in. He'd already found an easy one. He pulled over and cut his lights off. He saw her crank up her car in his rearview mirror, and then she pulled out and passed him without even a glance. He pulled out behind her plus about fifty yards. She drove about ten blocks, made a few turns, and pulled in front of a small house, quickly got out of the car and went inside.

Jim made a note of the address. "Well, what do you think?"

Stephen sighed as he pulled away. "Obviously getting the key from her makes everything easier, but I still think we were tailed."

"By whom? No one knows we are in town, and if they did, they don't' know who we are."

"How long have we been doing this?"

Jim laughed. "Since you were seventeen and I was sixteen. You took advantage of my youth."

Stephen chuckled. "Yeah and you took advantage of my relentless horniness."

"Is that a word?"

"I don't know. Let's drive back to the front of the house, and this time ignore the house, and look at all the cars and windows across the street. Let's see if someone is expecting us."

"Good grief, you are so paranoid," protested Jim.

"I do it for you because you would look shitty in prison garb."

Jim laughed. "Okay, good point. Let's go."

While they were gone, Larry wisely removed himself from his car, as did his men, and they each hid in the trees in nearby yards. This left their cars empty. Larry saw them coming in his side mirror and radioed to his men to duck down. The other car was parked a few cars down and parked on a side street facing the 211 house. There was a street light above the car. A normal surveillance person would not park under a streetlight. The officers were hidden in a row of bushes.

Stephen noted the cars along the side of the road, ignoring Larry's car in the dark with ticket in the wiper, but when he saw the other cop car he slowed down. "Jim, look at this car. Do you notice anything unusual?"

Jim looked where he was nodding and studied the car. "No, I don't. What's up?"

"Two things. I can see steam coming off the hood, so the engine has been running, but the second thing is really important. Do you see which way he is parked on that street?"

Jim replied, "Yeah, he is facing the house."

"I think it is a cop car."

Jim said, "How can you tell that?"

"He is facing the wrong way on a one-way street while facing the house. I saw a ticket on another car just fifty feet away, but the owner of this car is not afraid to get a ticket."

"So you assume it is a cop?"

Stephen smiled. "I would bet on it, but there's only one way to be sure."

"How's that?"

Stephen smiled slyly. "Go over and tap on the window, and see if a cop raises up and if so, ask him if he has a light?"

Jim looked at him like he was crazy. "Not on your life."

"That's my point. Why should we risk our lives when my brain says this could be a trap?"

"But how would anyone know we might come here?"

"I can only thing of one person."

Jim's face went somber. "You mean Tyler, don't you? But he didn't know we were coming."

"No, but he might have guessed. It wouldn't be the first time we came after a mark's home. We did it just last year after that creepy college professor that wanted to paint a nude Tyler in red paint."

"You're right. I forgot about that."

"I think we should leave town."

"Okay, I'll miss the fun of stealing from your friend, but what the hell, let's go to Acapulco for a few days and work on our tan and tequila."

"Sounds good to me as it is south of the border. I'll drop you by the hotel. You go get our bags and walk out the back entrance like an employee, and I'll pick you up. While you're in there, I'll make sure we aren't being watched. Keep your phone handy and make it fast."

Stephen drove slow and easy until he topped the hill and out of sight of the car he spotted. He made a few quick turns and then sped on to the hotel. He dropped Jim off, drove around the block several times while carefully watching the parking lot. He memorized the empty parking spots and counted six. Each time he came around, he checked to see if all six were still empty. His phone rang.

"I'm going out the door now."

"Okay," replied Stephen as he made a left and then a right and swung alongside the hotel in the rear. Jim threw their stuff in the back seat and Stephen stepped on the gas. He watched his rearview mirror, but spotted not a single car following them. When they hit the freeway he turned east instead of west and on to the airport.

Jim gave him a look. "I take it we're going somewhere other than the San Diego airport?"

Stephen smiled. "If we lost the tail, and they discovered our rooms our empty, where would they go to look for us?"

128

"The airport."

"So we'll drive north to San Bernardino, which is in the opposite direction I believe they would think we would go. They would assume we would flee to Mexico, so they'll watch the airport and maybe the border. They'll be looking for our names on the tickets or the names we used to check into the hotel. We'll use different identities to buy new tickets and fly directly to Acapulco. It's just under two hours until we get there, so get busy on your phone and get us two tickets for the next possible flight out of there. Then find a hotel near the airport and get me directions to it."

"We're going to stay overnight?"

"No, I'll pull in the hotel parking lot like we're staying there and we'll catch a cab to the airport. That'll slow down the finding of our rental car."

"You're so smart. Okay, I'll take care of everything."

Larry walked down the street to talk with his men. When he saw their car, he cursed. "Damn! What the hell are you doing parking the wrong way on a one-way street? You idiot. They made us! Let's go!"

He ran back to his car and drove immediately to the hotel, scanning the parking lot for their rental car. By dawn, he had a maid let him into the room only to find it empty, except for a pile of empty UPS air boxes. He knew then they had been discovered. When he got back to his car, he called Eric.

Eric was very happy with Tyler sleeping on his shoulder with his soft hair almost tickling his nose. The sex they had last night topped anything he had done in his life, and not because they invented some new ways to do it, but because he absolutely loved every square inch of Tyler. He could tease his tits with his tongue, but he also enjoyed playing with his belly button, or tickling his bare feet. He loved the way Tyler French kissed him, and how he finished by lightly sucking his tongue as if it could produce milk.

The phone rang at the same time the alarm went off. In a flash he hit the alarm and opened the phone. "Hello?"

"This Larry Anderson in San Diego. I'm sorry to wake you, but I've been up all night following Stephen and Jim. We were very careful, but something we did must have spooked them." He was too embarrassed to admit the error his men made in parking their car.

Larry continued, "They drove by the house several times and around the block so they were obviously casing the place, but suddenly they disappeared. We waited about an hour before I came back to the hotel to see if their car was there. It wasn't too long before I got into their room and it was empty. They fled sometime after three this morning our time. I sent men to the airport but my gut says they are gone. They left behind a pile of UPS air boxes."

Eric said, "The boxes are how they send the loot to their fences, so it is hard to catch them with the stolen property. I assume the labels were not yet on the boxes.

"Yep, you're right."

"Dang. You're probably right. They are long gone. Thank you for trying. I have surveillance on their property in Miami, so we'll know soon if they came home. I'll keep you posted. Thanks again."

Tyler yawned. "Who was that?"

"A detective in San Diego, and your friends Stephen and Jim gave them the slip. Time to get up."

"But I like sex in the morning," replied Tyler as he reached over and held on to Eric's penis.

Eric kissed his forehead. "You like sex any time of the day. Come on, sleepy intern, you have a lot of work to do today."

Tyler cussed, but they got up and moved on to the shower, and forty minutes later, they were on the way to the office.

THIRTEEN

...Three months later.

Eric sat on the bleachers in the shade overlooking the obstacle course. Every person that went into the field as an agent was required to master and tackle the course, and pass in a reasonable amount of time set by George Harishita. He maintained strict, physical test results on every person. The only employees excused were secretaries and other personnel that would never work on an outside operation. You could delay your testing if you were wounded or disabled at the discretion of George. Eric ran the course with everyone else, and made sure he remained in the top five percent of the entire group.

He was scheduled to run later in the afternoon, but preparing to run in the first group was Tyler. The intern was dressed out in battle fatigues, combat boots and helmet. He carried an M-16 rifle in both hands, and wore his 9mm pistol on his hip in a covered and padded holster. Besides the usual swinging on ropes over water, walking telephone poles, belly crawling through pipes and under wire strands, they each had to stop at the rifle range, and fire ten shots. Nine of the ten shots had to be kill shots either in the head or dead center of the chest. They also had to draw and fire their pistol at a slightly shorter distance and achieve the same results.

Eric opened the folder on Tyler's training record prepared by George, Rob, and other team members as well as Oscar. His medical exam was in the back of the folder. Tyler was pronounced very fit with a very low body fat count that was actually lower than Eric's. He had excellent hearing and vision. Thankfully, he was disease free including AIDS. Like every team member, he received an unannounced battery of shots protecting the agents from known diseases around the world, including malaria and hepatitis.

Many of Tyler's friends would have bet he would quit the physical program after one just day, but he had surprised all by making it the full ninety days. Early on, Eric surmised that Tyler did suffer from low self-esteem, which he counterbalanced by being outgoing, friendly, and a bit verbose, but he was a bit like a small dog that barks loudly, while remaining safely behind a fence. Eric gave him lots of praise for every step and goal he made during his training. The more positive words Tyler heard, the harder he worked.

Eric was greatly relieved at Tyler's effort, because if he slouched off, it would have made it hard for Eric to keep him with the firm, or he would have to take an inside job only, and Eric loved to travel and wanted Tyler on the road with him as well.

He heard a whistle and set the folder down, and picked up the binoculars he had brought with him. There was a squad of twelve agents jogging on the beginning of the course, and Tyler was right in the middle of them. He hardly recognized him with the helmet and gear, but he would know that ass anywhere. They jogged a half-mile before veering off to go through the first phase, the obstacle barrier course. Tyler leaped over various poles and barrels, walked a log, and remained in the middle of the group.

When they reached the rifle range, he was the second man to begin shooting, and fired rapidly, hitting ten for ten. Eric was thrilled. Tyler swung his rifle strap over his shoulder, and pulled his pistol all in a quick fluid motion. He fired his full clip, and again put all in the black center. He didn't wait for a result, but turned to run while changing out his clip in his pistol and stuffed it tight in his holster, and removed his rifle and changed the clip on it as well. Tyler now had a head start on the group.

He did the last phase very well, and ended up second to the finish line. Eric had to bite his tongue, so he wouldn't let out a cheer as he left the bleachers and went back to his office.

He watched the clock. At eleven, he went down to the gym, but over to the catwalk so he could look down into the floor mat training area. He spotted Tyler, but Eric positioned himself so that he was behind and out of Tyler's view. George was giving the group of ten instructions on how he wanted this exercise to go. George picked the first two men and blew a short whistle for them to start. They rapidly went through some fighting maneuvers by using their martial arts training, and they did them all correctly. Two by two, the rest of the group did the same.

George then divided them into two groups, and designated which team was to be the attacker, leaving the other group as a defender. They went through the line with frontal assaults, and the defenders handled themselves very well, and then they attacked from the rear, with rubber knives and guns. Then the squad swapped roles and started over again. In each maneuver, Tyler did very well, and appeared be a natural at martial arts. Tyler had a told him he liked it a lot, and said it was like dancing. Eric could not fathom that at all, but if it worked for Tyler, it was fine with him. Tyler had put on fifteen pounds of muscle, developed an iron stomach, strong calf and thigh muscles, and for the first time in his life chest, shoulder, and arm muscles. He looked even better, thought Eric.

Eric went back to his office and began reading through Oscar's notes. One of Oscar's earlier comments about Tyler was that you only had to tell or show him how to do something once. He considered him proficient in setting up the field command networks for radio, phone, and satellite links. He knew how to rebuild a radio in the field, and how to determine what the problems were, and apply solutions.

He said Tyler loved to attack a new research assignment like a crossword puzzle. He was still learning the tricks of the trade, as to finding important data, but he had shown creativity in discovering all possible details concerning a suspect. Tyler showed Oscar how to use Twitter, Facebook, and YouTube to find suspects as well.

He also liked the fact that Tyler could handle more than one computer at a time, and stated he surrounded himself with three monitors and keyboards so he could start one on research, the next on logistics, and so on. He suggested Tyler be assigned as an assistant field tech on the next assignment to see how he handles himself in the field and under stress, but he was willing to bet he would do very well.

George knocked on his door and brought in a stack of folders. "I have the results of today's testing in the field and the gym. I think our teams did very well. I hope you agree."

"From what I saw, they all did very well."

George smiled. "To be honest, except for Tyler, they all had done similar work in the military. Tyler is the only civilian. He should have joined up because I think the boy likes the job as much as we do."

"What do you suggest as his next step?"

"I would take him on to phase two which will be more intense martial arts training that I will handle, and Bob will I'll teach him how to use grenades, an Uzi, and other weapons. In a year, he could be a field agent. How's his electronic work coming?"

"Oscar says he is has taken to it very well, and suggests we book him for an assistant tech on the next op."

"Good for him. Any questions?"

"No, George. Thank you once again for doing a great job."

"The job's not done yet. I expect you on the track this afternoon."

Eric smiled. "Roger, will do."

Tyler and Eric went to lunch a little late, made their orders from the menu, and began talking. "Tyler, let me quickly say your reports on your field exercises, shooting performances, and martial arts skills, are outstanding. I could not have been prouder. Your work with Oscar is top notch, and he has recommended you for a field trial to work as an assistant to the tech in charge. Would you like to do that?"

"Absolutely."

"I have some bad news and good news. You're no longer an intern. That job is over. If you want it, you're now part of the team."

Tyler grinned. "Yes I do."

"Okay, when we get back to office, you have some more paperwork to fill out. You still have about a year of first level training to do, and every person keeps training and learning as time goes by. We'll get you on all our benefit programs. You'll earn fifty thousand a year, and if your reports are good, you'll get a raise at that time. You'll have three-weeks paid vacation, health insurance with full coverage, and if wounded on the job, you'll be taken care of by the best. You'll also have a five million dollar life insurance policy, and the firm pays that, as no outside carrier would cover us. Our work is considered hazardous for obvious reasons. You have to decide on a beneficiary."

"What is a beneficiary?"

Eric tried not to smile. "Let's say one of my men is killed on the job. He has probably set it up so that the life insurance money goes to his wife, his children, or someone he loves.

"Oh, I have never had life insurance before. Heck, I never had health insurance either."

"Well, God forbid, if something happen and you were killed, the money would go to your beneficiary. Do you want to name your parents?"

Tyler went instantly silent. "I guess most of the single guys would probably do that, but my folks hate my guts and haven't spoken to me in years. I don't feel close to them at all."

"Well, you think about it, and if you can't think of anyone, you can always do it later. Congratulations, you now have a full-time job and career."

"Thank you. Thank you very much," beamed Tyler. After a pause, he softly said, "How much can I earn with your company?"

"Well, I can't discuss any specific salaries with you, but I can tell you our top field agents make over three hundred thousand a year."

"Oh shit! That's a lot of money!" exclaimed Tyler.

Eric laughed. "You can get that, too, but I promise you, you'll have to work harder than the rest, so it doesn't look like the boss is playing favorites."

"I know. I have been thinking about it. Do we have to keep our relationship a secret?"

"Not anymore, but on the other hand, I think it would hurt morale if I displayed affection in front of the others, or gave you more attention than the others. So at work, I'll be like a fearless leader and at home..."

"You'll screw my brains out!"

Eric busted out laughing. "You're right about that, but I'm still a little sore from last night while I was the bottom. I guess you were getting even with me."

"It was fun. Just wait until tonight. I have more sex planned for you!"

About three o'clock, Oscar buzzed Eric's office. "Hey, boss. Your boys in Miami are home. They got in about twenty minutes ago."

"I'll be right down."

Eric arrived while Oscar moved the live streaming video to the large screen on the wall and turned up the audio.

"I heard him say something about Acapulco in the beginning as they talked to a..."

Tyler rolled his swivel chair over so he could see the video and interrupted, "Marvin. He is the housekeeper, cook, and former criminal, at least as far as I know. He makes great omelets and a pot roast. He was asking them about their vacation in Acapulco. He then asked if they stayed the whole three months there and Stephen said no, they only spent two weeks there before moving on to Costa Rica. Jim breezed into the room and said he was on the way to the pawnbroker, so that probably means they did a job somewhere on their trip."

After thinking Eric asked, "They own an island in Costa Rica, don't they?"

"Yes."

Oscar was getting confused, so Eric decided to tell him more about Tyler. "Oscar, this is confidential. Until a few months ago, Tyler was involved with this group. Think of them as the Charles Dickens character Fagan and Tyler played the part of Oliver Twist. Stephen and Jim are also killers like Bill Sikes. Tyler saw the error of his ways and ran away after receiving a bad beating. He is the Tyler they want to find and kill just to shut him up, so he could never turn them in."

"Okay. Thank you for filling me in. Well, we'll keep watching them because they are not going to kill my new expert technician."

Eric smiled and winked at Tyler. Tyler smiled slightly.

Eric said, " I'm surprised our camera is still working."

Oscar said, "Oh it could survive for a year or more, unless a hurricane comes through."

Eric replied, "I bet they have been thinking of their next project. We need to find out where and when they'll be flying out. Let me know when you figure it out. I've got a few plans I have been working on that perhaps will make them more desperate. I'll talk to you later."

Eric had been thinking for about an hour when he called Ted Rivers to his office. Ted was his financial expert and along with Oscar, the two of them could figure out and handle just about any financial scheme. He wanted to talk with Ted first before bringing in Oscar. He gave Ted a file he prepared, but began by telling him the highlights.

"Obviously, we'll soon have enough evidence for the cops to arrest them, but they'll hire the best lawyers, get out on bail, and they'll be gone. They put tons of their money in offshore accounts, most of it in Cayman, and they own an island in Costa Rica where they could hide out forever. We have no extradition treaty with the government there."

Ted asked, "What do you have in the mind?"

"These guys are very good, and they can smell a cop or trap with ease. I want to force them into making a mistake, and I want to hurt them financially before they are arrested, so they'll have no means of getting out."

Ted smiled. "So we need to bankrupt them. Money is their cushion, and it sounds like they have a lot stored away plus gold and jewels. I'll have to do some research, but I think we should buy their island."

135

Eric's jaw dropped. "How could we do that?"

"Well, what I will propose will be a little bit of creative accounting. We'll beat them at their own game, but using a much higher level of technology and documents. I'll create paperwork just like we were going to a real closing to buy the island from them. We'll need to find out what names they used to record the deeds and their signatures. Oscar will find that for us. I think you should pay about five million for it."

"Ouch, I better call the bank."

Ted laughed. "Oh, we want be using your money. We'll be using theirs."

"I get it. Oscar will move money from their accounts to do so."

"In fact, I think we should move all their money into our hidden accounts, and we should buy their house, cars, and anything else they own."

Eric replied, "They have more money and jewels in a safe room in the house."

Ted said, "Okay, so we'll buy the house and furnishing as well."

"This also should happen at the same time," began Eric, "so that they go from rich to poor in less than a few hours."

"Precisely. Do you have anything else? I have a lot of work to get started on. This is going to be fun."

"No, go ahead, and I'll brief Oscar. Thank you very much. Keep me posted on your progress so we can coordinate the timing. It'll have to be when we know they are faraway and not able to return in time to stop it."

After Oscar arrived, Eric briefed him on his meeting with Ted. "I need to make sure we have all their offshore account information, passwords, and more so that when we're ready to drain their accounts, we don't leave them a single loophole."

"Okay, I'll probably lose my eyesight, but we'll zoom in and start counting keystrokes. He's a pretty good typist, but we can record what he types, and slow it down."

"Very good, please keep me posted."

Three days later, Eric got a call from Oscar. "Good news, Tyler and I believe we have discovered and broken pass codes on all their accounts. There were thirteen of them in four countries."

"Thirteen. Hmm, I guess that will be an unlucky number for them. Any progress on the information Ted needed."

"Yes for Stephen. We have his signature, and at list of aliases for him. We had to hunt long and hard for Jim, as apparently Stephen does all the legal stuff. Jim better be nice to Stephen."

"Why's that?"

"Everything is in Stephen's name, or one of his alias names, and nothing is in Jim's name. If Stephen got mad, he could cut Jim off from all the money and property."

"Stephen wouldn't cut him off." He paused, "He'd kill him. He just wouldn't have any trouble with his money and possessions tied up in probate. Good work. Thanks."

On the way to work the next day, Eric broke the news to Tyler that he had been selected to assist with tech support for an operation. His client Larry Menard was speaking at a computer convention in Chicago next week. The firm would take Larry to and from the event and protect him at all times.

Tyler laughed. "What could happen to him? He develops software, some of which doesn't work very well."

Eric grinned. "That in itself might be reason to kill him. I've thought of killing the people who invented the computer many times when my laptop froze, and I lost all the work I had done for the past few hours. But Larry is also very rich, and most likely to be kidnapped for a large ransom. I should also mention that he is gay, so he likes to throw us a curve by going out to gay clubs."

"Oh, I get it. He is the guy you were protecting when I met you in Miami."

"And they said blonds are stupid," laughed Eric. "You are very right. Are you up to the assignment?"

"Yes, I am."

"Okay, they'll be a team meeting this afternoon at three. Bring your pad and pen, pay attention to details, and memorize as much as you can. If something bad happens, we don't have time to look up a detail. We have to know it as well as our own birthday."

Oscar assigned Ronnie Beam as tech leader for the Menard assignment detail for the Chicago job. Tyler would assist. Eric met with the full team that afternoon, and began with the schedule and timetable. They would be in Chicago for four days arriving midday. "We'll be staying in the Conrad Chicago, a luxury, five star, top of the line hotel, and take over an entire floor and dozen rooms. Menard will be staying in their top suite, along with two of his associates, and his personal assistant.

"The computer show will be in the heart of the financial district and just a few blocks from the hotel in the Merchandise Mart, where many conventions are held. While there are some in this room that may like to strangle our client from time to time, he does spend about ten million a year with our firm. We should be prepared for anything. Obviously, kidnapping is the top of our worry list, but the notoriety of killing him is possible, too, hence the killing of John Lennon and Robert Kennedy, among others.

"Gil Allister will be in charge of this mission. I will go along as an observer, and to keep Gill from killing Menard after a few days of his whining." The group laughed. "Okay, Gil, you're in charge. Call me if you need me."

As Eric left, Gil took over and brought up slides of the hotel and the Merchandise Mart, and began talking about the operational plans he and Eric had been working on for several days.

Eric was walking pass Oscar's office, who waived at him while getting off the phone. "Our boys are on the move."

Eric asked, "Where to?"

"That is the weird part. He has discussed the trip with Jim, but not one word as to where they are going?"

"What about plane tickets?"

"They haven't booked anything yet, but I'm monitoring him closely, as well as watching his emails for ticket, hotel, and rental car confirmations. So far nothing like that has arrived."

"So they're planning a mission, but we don't know where. Do they own a plane in the States?"

"Not that I could find, however, Ted has done a full detail analysis of all their accounts. I'll ask him."

"Print out their credit card transactions for me, but be aware they often steal credit cards, and may have access to other illegal cards. I doubt we'll know which ones unless you can spot their use. Please let me know if we get lucky."

On the way home, Eric told Tyler of his discussion with Oscar.

Tyler remarked, "Well, I was happier knowing they were out of the country, but I'm no longer afraid of them. I will feel better when they are in prison."

Eric sighed. "We're trying to create a situation where they can be caught in the act, but burglary in itself does not create a long prison sentence. If we can stack up a bunch of their crimes, we might get them up to ten years."

Tyler asked somberly, "What happens when they get out?"

"Well, most grifters, with the skills and intelligence of these guys, go underground and surface with new names, identifications, a new house, and new cars. They never change, and they always start over."

"Do you think they'll come after me?"

"Yes, I do. They will assume you turned them in because they think they are too smart to get caught otherwise, and that may well be true."

"What if I become the government's prime witness?"

"I have been thinking about it, but there are several problems. First of all, although we would bargain for your slate to be wiped clean, the court rarely does, and you could serve a lesser sentence. Secondly, if you did become their witness, I don't think it would change the length of their sentence, only an easier conviction, but you would be marked as a thief and every job you applied for you would have to check you had been convicted of a crime. No one ever trusts a thief. They say 'once a thief, always a thief' but of course, that is not true for me.

"However, I do think we should pay for our crimes, and I think it essential to turning over a new leaf. If the price of your crimes is paid, you are then free to be an honest person. Most criminals don't make it after doing their time, as they find it hard to find a good job. They are forced to live in poor apartments, do menial jobs like washing dishes to get by, and so sooner or later, they fall back to the easy money and back into prison.

"I don't want to take that chance with you. I will think of a way out of this. I will find a way I can justify you paying for your crimes without being a witness and without going to prison, and of course, I plan to put your friends out of business for life."

Tyler smiled slightly as they pulled into their driveway. "How will you do that?"

"We're working on it. I want you to meet tomorrow with Ted. He is working on an analysis of all Stephen and Jim's assets. We're going to take every single penny and object away from them. Maybe you can help him fill in the blanks, as if you were a witness, which you are. I'll talk to him about your situation first. Helping to convict them could satisfy any need to prosecute you.

"If we get them in prison, I want them to come out with nothing, so it is harder for them to get back to the level of living they have now. By the way, do they own a plane?"

"A small plane in Costa Rica, but Stephen does charter one now and then to get there from Miami, and we sometimes went diving in Cayman."

Eric smiled. "You may know this already, but Cayman has a large amount of international banks, and that is where many wealthy folks, honest and dishonest folks, as well as crooks and drug lords put their money. Did you ever note whether they did some banking while there?"

"Stephen would. Jim would get mad because he wanted to go diving, but we would have to wait in the car while Stephen when in with a briefcase. He usually did this several times while we were there."

"They have a lot of money in those banks and in a few others in other countries, and of course, they have the island in Costa Rica. Do you recall anywhere else they owned property?"

"Yes, they have a place in Spain."

"What city?'

Tyler frowned. "Ugh, this hurts my head. It rhymes with fizz."

Eric laughed. "You mean Cadiz?"

"Yeah, that's it! How did you know?"

139

"I was in the Navy Seals, and there is an American navy base there."

"Hey, that's right. When I would walk the streets, I would see all these cute sailors in their uniforms. They packed into the bars, even the gay bars. I would sometimes act like I didn't speak English, but it didn't work too well, as I don't look like a Spaniard at all."

"Give this information to Ted," Eric said as they went inside. "Would you fire up the grill? If it is okay, I'll think we'll have steaks tonight. I'll get them marinated and ready."

"Yum, yum. No problem. I'm starving already."

"I'll get the potatoes started and fix some salads. Tea or wine?"

Tyler laughed. "I'm not smart enough to know anything about wine, but I do love sweet iced tea."

"That's okay, I have southern friends who call sweet iced tea southern wine."

"It is good without a hangover," replied Tyler as he went out on the deck.

Eric smiled. He hadn't been this happy in a long, long time. During the last few years, he had poured every ounce of his energy into the firm. He was satisfied with the progress and felt they were set for life. Tyler returned to the kitchen, came up behind Eric, gave him a hug, and kissed the back of his neck. He smiled again. Life is good, he thought.

FOURTEEN

Stephen drove the Porsche rapidly out of the gate and began zipping along the freeway, and a half hour later, he arrived at Kendall-Tamiami Executive Airport. This airport handled only private jets and charters. He parked the car, picked up his briefcase, and walked to the entrance for the small office that was adjacent to a large hanger. He walked up to the receptionist, and asked to speak to Bobby Henson. He sat down and waited a few minutes until Bobby came out, shook hands with him, and invited him into his office. Bobby was nearing sixty, wore his gray hair in a short crew cut just as he did as a pilot in the Air Force for twenty years. He started his charter service with one plane and it grew. He now had fourteen Learjets in service. He maintained another seventy private jets and planes as part of his storage and maintenance programs. He obtained his Florida tan from being on the tarmac so much as well as playing golf on weekends. At just over six feet, he continued a daily workout at six every morning.

After he closed the door, Bobby said, "I take it you need to charter a flight again?"

"Yes, here's the schedule and destination," replied Stephen as he gave Bobby a sheet of paper. "We'll leave on Friday."

"Give me just a second to check our aircraft availability," he said as he punched a few keys on his computers, rechecked the dates, and then scrolled down the list of crews available. "Good news, we can handle this schedule for you. How many people are flying?"

"Just three, and only five pieces of luggage for the short stay."

"And the average weight for the passengers?"

"Stephen smiled. "Very average, and you've met Jim before. He and I will be making the flight along with our personal assistant who weighs about a hundred thirty-five pounds. How much is this going to set me back for?"

"Six grand. It would be less if you didn't want the crew standing by."

"I know, but I'm not sure what time we'll be ready to leave. How much notice do I need to give the pilots?"

"A couple of hours will be fine. I'll warn them you could leave at any time. Once they get eight hours of sleep each night they are good to go."

Stephen chartered a flight several times a year, and had already configured the flight cost, and had the money in an envelope. He tossed it to Bobby. "This should pay for everything in advance."

Bobby smiled. "It's not often we are paid in cash."

Stephen laughed and lied. "Well, I have to keep this trip secret from my ex-wife, if you know what I mean."

Bobby chuckled. "My lips are sealed." He stood and shook Stephen's hand. "We'll be ready. Would you prefer steak, pork, or chicken?"

Stephen replied, "At these rates, I expect excellent steaks and cooked medium rare."

"Done."

With Tyler's help, Ted was able to find the details on the house in Cadiz. He prepared the paperwork for obtaining the property. He also told Ted what he knew about their cars and more details about the house.

Tyler also began helping Oscar with the surveillance of his former home in Miami by taking computer screen shots and making notes on the bank accounts. His martial arts training with George was down to an hour a day plus his physical workouts. However, he spent most of his time with Ronnie Beam, as they prepared all the radios and other communication gear for their upcoming trip to Chicago. Together, they attended the detailed planning meeting with Gil until they knew every scenario and all the details of the mission. Tyler was impressed that the team actually planned three or four alternate plans in case of problems, attacks, or what Eric called an odd feeling. He always trusted his instincts.

Later in the day, Eric welcomed Ted into his office. He presented Eric with both his report on Stephen and Jim's possessions, and his thoughts on how they could take it all away. Eric asked many questions, but Ted anticipated every one of his inquiries. Eric smiled and congratulated him on an excellent job.

The end of the week came quickly, but they were up before dawn, with their bags packed, and dressed in business attire. Eric helped Tyler adjust his gun harness over his new shirt until it fit like a glove, undetectable under his suit jacket, but ready for quick draw should a situation occur. In Tyler's wallet, he carried his new gun permit issued by the FBI. He also carried a typical black leather, wallet-style folder that looked exactly like the one the FBI used for their field agents. It showed Tyler's official security team ID with his picture, a copy of his gun permit, and at a quick glance, most folks would assume he was a government agent instead of a private one. Tyler kept Eric in stitches the night before as he practiced flashing his ID with stupid names. "This is Barney Rubble, ma'am, I'm here on official business." Eric inspected him from top to bottom, adjusted just slightly his Windsor knot in his tie, and gave him a ten on his overall appearance, including his new military-style haircut. He then kissed him and smiled.

Eric and Tyler arrived just minutes before the rest of the team. Tyler and Ronnie carefully re-checked every piece of equipment. With Tyler doing the final packing, Ronnie checked each piece against his checklist. Then they began issuing each team member their radio, sleeve microphone, and earpiece for the day. Each person did a quick sound check on the assigned frequency, and then left to pick up their firearms, and load the transport van. They locked the rest of the team's electronic gear inside heavy-duty, special made footlockers, and moved the trunks to the loading dock using hand trucks.

Tyler put his luggage just outside the van alongside the rest of the team. They rolled the weapon footlockers out last and loaded each into the second van. Equipment was loaded first and then the luggage. Members of the team carried a 9mm Glock pistol under their left arm, spare clips under the right arm, and just in a case, they carried handcuffs in a pouch at their left hip. Tyler felt funny caring the handcuffs, but his training included how to take down a bad guy, and the handcuffs made it possible for him to secure a suspect while continuing the mission.

Gil came up with his clipboard and checked off the name of each member. They boarded the two vans, and then along with their gear they drove to Lee airport, where they boarded a chartered flight to Chicago. Two hours later, they landed at Chicago Executive Airport and rolled into a private hanger. They quickly disembarked and moved their gear and bags into two waiting black Toyota Sequoia SUV autos. There was a black limousine waiting as well. One of Gil's men would drive the limo, while a second person rode in the passenger seat armed and ready. Eric would ride with Larry Menard in the back. No one else wanted to as Larry was always difficult, but he paid the firm well, and thus, Eric paid the crew very well, so he made the sacrifice of sticking close to their sometimes, somewhat obnoxious client.

Eric checked his watch, looked to the west, and saw a second Learjet approaching with landing lights on. He put his combo briefcase/laptop case inside the limo, and walked to the front of the car as the jet slowly taxied into the hanger. As the steps motorized down to the tarmac, out bounced a jovial Larry Menard.

"Eric, you old shit, how are you?"

Eric stuck out his hand to welcome his client and rolled his eyes, "You just love embarrassing me in front of my men, don't you?" He paused, "I'm fine. Are you ready to roll?" Eric watched a flight assistant load luggage into the back of the limo.

"Let's do it."

Larry entered the car, followed by Eric who closed the door, and locked it. They started the vehicles and pulled out with one SUV in front of the limo and the other one behind. As they approached the airport expressway, two police motorcycles pulled in front, providing escort service into the city. The planned routes were approved last week with the Chicago police department and Gil.

As soon as they reached the hotel's parking garage, two thirds of the team quickly disembarked and began preparing the route to Larry's suite and their rooms. The hotel manager met Larry at the private entrance, where he quickly signed their forms, and received the key to his room. Eric obtained a duplicate key. A few minutes later, Eric heard the all-clear signal on COM1.

Gil and two agents began moving Larry through the hotel to the elevator. Ronnie and Tyler unloaded the equipment lockers and took the service elevator to the eighth floor where a hotel staff member met them with the electronic keys to all their rooms. Ronnie signed for them as Tyler pulled the footlockers into the room. The requested banquet tables and chairs were set up in the living room of a nice suite.

Tyler knew exactly what to do and began setting up while Ronnie passed the packet of room keys to Gil, and then came into the suite to help Tyler. They immediately checked the quality of the power with an electrical testing device, and after obtaining a green light that indicated clean power, they began preparing the control center. They lifted one of the footlockers into a vertical position, unsnapped the lids from front and back, and plugged in a heavy-duty power cord to a wall outlet. Tyler placed big strips of gray duct tape over the plug to prevent accidentally unplugging. He also taped the cord to the carpet to prevent anyone from tripping over it.

Power ran into the bottom of the rack and into an inverter that continuously charged special-made, deep cell batteries similar to golf cart batteries, providing clean and consistent uninterruptible power. A second inverter took the twelve-volt electricity and converted it back to standard household AC power. With the batteries in the loops, no surges or temporary browns outs, or power failures could harm their equipment. With some power management, they could run almost twenty-four hours off the batteries if required. Every electronic device became part of the clean power system with branches of power feeding outlets running down the length of the banquet tables and to the rear.

Tyler clicked a switch to power up the fans that kept the equipment cool, then removed a cap in the top of crate and raised two antennas. He then went to the window, and taped another antenna onto the glass. He ran the connecting wire to the back of the rack, and plugged it in the appropriate jack where he had memorized the location inputs for all the required equipment.

Ronnie flipped several switches and lights as one by one the various pieces of equipment came to life, including a portable fax machine and a high-speed printer and copier. Tyler opened the patio door and set up a portable satellite dish on the balcony. After securing the base, he touched a button on the back of the unit, and the dish began unfolding and searching the sky for the proper satellite signal. They requested a room with southwest view for this purpose. He also installed a fourth telescoping antenna to the corner of patio and raised it upwards about twenty feet. He rolled all the wires back to the crate and plugged them into the rack. He placed some insulation in the door crack, taped it in place, and then used an adjustable, locking rod jamb to secure the door. Ronnie verbalized a mental checklist and began checking each piece of equipment for power, while Tyler opened the second crate and began setting up a bank of computers on the tables, firing them up, and together they began testing their highly secured and encrypted Wi-Fi system that all the agents would use on this floor. They also tested their private, cell phone system that allowed all agents to use their office cell phones anywhere in the county. The high-powered system was granted a special license from the Federal Communication Commission.

Back in the home office, Oscar checked his watch and waited while staring at the monitoring blocks on his computer screen. Tyler logged in while listening to Ronnie run down a radio check with each member of team. Just as the last person responded, Gil came on the radio, announcing they were bringing Larry up after his team checked and cleared each room very carefully with a variety of sensors and detecting devices. This eliminated both bugs and bombs. Tyler adjusted his earpiece as it made his ear itch. He tapped rapidly on the various keyboards while watching the screens, and in just a few seconds, they were linked and synchronized to Oscar.

Oscar hit the chat link and an instant iChat audio-video window opened on Tyler's first monitor. Oscar and Tyler could see and hear each other. "Way to go, Tyler. Links look good. I am uploading coded email for the team, and other documentation for Gil. Also tell Eric that Marti said call him."

Tyler spoke towards the built-in computer microphone, "Roger, will do. Thanks."

"Oscar is out but standing by." Tyler closed the chat window.

"All radios, and satellite links are a go," pronounced Ronnie, as he began tweaking.

"All computers are good to go as well," said Tyler.

Ronnie checked his watch. "Sixteen minutes. Not bad for a newbie," he teased.

Eric came in the room, as did other team members. Larry was now safely in his room with a security detail at his door. A second team was stationed in opposite directions monitoring the hallway. "Are all systems go and ready?"

"Roger that," replied Ronnie.

"Very good," replied Eric as he set down his briefcase and pulled out his laptop. "Wi-Fi up and running?"

"Roger that," replied Tyler. "You have communications from the office, and Oscar said for you to call Marti."

Eric tried not to smile as Tyler was exactly copying Ronnie's military sounding voice and not his own. "Thank you, go ahead."

Tyler hit a key that deciphered the email packet from the office, and instantly sent it to the proper team members. Eric picked up his cell phone "Phone network secured?"

"Roger that," replied Ronnie and Tyler in unison.

Eric laughed. "What are you guys—twins?"

While Eric made his call, Ronnie and Tyler installed a few safety items for the command center. Three hidden buttons were activated along the under edge of the table that were like those used by a bank teller during a robbery to call in the cavalry. They were to only use these buttons if the room was compromised, so that an enemy couldn't send out incorrect messages and instructions to the team. Each button downed all equipment immediately, and a small cylinder blew a puff of smoke from the equipment racks, indicating the gear was actually fried, but it wasn't. However, it could only be restarted via a hidden power switch in the back of the vertical rack that looked like a tweeter speaker. If any of these buttons were touched, a small bell tone would sound in every agent's radio within range of the command center. If heard, Gil could punch in a code on his radio and actually listen to conversations in the room to determine if their command control center agents, Ronnie and Tyler, were still alive, and the status of the situation they were in. Lastly, they taped two pistols in quick-draw holsters to the bottom of the table in case of a breech by an enemy.

Eric explained to Tyler that much of these security precautions were not necessary for this trip, but done because they were part of their routine, and created a habit, so that in the future, they did everything as they always did, leaving knowing to chance.

Eric talked with Marti about several messages she received, and when finished, she transferred him to Oscar.

"Boss, I think our guys are on the move. I came in early today to prepare for your links, and there is no sound or activity in the house at all. I think they give the housekeeper time off when they are gone. Stephen did not turn on his monitor. I became suspicious and rewound the video until late last night. Just before midnight, Jim went in the safe room. He took some cash out of the vault and two Glock pistols, and then closed the bookcase and left. The house went silent after that.

"Did you say two 9mm Glocks?"

"Precisely. They are armed."

Eric thought for a minute. "Well, they aren't flying commercial. See if you can download the data for all charter flights out of that area and log their destinations."

"Eric, that is Miami. There are probably hundreds of flights this morning from Fort Lauderdale on down to Miami and on to Key Biscayne."

"I know. I hope you can find them, but please let me know if any of those flights are coming to Chicago."

Oscar let out a long sigh. "Oh, I see. That'll narrow down the list. Roger, will do. Out."

Larry wasn't scheduled to arrive at the computer show until that evening, so until then, Eric enjoyed some free time. He went to his room and setup his laptop, took off his shoes, took a water bottle from his bag, and set down on the couch, putting his feet up and then began thinking.

Where would Stephen and Jim be heading? He didn't believe they were going after Jim's mark from the Las Vegas encounter, but he made a note anyhow to ask Oscar to see if any flights where going to San Antonio, and the mark's house.

He went online and began searching for any gay event anywhere in the country. He knew it was a long shot, but he couldn't find even a single, gay pride parade. There wasn't a gay charity event, or a gay day on Oprah. He failed to find any gay events anywhere in the country. He laughed as it was like a gay hibernation day. He began searching to see if there was some big grand opening for a new, gay nightclub, and started with all the major cities and again found nothing.

He thought back over when he first discovered Tyler. He then recalled it wasn't a special event, just another night at the strip bar. He looked up the major cities again and found twenty well-known, gay strip bars. He made a list and waited for Oscar to report.

He also wondered why this trip required 9mm pistols and an expensive chartered flight instead of their usual commercial flights.

Finding no easy solution or even a good probability for their destination, he began to go back over in his head the trap they were setting for Stephen and Jim's money and loot. That part of his plan had been the easy part. What he couldn't solve yet in his mind was how to catch them in a crime that would put them away for a long, long time. Whatever he came up with, he thought, it had to be done in such a way that Tyler wasn't involved, but a way in which Tyler was instrumental in apprehending the thieves. That way, if his name came up, Eric could testify that Tyler highly assisted the team in catching the real bad guys, indicating that Tyler was actually a victim, too. However, as long as Stephen and Jim thought Tyler was dead, there would be no need to involve him.

Now that Ted had 'act one' ready to go, Eric decided that when this operation in Chicago was over, he would assign a squad to Miami to put constant surveillance on Stephen and Jim. He knew they would have to be very careful, as he was convinced the cops had blown the last attempt in San Diego. To catch and put them away for a long sentence, they would have to know where they were at all times, and they would need to know what they planning.

To do that, he would have to go back into the house, and plant lots of audio bugs for other rooms and their telephones, as well as surveillance-tracking bugs on all their vehicles, so they could be tailed from a longer distance to avoid discovery. He smiled while recalling he safely entered their house once, and he could do it again, as he knew the secret alarm code he had activated. He suddenly realized that he just missed the perfect time to be inside their house, because the thieves were out-of-town, but Eric was here in Chicago with an important client. "Damn!" he said to no one but himself. "Damn, damn, damn."

He picked up his cell when it began ringing. "Eric."

"Boss, this is Oscar. I have compiled a list and emailed it to you because it is a long list."

"That's good. While I am checking my email, how many flights to Chicago?"

"Ten."

"San Antonio."

"One."

Eric opened the email, and then began scrolling down the list. Half the flights to Chicago had already arrived. "Dang, it. I'm going to the airport to meet the other flights. I pray they aren't coming here. Good job, Oscar, see if you can find out who was on the flight to San Antonio and let me know."

Eric poked his head into the command suite and said to Gil, "I'm going back to the airport to meet some other flights."

Gil asked, "Need any help?"

"No thanks, just surveillance. I've got that old itch again."

Ronnie quickly spoke up, "The airport will be out of normal radio range. Shall I run up the balloon?" Oscar created the balloon antenna a few years ago. It was a typical weather balloon that carried a battery and solar powered repeater antenna. To launch it, they used a can of helium to inflate it, and a motorized fishing reel. They normally launched it a bit higher than the buildings, but could go as high as five hundred feet. However, in metropolitan and surrounding areas, they rarely went too high due to airplane traffic. The repeater antenna extended their radio signals from fifty to a hundred miles.

"No, that's okay," replied Eric. "I'll just use the cell phone. I won't be gone long."

Eric left after nodding at Tyler's smile as he glanced up from the computer where he was doing some equipment checks, while monitoring satellite and cell signals on another computer. He noted Gil and another agent were preparing Oscar's new mouse chaser that was actually a lot like the metal detectors folks used on the beach to find coins and other valuables. However, Oscar's new toy produced a far stronger signal allowing the operator to see in a viewfinder an image of what was in the ductwork in the hall. It could also hear the tick of any bomb timer, and would pick up any hidden electronic devices. It became part of their new arsenal of weapons after the Buenos Aires episode with the bomb in the hall ductwork.

Eric took a cab back to the Chicago Executive Airport. He got out of the cab near the flight tower. He went inside and sat where he could see the arriving flights. He opened his laptop and began studying Oscar's long email. He realized that Oscar had listed not only the flights and anticipated landing times, but also the name of the charter company and tail number. He quickly memorized the ID numbers of the five remaining planes. He used his air-card via his USB port on his laptop, and loaded the national, fight-status website. He punched in the five tail numbers and in seconds he had blips on his screen as to their location. He could click on any single blip for details of the plane, flight origin, and destination. It took just over an hour, but one by one they all came in, and using a small but high-powered set of binoculars, he determined Stephen and Jim were not on any of the flights. He hailed a cab to return to the hotel. In the cab, he called Oscar.

"They weren't on the last five flights, but I saw surveillance cameras at the corners of the flight tower. See if you can get footage of this morning."

Oscar grinned. "Oh, that's too easy. I will be back with you soon." He almost hung up, but then quickly said, "Oh, by the way, there was a priest and three nuns were on the San Antonio flight flying home with a dead parishioner for his funeral. He was very wealthy."

Eric sighed. "Okay, that unfortunately either makes Chicago the more likely target, or they are on any of the other flights. Maybe you can get footage of all of them."

"Sure," laughed Oscar. "I just need about forty hours and twelve hands."

"Why not start with the Miami area executive airports. Maybe you can get the name of the company or the tail number. Tyler said they flew out of there several times a year. Thanks," grinned Eric. "I'm counting on you."

Ronnie returned from his break, and told Tyler to take a walk and get familiar with the hotel, especially elevators and stairwells, and the route to the parking garage. Tyler had already memorized the floor plan, as did the rest of the team, but he realized that Ronnie was just telling Tyler to chill out and get some fresh air.

He chatted briefly with the other team members on duty in the hall and took the elevator down. The elevator was one of those fancy, upscale units with all glass on the back so the guests enjoyed a view of Chicago, once they were above the fourth floor, and a view of lobby as they descended. Tyler was a little afraid of heights, but gradually moved to the rear, so he could look through the windows and down into the giant lobby of Conrad Chicago Hotel. As he passed the fourth floor heading down to the lobby, he suddenly caught sight of someone that made his heart skip a beat. He stared in disbelief as he realized the first person he saw was Stephen, but soon he spotted Jim walking with a tanned, good-looking young man at his side. As Tyler passed the third floor, it dawned on him they were walking right to the elevator area and in his direction. When the door open, he could be standing right in front of them.

He started to panic, but his training helped him remain calm so he could think clearly. He looked at the elevator buttons just as the light for floor number three went off, and the next stop was L for lobby. He dove at the buttons, and hit the white square for button two.

He held his breath as the elevator came to a sudden stop. He looked up at the numbers, praying he wasn't in the lobby. The lights remained out, and he felt the elevator rise just a little and stop. The door suddenly opened at the same time the number two appeared on the display above the door. He took a giant step out and found himself on the convention floor with people everywhere.

He took a deep breath as he exited the elevator, and brought out his new, company issued, cell phone, and hit the speed dial for Eric.

Eric was just paying for the cab in front of the hotel. "Eric here, how may I help you?"

"This is Tyler. I just spotted Stephen, Jim, and another man in the hotel lobby. I was on a break and coming down the elevator, and saw them pulling their luggage to the elevators, so I got off on floor two, the convention level. What do I do?"

"Find a plant or a tree to stand behind just in case they get off on your floor. I am coming through the lobby. Hang up your cell phone and listen in on com1." He walked briskly to the elevators, but didn't see them. He ran back into the lobby and watched four elevators going up. He scanned each one and in the last one he spotted Jim standing next to the glass with the young man.

He pressed the button for his radio. "Gil, suspects are three men currently in the fourth elevator." He quickly described all three. He then said, "That is the last elevator to your right if you're facing the waiting area." He ran back to the elevator entryway and watched the floor read out for that elevator. "The car stopped on nine—one up from ours. Get a man there fast and find out what room they check into, and tell him to act cool or even lost. Hurry!"

Eric knew the entire team was listening so he continued, "We have three suspects that could be after Larry. Gil, get Oscar on the horn, and have him email the pictures that we have for two of the men, known as Stephen and Jim, but they will be using aliases. We need a briefing in ten minutes in the command suite. Out."

Eric took the escalator up to the second floor and walked around the hallway to the elevators where he easily spotted Tyler hiding behind a big fake fichus tree. Eric smiled. "Come on out, Tarzan."

Tyler walked out, but he was as pale as a ghost. "Where are they?"

"I suspect the ninth floor. Gil sent a man up to confirm."

"That's just above our rooms. What are they doing here?"

Eric smiled. "I think they are after one of the richest gay men in the world."

Tyler's face became puzzled. "Who in the hell is that?"

Eric winked at him. "Our client, Larry Menard."

"Did the pictures arrive?" asked Eric as he entered the room with Tyler right behind him. Tyler quickly took his usual seat in front of the bank of computers. Ronnie was printing the pictures out on their portable printer. Except for the agents guarding Larry's room and George who was an errand, the rest of the men were assembled and using every available chair and couch.

"Oscar and I have been working on surveillance of two of these men for over three months. We know where they live, but we also know they are master crooks and target, rich gay men. They have pulled all kinds of grifting and swindling schemes to rob their marks of cash, jewels, and any other items that suit their fancy. They give the mark a knockout drug and then steal their credit and debit cards, and quickly move money to foreign accounts before transferring that cash into their offshore banks. If need be, they are willing to kill to keep themselves from discovery and conviction. We almost had them in a trap in San Diego three months ago, but they sensed a tail from the cops and escape the country. They are extremely smart.

"Just minutes ago, Tyler spotted them in the lobby heading to the elevators. I think it is safe to assume they are after our client, Larry Menard." The door to the room pushed open and George entered. Eric asked, "Did you confirm where they are staying?"

"Yes," he replied. "They are in room 904."

"Thanks," replied Eric. "Ronnie, bring up the floor plan for the ninth floor. Put it on the wall projector." He waited a moment for the information to appear. Ronnie zoomed into room 904. Eric said, "It is a suite of two bedrooms, living and small kitchen, and similar to this one.

"Gil, make notes so you can brief the men that are on duty and missing this conference. After we are finished, send replacements to take their place, and bring them up to date. Now we have a problem. Though tempted to do so, we can't kill these targets in the United States. We need to find a way to protect Larry, while also setting a trap to catch them in the act of committing a crime, so the cops can put them away for a long spell. Once that is accomplished, Oscar, Ted, and I have a plan to put them out of action permanently." Eric paused to let his information settle with his group.

Eric then said, "Tyler? Get Oscar and Ted online and conference them into our discussion with the audio-video link." Tyler made a quick call to the office, gave the orders to Oscar, who also called Ted, and sixty seconds later they could see both men on the projected wall image in separate squares.

"Can you hear me guys?"

"Yes sir," they replied in unison.

Eric replied, "Very good. I have briefed the team on our surveillance work on Stephen and Jim. We have discovered they are in the very hotel we're staying at and just checked in. Since we know they always target rich gay men, of course I suspect they are after our client Larry Menard. While we're thinking this through, Tyler, I want you to run an analysis of all attendees and speakers for the convention, and search for any other rich gay men that are most likely out of the closet. I want to know if there is a possible second target, or is Larry indeed their focus.

"While he is working, Ronnie, I want you to search hotel records and find out how long they are staying, and if they used a credit card to pay for their bill. They won't be using their real names.

"Oscar, we know they were probably on one of the flights to Chicago. Find footage of them. I want to know what private jet company they used, and what are their plans for a return trip?"

"Ronnie, also find all footage of them in the hotel lobby, hallway and even in the elevator. Also check to see how they arrived? Do they have a rental car we need to know about, or did they arrived by taxi?"

"Men, we need our eyes and ears on them, but we can't tail them as they are too smart. This is open to the group, how do we keep a step ahead of them?"

Oscar spoke up first while punching his keyboard rapidly and grabbing security footage, and then putting it together. "Boss, I think I can help technically. Do you think you can get in their room while they are away?"

"Sure, that would be easier than their house."

"Why don't I FedEx one my new little cameras to you. You could put it in their room, and you'd have video and audio. Since you already have a local Wi-Fi set up, you only need the camera in place.

"I will also send you a box of new bugs. Ronnie? I'll send you a dozen dots. You'll have to program your GPS Locator Unit. They'll all start with frequency 12161.2 and up. I'll send some Green Boot as well."

Eric replied, "Okay, I know what to do with the camera. Send two of them. What are the dots for?"

"Boss," laughed Oscar, "you missed my memo?"

The team snickered. Eric sighed with a slight smile. "Perhaps, I did. Enlighten me on great wizard."

"The dots are a tiny GPS tracking device about the size of a pencil point. They are sticky and will attach to anything. All you have to do is brush against the target, leaving it on their coat or shirt. They'll never feel it. As a matter of fact, you can take a small swizzle stick from the bar and blow it like a dart."

The group laughed. Eric said, "I know you better than to doubt you, but get the stuff to me in the next two hours. What is Green Boot?"

"I wish I had invented that stuff, but all you do is spray it on the carpet in the entrance of their hotel door. It is invisible. Every time someone goes out the door, it sends a pulse back to the command center to alert the team. A tiny piece of Green Boot will stick to their shoes and you can track it.

It has a range of just a mile, and of course, eventually it wears off their shoes. Ronnie knows how to set up the GPS tracker for it."

"My friend, you are indeed a wizard. Send it to me."

Oscar replied, "Roger that. No problem. I've uploaded their flight footage. They arrived on a Briscoe Air Charter, tail number 192621. Tyler, that's also the digital file number. Double-click it and the video will begin rolling."

Tyler quickly ran down the list of downloaded files and double-clicked file 192621. Seconds later, the team was watching Stephen and Jim step off the plane, but Tyler became very interested in the next person off the plane. He looked sixteen, with a tan, and dark eyes, and probably of Spanish decent, but then he had another idea. After San Diego, Stephen and Jim laid low for some time at their Costa Rica island paradise. The boy was probably picked and groomed to take his place. It almost made him throw up, but he stifled the instinct, and kept working.

"Oscar, keep tabs on that charter. Find out if the jet is waiting for a return flight, and if so, has the flight been scheduled. Let me know. They will make their hit and fly out quickly thereafter, so if you can get a time for the flight, we'll have an idea of their plan. Good job on the video and your surveillance tricks."

Ronnie spoke up, "I have the footage from the hotel cameras. Rolling."

The team watched the threesome climb out of a cab, then enter into the hotel, and walked over to the front desk. Stephen took care of their registration while Jim and the boy stood off about twenty feet away. The next footage showed them walking to the elevator where Tyler first saw them. Amazingly, they had excellent clear shots of the three in the elevator. Ronnie froze the footage, zoomed in on each man, and Tyler captured the pictures to a file.

When they got to the boy, Eric said, "Who is this kid? Oscar, Ronnie, Tyler—find out?"

There was a slight pause when Tyler suddenly spoke up, "The kid is the bait."

Eric turned and looked at the serious look on Tyler's face, but he also noted his eyes were watered. "I see. I understand. They will use the young man to attract Larry. Tyler, run his picture through the Immigration Network System, and see if there is a passport match."

One of the agents spoke up, "How about we just shoot Larry, so they can't pull off their sting?" The team members laughed.

Eric smiled. "That thought has crossed my mind several times through the years, but he pays us millions each year to protect him. Did everyone enjoy and spend with delight last year's bonus on our earnings?"

They all nodded. "Ronnie, is there a camera on that floor?"

"Yes, sir. Coming up." Ronnie typed rapid strokes and soon in the far left corner of their temporary wall screen they could see the ninth floor hallway and a picture of a maid pushing a cart.

"Very good. Make sure you team monitor that hallway."

"That's it for now. I need to do some thinking. Let me know when the surveillance gear gets here from Oscar. Back to your posts."

Eric gave his boyfriend a slight smile and Tyler nodded slightly in reply, but kept his search operation going on his computer looking for a match, while wondering how Stephen and Jim were treating this new kid.

Eric went to his room and sat down on the bed for a minute while thinking, but soon he stood up and began pacing back and forth across the room. He knew that his first responsibility was to protect Larry. He could tell the police what he knows, and they could arrest them, but no crime that he knew of had been committed in Chicago, even though Tyler could testify as to their criminal activity. He knew he didn't want to do that, as it would implicate Tyler as well.

Although tempted to do so, it would be a crime to kill them, but how to put them away and still protect Larry, he wondered? He knew Tyler would have to remain out of sight, or Stephen and Jim would flee. He wondered if he should try to get the new boy away from them? Would the young man know what was in store for him?

Two hours later, he had a plan set in his mind and returned to the control suite. He called Gil in, and together, with Ronnie and Tyler listening, Eric began telling them what he had in mind. "First of all, give me a status on security."

Gil quickly replied, "I have two men at Larry's door, and two more at each end of the hallway, with one stopping just before the elevator. I have another man watching our vehicles. The rest of the men are on stand-down waiting for a shift change."

Ronnie spoke, "Boss, the package from Oscar just arrived at the front desk. I'll send Tyler to go get it."

Eric immediately broke in, "No, Tyler must remain in this room at all times. I don't have time to go in to a discussion right now, but these men know Tyler. If they see him, they'll run, or they may try to kill him. He must stay here. If you don't mind, take a break, and go get the box yourself, and thank you for your patience."

Ronnie stood up to leave. "Yes sir, and no problem."

Eric said, "Gil, in order to trap them in a crime, we have to give them a feeling of confidence, and that Larry is an easy target. I'm going to level with Larry, and ask him if we can step back from tight security at certain areas in order that these men attempt to make their plan work.

"How is that possible? What about other attackers?"

"I didn't say it would be easy, but I think we should protect him in public with full force, but at the welcoming party, convention speech, and the banquet, we'll back off a little, and see if they make their move."

"And if they do?"

"First of all, we need a secret camera running at all times. I also think we need to wire Larry for sound and a GPS dot. We never let him out of our sight, however, we must make him approachable."

"Let me see the itinerary again."

Gil quickly handed him a sheet of paper from his planning folder. Eric studied it.

"There's a welcome party with open bar for gold ticket holders tonight. He'll meet them there. There are metal detectors at the entrance so Larry would be safe in that room."

"What's a gold ticket holder?"

Eric smiled. "It's for the super rich or the super brilliant computer software inventors, and Larry, our friend," he added satirically, "is invited on both counts. I'm betting the thieves have a gold ticket, too."

"Tyler," he said suddenly, "what names did Stephen use when they checked in?"

Tyler scanned down through the report. "Bob and Ted McKenzie. They're pretending to be brothers. There's nothing listed for the boy."

Eric replied, "Pull up the list of the gold ticket invitees you and Ronnie ran security checks on."

Tyler brought the list up and displayed it on the wall electronically. "Larry is the seventh one down." He scrolled down the list and near the bottom was Bob and Ted McKenzie and nephew Juan Jorge. I think Juan came from Costa Rica where they spent the last few months."

"You're probably right, but now we know they are going to the party."

Ronnie came in the door carrying a FedEx box. "I got Oscar's presents."

"Very good. Ronnie I want you to install and operate one of our regular video cameras in the convention room for the welcoming party tonight. We'll use Oscar's goodies on Larry's room, and if we get the chance, we'll put the other toys in the room for the grifters. I also need an audio wire for Larry. I'm going to see Larry now and ask for his help."

FIFTEEN

Larry gave Eric a look as if to say you're absolutely crazy, but then asked again, "You want me to do what?"

Eric knew Larry would not be excited about going into a room where a known crook would be trying to fleece him. He began his planned approach, "Larry, they could return with a different tact, maybe a new guy, or they just decide to rob your house and beat the shit out of you. They are mean and cruel people, and could do nasty things to someone if they wanted to. What I'm proposing is a carefully controlled, choreographed sting, you know like Robert Redford and Paul Newman in the movie. You get to set these guys up and you'll get the credit when they are arrested. Don't you just hate it when a gay person does bad things, especially to another gay person, when we're all trying to show gay people are good folks, too? You donate millions to gay youth groups so they'll have a chance at an education and obtain good jobs. How would you feel if this gang picked one of those kids as their next grifter? This is a cute good-looking young man, and all you have to do is savor his infatuation with you. It'll be good for your ego. This may be his first time to do this, and you'll have chance to set him on the right path."

"Okay, okay. Let me see if I have this straight. You'll be right there with me," said Larry.

Eric replied, "I'll have my men in the party. We have a camera monitoring the room, and we can pick up your conversations, and besides the wire, you'll have this." Eric handed Larry what appeared to be a thick button about the size of a quarter, but there was a recessed button in the center. If you feel uncomfortable or need help, just press that button. I'll casually walk over, and we'll start talking like long lost friends. I'll put my arm round your shoulders, and we'll head to the bar for a drink. What could be easier?"

Larry sighed. "Okay. I wish you would just shoot them, but I'll do my part. What time do we leave for the computer show?"

"Two o'clock. I'll be back to get you, but Gil and his team will take you to the show. I will be watching from the control room. I will keep my face out of view for now in case we have to use plan B as we discussed. Thanks again, Larry. I want to nail these bastards."

"Gil, we're all set with Larry for tonight. I told him you would lead the detail at two."

"Roger, no problem."

Eric turned to Ronnie and said, "I want a camera on Larry this afternoon. How can we do it?"

Ronnie replied, "I could operate a handheld unit from the balcony and look down into the room, and Tyler can capture the feed up here in the control room."

"Sounds good. Let's get ready." He turned to Tyler, "Have they come out of the room?"

"No not yet, but it is lunch time, and Jim never misses a meal. You can probably get in while they are at lunch."

Eric replied, "Okay, get the camera ready and that boot stuff." He turned to Gil. "Have a man in the lobby watch for them when they come down. Staying way back, follow them to a restaurant, and let me know when he has them in sight. Of course, let me know when he sees they are returning. I shouldn't be in there very long, but we don't want to blow it on setting up surveillance. "

Tyler spoke up, "How about the dots? Are you going to put a dot on each of them?'

"I guess so. We don't have enough agents for tandem triple tail teams to avoid detection and protect Larry."

Gil added, "I think I could do it, but I would need a partner."

Eric laughed. "And how do you plan to do it?"

"My partner and I will act like two friends who have had too much to drink, and we'll chat them up and stumble into them a little. It would be easier on the elevator. We'll wait on them say one floor down from us to avoid suspicion. That will give us a long enough ride down to do the job."

"It's okay with me."

Ronnie added, "I'd put them about mid back or lower so their eyes don't just happen to see it, but it is pretty hard to see the dots on fabric."

"Okay, hurry it up, as they could exit at any time."

After their men moved away from the control center to get ready Tyler said, "I can't believe Stephen and Jim are here. They make me real nervous."

"I know, but this is best chance we've had to catch them. You just stay here and out of sight, and all will be well."

"How are you going to get in their room? Is there a lock to pick?"

Eric smiled and removed a key. "I insisted the management give me a pass key. It will be easy."

Tyler advised, "When you go in, you'll see a simple piece of paper on the floor. Just leave it alone. It must remain exactly as you found it."

"Why is that?"

"Stephen has this thing about people coming into the room. He won't even let them turn the bedspreads down and leave a mint on the pillow. Often, I sat in the room standing guard while the maid staff went about cleaning it. He was a pain, but the paper looks like some simple trash, but it is placed so he can tell if someone came in, especially if they tried to help by picking it up and throwing it away."

"I understand. Thanks. You're doing a great job. Hang in there."

"When do we eat? I get hungry when I'm nervous."

"Eric laughed. "You get hungry when you're breathing!"

Ronnie wired Larry for audio, and then went to the merchandise mart to set up for Larry's appearance at the computer show. Larry would make a brief speech, and then wander the room meeting his fans and doing autographs. He set his camera up on the balcony inconspicuously, and made a radio call to Tyler.

"Okay, camera one is set up, and I'm feeding the signal to you. How does it look?"

Tyler punched a few keys on this computer, and instantly the picture came up on the projected image on the wall. He created a video square and put the picture in the upper right. The ninth floor camera was still in the upper left.

Tyler replied, "Looks good. Excellent picture. Will the lighting remain the same?"

"Good thinking, I'll find a manager but from the look of the room, I suspect it all fluorescent lighting fixtures and can't be dimmed. Larry is wired for sound. Make his input as audio one and test his signal."

Tyler clicked on shortcut button that was marked audio, and brought up a mixer board on his computer that was much like those in a recording studio or radio station. He selected audio one and began bringing up the signal. He started laughing. "It works too good. Larry is singing Motown and he is horrible."

Ronnie laughed as well. "Okay, let's test how his audio will be in here. I have temporarily put a microphone on my shirt, and I want to walk around the big ballroom. Bring me up on audio two." He began walking around the room. "Testing, testing, and testing one, two, and three."

Tyler clicked on the audio circuit, brought up the microphone level, and could hear him just fine. "You're coming through the external signal, so I used the booster amp, but clarity is good."

"Okay, I'm going down one floor to the main room and will walk and talk. Let me know if you can't hear me."

Once again the testing went well, so he packed up his camera and returned to the hotel.

Ronnie arrived as Tyler was showing Gil how to handle the dots. He put one on two fingers of his left hand and one on his index finger of his right hand. Bill arrived and they went over their drunken routine before leaving to wait two floors down at the elevator waiting area.

Ronnie had just returned to his seat when Eric walked in. "Status," he said.

The senior officer in charge spoke up. Ronnie said, "Larry is wired and tested. Camera one has been tested and ready for quick set up near the time. Audio in the ballroom is set up and tested. Excellent signals. Gil has the dots, so he and Bill have gone to the seventh floor to wait for the targets."

"Excellent. Do you have the camera for their room ready?"

Tyler said, "I just finished testing it. It has an amazing picture quality and control." He handed it to Eric who was already familiar with the setup procedure from his excursion in Miami.

They all sat comfortably watching and waiting for the suspects to appear on the hall camera. Seven minutes later they stepped out of their room.

Eric spoke into his sleeve microphone. "Gil?"

Gil lifted his wrist as well, "Roger."

"They just left their room. They are walking to the elevator area. They hit the down button in front of elevator four."

"Roger." Gil waited until he saw elevator four pass them going up and stopped on the ninth floor. He hit the down button for the same elevator and waited. They saw the floor digital red light counting the floors down. Thankfully, it did not stop and pick up anyone else. He unbuttoned his collar, twisted his tie far from straight and messed his hair up a little.

The elevator stopped as he said to Bill, "Man, that Long Island Iced Tea was strong. They must have put more than the usual five shots in it." He stepped into the elevator and into the middle of three men waiting. "Dang, I've got a buzz."

Bill replied as he stepped between two of the men on the left side, "My head is spinning. That was some stripper. I like these private, company welcome parties. Whoopee!"

Stephen rolled his eyes, Jim frowned, and the kid started laughing. Stephen gave the kid a frown filled glance, and the boy immediately covered his mouth.

Gil said, "Man, I'm hot." He started taking off his coat and in so doing he accidentally bumped into Stephen with his right hand, and successfully put the dot on the back of his coat. As he spun around to pull his other arm out, he twisted near Jim, and managed to get the next dot on Jim's back. "Sorry, dude. My legs feel like they've been at sea for years, and this elevator is making my head float around."

Gil looked at the kid. "Dow, man you look twelve years old. Are you some kind of computer genius?"

The kid replied, "No, I'm just a computer geek, and I'm nineteen."

Gil laughed. "Sure you are. You've should have seen the stripper in the room party. She had huge tits."

The kid started to laugh again, and Gil tried to move closer to him. Suddenly, the doors of the elevator opened and they were out of time. Stephen and Jim roughly pushed through and around Bill and Gil as they made a quick exit. The kid started out last.

Gil quickly threw a five-dollar bill down on the floor of the elevator near the entrance. "Hey kid? You dropped some cash."

The boy quickly turned around and returned to pick it up. Gil timed it perfectly, bent over at the same time, and losing his balance, he bumped into the kid, and then stood up and started apologizing while transferring his last dot to the kid's back as he patted him. "Sorry, little man. Have a great day."

The kid took the money, and quickly caught up with Stephen and Jim. "No one likes a public drunk," complained Stephen. "I was just seconds away from blowing the guy away."

Jim smiled. "Now dear, killing him would have upset the applecart, and we could have lost a chance for millions of dollars. Let it go. I'm starved. Shall we try to the buffet?"

Stephen nodded, though still seething at the drunks, and followed Jim and the kid to the buffet.

Gil and Bill watched them walk across the lobby before moving out of sight. He lifted his sleeve microphone to his mouth, "Eric?"

"Stephen, the dots are online. You were successful for all three. You can leave them there and head back to control. I'm going in the room."

Eric caught the elevator and went up a floor. He went to room 904 and used his passkey to go in. He watched for the paper as he opened the door very slowly, avoiding a small wind draft. He spotted the paper and noticed one corner pointing precisely at a leg of a narrow hall table. Into his radio microphone he said, "Way to go, Tyler. You were right about the paper."

Eric moved around the room looking for the best angle for the camera. He noticed Stephen's laptop on the desk, so he settled on putting the camera in the frill at the top of the long window drapes. "Camera in place. Do you have a picture?"

Tyler activated the camera, and it instantly came up on the projected image in full color. "There's a piece of fabric right at the bottom."

Eric adjusted the camera. "How's that?"

"Good."

"Tyler, do you see Stephen's laptop? Do you think you could read the screen?"

Tyler operated the electronic joystick on his computer screen and zoomed in on the laptop. "The book on the shelf behind it is by Clive Cussler."

Eric had to walk across the room to the desk and bend over to read the title on the edge of the book's spine. "Amazing. How is the audio? I'll put my hand microphone down. Can you hear me now?"

"Loud and clear."

"Are the suspects still in the buffet?"

Ronnie broke in. On his computer he could see the dots. He had programmed in the floor plan of the hotel as layer beneath the dots, and thus he knew they were indeed eating lunch. "They're still there. You're clear."

"Good, I'm going to poke around a bit. Remind me to spray the green boot stuff when I leave. Out."

Tyler followed Eric with the camera giving him a chance to practice with the controls. Eric studied the papers on the desk, and he found three name badges for the computer show, and the invitations for the private gold party printed out for Bob and Ted McKenzie, and Juan Jorge.

Eric went to the closet and spotted their luggage on the racks. Tyler spoke up, "Stephen's is the gray one, Jim is the brown, and I guess that purple duffle bag is the kid's. In a hidden compartment in the bottom of Stephen and Jim's bag will be 9mm pistols. I doubt the kid has any weapons." He almost said they never allowed him to be armed, but bit his tongue instead.

Finding nothing of interest, he left the room by once again being very careful with the door to avoid messing up the angle of the paper on the floor. He looked up and down the hall, shook a small spray can of the green boot stuff and then sprayed it back and forth across the floor just inside the door, and then slowly closed it. He returned to the control room.

"Ronnie, when I sprayed the stuff it was clear, which I guess makes sense as the green paint would have been easily seen, but why did Oscar call it Green Boot?"

Ronnie laughed. "Okay, on the lower part of the screen is our GPS system. The three red dots represent the location of the suspects in the buffet. When they step on the spray you put at the door, they'll show up on the screen as green dots."

Eric smiled. "Got it. You computer geeks are weird."

Tyler laughed. "We're also hungry."

Eric replied, "I'll order room service. Ronnie, go ahead and go to lunch with the rest of the team. Tyler and I will hold down the fort."

"Roger that and thanks." Ronnie, Gill, and Bill went to lunch. Most of the rest of the crew had been eating except for the two men on Larry Menard's door. Larry was eating in."

Eric ordered their food on the hotel phone and then using his secure cell he called Oscar. "All your toys are in place? Do you see them at home base?"

"Roger. Quality is excellent for audio and video. I am anxious to see how my Green Boot stuff works. It will be a good backup in case they change clothes or lose the dots. You have more dots you can use, they just have to be applied."

"Okay, good work. Transfer me to Ted."

Ted picked up his phone. "Ted here."

"This is Eric. We have the three suspects in our hotel under electronic surveillance. I can't use our men to tail them because they are too smart. We're hoping to catch them in their attempt to rob Larry."

"How was Larry with this plan?"

161

"He balked at first, but I convinced him it was better to catch them here than being attacked later while alone."

"Roger."

Eric asked, "Is your plan ready to go?"

"Yes, it is."

"What part can you start without them knowing it?"

Ted replied, "I would say we go ahead and buy their island, the house in Spain, and I discovered they own a condo in Cayman. In a few hours, you'll be the proud owner of all three and paid for with their money. I discovered that although they have numerous accounts in various parts of the world, the accounts in Costa Rica are checked the least. Their accounts total over ten million dollars and are just sitting there drawing interest. The accounts in Cayman are checked more often, but primarily they use one account for putting money into and then transferring it to the others. That's the one we need to stay away from as long as we can."

"Okay, take their properties."

Ted asked, "What about the housekeeper? His name is Marvin. He might call them."

Eric said, "I have a cop friend in Miami. I'll get him to handle him."

"Let me know when you have the bastards, and I'll bring down their house of cards."

Eric smiled at the thought. "Roger, will do. Thanks. Out."

Eric made the call to Miami. "Harry Feinstein, please."

"One moment," said the receptionist at the police station.

Eric waited for Harry to come online. He began recalling they served his first year in the Marines together. Harry had been wounded in his second tour and send back home.

"Harry here. How can I help you?"

Eric replied loudly, "Stand at attention! You're talking to an officer!"

Tyler laughed. Harry responded, "Yeah, right. An officer of the latrine, I suspect! Eric, how are you?"

"I'm good and you?"

Harry replied, "Bored and happy. Molly is pregnant again. It'll be our fourth child."

"You dog! You're a lucky man to have found Molly."

"Yes I am, and what are you up to?"

"I need a favor." Eric continued with a short version of his involvement with the three suspects, and his protection of Larry. He explained that the housekeeper called Marvin had done crime a few years ago, but he needed him held, so he couldn't warn the suspects. Harry agreed to pick him up.

Harry asked, "What about the house? There could be stolen property in there."

"You're right, but I doubt you could obtain a warrant on just my word. Today I bought the house so once they are arrested, I'll fly down and we can go through the house at our leisure. Is that okay with you?"

"You had the cash to buy a house in that neighborhood?"

Eric lied, "I had a few nickels saved up."

"Yeah, and my aunt has three tits. Okay, I'll call you when we have him. See you later."

"Thanks, Harry. Bye."

There was a knock at the door. Tyler checked through the peephole and opened the door so the waiter could roll in a food cart. "Lunch has arrived."

Eric signed the check, the waiter left, and he and Tyler sat down to eat. "You're doing a great job," said Eric between bites.

"Thanks. I like the work a lot, except for being cooped up in here."

"I know, but on this particular project you're safer here, and our sting is safer, too. Your work is valuable. We must keep Larry and our team safe. What do you think of the kid?"

"He's new and I bet he's green. They didn't waste too long in replacing me."

"Do you think he's gay as well?"

"Yeah. There isn't much of an age of consent in Costa Rica. We went to a nude gay beach one time, and there were teenagers as young as eleven hanging out with gay men and everyone was nude. Now and then they would go in the woods with a man for sex. You would see thirteen year olds dancing nude in the gay bars. Picking up a kid there is as easy as picking up a pineapple."

"So you don't think he is experienced at their level of crime?"

"No, but Jim would have taught him how to pick a wallet, remove a watch or rings, and how to flirt. Stephen would have drilled him over and over as to what he could say and what not to say. He would have already taught him how to case a room and look for a safe, cash, credit cards, and more."

"Boy, they sure give gay folks a bad name. I'll look forward to taking them down." Eric paused and asked, "So he'll be the bait as you said?"

Tyler sighed. "Most definitely. If I were still with them, I would have Larry drooling over me. We would have sex tonight, and he would wake up robbed. By dawn, his bank accounts would have been emptied, and if they are really greedy, they would have his house key and catching a plane to beat him home."

Eric smiled at him. "I'm sorry they treated you like that. Now all you have to worry about his putting up with me."

Tyler laughed. "That and your gorilla looking face early in the morning."

Eric laughed. "Funny, you're so funny. Revenge will be coming soon."

The agents returned to the command center as Tyler finished his lunch. They were all there except for the two men changing shifts with the crew on Larry's door. Gil checked his watch and prepared the men for moving Larry to the Merchandise Mart for the computer show appearance.

Ronnie spoke up, "Suspects on the move."

Tyler added, "They're splitting up. Two moving to the elevators and one to the front door of the hotel."

Eric spoke into sleeve microphone, "Bill, which one went for the door?"

Before he could reply Tyler said, "It'll be Jim. He eats too fast and is always buying Rolaids or Tums. He just can't help himself at a buffet." He stopped himself from saying they should have seen him at the giant hotel buffets in Las Vegas.

Bill came on the radio. "He went into a corner market. He's popping Tums and returning to the hotel."

Gil said, "Jeez, kid. You're psychic. Listen, I need for you to pick some horses for me in tonight's race."

The rest of the team chuckled as Eric said, "Okay, let's get ready for Larry's walk to convention floor."

Ronnie spoke up. "Boss, do you see the green dots."

Eric looked at the GPS block in the lower left. There were two red dots on top of two green dots and he could the double dots moving in unison around the room. "Two of the suspects have returned to their room and stepped in the green boot paint. Amazing."

Tyler shifted the picture to a 3D side view so they could see Jim making his way to the elevator. He GPS surveillance disappeared while inside the elevator, but instantly came back online in the hallway on the way to his room.

Eric said, "Excellent. Okay, I'll go see if Larry is ready."

Eric asked as he entered the room, "Are you good to go?"

Larry stood up beside his desk. "Yeah, the speech will be short."

Eric spoke into his sleeve microphone, "Do you copy Larry loud and clear."

Ronnie replied, "Roger. We're good to go."

"Gil?"

"Yeah, boss."

"Is your team ready?"

"Roger, we're outside the door. The vehicles are waiting for us in the garage."

"Okay, here we come."

Eric followed them out, but returned to control as Ronnie joined the team with the field camera. Eric took Ronnie's chair and waited with Tyler. They listened to the team's audio channels, as they made their way down and into the limo, and then took the short drive to the Merchandise Mart. Gil and three men went inside the big mart to make sure the promoters were ready for Larry. He then ordered the men to move Larry to a waiting dressing room just outside the big ballroom.

Ronnie went up to the balcony once again, set up his tripod and camera, and turned it on and checked the signal with Tyler. Soon Eric could see the entire room, and he couldn't resist checking it out.

"Ronnie slowly scanned the room, looking for anything unusual."

"The room is full of mostly men and some lady geeks as well. I don't see any obvious bad guys."

Eric studied the picture carefully, but saw nothing of interest. He looked back to the left square and said into his microphone, "Suspects on the move. All three are together."

Eric felt like he was watching the foxes making their way to the hen house. He wished he could think of a better way of taking them out. He knew if they were out of the country, and given the opportunity, he would have used a high-powered scope on his rifle and taken Stephen and Jim out. He had no worries of doing so, but he couldn't do that in the States without putting his career and his company in jeopardy. Ten minutes later, they saw the green dots enter the ballroom. Eric said into his radio, "Suspects have arrived."

Gil was backstage with Larry. The promoter knocked on the door and said they were ready. He returned to the stage and began welcoming the audience to the meeting. He followed with a few announcements before beginning his introduction of Larry Menard.

Larry made his way to the stage, and Gil's men filtered around the room with two men at the corners of the small stage in case some idiot rushed the stage. He couldn't imagine anyone interested in bothering Larry, but as Menard began his remarks, the audience fell silent in admiration for the guy who invented and developed so much software. At the end of the twenty-minute speech, he left the stage and made his way to the main floor, where he began shaking hands and signing autographs.

Eric had purposefully not shown Larry pictures of the suspects, so that he would act naturally. Larry was always making speeches, so in doing so, he forgot about being wired for audio, and easily went from person to person shaking hands and chatting. He also answered specific questions about a problem someone was having with their software. Eric marveled that he always had the answer they sought on the tip of his tongue.

Ronnie zoomed in so they could easily see a twelve-foot diameter circle around Larry in case someone pulled a gun, but everyone in attendance went through a metal detector to enter the room, so they were pretty sure there were no weapons to harm him. Larry had been instructed to only drink from his water bottle to avoid the possibility of ingesting poison in a drink some offered him.

"There's the kid," said Tyler.

"He's pretty well dressed for a kid from Costa Rica," replied Eric.

"Stephen would have bought him a whole new wardrobe. I bet even his hair was styled and his nails done." Tyler looked around to be sure they were alone. "Stephen and Jim would have worked with him sexually to make sure he could perform with great expertise. The guy will have a big dick, and he'll use it as a tempting lure."

Tyler became almost sick to his stomach as he watched the kid. It felt like he was seeing himself in a video. The kid shyly made his way to Larry and shook his hand, but lifted his right hand to also gently rub Larry's outside palm. He got Larry's immediate attention with his soft face, and beautiful eyes. He asked a question he and Stephen had rehearsed.

Larry answered and then asked the boy his name, learning he was called Juan, which was just small talk as the kid was wearing a name badge just like everyone else. Larry began to ignore other conference attendees while giving Juan his full attention. Eric grinned, knowing Larry could not ignore the attention of a handsome young man. Of to the side, Stephen and Jim smiled at each other, as they went to work on two other incidental marks. Stephen selected correctly on his first try, but Jim went through a few idiots until he found another software developer who was also gay.

While others waited to speak to Larry, he leaned over and whispered to Juan, "Please stick around while I make these other folks feel welcome." He winked at Juan, and the boy smiled back approvingly.

Larry began quickly meeting each person, and politely but rapidly answering their questions. Once done, he led Juan away from the crowd, and forgetting his wire microphone, he began chatting away with the young handsome man, who agreed to have dinner with him in his room.

Eric said to Tyler, "Larry's an idiot."

Tyler replied, "Yeah, but Juan is good. Just think about it. He just innocently seduced one of the computer world's richest gay men."

Eric spoke into his radio, "Ronnie, get close-up shots of Stephen and Jim and their new friends. Tyler, see if you can capture their pictures and find out who they are. Ronnie also watched for a pickpocket attempt.

They were too late to catch Stephen lifting his mark's wallet, but Ronnie did catch Jim's successful attempt. They now had the evidence for Jim's arrest, but he'd be out in less than a few hours on bail, and back in Miami in another two hours.

They heard Larry get the kid's cell phone number, and Larry said he would call him when dinner was ready. They talked for another thirty minutes before Juan said he had to go. Stephen and Jim also excused themselves from their marks, promising to see them later.

Eric and Tyler watched the three suspects make their way back to the hotel, each taking a different out-of-the-way route in case they were being followed.

Gil and his team began returning Larry to the hotel via the limo as Ronnie dismantled his camera setup.

Eric turned to Tyler before the team returned. "What are they doing now?"

"Once they are in the room, Stephen will debrief them."

"They are that organized?"

"You bet. Stephen is a fanatic about details. He will decide if the other two marks are worth pursuing, or just go to work on their wallets. He'll ask Juan about everything they discussed, and he'll go over it many times. He never believes you told him everything." Tyler paused and then asked, "Did you notice what Juan said about his hotel room?"

Eric replied, "He gave Larry the wrong room number?"

Tyler smiled. "He gave Larry the wrong hotel and wrong room number. Larry won't know he is staying just one floor up because Juan gave him his cell number. That cell by the way is one of those throwaway units. Stephen gets them for a thousand minutes. It is the only kind they use on a caper."

They watched the three suspects via the dots as one by one they returned to the ninth floor and their room. Eric and Tyler watched at Stephen and Jim went through the wallets they had stolen. They removed cash, credit cards, and any notes with passwords on them. They put the wallet and the rest of the stuff in a trash bag. Juan was told to take it up a floor and put it in the trash bin by the coke machine. They watched as he left the room. Stephen and Jim began discussing the marks.

Stephen asked, "You think your guy is worth attacking?"

Jim replied, "He was wearing a cheap suit, no valuable rings or watches, he had only two credit cards and one bank card, and only three hundred in cash. I don't see him as a mark."

"I think you're right. My guy was loaded. I have two thousand in cash, he wearing an Armani suit, and a very expensive Rolex watch, plus a diamond ring on one hand and gold nugget room on the other. I also thought he was good looking. I'd say he is a mark, and I'll work him so more, starting with sympathy that he lost his wallet."

They both laughed as Juan returned.

"Okay kid. You did well. Now strip naked."

Juan asked, "Why?"

Stephen expected the reply and forcefully said, "Because I said so. Now strip!"

Eric leaned over to Tyler. "Why is he making him strip?"

167

"Two reasons. They don't trust him yet, so they will check his clothes for anything he stole, but didn't report, and two, it'll make him feel vulnerable. He'll tell them the truth right away, so he can put his clothes back on. If he did well, they'll probably reward him by both fucking him."

"Jeez, these guys are sick."

"They own the boy now, physically and mentally. You get sucked in, and they probably already told him that if he crosses them, they'll turn him into immigration, or they'll bury him alive. I have to tell you being shot and killed is not as scary as being buried alive. It really caused me a lot of nightmares."

Once Juan was naked, he was told to stand on the bed. Tyler added, "See I told you he would be hung."

Jim started going through the boy's clothes while Stephen began the questioning. He didn't write anything down, but stored the information permanently in his brain. Jim found nothing and began getting out of his clothes. Stephen was soon satisfied the boy had nothing to hide, and went over to the desk and fired up his computer. Jim crawled on the bed and pulled Juan to him. They started making out.

Eric said, "Move the camera to the computer screen and zoom in while I get Oscar on the phone." He waited for Oscar to answer. "Are you online with us.

Oscar replied, "Yeah, those boys are sick. What's up?"

"They stole two wallets so try to capture Stephen holding the evidence. I assume he is going to attack their credit and debit cards."

"I get the picture so you want me to stop him."

"No, let him be successful, just track every single click and decision he makes. After he completes the theft of the man's accounts, he'll transfer the money. Once it has arrived at their bank, transfer the money to our account, and then ask Marti to mail the victim a cashier's check with no company name on it."

Oscar smiled. "Yes, Robin Hood. You're supposed to give the money to the poor. My 'poor' name is Oscar…"

"Yeah right. I believe you are driving a new BWM sport coupe."

Oscar laughed. "Oh yeah, I forgot about that. Okay, you got me. I'll get back to you when done."

Eric smiled. "Thanks."

Tyler studied the computer screen. "He's using a software program called Halo and Horns. Oscar told me about it. It rapidly guesses passwords by first downloading their credit files, account history, family history, and more. It analyses the data and comes up with high probability passwords. It is amazingly successful. He said humans choose easy passwords, often only four to six letters, and it is usually something associated with them. A wife's or kid's name, their favorite pet, etc."

Gil came into the room after depositing Larry. He left two men on duty, and the rest stood down to prepare for the upcoming evening activity.

Eric suddenly had an idea and called Oscar again. "Hey, using the data you gave me earlier on their charter, I need for you scare off the charter. Tell them you are with the FBI, and their passengers are involved in a bank heist. Threaten to involve them as accomplices unless they fly away to their homeport. That'll leave the boys with no ride."

"No problem. I can handle that. Out."

Gil began debriefing his team including his boss and Tyler. Ronnie and Tyler quickly typed notes into the support file. They also logged footage and audio recordings in case there was a need to bring them up again now or in the future, or to support a court case. Once completed, he told the men to take a break, but also reminded them to be ready for Larry's seven o'clock departure. He then dismissed the group.

Tyler whispered to Eric. "Can we get away for a while? I don't want to listen to them fuck this boy."

Eric nodded yes. He told Gil that he and Tyler were going to an early dinner. Ronnie said he would cover, sensing something was wrong with Tyler.

SIXTEEN

Eric checked the GPS blips in the left square on the video feed displayed on their large, portable, wall screen that told him the crooks were still in the room. Satisfied the coast was clear, Eric and Tyler quickly walked to the elevator and went down to the garage level. They drove one of their SUV's as Eric made a quick call on his phone and obtained a reservation. They parked on a side street, and began walking a half block to Prego's Italian Restaurant. Eric knew that Italian food was one of Tyler's favorite. They ordered salads and decided to split an order of fettuccine Alfredo with grilled chicken because he knew they would fill up on the Italian garlic bread and salad, which was exceptionally good.

Eric talked about how fascinated he felt with what Tyler learned to do in just three months at the firm, and how efficiently he handled his training. He tried to cheer Tyler up, but his boyfriend was definitely in a funk. Finally, Eric gave up talking about other things and just spoke softly to him. "I know you're down. Talk to me about it."

Tyler gave a small hint of a smile. "I didn't know they were going to recruit someone in my place, although I should have guessed they would. It makes you wonder who was before me. I never speculated about that until today. When I first moved into the guest room in Miami, I found a watch under the edge of the bed with a guy's name on the back. I put it in a drawer and never asked about it. They might have killed him."

He stopped for a moment, deep in thought, and finally with his appetite disappearing, he set his fork down. "I didn't think much about it, but today I realized they trained me to think like they wanted. They gave me presents, but they demanded a lot as well. Sometimes I had to do sexual things I didn't want to do, but I was living good, so I just went along. I was good at learning how to be a grifter. I could pickpocket, trick, and steal anything. I could lie with a straight face, and I used my natural good looks and big dick to get the mark to do what I wanted.

"They will both fuck him to remind him who is boss, and to break him down a bit more. He'll get some praise for his work with Larry, but Stephen will threaten him should he mess up this opportunity. His favorite threat is that he'll cut you where it doesn't show. You knew that wherever he targeted his blade that it was going to hurt a lot."

"Did he cut you?"

"Yes on the bottom of my foot. I limped for a week and it throbbed when I tried to sleep. He also put the tip of the knife into my testicles. Jim never used a knife. He would either bite your tits or penis, and once he actually put deep, teeth marks into my right buttock."

"Do you think this is the young man's first time?"

Tyler shook his head affirmatively. "The way they are treating him, well, I would say yes. For example, after my first ten or so times, I would return to their room and just start taking my clothes off. I would dive for the bed and start masturbating. They always loved to watch me beat my meat, and would go a bit easier on me. After a while, I no longer had to strip like this, as they trusted me, even though they were stealing part of my share.

"Now I realize that the cute guy is the one that is most exposed, and taking most of the risk. It is not their face the mark will remember, it is not their face he'll report to the police, and it not their body that could be caught and killed by the mark in a fit of rage. "

"What do you think they have planned for Larry?"

Tyler fiddled with his napkin for a minute before saying, "Juan will say he wants to go back to Larry's room. They'll have a good time, lots of drinks, and sex. Juan will have a small vial of a clear liquid in his pocket. In one of Larry's drinks, he will secretly place the drug. It'll knock Larry out for about eighteen hours, unless someone shakes him awake. I never knew what the stuff was, but it always worked.

"After he is out, Juan will probably call Stephen on his cell, and they may join him in the room. I always dressed while they were coming, so that I was ready to leave should a discovery happen. We'd take the cash with us, and put the rest of the stuff in a FedEx or UPS box. Our bags will already be in the car, and we'll rush to the car and head to the airport. We drop the boxes in an overnight drop and catch the next flight out-of-town. We never see the mark again. They never leave a city with the evidence on them. Should they have a car wreck, or any other calamity, no one would be the wiser.

"Once home, we go get the boxes at a mailbox service store, and Jim takes them to the pawnshop to fence for our cash. Meanwhile, Stephen would go to work on the bank and credit cards. I never got a share of that. He would always say they had closed their accounts."

Eric said, "That's not true. He has millions in offshore banks, and I suspect there is a lot of cash and jewelry in the safe room. What about Larry's house? Will they go for it?"

"I don't know. Sometimes we went immediately to the person's house and added to the crime. It is easier when we are visiting their town, and they take me to their house for sex because there is no alarm system to worry about. When you hit a mark out-of-town, it is possible an alert will have gone out, or perhaps a friend of theirs drops by and knocks on the door. Stephen has this mold stuff that he used to make a copy of the person's house key. If we do hit their house while they are out-of-town, he already has a key.

"Probably the best thing to do is to put Larry's keys in the command room, and then they can't be stolen or copied, and it is less likely they'll go to his house. I think they will assume a man as rich as he is would have a top security firm wire the house."

Eric smiled. "He does. We put the system in and hired the selected crew that maintains the gate." Eric paused and looked into Tyler's sad eyes. "I

171

have some good news, and if you are considering getting even with them, I have very good news."

"Shoot, I'm ready for anything."

"Today, I bought Stephen and Jim's house in Miami, as well as their place in Spain, and their entire island near Costa Rica. I also bought their cars, and the police have Marvin in custody."

Tyler laughed. "They are going to shit a brick!"

"Here's the best part. I used their money to buy everything. We took their money from some lesser-used accounts in foreign banks. Once we have them in custody for a crime, Ted will take all their money from all their accounts. They won't have a dime to call an attorney with."

"Their attorney is Albert Smith."

"Thanks, I'll let their attorney know a witness has testified that he knowingly helped these criminals. I'll suggest he no longer have any dealings with them." He paused. "Had enough of dinner?"

"Yeah, sorry. I wasn't as hungry as I thought."

"That's okay. Let's get a to-go box in case you're hungry later, and then we'll get out of here."

They left the restaurant and Eric soon felt Tyler put his hand in his. Eric gladly held it and walked him to the car on the side street. Inside the car, he leaned over and kissed Tyler, who smiled and began French kissing Eric. They made out for about twenty minutes and ended with Tyler sucking Eric off. Eric noted he almost instantly looked better. He hated to go back to work, but it was nearly time for the night action.

Once back to the garage, he checked in with Ronnie to be sure the suspects were still in their room. Ronnie told they were and to come on up. Tyler and Eric quickly made their way back to the control room.

Eric was amazed at how stupid Larry could sometimes act, and yet he was such an amazing genius when it came to anything related to a computer. He knew Stephen and Jim were after him, and they had a younger guy set to flirt with him, but all he could think about while dressing for the gold, dinner party was spending time with young Juan. To anyone that asked, he said he couldn't wait to fuck him, but in reality, he wanted Juan to fuck him. Before he became rich, he had nothing to attract a good looking bottom, so he became a bottom and a good one, and even guys that had not an ounce of love for him—loved to fuck him.

Eric just rolled his eyes as he checked his microphone, while Larry talked on and on about Juan, completely ignoring the fact that Juan was working with Stephen and Jim. Larry planned to outsmart him and fake drinking his cocktails, delaying Juan from his mission, and forcing him to put out. He felt no one could outsmart him. He was ready to take on the challenge.

Eric decided to say nothing. He figured things would go better for Juan and the taping from the camera for the court case. He turned Larry over to Gil while he returned to the command center. Ronnie left the room to setup the camera for the dinner. They held the event in the big ballroom at the convention center, but Ronnie set up the camera in a sound and audio booth near the ceiling at the back of the room, affording him a bird's eye view of the entire floor below, but keeping the camera out of view.

Tyler spoke to Ronnie on the COM2 circuit while they tweaked out the signal. Once completed, Ronnie left the camera in the booth temporarily, and walked around the room as Tyler switched to COM1 to test the audio transmissions from the ballroom. To obtain excellent signals, Ronnie placed a repeater antenna just outside his post in the booth. Tyler made several adjustments and pronounced the audio loud and clear. Ronnie returned to the booth while checking his watch and noting the start time was close.

Gil and his men began moving Larry to the garage area for the ride over to the Merchandise Mart for the dinner in the convention center. Eric and Tyler listened to the COM1 communications as each member of the team did their duty, preparing the way for Larry's path. Eric knew all would be well, but he didn't relax until Larry reached the limo. He tensed up again as they arrived at their destination, then moved Larry across the walkways, down the halls, around the corners, in and out of an elevator, and finally into the ballroom.

At that point, Gil and his team reluctantly backed off to the corners of the room and the entrance. There was also a team member watching the food servers coming in and out of the kitchen. Gil sent Arnold to test Larry's food and stood guard. He used a very expensive device with a small sharp probe, attached to a digital readout. Arnold poked each dish and in seconds the little device's computer began whirling and soon displayed an analysis of the foods contents. It would flash red if it detected a poison, but today's meal was clear and safe. Eric knew that rarely were poisons cooked with food as they might break down, but generally added to the food right before serving.

Larry contacted the promoters and arranged a last minute free seat beside him. He smiled when he saw Juan, and while trying to be casual, he made his way directly to him. They talked for a bit about stupid stuff, while Eric and Tyler rolled their eyes as they easily heard everything on Larry's wire microphone on COM2. They were recording Larry and Juan's conversations.

"Well, at least the signal is good," stated Tyler.

"I'm not sure I can stomach Larry's benign, pathetic small talk. I should have written down some stuff for him to say."

"It won't matter to Juan. Larry could be speaking in Russian and Juan will still pretend to be happy and attracted to him. Remember, it's a sting. The bad guys always win."

"Not tonight. The good guys will win this one. Any sign of Stephen and Jim?"

Tyler scanned the picture of the entire banquet hall. "Stephen is over near the center wall with his mark. He is a smooth talker and his mark will fall for him like a fish after a dangling, juicy worm on a hook. Jim just came in the door, and his mark walked up to him. I guess Jim can play hard to get, but actually, he is easy. He plays with his prey, playing hard to put out, and testing his mark to see how desperate they are for sex by asking them stupid stuff like would they suck his toes, put their hot tongue in his nose, kiss his hole, and worst."

"Jeez, I'm glad I already ate."

Tyler laughed. "I just hope we put Stephen and Jim in jail. Is there a way to get Juan off and send him home?"

"Yeah, a very good way. We'll get him to turn against them and become the prosecutor's prime witness against Stephen and Jim. He'll be a big help to them. Let's hope he is underage and if so, the FBI might be able to get them on kidnapping, transporting a minor, illegal immigration, and more."

As they settled down to dinner, Gil's men reported in from time to time but all was going well. Steve frisked the waiter and once cleared he gave the man the secured food tray and pointed at Larry. The young man did as directed. After he returned, Steve gave him a fifty-dollar bill as a tip.

Juan and Larry ate and chatted while totally ignoring everyone else at the table. An hour later, after a few boring speeches, the dinner was over. Guests approached Larry for autographs and small talk, which he quickly did. Gil had a pair of men for loose tails for Stephen and Jim. He also had new GPS dots ready, but so far, the boot stuff was still working, and so were the old dots. Eric and Tyler could see every step the threesome made. Just to be safe, Eric also placed a tiny dot on Larry.

As the parties began to separate and make their exits, Eric and Tyler became busy by making sure they had visible and GPS coordinates on each of them. Tyler adjusted various COM1 signals, while Ronnie hurriedly took down the camera and audio repeater, and began making his way back to the hotel.

Larry and Juan rode in the limo, and the boy loved the car. This time there was only the chauffeur with them to avoid suspicion, and the two SUVs that were trailing them. Larry's apparent wealth mesmerized the boy. Following his training, he began counting the mark's pieces, and so far, he counted seven items to take: one diamond ear stud, two gold cuff links, a diamond ring and a gold ring, an amazing gold watch with diamonds, and of course his wallet.

It wasn't long until they were in Larry's room, where he and Juan were alone, except for the planted camera and audio. While Tyler confirmed all the audio and video signals were good for Larry's room, he and Eric continued monitoring the GPS signals for Stephen and Jim. They used COM1 to tell the agents that the thieves separated and the directions they went.

Eric hoped the marks would be staying in the same hotel, but they went in opposite directions. Eric advised the tails to change to plan B and their assigned COM signals. The tails remained out of sight as Tyler guided one team using COM3 to the correct floor, and Eric guided the other team on COM4. Everyone could also hear COM1 as well. COM2 continued recording Larry's audio. Once all the marks were in the room with one of the grifters, they all had to sit back and wait.

Larry's security detail and Gil hid in the control room until Larry and Juan were in the room. After Larry closed the door, the team stood by, waiting to see what would happen, and would Juan begin making his moves on Larry.

Earlier, Eric met with the local cops, who agreed to be standing by in a conference room downstairs once they realized they would get the collar, and if the sting went well, they would have all three bad guys and a victim ready for testimony. Eric would also provide copies of all their audio and video surveillance of the marks.

Eric had done all he could to prepare, wishing things would go as planned, but he had no control at this point. He decided to send two cops to each location for Stephen and Jim's marks, so they could be detained upon exiting with the loot in their possession, preventing a return to the Conrad Chicago Hotel. He warned the cops the suspects could be armed and most likely dangerous.

Eric and Tyler watched the projected screen showing the GPS locators and Larry's room. Tyler slowly turned the command center's speaker volume down for Larry's microphone, leaving just enough sound so Eric could hear, while Tyler tried to block it out. Listening to Juan was like listening to himself. It made his stomach churn.

The moment the door closed, Larry began pulling Juan to him. He made a couple of drinks. They groped and kissed, and finished their first drink. Larry took his coat off and quickly excused himself to the bathroom, where he removed the wire and his shirt.

Tyler killed the audio microphone from COM2, and brought up the room audio from the camera Eric planted, and patched it to COM2 and continued recording.

Larry sat down on the edge of the bed and Juan came to him. Larry kissed him while his hands began unbuttoning Juan's shirt. He soon took it off as well as his tee shirt. The boy possessed beautiful, bronze skin, and Larry's hands began touching every square inch of it. He unbuckled the boy's pants and let them fall to the floor. Juan stepped out of them.

175

Larry adjusted his crotch as his erection grew. Juan tried to talk but Larry planted another wet kiss to his lips, thrusting his tongue deep inside the young man's warm, wet mouth, and moved his hands down to his soft, white briefs and slowly began pulling them down. By the time the kiss ended, the boy was completely naked.

Juan began taking Larry's clothes off, while Larry took another gulp of his second drink.

Eric reluctantly watched as Juan took the last of Larry's clothes off, and made a pile of them on the bed. Eric tried to lighten the situation by saying to Tyler, "You know in all the years I have protected Larry, I have never seen him nude, and I hope to never see him like this again."

Tyler didn't reply but continued staring at the screen. Eric glanced over at him while touching his shoulder briefly to remind him that he was there for him.

Larry and Juan fell onto the bed. Larry began sucking Juan into a large erection. Larry's hands constantly roamed the boy's nervous body, while inserting a wet finger into his butt. Larry twisted his body so Juan could suck him.

Larry managed to take another swig of his drink, draining the glass dry, forgetting he was going to fake drinking. Larry pinched the boy's tits to make them hard, and then nearly sucked them off his chest. Larry was close to ejaculating, so he pulled Juan off and said, "Give me a second. I've got to pee like a race horse."

Larry went to the bathroom, peed, and then put a dab of lubricant in his anus. Eric and Tyler watched as Juan quickly remade their drinks, went to his pants and retrieved a tiny vial. He poured it into Larry's drink. He was sitting on the corner of the bed sipping from his glass when Larry returned.

"I filled your drink for you. I don't want you to run out of steam. We have so much more sex to do," he lied as he handed Larry's his third drink.

Larry forgot about the sting and the thieves, and dove on the bed for his drink and more of Juan. "I want you to fuck me."

Juan laughed. "I thought you would want to do me."

"I do, but I like to be done first. I want that long, hot rod of yours in me as far as you can go."

Stephen and Jim had never let Juan do them, and for a few minutes, he forgot about his job. "Okay, down your drink and let's ride cowboy."

Juan downed his drink and so did Larry. Juan put a condom on as Larry moved to the center of the bed and on top of their clothes. Juan rolled him over and climbed on top. Larry moaned with delight as Juan entered and began pumping soft at first, and then faster and deeper. He soon exploded as Larry gave out a huge sigh and then abruptly passed out.

With Eric and Tyler watching, Juan quickly began dressing. Following his training, he flushed the spent condom. He got his underwear and socks on, but Larry was lying on top of his pants and shirt. He sighed. He pulled Larry's arm until he managed to free his pants. With more tugs, he finally freed his shirts, as well as his socks, and finished dressing. He produced a bag from one of his pockets, put his shoes on, and counted aloud. "One," he took the diamond stud from Larry's ear. "Two." He removed the cuff links, and so on, until he had all but the wallet.

He tugged left and right, but Larry was laying dead on it, and he was heavy. He bent down and started trying to worm his hand under Larry's stomach to retrieve the wallet. Suddenly, Larry's eyes opened. Juan shrieked in fear. Larry yelled at him, though he couldn't move his limbs. Terrified, the boy yanked his arm back from the bed and ran for the door. He left as fast he could and ran to the elevator to his room.

Eric said, "Tyler, keep monitoring the teams. I'm going to make sure Larry doesn't suffocate himself."

Slow tears began sliding down Tyler's face as he recalled all the times he had done just what Juan had been doing with Larry. He had sex over and over with men he detested, just so he could steal for Stephen and Jim.

He quit crying when Ronnie came into the room with his camera equipment. Tyler quickly brought him up to date.

"Look," said Tyler. "Jim is on the move."

"He's moving fast."

Jim saw the cops waiting for him when he came out of the room and bolted down the hall looking for an exit. While running, he pulled his cell phone from his pocket and speed dialed Stephen.

Stephen was almost done with his mark that lay unconscious on the bed when the phone rang. "It's me. What's up?"

"The cops were down the hall when I came out of the room. They are chasing me."

"Lose them! Do everything you can to get away. Out!"

Stephen quickly grabbed his shoes in his hand and made for the door. He opened it slowly, peered out, and saw two cops waiting on him as well at the end of the hallway. He closed the door and locked it with the deadbolt. He went to the patio door, opened it, and stepped onto the balcony that was three floors up. He thought perhaps he could leap to the next balcony, but if no one were in that room, he would have little chance of breaking in. He glanced down and sighed.

He stared at the pool and wondered how deep it was. He would have to leap pretty far out from the balcony to make it. He looked back across the room and caught sight of a pair of black shoes under the door. The cops were about to enter. He dropped his shoes over the rail without noticing they fell in

177

some tall bushes as he leaped through the air. With his arms flailing, he tried to steer himself, but finally rolled to his back, and grabbed his head as he did a splat on the water, which kept him from hitting the bottom harshly. However, it did knock the breath out of him.

He would have drowned, but a man happened to see him fall, and jumped in and pulled him out of the pool. Stephen coughed but began getting his breath back. He got to his feet and ran away without a word to the man who saved him.

Tyler said, "Stephen's boot paint dots have stopped moving, but they are on ground level. Did they arrest him?"

Ronnie called out on to COM3 to see if they had Stephen. They reported no, but a cop was trying to listen through the door, but heard nothing. They summoned the hotel manager for the key.

"Where did Stephen go?"

Ronnie spoke up excitedly, "Look at Jim's dot! It's still on his jacket, and he is moving quickly."

Jim ran down the stairwell several flights. He pulled the fire alarm, yanked a fire extinguisher off a wall bracket, and flung it onto the stairwell. He entered another floor, broke the glass for a nearby fire hose, and quickly threaded it through the handle of the stairwell and tied a knot. He turned on the water and the hose tightened securely. He ran down the hallway, took another stairwell exit, and went down to the ground level.

The cops couldn't get in through the stairwell due to the tied hose, but Ronnie guided Jim's tail team to the ground floor of the hotel and around to the back. They went out the side door into a parking lot.

Jim managed to run through the kitchen and came out to the shipping dock. He ran around to the right and saw two men talking to each other, but they weren't cops. He began running down the sidewalk towards them and hopefully to the corner to hail a taxi.

Just as he was about to pass the men, Steve flung out an arm and punched Jim hard in the mouth. Bill flung a judo chop to the back of Jim's neck, and he hit the cement face first, breaking some teeth and bones with a nasty sounding crunch and fell limp.

Steve spoke into his sleeve microphone. "Ronnie, tell the cops the suspect is on the north side. He's on the sidewalk waiting on them."

One cop remained to check on the mark when the manager arrived with the key, while the other ran down to the parking lot. "What happen to him?"

Steve smiled. "I guess he slipped."

The cop laughed. "I'll call an ambulance." He handcuffed Jim while waiting. He had already seen how slippery and adapted Jim was at getting away. He wasn't going to give him a second chance.

Steve reported in via his radio. "Jim has been captured and in police custody. We're returning to base."

Ronnie and Tyler listened to COM1 as Gil and his men were all searching for Stephen. They heard sirens as the police formed a human net by surrounding the area with a dozen police cars in an all out effort to find and arrest Stephen.

Tyler said, "Ronnie, if it okay with you, I'd like to go check on the young man."

Ronnie checked the gear on Tyler's part of the table and replied, "Sure, but don't be long."

Tyler grabbed his jacket to hide his firearm, left the room, and took the elevator up a floor. He moved down the hallway to Stephen's room. He hesitated to enter. Juan apparently left the door ajar. He pushed it open slowly while drawing his weapon.

He found Juan alone and sitting on the bed. Beside him were the six items he had stolen but no wallet. He was crying. He knew Stephen would beat him for failing to get the wallet. Suddenly, he looked up in fear at Tyler and his gun.

Tyler put his gun away and said tenderly, "It's okay. It's over. You're safe. You no longer have to fear Stephen and Jim."

Juan looked through his tear-stained eyes and sighed with relief. Tyler smiled at him as he added, "I'll protect you, but I think we should get you out of here right now. The cops will swarm this place in a few minutes. I'll take you down to a safe room with the rest of my team. Let's go."

Tyler reached out and took Juan's hand. He then noted the color fell from Juan's face as his eyes went white with fear. Tyler started to turn, but as he made his turn he received a hard hit to the jaw from Stephen. The blow knocked him down to the carpet and over against a chair. Tyler was dazed, but he could hear Stephen yelling at him. He decided to play possum, pretending he was hurt more than he really was.

"I should have known you were behind this. You're a traitor." Stephen noted Tyler's handgun.

Tyler's anger began to boil, he opened his eyes, and managed to say through his sore and rapidly swelling jaw, "You're a thief, a bully, and they suspect you of being a murderer as well."

Stephen screamed back, "I should have killed you long ago." He pulled his pistol and aimed it at Juan. "Get Tyler's pistol." Terrified, Juan hesitated, so Stephen screamed at him, "Do it now or I'll shoot you!"

Juan nervously moved to Tyler, reluctantly pulled the pistol from the holster, and brought it to Stephen. Tyler suddenly remembered he did not turn on the camera and audio in Stephen's room because they were all out with their marks. He sighed at the unfortunate revelation.

179

Stephen glanced at the bed and replied, "Where's Larry's wallet? Did you think I wouldn't notice?"

"Larry woke up. He was lying on his clothes and I couldn't pull it free. Suddenly he yelled at me, and I had to run before he captured me."

"You must have spilled some of the knockout drug. You idiot. Sit down on the bed." He turned to Tyler. "Lay down flat with your hands behind your head."

After Tyler did as commanded, Stephen quickly began changing from his wet clothes while keeping the guns close. After he tied his shoes and slipped on a jacket. He said, "Juan come here. Tyler, get up and put your hands up. Move around us."

Stephen put Tyler's gun inside the waistband of his pants in the front. He pulled Juan's arm and twisted it behind him. "Ow!" protested Juan.

Stephen poked him hard in the back with barrel of the gun. "Make another sound, and I'll put a bullet in your brain." To Tyler he commanded, "You'll go first. If you make any attempt to run, I'll shoot Juan."

"You'll shoot both of us when you think you're in the clear, but you'll never be in the clear. Your lives were like a stack of cards, and they've finally fallen to the ground. They arrested Jim and they have tons of evidence against the both of you. The cops are on the way up here right now. You're going down, and you'll be in prison for a long time, but if you kill us, you'll get the death penalty."

"I will be out of the country in a few hours, and they can't touch me where I'm going."

Tyler wanted to tell him about Eric and his purchase of all his property, but he thought that information would enrage Stephen to the point where he might just kill them.

Stephen pushed Juan forward. "Tyler, I want you to open the door and step into the hall, and tell me if you see anyone? If you run, I'll shoot."

Tyler brought his left hand down to open the door, and carefully clicked his sleeve microphone before touching the doorknob. Suddenly, the entire COM1 team could hear Stephen. Tyler stepped out and found no one in the hall.

"It's empty. They know this is your room. Give it up, Stephen. Let Juan go." Tyler just managed to let the team know the situation.

"Shut up and turn right." He pushed Juan out into the hall, and then glanced right and left. "Move down the hallway to the right."

Tyler began walking down the hallway slowly.

Stephen said, "Faster or I'll shoot."

They rounded the hall corner and made their way to the back stairwell. Tyler said, "They'll have all the stairwells guarded, especially the obvious back stairwell."

Ronnie got Eric to answer on COM1. "Change to COM2 now."

Eric quickly switched channels. "What floor is Tyler on?"

"He on the ninth floor and they are moving to the rear of the building."

"Get Gil and his men here on the double. I want two men guarding Larry. Do it now!"

Eric wanted to run after Tyler, but he knew he had to protect Larry as well. He was partially afraid Stephen would come after Larry and his wallet, but most likely, he just wanted to run.

Tyler started down the second flight of stairs just as Juan was the making the turn from the previous flight, and Stephen was a step behind him. They went down the next flight and suddenly, Tyler shot a hand up and through the spindles. He grabbed Stephen's leg as he was lifting it to take the next step. He was already off balance and forced to let go of Juan as he fell hard into the wall on the landing. Tyler reached up and yanked Juan down the stairs.

"Run!"

Tyler took a strong grip on Juan, and just got him down and around the next turn as Stephen fired his weapon but just barely missed Juan. He got to his feet and started downward chasing them. He fired over the railing just missing Tyler as he rounded two flights ahead of him. This continued for several more flights, but at the fourth floor, Tyler made a quick decision and pulled on the door leading to the floor. He knew they would have to get down the hall around the corner before Stephen could see which way they went.

They almost made it to the corner, but as Tyler started the turn, he heard the gun, and the shot hit wall near his face. He kept running. The hotel floors were in a pentagon shape. He knew they had no time to wait on an elevator to come all the way up, so he hit the button calling the elevator and hoped it would arrive from a nearby floor, and that the door would close before Stephen got there.

Eric sprinted from Larry's room as two of Gil's men reached the eighth floor. Eric and Gil ran up to the ninth floor and to the room. Two more men reached the same room seconds later. Finding it empty, he turned back to the hallway.

"Gil, take a man and go left to the next stairwell. I'm going to the right with the other man. They probably went down, hoping to exit the hotel so Stephen can run."

Eric didn't wait for a reply, but as he made his way down the hall, he sent orders through his sleeve microphone. "Ronnie, get a cop up here to protect evidence in the Stephen's room. Tyler, Juan and Stephen are gone."

Ronnie quickly responded, "Shots were heard in the stairwell and on floor 5."

"Damn!" he exclaimed and then to Gil. "Gil, go down. They are on the fifth floor."

The two teams began rapidly working their way down the stairwells.

Tyler and Juan weren't lucky with the elevator as they all were too many floors away. They began running once again. Tyler just made it to the next corner when Stephen fired at him. He rounded the bend and whispered to Juan. Run to the next corner and yell, "Tyler hurry, as loud as you can. Then run to the next stairwell and go down to the second floor and exit. There will be many people on that floor. Get in the middle of them until I get there. Hurry."

Tyler crouched down in an alcove for the ice and soda machines. He twisted around so his stronger right leg would be ready, and his weight would be on his left. He closed his eyes so he could hear Stephen's footsteps on the carpet. He closed his eyes as George Harishita had taught him in their marital arts classes. He heard Stephen's shoes. Swish, swish, swish...

Just before Stephen reached the corner, he heard Juan yell. "Tyler, hurry!" Stephen took the last two steps even faster, and prepared to make the turn and fire at Tyler. He thought Tyler must have been falling behind for Juan to yell at him. He began the turn.

Suddenly he saw just a slight flash of Tyler's hair as the young man let loose with all his strength and speed he had learned in his judo classes with George. He had only a hair of a second to aim, but he hit Stephen's knee solidly. The blow sent Stephen slamming into the wall. Tyler's gun spilled free from Stephen's pants.

Tyler snatched the pistol from the carpet with his right hand, gave Stephen a hard punch to the chest with his left fist, and a quick chop to his right arm, sending Stephen's gun flying down the hallway.

Tyler took off running once more. He got to the stairwell as he saw the door closing. "Run Juan! I'm coming!"

Stephen struggled for breath and slowly walked back to his pistol with a bit of a limp from the blow to his knee. Just as he bent to pick it up, Eric and his team members stepped onto the fifth floor. Stephen snatched up the pistol, fired at them, and dove around the corner as they quickly fired back.

Stephen ran to the stairwell door that Juan and Tyler had taken. He made a quick decision, and pushed the door open but didn't enter. He kept running down the hall. He managed to just get around the corner before Eric made it to the stairwell.

Eric was well trained and disciplined. He heard Tyler say into his microphone they were going down the stairwell. He made an instant decision and flew down the stairwell because he knew that Gil and another team would be coming down the fifth floor from the opposite direction he had taken. He felt if Stephen had fooled him and not followed Tyler, then Gil would take him out. However, if Stephen took the stairwell, he might just be able to kill Tyler and Juan. That was an option he was not going to allow.

Tyler and Juan reached the second floor and spilled out into the room of business convention folks. He quickly stuffed his pistol into his holster and pushed Juan through the crowd until there were a hundred people between them and the stairwell door. They quickly moved into alcove on the opposite side to hide behind the plants as Tyler had done previously.

Before Tyler could pull his sleeve up to use the radio and call for help, the stairwell door suddenly opened. Tyler and Juan held their breath. The moment Tyler caught sight of Eric's face he broke into a huge smile. He whispered to Juan, "The cavalry has just arrived. We're saved."

Tyler spoke into his sleeve microphone, "Eric, turn left. We're in the alcove."

He watched as Eric's head spun and stared through the crowd until his eyes caught Tyler's smile, and then quickly he and Tim made their way over to him.

"Are you okay?"

Tyler replied, "Yes, but he nearly got us. Did you see him?"

"I had a glimpse of him as he fired at us, but I guess he faked following you down the stairwell and continued on. I hope Gil gets him. Hold on." Eric spoke to Gil on the radio, "He gave me the slip by not coming down the first stairwell. Find him!" He then said to Tyler, "Let's get you back to the command center."

"Eric, this is Juan."

Juan tried to smile, but he was still shaking with fear. Eric smiled at him. "Son, you're safe now. My men and I will protect you. Come on, we'll take the elevator this time. "

Stephen's luck took a better turn. Before the next turn in the hallway and running into Gil, a room door on the left side abruptly opened. He barged in and shut the door gently while slowly turning the knob so it would not make a sound. He put his finger to his lips and pointed the gun at the astonished lady standing near him. "Say a word," he whispered, "and I'll kill you." He began rubbing his sore knee.

He listened as Gil and his partner ran on down the hall. Stephen then opened the door and ran the opposite way, down the back stairwell once again and made it into the parking garage, over a wall, and crossed the street as a swarm of police cars began surrounding the building.

He ran for several blocks until he was positive he no one followed him. He hailed a cab and told the driver to take him to the Executive Airport, but after catching his breath, he had a second thought. He asked the driver, "How much to take me to South Bend?"

The driver laughed. "Five hundred."

Stephen counted out three hundred dollar bills. "Here's more than half and you'll get the rest when we get there. No speeding tickets. I've got to rest a while."

SEVENTEEN

Eric walked with Larry to his private jet in the hanger. He more than had enough of his experience in Chicago and was ready to go home, so Eric made the flight changes for him. Though he apologized several times for the way things turned out, he felt Larry should be congratulated for helping to put two major gay grifters out of business. With Jim in jail and Stephen on the run, Larry played a significant part in their downfall.

Larry accepted the apology, told Eric he was going to Europe in six weeks, and would have his travel director get in touch so Eric could arrange the security team for the journey.

Eric politely said he would look forward to another normal trip and no more crime fighting escapades for Larry. Larry laughed and said that at least he got laid by a good-looking man. Eric didn't tell him that he had video of everything in case the police needed it, but he hoped Larry's statement and Juan's confession would be enough. He waved goodbye as Larry turned to head to his seat and minutes later, Eric watched as the Learjet left Chicago.

He turned around and found Gil waiting off to the side. "Are we loaded and ready?"

Gil replied sharply, "Yes, sir. Are we going after Stephen?"

"How'd you guess?"

"Because I have been in the marines with you for four years, and worked for you for six years, and I have never seen you let a bad guy get away, one way or another. So where to?"

"Miami," replied Eric with a slight smile. "Stephen will lay low somewhere and choose alternative routes to Miami, but he has lots of cash and jewels stored in that house, plus luggage and clothes, cars, and computers. He may need to go on the run, but he is a spoiled, rotten, greedy crook, and he'll want to take some nice things with him when he leaves the country."

Gil asked, "Shall we discuss the plan in flight?"

"Let's go."

Stephen paced his room in the Holiday Inn next to the South Bend Airport, thinking carefully about his situation. He knew there was nothing he could do for Jim personally except call their attorney and try to get Jim out on bail. He purchased another throwaway cell phone and called the attorney. The receptionist told him that his attorney was out of the country for an extended vacation. When he asked for associate he was told there were none available. This had never happened before. They always welcomed his business. He cursed and hung up.

He knew he that he couldn't leave the USA without first going to Miami and getting his stash, especially all his fake identification cards and passports, all their cash in the safe, as well piles of jewelry, and get out of the country as fast as possible. He assumed the FBI was involved, as the men chasing him had been highly trained, and they wore the same headsets and microphones as the FBI or a Secret Service agents. However, he could not figure out where Tyler received training for the judo move he made on him in the hotel, nor why he, too, wore a headset, and carried a 9mm pistol. He thought Tyler was too young to be an FBI agent, but perhaps he just looked a lot younger than he was, if so, he knew way more than Stephen wanted him to. He hoped he had a chance to kill him before he left.

He stayed in the hotel and waited twenty-four hours while he ran various scenarios through his head. He ventured out for some accessories and props to change his appearance, clothing, and food, but the rest of the time, he stayed in the room. Using a fake credit card, he booked a flight but not directly to Miami, but to nearby Fort Lauderdale, using another identity. He also rented a car with a different credit card under yet another false name. He left early the next morning wearing a gray mustache and partially grayed hair with dark sunglasses.

Jim's mark would be Chicago's prime witness against him, but the FBI had been brought in because their crimes crossed over state lines, and Stephen and Jim brought Juan in the country illegally. Juan told the FBI investigators he was forced to have sex with Stephen and Jim, and their marks, even though he was underage. Eric didn't mention that Larry had sex with Juan, too, justifying that he was part of their sting on this group. Juan gave them six hours of taped interviews and signed various affidavits. Eric promised to return him for any follow-up testimony, and for a trial, although Eric was pretty sure when faced with a long sentence, Jim would turn on Stephen, relieving Juan of any need to stick around. Eric told the FBI that all their legal property was in Stephen's name, and he suggested that probably Jim didn't know that. He would then understand that Stephen was going to leave him hanging in the wind. Eric's attorney handled the paperwork on Juan's behalf, so for now, he was free to return to Annapolis with Eric, and hopefully soon he could return to his homeland. He also agreed to pay all of Juan's legal bills.

Tyler learned through their long talks that Juan was indeed gay, and made the mistake of telling his mother, hoping she would keep his secret and keep him safe. She did the opposite by telling his father. His father and his older brothers beat him, and then chased Juan from his hometown. He ended up in a large city where another boy taught him how to make money with his body. In a month, he knew all the ways to please a man with dollars in one hand and his dick in the other.

He had learned to speak English from a Christian school when he was younger, and it came in handy when trying to attract the richer, American and Canadian tourists. Stephen and Jim picked him in a gay bar where he was dancing naked on the bar. The audience put dollars in his socks, and for twenty dollars, they could suck him right there on the counter with everyone watching. Sometimes, he had four to five men standing in line to be the next one to suck him raw.

The boy leaned his head on Tyler's shoulder and fell asleep once the jet crossed through the clouds.

Meanwhile, Eric and Gil went over their plans for Miami. At the home office, Ted closed out all the transactions, and sent paperwork to locksmiths so they could change the locks on all the houses around the world. In Miami, he arranged for the locksmith to stand by for Eric's arrival.

Eric decided they would set up a command post at a nearby hotel he spotted on his previous visit to Stephen's house. He made reservations for several rooms. Oscar flew in additional cameras for them to set up. Ronnie made a checklist of everything he and Tyler needed to do upon arrival. Juan would stay in the hotel room at all times where Stephen could not find him. At first, Eric thought it might not be good for Tyler's mental health to be around Juan, and digging up bad memories, but as he watched them talk, he realized that no one else knew more about what Juan went through than Tyler. He also realized as they compared their time with Stephen and Jim, it brought about a catharsis for Tyler, perhaps releasing him from the guilt and fear of his old life. He saw in Tyler's face and eyes, a more mature, positive, and leadership role. He smiled because he realized that Tyler was now acting like a responsible adult, using his new skills the firm taught him. Eric felt very proud as he winked at Tyler. He also laughed as Tyler told him about the kick to Stephen's knee. He didn't fuss at him for not holding his gun on Stephen while he was down, or at least shooting him in the leg. He knew that Tyler would probably beat himself up for that. Eric also knew that Tyler was terrified of the man that threaten to bury him alive. This made him very determined to get Stephen.

Eric and Gil decided to use about a dozen cameras for the surveillance of the grounds, keeping all of the team members out of sight. They knew from experience that Stephen might spot a surveillance car, and naturally, he would be wary of anything that piqued his curiosity. They wanted to trap Stephen inside his own house. The local police force had been briefed as well as the FBI. Harvey Feinstein, a friend of Eric's on the police force, vouched for Eric. His ex-Seal buddy at the FBI appointed a single FBI agent in charge of the government's case, and he, too, went along with Eric's plan. As they discussed the details through in-flight video conferencing, both jurisdictions accepted the obvious fact that Eric's team had more knowledge and equipment than they had, and far less legal barriers in the way of action. They were happy for the firm to do the grunt work.

Two hours later, they touched down in Miami and immediately made their way to the hotel. They dropped their bags and changed into their black assault uniforms and gear. Ronnie and Tyler began setting up the equipment, placing all of the external antennas on the roof of the hotel, providing far better range and quality of their communication gear. Juan plopped down on the couch anticipating a long wait. In addition to the two SUV autos they rented, they also stopped at a small rental agency and rented two of the oldest cars on the lot, vehicles that Stephen would take little notice of.

Oscar confirmed there had been no human moving about in Stephen's office from their video link. Tyler brought the same link up on the makeshift wall screen in the hotel room. This left Eric highly confident that Stephen was not yet there.

Using one of the old cars, Eric, Gil, and two team members made their way to house, parked a block away, and cautiously approached the house in preparation of confirming whether Stephen was there or not. Eric picked up the keys from the locksmith parked on the side road. Once confident Stephen was not about, he opened the back gate, and they all went inside. It took a few hours, but they checked everything in the house and especially the safe room, making sure Stephen had not arrived and took everything before making his escape.

Eric radioed to the control center in the hotel, and soon the rest of the team, quickly made their way to back gate. Ronnie and Tyler were manning the command center, while Steve waited for Oscar's package. The local FBI agent also stayed in the control room at the hotel, so he could see everything at once. He was jealous of the electronic gear and toys Eric's firm possessed. His name was Hank Barlow. He was forty, and far up in the investigative branch of the Miami FBI office. He and Gary Roberts were friends and he highly respected him. Hank was in top shape, an excellent shot, and just loved putting the bad guys away.

A sudden knock on the door made them all jump with Tyler, Steve, and Ronnie pulling their pistols. Ronnie looked through the peephole and smiled. "It's the FedEx man."

He stepped outside so the man could not see their equipment, signed for the delivery, and quickly gave Steve the gear Eric would need. Steve immediately left for the house.

Eric and Gil quickly made a survey of the grounds and showed the various men where the cameras needed to go. After Steve arrived, the agents quickly installed the gear, checked with Ronnie or Tyler to verify signal and audio, and then returned to the house. An hour later, they had a dozen cameras working on the outside, and six more fixed on the entrances to the house. There were two more entrances they secured with metal screws so no one could open them.

Eric and his men then retreated to the second floor, and chose a room with no windows and a door that didn't face an open area, so their monitoring lights could not be seen.

Eric set up a table and placed four laptops on it. Using their COM2 audio circuit, he worked with Ronnie, Tyler, and Oscar at home base to organize and setup the various signals so Eric and command could see all the camera channels at the same time.

Meanwhile, Gil divided the men into two-man teams. One of each pair carried a pair of night goggles. They now carried UZI machine guns to protect themselves. The agents were stationed well back from the stairwells out of sight, or buried in the landscaping on the property. They would remain hidden for as long as it took. The trap was set. Steve and another man removed all their vehicles from the property, locked the rear gate, and parked their cars in various spots at least a two blocks away. There would be no one sitting in a vehicle just in case Stephen cautiously rode through the neighborhood.

Remaining prudent, Stephen landed in Fort Lauderdale and checked into a hotel. He changed his disguise and then went out to do some shopping. He drove twenty miles away before choosing an ATM, and put in his debit card to withdraw some cash. He had already assumed the credit card he had been using had been traced to the airline and hotel in South Bend. He had thrown that card away in the airport.

He put the card in and typed in his security code. Suddenly, the monitor flashed a warning message that the card was stolen. Stephen tried to cancel the transaction and get his card back, but the machine would not give it back. Suddenly, a siren went off and he began running to his car and sped off.

"Boss, this is Oscar. Are you there?"

"I'm here. Report."

Oscar sipped a little of his soft drink while sitting in his office in Annapolis. "You know it is cold up here today with the temps hovering at freezing, and my home page says it is at least eighty degrees down there in Miami. Don't you need me to do a field analysis or something?"

"You're too old for the field," teased Eric.

"I'm only thirty."

"I meant your body. You're out of shape and look forty."

"Gee thanks. Never mind. I have news for you, but I guess I'll head to the gym and get a workout done."

Eric smiled. "Shoot. What do you have?"

"Our boy just tried to use his debit card in Fort Lauderdale. You can call off the cops at the Miami airport and the private field. He's smart. I bet he flew into Fort Lauderdale and rented a low profile car. I ran a report on all cars rented matching his description. Over two hundred cars were rented this morning, but his name didn't show up in any of the reports. He probably has a disguise, but I faxed his picture to all the rental car offices, and asked them to call me if they saw him."

"Good boy. I take that back. You don't look a day over thirty-eight!"

"Gee boss. I'm feeling better already."

Eric laughed. "Do you have the audio and video feeds on your systems at base?"

"Roger, loud and clear. I'm running digital recording on everything in case of a court case or field assessments."

"Okay, you're down to thirty-six. Thanks. Good job. Out."

Eric alerted the team that Stephen was indeed in the area.

The news made both Tyler and Juan nervous, although they were safe in their hotel room on the top floor.

Stephen drove several miles before calming down and thinking the situation through. He didn't believe it was bad luck, but rather somehow they had shut down his ATM card. Although he had another fake credit card, he did not have another ATM card. He always kept a spare check in his wallet, so he walked into a nearby branch of his bank and up to the teller. He did not like their surveillance cameras staring at him so he kept his hat and glasses on. He showed the teller his identification for the name on the account, and gave her the blank check so she could pull up his account. He said he wanted to cash it for two thousand dollars.

He nervously waited as she tapped the account number in, frowned, erased the number and then re-entered it. She tried again, frowned, and then looked up at him. "Just a moment. I'll be right back. My computer is really acting weird." She didn't wait for an answer, but turned and walked to the door to the teller area, and Stephen watched as she went into the manager's office.

Stephen quickly reached through the teller slot and bumped the computer screen so he could see it. He read the screen twice not believing what he saw the first time. The screen showed a withdrawal yesterday for twenty-six thousand dollars and change, and leaving a balance of zero. The account was now closed.

His heart skipped a beat as he immediately turned and made for the door. He could hear the lady calling his name as he went through the door and raced to his car and drove away.

"Uh, boss?"

Eric smiled. "Oscar, long time no hear from. Report."

"Our boy just walked into a bank branch and tried to cash a check and discovered his account had no money and was now closed. I guess easy come, easy gone! He fled the scene. I'm sending the footage to you now."

"Thanks. Amazing technology. You're down to thirty-five years old."

Oscar grinned. "It's a digital age. Everything is fast. Enjoy. Out."

Stephen returned to the safety of an anonymous human being in his hotel hideaway. He bolted the door and began pacing from the rear wall to the door, and back again, running through what was happening to him over and over in his mind. He felt only a slight tinge of guilt that he quickly dismissed from his soul like leaving a sip of orange juice in the bottom of a container, and tossing it in the trash and forgotten forever, which is exactly how he felt towards Jim. He wanted to know if a lawyer had gotten him out, but the ways things were going for him, he knew Jim was pacing a small cell like a lion longing for freedom to run on the plains. He was not about to let that happen to him.

Slowly, he began to sort things out. Someone high up in the police world was hot on his trail, but it didn't make sense to him that this group would for some unknown reason train Tyler to be a cop and carry a gun, and to fight. He recognized the judo move that he caught just a slight glimpse of before Tyler's powerful kick sent sprawling into the sheetrock wall, leaving head and body dents on impact. He could feel the swelling and bruises. He cursed Tyler aloud.

He could not figure out why Tyler had not been arrested, and then an idea hit his brain. Tyler was their mole, an important witness, their guy with the inside information, but even as he thought it, he became even more confused, because he made sure that Tyler never knew about his finances, his cash in the bank, or anything that he did on the computer.

"To hell with all of them," he said aloud to no one as he grabbed the car keys, and drove to Walmart to purchase some dark clothing that wasn't so easy to do in the south Florida, known as the land of the loud neon pastels and Hawaiian-style shirts, but he managed. His goal was simple, get in the house, and fill the stack of black duffle bags with all their stored cash, gold, silver and jewels, his stash of credit cards, licenses, and passports, grab some luggage and clothes, his laptop computer, the external drive on his desk computer, and then disappear.

He would first get to Spain and hold up there, as it put him far away from America. He would have enough cash to live well and never step foot in the USA again.

He went back to the hotel after picking up some takeout food, and began waiting, something he was never good at.

Wearing his latest disguise, he arrived at the Miami house just half past midnight, and thankfully, for his sake, the moon remained well hidden behind some dark clouds. He stopped just a half block away and listened, as if trying to hear or feel a trap that might lie ahead for him, but he heard nothing and felt nothing. He drove back and forth on the perimeter roads, staring at every parked car, but this time, nothing seemed out of the normal. He parked his car, crossed the street, and moved forward with cautious steps like a panther approaching a prey in complete darkness.

191

He stopped behind a tree near the gate. He fingered his house key in his pocket, while studying his own house, looking for anything that might give him a hint. He studied the palms and plants, the pool furniture, but all looked in place. He looked at the fountains, which were running, and studied the blue water in the pool. Everything looked in place.

"Eric? He's here," said Tyler as he studied the camera angle on his monitor. "He's across the street for the main entrance."

"You'd think he would have come in the back way or over a wall."

"He an arrogant prick who believes he is invisible, but don't take him lightly. He's smart, intuitive, creative, and can think faster on his feet than anyone I have ever met." Tyler paused before adding, "Present company excluded of course." He smiled at Eric.

"We'll get the bastard. You'll see."

"You had all the locks changed on the house and grounds, but why did you leave the gate lock untouched?"

"You can't catch a wolf if you don't leave the trap open. I want him on the grounds, but outside the house so we can capture him within his own fence walls. Steve is hidden not far from the gate behind some big palms and just waiting for my signal to secure the gate with a pair of thick twist ties like the cops use when there are too many suspects. They're silent and impossible to get off without wire snips."

Eric whispered into his sleeve microphone on COM1. "Stephen is approaching the front gate. Just as he reaches the house, Steve will secure the gate, and then will spring the trap on my command. Stand by."

Stephen felt like he was betting ten thousand dollars at the casino playing twenty-one, and he was already at twenty, but so was the dealer. His next card could give him the magical twenty-one, or it could deflate him with a twenty-two or higher. He was about to make a momentous decision by just stepping out from the tree. He scanned the streets and failed to detect a single cop car, which would have easily stood out in his neighborhood of Mercedes, Bentleys, and Jaguars.

He almost moved forward a foot, but sensed something was wrong, and he had no idea why. He needed the cash, the passports, and more, but at what cost, he wondered? He paused for a few minutes and decided he was not willing to take the chance. He would get the money another way, and he knew where to go to obtain a fake passport. He would fly to Spain, get the cash from his bank accounts there, and with the purchase of a new computer he would get access to his cash in the Cayman banks.

He moved from tree to tree and disappeared into the shadows.

"He's gone. I don't see him," complained Tyler.

Eric replied, "Scan all the monitors. Where is he?"

192

Ten more minutes passed, so Eric knew it was over, but he made the call anyhow. The cops had been a half-mile back and out of sight. Suddenly, they swarmed on the scene from all directions with sirens and lights flashing. Fifty men searched in all directions, while Eric's men checked the grounds, but he knew he was gone. Now that the fox had escaped his trap, Eric decided to go to work on the house.

Quickly, he and men began working on the safe room. Eric found the unlocked safe deposit with not only the keys, but also the combination code written backwards. In twenty minutes, they packed everything in Stephen's duffle bags. Their vehicles were brought to the rear gate, where they loaded all their surveillance gear and the loot, locked Eric's new house, and left. The locksmith was on the way to change the lock on the front gate, and would mail the key to the Annapolis security office.

Stephen looked back from hill, and watched the cops in action. Though he knew he had made the right decision, it angered him that he was so close to being captured, and they had already taken possession of his house.

Once he made it to his car, he drove straight to the hotel, packed his stuff, and drove to Fort Lauderdale, where he woke an old friend up in the middle of the night. By dawn, he had several sets of new passports, and spent the last of his cash. He drove to a busy breakfast buffet and lifted two wallets in five minutes, exiting without eating. He drove to a McDonalds drive-thru, bought some breakfast, and went through the wallets, removing the cash, credit and debit cards. He tossed the wallets in the trashcan as he exited the drive-thru, and drove north for several hours before veering left to Orlando.

He waited three hours before catching a flight to Europe with two stops before finally getting him to south of Spain. He rented a car and began the five-hour drive to house.

By dawn, Eric and his team were packed up and on their way back to Annapolis. Juan went home with Gil so he could experience a normal family setting, but also because there was no way Stephen could find him. He might find Eric and Tyler, but he remained doubtful that Stephen would take a chance on revenge. The men were tired from their work in Chicago and the all night surveillance in Miami, so he gave them some time off. He and Tyler drove to his house.

Tyler stated strongly, "We almost had him."

Eric grinned. "Yeah, but he now knows we are on his trail, and that we know more about him than he thought we did. He might assume you told us about the house in Costa Rica, so my guess is he'll play it safe and go far away and most likely to Spain.

"The American Embassy has alerted Spain's secret police and so they will handle things there. I hope they catch him because their punishment

193

for grifters is far worst than here. He could get twenty-five years of horrible prison conditions."

"My heart bleeds for him," replied Tyler slyly. "I hope he rots in hell."

"Jeez, you sound like you're in a foul mood, and I was hoping for sex tonight."

Tyler laughed. "I think we should start right now." He reached over, unzipped Eric as he drove, and began playing with his penis. "Umm, this gear shift feels wonderful and warm."

Eric began driving a little faster. "I'm hurrying as fast as I can."

"That's what they all say," laughed Tyler.

Stephen gave the man fifty dollars after convincing him to go to his house for him. They stopped at a store and he bought a jacket, hat, and glasses for the man. He had been watching people go back and forth across the square until he found this man, who indeed not only was the right height and weight as a match for him, but actually even looked a little like him.

He adjusted the man's clothes, gave him the key to the front door, and sent the man on his way down the street to his house. Stephen then ran around the block, so he could watch from a different direction than where the man left him.

The Spanish agents watched the approaching man from across the street on the second floor of another house. They glanced back and forth from the emailed picture of Stephen, and decided the man certainly looked like the same height, body shape, and hair color although the hat covered most of his head, and the sunglasses hid part of his face.

They prepared to make their arrest, but just as they were about to pounce, the man walked pass the front door and continued on for a few steps per Stephen's instructions, and then abruptly he turned around and returned to the door. He took the key and put it in the lock, but as he tried to turn the key it would not bulge.

Stephen saw this and wondered why he could not turn the lock and step inside as instructed. Stephen wanted to make sure there were no cops inside the house waiting for him.

The man tried a few more times, and then turned around facing where he had last seen Stephen, but of course, Stephen was watching from a block south.

Suddenly, the cops sprang into action and came running out of the house, yelling at the man to get down on the ground and place his hands behind his head. They cuffed him and pulled him to his feet, and began rapidly asking him questions. As they pulled his hat and glasses off, they realized immediately they had captured the wrong man.

The man began telling them about Stephen and then pointed to where he last saw him. The cops rushed to the area, as Stephen began moving south in the opposite direction. When he reached his rental car, he got inside while cursing, slamming the door, and pounding his hands on the steering wheel, and then calmed down a little before driving away.

He drove in a northwest zigzag pattern and crossed the border into Portugal using his fake passport and drove on to Lisbon. There he found a coffee shop with computer access, and paid a small fee to use a workstation. He sipped the hot coffee, took a bite of a breakfast cake, and began typing in the browser window for the bank in Florida, hoping to figure out what happen to his account. He was able to log into his account with his password, but the next screen displayed in big letters "ACCOUNT CLOSED".

He cursed and began typing in a different login name for his bank in Spain. He had several accounts and began checking them one at a time, but every single one displayed the same message. All his accounts were closed.

He used the bank's online chat program to talk live with a support person. He explained that he had not closed his accounts, but they all displayed closed. The tech support rep quickly attempted to open the accounts but couldn't. He then scanned activity history and could see where all the funds had been transferred to the states with no name only an account number. When he told Stephen, he cursed and closed the chat window.

He also tried his Cayman Island accounts, and they were closed, too. He took a tally, and felt sick when he realized someone or some government just robbed him of just over fifty million dollars.

He decided to see if he could figure out what had happen. He searched title changes for his house. Near the top of the recent transaction list was the purchase of his house for two million dollars and sold to an Eric Hanson. He then searched for his autos and they, too, had been sold to this Eric.

He then did various Google searches and couldn't find anything on an Eric Hanson. Oscar routinely checked the Internet to keep all of their team members off the web, fearing reprisals from various enemies.

Stephen had trouble with the Spanish, but managed to find a list of recent house transactions in Cadiz. At the top of the list was his house. It had recently sold for eight hundred thousand American dollars to Eric Hanson.

A knot formed in his stomach as he began to take stock of his situation. The only remaining large stash of cash was hidden in his island home of Costa Rica, and he was confident that the bribes he had paid to local officials would protect his property.

He spent a half hour searching Costa Rican web sites, but they were not as advanced as other major countries, and he could not find a list of any transactions. He felt he could not let them beat him out of all of his cash, so he decided to go immediately to Costa Rica.

He left the Internet coffee shop feeling deflated and frustrated. He decided to get a hotel room and some food, and to think a while. After a long nap, he took stock of how much cash he had left, and it was not enough to pay cash for a plane ticket. He was tempted to use one of the fake credit cards, but he sensed the FBI computer gurus were searching electronically for his trail, so he was afraid to make it easy for them. However, he needed more cash.

He and Jim had been to Lisbon a few years earlier, and he knew what clubs to go to. He shaved and showered after dark, and soon hit the streets to find the busiest shopping district. He watched the crowds carefully, and managed to pilfer a wallet from a lady's purse, and wallets from two men as well. In a restroom, he removed the cash and cards as usual, tossed the wallets, and walked to a different area, and began working another crowd attending a street festival. He stumbled into a wedding party as they awaited for the bride and groom's exit from the chapel and into their decorated car. He worked among the jubilant alcohol fused crowd, and easily lifted two more wallets.

He made his way into the church, and quickly ducked into a broom closet to avoid being seen by the bride and groom, as they excitedly made their way to the door of the church to leave for their honeymoon.

Stephen quickly opened door after door until he found the room where the grooms changed clothes. He laughed at the field day where he snatched eight wallets. He went down the hall and found a room with piles of ladies clothes and purses for the bride maids. He grabbed what he could and made a quick exit out the back of the church. He once again found a bathroom and took a tally of his cash. He now had almost a thousand dollars, and eight credit and debit cards. He tossed the debit cards because he had none of his laptop tools to break into the accounts.

He returned to his hotel and ate some dinner in the restaurant. He went upstairs and hid the cash and cards. He checked his clothes to appear as handsome as possible, and left the room to head to the largest gay nightclub in the area.

Although he had given his team a couple of days off, Eric and Tyler came to work the next day. Oscar was busy searching for signs of Stephen. Ted paid Eric a visit and gave him an accounting of his work. He was pleased to announce that Eric now possessed all of Stephen's possessions, and all of his cash. Eric and Tyler stored the duffle bags of loot and cash in the armory in the basement for now.

Ted asked, "What do you plan to do now?"

Eric smiled. "Well, I think he would have taken a safe route while making his way to Spain. Extradition is a long tedious process, and the cops in Spain haven't caught up with the rapid technology we enjoy in the states. After he learns he has no cash there, he might fly to Cayman, but I suspect with his computer knowledge, he'll check the accounts there and decide there is no point in taking the chance of getting caught on an island with an excellent police force."

Ted asked, "So he'll head to Costa Rica?"

"Well, we have a fifty-fifty chance of that. He could stay in Europe and begin pickpocketing for cash until he can begin scoring more successful marks as he did here. It would take a long time for him to get back to the level of comfort he had before, and years before he could take a chance on returning to the United States. The FBI and Interpol have bulletins out for him all around the world. He'll have to use fake passports and disguises to move around, and those items take a lot of cash. I suspect he has a stash in Costa Rica of cash and gold. I think he'll try to get it."

"Can he do that?"

Eric replied, "That's the conundrum. He'll either play safe and stay underground, or he'll be revengeful and start planning either A, his comeback via his money in Costa Rica, or B, he'll want to find this Eric guy who bought all his property, while surmising I may have all his money and loot in my house."

Ted frowned, as he was more of an accountant than an agent, though he trained as did the rest of the teams, but he was better at handling pencils and keystrokes as opposed to knives and pistols. "What are you going to do to protect yourself?"

"Well, first of all, my house is not in my name so he won't find me listed anywhere, so I feel safe. I'm betting he will steal wallets and anything of value not glued down in Europe until he has enough money and safe passage to Costa Rica. He'll want to pay cash for a ticket, making it more difficult to track him. He'll hope that the poor government of Costa Rica will not have cooperated with the American government, so his house and stash are still safe. I believe he hates this Eric guy enough that he will eventually take the chance and make his way to the island."

"So you're going there with a team?"

"I hope to leave tomorrow. Oscar is sleuthing for any sign of Stephen in Europe. The moment we think he has made his move, we'll be ready for him."

"I have prepared copies of the transaction documentation, just in case you have a problem with the authorities there. Be careful and I wish you good luck. I hope you nail the bastard. I have also put in the contact information for the Costa Rican attorney we hired for the process."

"Thanks, and we will capture him."

Eric made his way down to Oscar's office where he found Tyler working alongside of him. They had multiple video blocks on the big LCD monitor on the wall. "Hey, guys. Any luck?"

"Hey, boss," replied Oscar. "Yes and no. Tyler, bring up the photos of the suspects." The screen on the wall filled with forty-five male pictures. "These are the photos of the men about Stephen's height and weight who flew out of Florida the next eight hours after Stephen disappeared in Miami. We have run visual and physical analysis on each photo. We eliminated twenty-five men due to their age. Although he probably used a disguise while making the flight, I doubt he had time to create prosthetics to age his body by forty years. In a hurry, he could make a large stomach, but not double chins. So anyhow, Tyler put up list number two. These are the remaining fifteen men.

"We tracked their arrival in Europe and not one of them flew directly to Spain. So we found twelve that had connecting flights, and seven did fly on to Spain but none to Cadiz."

Eric replied, "So he is smart and would have flown in to a bigger city and drove to Cadiz."

"Yeah, because none of these men took a flight anywhere near Cadiz. So we began to study car rentals, and they were almost fifty car rentals, but unfortunately, there were no photo ID picture online."

"But foreigners would have been required to show their passports."

"You're right, which dropped the list to ten. It took us a while to get the passport numbers from these agencies, but we did. I must work on my Spanish. Tyler put this list on the screen. So then we did a comparison of our seven that flew from Florida to Europe, and on to Spain with the list of ten who rented cars."

Oscar hit a few keys. "Once the comparison analysis was completed, we now have a list of two men that flew from Florida to Europe to Spain, and rented a car. Tyler put the final list on the screen."

Eric laughed. One man was white and the other black. "I take it you were able to narrow this list of two down to one." They all laughed.

"You're right. The guy on the left, the white guy, is Stephen." Tyler hit a key, and Stephen's face came up full screen.

Tyler said without emotion, "This is definitely Stephen, though he is wearing a disguise. You see that small scar under his left eye. He got that after debarking a flight to New York two years ago. He opened the upper baggage compartment and the contents must have shifted, and a fold-up baby stroller fell out. A corner of one of the handlebars caught his eye. He bled like a filleted pig, and Jim and I had to clean him up. He threatened to sue the airline and the lady with the baby. He was not happy."

"How about his eyes? Is he wearing contacts?"

"No," Tyler replied. "Those are his natural eyes. He has worn colored contacts before but he hated them. I don't think he brought them to Chicago, but even if he did, they were most likely with the rest of the stuff he had to leave behind while making his escape."

"Oscar, send this photo to the FBI and the Interpol, and directly to the Cadiz police authorities."

"Roger, will do."

Eric sighed and asked Tyler, "What do you think he'll do when he discovers his house has been compromised in Cadiz as well? Will he flee or seek cash?"

"He'll do both. I don't know how much money he had on him in Chicago, although I'd guess a few thousand, and he had to use some of it to get out of Chicago, back to Florida, and then fly on to Spain. He is probably getting close to running out, so he'll steal by pickpocket, and once he has enough cash, he'll leave to avoid an arrest."

Eric smiled. "Oscar, search Cadiz for complaints for a thief."

"They may not be as sharp as we are with putting everything online."

"Okay, so if you can't do it by keystrokes, punch the keys on your phone and get some answers," teased Eric. "Let me know, I'll be in my office."

EIGHTEEN

An hour before midnight, Stephen left the hotel and walked to a large gay dance bar. He was fortunate as it was a holiday in Portugal, as men and boys, rich and poor alike, handsome and not quite so, were more than ready to party. He had to wait in a line to get in and it irritated him, but once inside, he found the large facility already packed with a thousand, dancing gay men, and half as many sitting on every available stool and couch. The lighting was very low, but the robotic dance lights were swirling all about. His mood changed instantly, though not for the want of finding a cute man to make love to, but rather a licking of the lips in seeking a rich gay man ready to unknowingly give up his cash. The loud music made his ears ring, but he kept his focus as he began searching each section of the bar for the type of mark he wanted. He had been preying on gay men so long that he could easily and quickly make a decision as to those he considered junk, worthless, promising, or gold.

He saw many opportunities for pilfering wallets and wads of cash, so he helped himself as he managed to easily collect some cash. This time he rapidly took the cash, dropped the wallets to the floor in a darkened corner, and moved away from the mark. Caught in a club with evidence might result in an arrest, or a severe beating from an angry crowd. He noted a few wealthy men, but none that he would score a ten. They were more of a six or a seven.

Two hours later, near the back wall, he spotted what he was looking for. The man was older and doing his best to look younger. He wore expensive rings, and at least a two thousand dollar watch. He took out a thick wad of bills, tipped a cute waiter with a large bill, and received a kiss in return, so he speculated that the man was generous, though handsome enough not to be.

He studied the man and his friends carefully, and soon surmised the man was without a boyfriend. Moments later, the man stood up and began making his way to the bathroom alone. Stephen followed a few steps behind. Once the man went inside, Stephen watched from the shadows as the man took a piss. As the man washed his hands, Stephen excited the bathroom, but since there was no door, he could glance in and see the mark was about to make his exit. Stephen took two steps back, and then walked briskly forward to the bathroom entry and head on into his mark.

Pretending to be a bit tipsy from too much alcohol, Stephen began apologizing for bumping into the man. He put his hands on the man's arms, and looked sweetly into his eyes, "I'm so sorry. The floor is moving around on me. Would you hold on to me for a second?"

The man looked at Stephen and liked him, as Stephen was indeed striking and attractive, if one considered only the shell of the man. "Come on, let's go sit down before you fall." Taking one of Stephen's hands, he led him to a nearby seat in the big room. They began talking, so Stephen let the man test him by allowing the mark to place a hand on his upper thigh, and from time to time Stephen would lean into the man allowing the man to get excited.

A few minutes later, he felt the man's hand squeeze his penis, and Stephen smiled. "Oh honey, that feels so good. You're going to make me hard."

"I should hope so," replied the man with a wicked grin.

Stephen allowed him to kiss him, as he moved his left hand's to the man's groin, and felt him getting an erection as well. They made out for about thirty minutes when Stephen suddenly said, "Well, I guess I had better go. I have rudely intruded on your party, your friends must be angry with me, and again, I apologize for running into you. I'm feeling better now. Thank you." He kissed the man and stood to leave with an obvious erection.

The man saw the lump, and was not about to let Stephen get away, which was exactly what Stephen hoped for, because it would be the man's idea that they leave. He felt it afforded any early suspicion by the man's friends, as well as the mark.

"Let's go back to my house. I live but a few blocks from here," suggested the man as he stood and enveloped his arms around Stephen and squeezed his butt.

"I don't know," feigned Stephen, suddenly shy and innocent-like. "You're not going to hurt me are you?"

The man laughed. "Heck, no, I'm a bottom. You're the one that will do the hurting!" They both laughed.

"Well, I guess it will be okay. I think I've had enough alcohol anyhow. Okay."

The man smiled and kissed him, then took his hand, and together, they made their way to the door. Cigarette smoke filled the club, so the sudden rush of fresh air brought a smile of relief to both men. However, a few blocks of idle chitchat nearly drove Stephen nuts, especially after determining the man was a complete and dreadful bore, but he played along as they entered his house, made their way to the bedroom, and began rapidly pulling each other's clothes off.

Stephen felt the man's wallet in his jacket, but left it alone for now, while counting as he had taught Tyler years ago. The man walked to a nearby table and removed all of his jewelry, leaving it in a pile. This is too easy, thought Stephen as he fell back on the bed. While the man was sucking him to a full erection, Stephen surveyed the room, looking for signs of a hidden safe. He also noted a few other items he could steal.

The man began to rotate his body around, and Stephen knew he would have to suck his victim as well, so he gave it a good show. A half hour later, Stephen had the man on his stomach, and he was fucking the bastard with great gusto, anxious to get it over with. He spotted a small statue of a naked boy next to the bed. During some heavy thrusting he snatched it, and pulled back out of the man's view as he continued pumping the man as hard as he could.

Just as Stephen ejaculated, he flung the statue at the back of the man's head knocking him unconscious. Stephen quickly pulled out, pulled the sagging condom from his penis, dropped it in the toilet, and flushed. He cleaned himself up, dressed, and retrieved the wallet, taking the cash. He put the jewelry on the table in his coat pocket. He searched his dressing area and found more rings and watches. He then began searching the room for a safe. He flung every picture off the wall, tried to move bookcases, but he couldn't find it.

He was about to leave the bedroom to begin searching the house, but he sat down on a dressing stool, and carefully moved his eyes about the room, looking for anything he might have missed. He soon noted just a slight rise in the middle of a floor rug at the foot of the bed. He jumped up and pulled the rug away. The floor was made of hardwood in long scattered length boards, but in the middle beneath the rug he noted a ten-inch square that didn't match the rest of the flooring.

Using his fingernails, he easily pulled the block of wood out, and beneath it was the safe. It was a digital keypad, and he didn't have the tools or the time to break it. He surmised that if someone went to all the trouble to install this type of safe, he would definitely fill it with cash and other valuables.

Reluctantly, he grabbed a handful of ties from the man's dressing room and returned to the bed. He tied two ties together several times, creating four longer ties. He rolled the man onto his back. He tied a pair to each of the man's hands and legs, and centered his limp body on the bed. He tied off the man's limbs to the corners of the bed. He took one of the man's socks, rolled it up, and stuffed it in the man's mouth. He walked to the sink, filled several glasses of cold water, and flung them in the man's face. The man stirred, and tried to focus his eyes, but Stephen had placed a wet washcloth over his face. He got more water and poured it on the cloth. The man thought he was drowning.

Stephen told him to shut up and if he did, he would remove the sock. He told the man if he screamed, he would cut his penis off. The man struggled to move his legs and arms for all of five minutes, but fell limp when he realized he could not move.

Stephen came close to the man's ear and said, "I don't intend to hurt you, though I will if you don't give me what I want."

"What the hell do you want?"

"I want the combination to your safe."

The man lied. "I don't have a safe."

Stephen poured more water over the man's covered face. "Have you ever wondered what it feels like to drown?"

"But I don't have a safe," pleaded the man.

202

Stephen hit him hard in the stomach knocking the wind from him. After the man coughed a few times, Stephen said, "The safe was at the foot of the bed in the floor. I have the wood block removed and need only the right digits to open it, and then I'll leave. So do I hurt you until you tell me, or do you tell me and avoid the pain?"

The man thought for a moment and reluctantly replied, "77771369."

Stephen left the bed, punched in the code, and heard the click. He opened the door of the safe. "Good boy," he said to the man as he smiled.

Inside he founds stacks of cash, lots of gold rings, some with diamonds, and several expensive watches. The haul required the use of a small pillow case to hold it all."

Once completed, he returned to the bed and asked the man, "Do you have housekeepers?"

"Yes, I do."

"What time will they come to work in the morning?"

"At ten, because I asked them to come in late since I would be out partying."

"Well, we had a good time didn't we? Now you just lay there and relax, and when your housekeeper comes, she'll let you go."

"Let me go now," began the man, but as he said the words, Stephen suddenly jammed the sock back into his mouth.

"Time to go."

Stephen didn't bother searching the rest of the house. He had what he wanted, and he stuffed the pillowcase in a shopping bag he found in the kitchen trash, and left by the back door through the dark yard, while all the neighbors slept. He went back to his hotel and packed his things. He left the hotel via a side entrance and drove to the next town some fifty kilometers away, and found a pawnbroker's shop. He parked across the street, and waited for the sun to come up by taking a nap. At eight, the man opened his shop, and Stephen entered with wet, teary eyes. He told the clerk his father had just died, and he needed to pawn his things until the will was settled, so he could fly his father back to Canada for burial. He laid it on thick, and the man gave him about thirty percent of the value for the gold and jewelry.

Although Stephen wasn't happy with how the pawnbroker cheated him, he was in no position to argue. He drove immediately to the airport and flew out on the next available flight.

The next morning Oscar was waiting on Eric and Tyler as they arrived for work. "You were right boss. There were several reports of pick pockets in Cadiz, and the local cops said that was unusual."

"Very good, so he has a little cash. How much did he get?"

"About hundred and fifty American."

"Not enough for a plane ticket."

"Probably not, but look at this. A man was robbed by a single white male with an American accent in Lisbon."

"He could fly out of there with ease. How much did he get?"

"About twenty thousand in cash, gold and jewelry."

"Jeez, he has plenty of cash now! Okay. See how many men flew from Lisbon for Latin America and perhaps Costa Rica."

"I'm already on it."

"Good job, Oscar!"

Eric buzzed Marti, "Assemble the troops." It was military jargon for the entire team to meet in the situation room. Once there, Eric began to speak, "I first want to thank everyone for your work on the Chicago project. We kept Larry from harm, and allowed him a little sex," Eric paused while the team laughed. "And in six weeks, Larry has another big assignment for us in Europe. We got one of the bad men, rescued Juan, and cut the financial resources of Stephen severely. Oscar and Tyler have tracked him to Europe, Spain, Cadiz, and on to Lisbon. He made a big score last night there, and we suspect he is on a flight to Costa Rica.

"This is not a normal mission for a client. This is personal project for me, so you don't have to join me, and it will not affect your status here if you decline. I don't like people who prey on young men like Juan, and steal and hurt others. I intend to put him out of commission forever. However, I do need your help. I want to fly to their island hideaway in Costa Rica in an hour, and prepare to take Stephen down when he gets there."

Eric paused. "Make no mistake, while he is a very good thief, he would kill us if he gets the chance. I don't plan to give him that chance."

He paused again and asked, "I want to ask for volunteers. Is there anyone that will help me get him?"

Without a pause the entire room stood. Eric was moved and smiled. "Very well, be seated. I will give everyone in the company a fifty thousand dollar bonus if we're successful." They cheered. "Okay, load up your gear we leave at nine-thirty sharp, and our flight's at ten. We're taking heavy weapons, grenades, shoulder missiles and such, and anything else that will help us. Think of this as a combat mission."

The room quickly emptied. Eric went to Oscar's office. "I need more of your cameras for surveillance. I'll take Ronnie and Tyler again to set up control. Can you handle the tracking of Stephen from here?"

"Yes, but I would be happy to go, too."

"I know, you're getting the bonus as well, but I need you to alert me of his movements if you can."

"Roger, will do."

"Thanks. I'll see you in a few days."

Eric returned to his office where Marti had a bunch of documents for him to sign, and then he went down to the locker room to change into his battle uniform.

Ronnie and Tyler quickly checked and packed their gear, and then loaded it in the van. They rushed back to the locker room to change clothes and load their weapons. By ten o'clock, Eric's team of twenty men was in the air and flying directly to the island's airport.

Meanwhile, Marti took Juan to the airport and put him on a commercial flight home. The boy was an illegal immigrant, and while Eric offered to help him stay in the United States, he wanted to go back home. He had been afforded the papers to allow him to fly freely to his homeland without hassle from immigration or airport officials.

Once in the air, most of the team followed their usual pattern of rapidly falling asleep, which Eric encouraged, as they never knew when they would get their next opportunity for rest once they were on the job. Sleep calmed nerves, while recharging their energy, and prepared their bodies for the upcoming mission.

Eric sat with Tyler in the front of the plane, and he knew Tyler was excited, nervous, and very apprehensive. Eric smiled at Tyler. "Are you okay?"

Tyler rolled his eyes. "Where we are going is beautiful. The island was built by drug money, and it has every option and toy you can imagine. The beautiful house has a waterfall in it, and the creek water flows through the center. There is a ten-foot tall by thirty feet long saltwater aquarium, and it is about six feet wide. It is filled with many exotic and colorful fish. There are eight bedrooms, twelve bathrooms, and an indoor pool that flows under a glass partition into the outside pool. The outside pool is one of those infinity pools that appear to flow over a cliff. The kitchen is better equipped than many restaurants. There's even a bunkhouse for the workers that maintain the property, and it also housed the guards for the drug lord when the place was built. I always had a good time there.

"Sometimes, Jim took the yacht to Quepos and picked up several gay couples that he knows that live there. They would party during the day, make a run over to the big gay beach, and everywhere Jim went, he would pick out good looking gay men and boys, and give them a card with the time and place to meet him at the dock for a trip to the island for a four-day party.

"I didn't think much about it at the time, but many of the young men he brought over were probably underage. His reputation was well known, and at the end of the party, he would give each boy a hundred dollars. If they were very good, they got two hundred. He would bring over about thirty guys. It was my job to prepare them for fun. They would put their clothes in the bunkhouse and go the shower area. Jim built this addition not long after we got there. It was an outdoor shower, sort of like you might see in a high school gym with shower heads three feet apart all the way around the room. There were at least twenty nozzles spraying water, and a shelf all the way around the room with every kind of shampoo and fragrance, shower gel you can imagine. Stephen and Jim insisted everyone shower very well, so it was like a party in there. I would arrive naked, and get them started by going from one boy to the next scrubbing, and getting them to scrub each other. I masturbated two at a time, and had them kissing and sucking everyone.

"Once cleaned, they followed me up to the pool where there was a buffet line set up and lots of alcohol. Although Stephen and Jim did not normally do any drugs, there were some drugs at the party, but usually they were ecstasy or any other sex drug. Jim was taking Viagra, and he placed thousands of condoms around the place. He created outdoor beds with lounge cushions around the pool area, and a big gymnastic mat area for the orgies.

"Stephen and Jim would walk through the men and pick out several guys like they were being selected for a basketball pickup game. I've seen Stephen take six with him to the mats, and the fun and the sex would begin. He'd have his dick in one boy, his balls would be sucked by another, he would be sucking another boy, while one of the bigger boys would be rimming his butt, and somehow Stephen would have a big toe in some boy's butt, and all at the same time. I would laugh my head off at the crazy looking scene. This party went on all day and into the night.

"Jim was not as multitasked as Stephen. He would line boys up and tell them to bend over, and he would go down the line fucking each one for a minute or two, then popping out, and thrusting into the next one.

"When we arrived on the island, they would insist I wear no clothes, except for riding on the four-wheeler. They said my body was too beautiful to be covered by clothes. I thought it was a compliment, but soon I felt like a prisoner. I did have fun at the parties, as I often enjoyed sex with boys my own age. I'd fuck underwater, in the Jacuzzi, in the steam room, on the grass, and on the flowerbeds. I liked doing it with three or four guys at a time. All these boys wanted the bonus money, so they put everything they had into making sure we were pleased.

"At meal time, a bell was rung and everyone went to the showers to clean the cum and shit off them, soon they were eating, and then back to fucking. Now and then, a boy would shy away from more sex with Stephen or Jim. This made Stephen very mad, and he would take the boy to the workout room, and punch the boy into submission. He would then fuck him as hard as he could. The boy would return to the group with his bruises, and no one rejected them again.

"Have you every heard of a conga fuck?"

Eric gave him his mystery look. "No, I am afraid I haven't."

Tyler teased him by saying, "You don't get out much, huh?" Tyler laughed and continued. "About once a day during the party, Jim would make all the boys assemble in a straight line from shortest to tallest. Jim was usually the tallest. Stephen would take pictures of them. I would be in the middle of the group, as Costa Rican men are generally shorter than Americans.

"Once we had everyone set, on Jim's command, they would make a quarter turn facing the rear of the man in front of them. Jim would put his dick in his man, and that man into the next, and so on. The conga music would start and we would fuck in rhythm, all thirty of us. It was hilarious. I bet I went through a hundred condoms in four days.

"At the end of the multi-day party, they would be sent home with their cash, except for a few young men Stephen and Jim selected to stay on. Jim liked the younger ones, as long as their dick was big enough for fun. Jim would sometimes have two guys fuck him at the same time. Stephen would select well-cut muscular men with a great dick, a cute ass, and an incredible mouth, as he loved having his dick sucked hard and fast. This select group was given a few hundred dollars a week, and all they could eat, for as long as we stayed on the island.

"I was in charge of this group, which meant they, too, were not allowed to wear any clothes. I was required to shave any body hair they might have, including their pubic hair and their testicles. A masseuse provided a sexy massage for each man, plus they were given haircuts, and they were required to wash their bodies several times a day. They were basically paid sex slaves, and I became friends with some of them."

Eric asked, "You said Stephen took pictures of everyone?"

"Yes, throughout the entire party."

"So he had pictures of the sex?"

"Yes, Stephen took pictures of Jim fucking some young men, and Stephen fucking as well."

"Do you think there are any pictures of Stephen fucking anyone underage?"

"Oh yeah, why?"

"Well, I would think the Costa Rican police would take a dim view of an American fucking their teenagers."

Tyler replied, "The cops in that country are weird. In San Jose, they are very military-like, although petty crime is still a problem. However, in Quepos, it was like being in another country with their own police force. They, too, wear army uniforms, but they are bribed all the time. You'd probably find that the cops there got a lot of cash from Stephen and Jim to look the other way. However, the government in San Jose might punish Stephen."

"Well, depending on how things go, instead of bringing Stephen back to the states for a ten-year sentence, he might get life in Costa Rica. I would think their jails aren't as nice as ours. Many people die in jungle jails, and they take a dim view of criminal foreigners."

Eric decided to shift the discussion to their plans. "Tell me about the airport. Oscar's satellite printouts showed it was more than long enough for our jet, and there were several buildings off to the side. Is that right?"

"Yes, there are several hangers. I was told the drug folks kept several jets and planes in storage, but Stephen and Jim only had a single engine straight tail plane. I always wanted to learn to fly, but they wouldn't let me take lessons in Miami." Tyler took a sheet of paper and drew out the airport, and then labeled the buildings. "Their plane is in this hanger. There are some cars in the other ones. Stephen flew in an airplane mechanic from San Jose when he needed any maintenance done on the plane. Stephen was the pilot."

"Can he fly a helicopter?

"No, I never saw him fly one or talk about doing so."

"I have the floor plan of the house, but tell me about the rest of the property, for example other buildings, boathouses, power plant, and so on."

Tyler chewed his lip a little until he formed a mental picture in his head, and began telling Eric everything he could think of. There were over thirty buildings on the property. Eric made notes on each one, and then began quizzing Tyler about how they obtained electricity for the island.

Tyler said, "There is a big diesel fuel tank on shore near the docks that is next to a pump house that feeds a fuel line up to the house area. I saw a fifty-foot boat arrive one day that was pretty grimy looking, and not like the yachts and sailboats that usually visited. I thought we were about to be attacked by pirates. Jim laughed at me, and said it was an old tanker ship bringing a load of fuel to the island. We used diesel for the big boats and apparently diesels for the two generators for power. The generators are in a building near the tool shed. We drove electric golf carts and four wheelers around the island. Our freshwater came from a deep well in the center of the island. A pump filled a water tank that was only twenty feet tall, but it was placed on the tallest point on the island, so we enjoyed very good water pressure. I could take a shower as long as I wanted to as we used several of those instant hot water units that ran off of diesel, too."

"This is good Intel. We'll need to protect the electricity station, docks, fuel tank and pump, water pump house and water tower, airport, and maybe the house. Which way do you think he'll come to the island?"

Tyler replied, "Well, when we first came to Quepos, we stayed at Big Ruby's Bed and Breakfast. It is a fabulous gay inn with awesome food and a friendly staff, but we made the mistake of hiring a taxi to get us from San Jose to there. On the map, it is only about two hundred miles I think, but we thought it was a paved highway. It started out that way, but about sixty miles or so out-of-town it went to dirt and on to mud. There were potholes bigger than the cab we were in. We had to stop for alligators and giant lizards to cross. It was nerve wrecking and exhausting.

"From then on we flew to the airport in a chartered plane. It only took about forty minutes, and you could easily see the jungle. I don't know what he'll do. I guess if he thinks no one is here, then perhaps he'll fly in as usual, but if he is suspicious, he might try to sneak onto the island by boat."

Eric sighed. "I think he is smarter than I wished he was, so I suspect he'll come by boat in the middle of the night. Is there any way he can check on his house from San Jose?"

"He'll call Alberto. He's in charge of the house and grounds crew."

"How many people on the island?"

"Eight."

"Very good." Eric stopped while thinking, and then said, "Hold on a second. I need to talk to Oscar." Eric lifted the phone receiver from the wall holder and dialed Oscar. "I need your help on a few things."

"Roger, go ahead," replied Oscar.

"I want you to forward all calls to the island to my cell. When Stephen gets there, he'll probably call a guy named Alberto for the status on the island. I don't want him talking to anyone. Can you handle that?"

"I hope so. It sounds like a primitive area."

"I assume the call will come from San Jose and into the city of Quepos, and then on to the island. Wait a second. I need to ask Tyler something." Eric turned to Tyler. "Is there a phone system on the island or did they only use cell phones?"

"There is no cell service in Quepos. The drug lord buried cable from the mainland, and rumors have it that he owned the local phone company. There are several extensions in the house, boat house, airport, and even the bunkhouse."

Eric gave the information to Oscar. "Have Ted put the phone account in my name right away. Let me know when you have figured out how to forward the calls to me."

Oscar replied, "Will do, but if there isn't cell service, you'll have to wait until Ronnie and Tyler set up the command center for you to receive or make calls."

Eric thought for a second. "What about the sat phone? Can you route the call to it until control is ready?"

"Good thinking. Yeah, no problem, just give me a test call when you land, and I'll update you."

"Thanks. Out."

Eric let Tyler rest, and hopefully fall asleep, while Eric began putting his plans together. He made notes for each section of the grounds, began assigning men, and in a few hours he had a long checklist of things to take care of.

About an hour before touchdown, Eric woke everyone up. On the overhead projector screen in the front of the plane was a hand drawn map of the property.

"Okay guys. Shake the sand from your eyes, as it is time to go to work. This is a layout of the island. We'll buzz the island to check for activity and land in about fifty minutes. I want everyone armed and off the plane in sixty seconds after we come to a stop. We are vulnerable and susceptible to attack while on the jet. We'll fan out and secure the area. There is a lot of military arms on the island, so even an RPG or short-range missile is possible. Once secured. I want two men to check out this hanger. Inside should be just one plane. We'll back our plane in there as well and shut the doors, so that no one can see it from the air. Our pilots should service the plane, refuel, and be ready to fly at a moment's notice if things turn bad on us. We'll leave two men and the pilots to protect the airport and the plane. Stay out of sight, but warn me if you see any flyovers or attempts to land.

He pointed across the runway to a hill. "This is the water tower. The rest of us we'll go the water tower. I want to set up a command center in a tent because this is the tallest point on the island, so our radio circuits should be clear in this tropical environment.

"After that I'll assign various teams to check out the main house, docks, bunkhouse, and so on until we know who is here. I think he has three options for getting on the island: airport, dock, or a small boat that could circle the island. However, since most of the island is a tall cliff, there are only two good areas for a small boat to approach. There is a beach on the backside near Quepos and behind the hanger, and the other one is on the open ocean side. I want cameras set up at each of these spots so we can keep an eye on them day or night. I want a camera on the airport and dock, as well as the house.

"There are only eight workers on the island, so I don't expect much resistance. We'll take their guns and arsenal, and move them to a hidden location. Tyler will explain that I have bought this island.

"Stephen will assume we're in the house like Miami, but this time we'll bolt the rear doors and put cameras everywhere. We'll hide out in the nearby jungle. We are not in America, so when in doubt, shoot to kill. We all have a blue dot on our lapels to identify us. It'll be dark in two hours after landing, so we'll have to work quickly. Use your dog whistles if approached and unsure if you are meeting a friend or foe. Two clicks on the radio mean danger nearby. We'll hunker down for tonight, and make more preparations tomorrow. If you hear a plane, stay out of sight under the trees. Surprise is our friend. Don't throw our friend in the ditch. Any questions?"

"No sir," they replied in unison.

"Good luck and Godspeed."

NINETEEN

Stephen did a lot of thinking and planning on the long flight from Spain to Mexico City, and contriving more revengeful thoughts during a three-hour layover there, before finally catching another two-hour flight to San Jose. He was exhausted as the plane finally stopped at the terminal just after dark. He endured a long entry customs, check-in line using a false passport, and caught a cab to a favorite small gay hotel where he knew the owner. He didn't have to show his passport on arriving, and was given a room on the second floor. He dropped his stuff in his room, and went right back to the street to a restaurant he also knew, ordering takeout. Once back in the room, he ate his dinner, downed two bottles of beer, took a shower, and immediately went to sleep.

In the morning, he bought breakfast, and arranged passage on a very small airline to Quepos. The flight would leave before lunch. He walked around the city for a while thinking and wondering what he would find at his island home.

Eric's team accomplished a lot on their first partial day on the island, but sunsets came quick in this part of the world. Thankfully, all was going well in spite of Steve stepping on a huge, boa constrictor snake, which raised his heart rate a bit, but no damage to man or beast, except for some ribbing from the other team members.

The command tent was set up quickly, so Ronnie and Tyler went to work on the control center. Tyler arranged a white sheet screen along a full wall of the tent to be used to project their images on. He used several bungee cords to pull it taut and flat. Soon they were testing with Oscar in the Annapolis office, and carefully tuned in the audio and video satellite dish to tweak for the best signals. All the COM networks were working, as well as the independent cell phone signal network. With their antennas placed on the high ground, their signals were peaking all around the island.

The men set up a second tent for meetings and personnel, and a third tent for their gear, and fourth for sleeping. Eric insisted the tents be accomplished right away after studying the weather charts and anticipating several tropical rains in next few hours. However, once accomplished, the men left in teams to scatter and install a few cameras before nightfall. They managed to secure the house and dock cameras, as well as the airport, but the rest would have to wait until dawn. Ronnie and Tyler would take turns monitoring the equipment, while the teams for the dock, house, and airport remained on duty, taking turns getting some shuteye. They begrudgingly ate their army-style MRE field rations.

Like most local airline flights in the Latin American countries, nothing left or arrived on time. Stephen arrived at eleven for the eleven-thirty

211

flight. He checked his watch and it was now quarter to noon, and he was finally on the tarmac waiting in line with a man and two chickens in a cage. Two women carried babies in their arms, and he was sure they would start screaming as soon as the plane fired up the engines, and scream until they landed. He was disgusted at the nauseating smells on the plane and already angry at the noise.

At least once a year, a plane like the one he was boarding would go down in the jungle with rarely a survivor, but he thought this was still better than taking the six-hour ride through the jungle dodging potholes and jungle creatures. He settled in the seat and debated on whether to use a seatbelt, half thinking not to use it, so that he would die quickly should they crash, as opposed to tumbling through the treetops over and over before slamming into ground.

The engine fired, the babies began screaming, and as they taxied out, Stephen put his fingers in his ears. He hated people that didn't control their kids. He thought of using his 9mm pistol to solve the problem. He had purchased the gun in San Jose that morning, but decided to be patient.

Eric pushed the men and they hustled, and by ten, they secured the island. He led a meeting in the tent, then afterwards the team grabbed some food and ammo, and made their way to their posts scattered throughout the grounds. Eric and Gil remained in the command tent with Ronnie and Tyler on technical duty.

Gil was checking communications with each team, while Eric took a call from Oscar.

"Hey, boss. How are the bugs?"

Eric smiled. "Animal or electronic?"

"I'd prefer the electronic ones as they're easier to kill. Our boy almost outsmarted me by flying into Mexico City and getting a late flight to San Jose. I lost him after he left Portugal because he is a genius and bought tickets for two different flights, one ticket to Costa Rica, and the other to Mexico City. I had thought he was on the first, but with a bit of research, I found that ticket marked 'no show.'

"I started over by working backwards from San Jose looking for a gringo like him. I got lucky as he was the only American on the flight out of Mexico City, and he got there, as mentioned, after dark last night.

"He didn't stay in a chain hotel, so I don't know where he stayed. I did some research and found there was an airline flight from San Jose to Quepos later this morning. Like most of the jungle tree croppers, the rubber band plane didn't leave on time. I think it left about noon and should land either in Quepos, or if he paid the pilot cash, he might land on your island about ten after one."

"Very good Oscar. Did you get all the calls to the island forwarded to me?"

212

"Roger, but I had to wire a guy five hundred dollars. I guess everyone has their hand out for cash down there."

"That may be. Thanks."

"What else can I do?"

"I'd like for you to monitor the cameras and audio traffic for anything we might have missed, and thanks again for a job well done. Out."

"Roger, boss. No problem. You're welcome. Out."

Tyler asked, "Eric, how long before he gets here?"

Eric smiled. "At the earliest, about an hour. We've done all we can do. We're as ready as possible, but I don't think he has any idea how many men we have with us. It would be nice if he thought he got away with keeping the house, but I decided to humiliate him as much as possible, hoping his anger and temper will easily lure him into our trap."

"Do you think he'll come by boat?"

"The easy answer is he would have to since we're on an island. The question is what kind of boat. I doubt he would take a wild chance by flying in without proper Intel and surveillance. I think he'll come under the cover of darkness, and I don't think he'll come alone. He seems to know people in Quepos and unfortunately, he picked up some cash in Lisbon. We may have to fight a small army."

Tyler frowned. "It'll be Tonto and the pineapple men."

Ronnie laughed. "Tonto?"

Tyler smiled. "There is this large man that owns a farm south of town. Stephen and Jim bought all our fruit and vegetables from him. He comes to town on Saturday's with a truckload of men ready to drink the town dry. Jim called them Tonto and the pineapple men. We would all laugh when we saw them, but I never wanted to run into them alone. They were big, tough, grimy, and appeared mean to me. Tonto liked Jim's cash, but the men hated us because we were queers."

"Great. Do they have rifles?"

"I don't know. I saw a shotgun in the truck, but mostly the men had machetes."

"Well, whatever he brings with him, we'll have to handle. I want this to end here. He must not escape. We might not be able to find him again, and I don't want to look over my back for him. Let me know if you notice anything on the monitors." He paused. "Tyler, if you see him, I want you to shoot to kill instantly. Do not think about it, just do it. The lives of the rest of us will depend on you shooting first. You're an excellent marksman. Use your skills. Kill him."

Tyler nodded, feeling a bit shaken from Eric's tone. He hadn't thought he might have to be the one that killed Stephen.

The day had gone by slowly on the island with no sign of any movement anywhere and this worried Eric, as he knew all soldiers lost their edge when boredom set in. He decided to rotate the teams to the next station to keep them as fresh as possible. The expected plane didn't land on the island, so they assumed it landed at the Quepos airport. Oscar confirmed the plane's arrival after calling the tower.

At just half past five, Eric's phone rang. He didn't recognize the caller ID. "Hello?"

"Is Alberto there?"

Eric replied, "There is no Alberto here."

"Doesn't he work there?"

Eric suspected the voice was Stephen's though he was trying to disguise it. "Not anymore. The place was sold to an Eric Hanson and all the workers were let go."

Stephen nearly cursed aloud and replied, "Oh." The realization that this Eric Hanson now owned everything he used to own, but why was he involved? Was he a friend of Tyler's?"

The phone was silent for a few seconds. Eric said, "Hello?"

Stephen sighed. "Is this Eric Hanson?"

Eric noticed he had dropped the fake accent "Yes, it is."

"Where are you?"

"At the moment I'm enjoying a barbecue with friends out by what used to be your pool." Eric enjoyed pissing Stephen off. "By now you've learned that I purchased every piece of property and vehicle you own everywhere in the world. You own nothing. Zero. The funny thing is, I didn't use a dime of my money to purchase everything. I used your money, or I should say the money you stole from others. You are broke. The FBI has moved you to their most wanted list, Interpol has bulletins out searching for you, and there are at least fifty countries that if you're found in, you'll be arrested on the spot. I have personally put a million dollar reward on your head."

Stephen became very angry. "Take a good look at the sky Mister Hanson. It is the last time you'll see it."

"Stephen, you are a lot of sad and evil things. Don't add stupid to your list of crimes."

Stephen yelled, "I'm going to cut your fucking balls off!" He hung up.

Eric looked over at Gil, as well as Ronnie and Tyler. Eric said, "That went well. I guess that means he is coming, and I don't think he is coming alone."

Eric warned the men he had just heard from Stephen and warned that the suspect made a big threat. He reminded them to stay alert.

After Eric concluded his radio message, Gil spoke up. "Eric, it seems to me this guy is pissed off at what we have accomplished. I suspect he'll hire a bunch of big guys with the promise of money and alcohol to take us. He probably thinks we're Custer, and he just hired the Indians. At the moment, we are prepared to capture him and are pretty much in a defensive mode. I suggest we shift to an offensive mode."

Eric nodded. "I believe you are right. What do you suggest?"

"I think we should welcome these guests with open arms and big bangs."

Eric laughed at Gil. "By arms, I think you mean weapons and by 'bangs' you mean…"

Gil cut him off. "Booby traps and hand grenades."

"Roger that," grinned Eric. "Come on, let's do it."

They used a golf cart at the hanger, loaded up several cases of grenades, claymore mines, and spools of thin wire. They drove to the locations for each team and instructed them to set traps where they thought their enemy might approach.

They set traps at the far corners of the hangers near the jungle. Trip lines were also set up on the steps from the dock, the corners of the house, the power station, and near the bunkhouse and the shed, where they found a stash of arms that they moved next to the command tent for safekeeping.

Eric and Gil also delivered boxes of military grade, food rations to each team and returned to the control center. It was going to be a long night.

"Ronnie, you and Tyler eat up. This could be an exciting night, and I need you to be sharp and alert. If Gil and I have to leave control, I need for you to tell me on COM2 what you see. We'll keep COM1 as an open channel to all the teams. Keep your guns ready and at your side. We don't know how many men are coming and from which direction. Stay on your toes. I will not allow anyone to take over our control center."

Gil and Eric ate their dinner quickly while talking tactics.

Gil spoke up. "Eric, I doubt we're going to get this Stephen character alive. If he's bringing a bunch of goons in, we'll have to kill everything that moves to stay alive."

"You're right and that's okay. I do not want any of our men to get hurt. Tell them they have permission to use lethal force at every opportunity, and that there will be a thousand dollar fine if they get injured or shot, but a two thousand dollar bonus on top of the fifty thousand I already promised if we succeed."

Gil grinned. "I like the sound of that."

As the hours slowly went by, Tyler became both nervous and sleepy. He had no idea how he could do it, but when he became too stressed, he could fall asleep in seconds. Ronnie had just relieved him. He immediately took a long overdue piss in the woods, and then returned to the cot to rest. He was already sleeping before Ronnie's chair was warm.

Twenty minutes later, he heard Ronnie called Eric on the radio, "Boss, there's movement on the back side of the island behind the hanger. I count eight shadows coming up the beach."

Tyler sprang up and nearly ran into Eric as he rushed into the command tent. "Roger," he replied to Ronnie, and then spoke on COM1 to his men, "Here they come. Hunker down! Lock and load! We have eight men on the beach behind the hanger. Expect other entry points and targets. Stand by."

Tyler spoke up from his computer. "I'm picking up movement on the ocean two hundred yards from the dock. It's probably a small boat."

Eric relayed the message to the teams near the dock, but as soon as he finished, Ronnie alerted him again. "There's a boat on the beach to the south."

Tyler got excited. "The satellite has picked up a helicopter coming due west from Quepos."

After Eric relayed the message, he called the team at the hanger. "Use a shoulder-launched missile, and take out that helicopter before it lands."

"Roger, boss."

Steve had already loaded the launcher, but he made a few final adjustments as he brought it up to his shoulder, while getting a feel of the weapon. It had been about two months since the last he tested with it, but he was one of the best shots in the firm.

Eric now knew there were at least three ground assaults in progress and one airborne team. He had handled far worst situations both in the military and as a security firm, but he didn't like the lack of Intel in this situation. He had no counts as to how many men Stephen had been able to line up, but he doubted if any the locals had military training. The firm also had surprise on their side.

The group coming in behind the hanger had split into two parties. Steve and his partner heard them try to open the back doors, but they were nailed shut earlier in the day. They cautiously moved around to the far corners. They were forced to move away from the building to go around several stacks of empty barrels. The first man hit the trip wire, and though his bare leg felt something, he didn't know what it was. He only had a second to think before the grenade bomb went off. They also tied the trip wire to a second grenade, exactly twelve yards back, and it went off as well, trapping some of Stephen's men in the middle of the flying shrapnel that instantly cut them down. One of the four men did survive, but he screamed horribly at the pain and soon bled out. The bad guys had no medics and no first aid kit.

216

Eric, Ronnie and Tyler watched the blast on the big projected screen. He spoke quickly into his radio. "Steve, the other team will work their way around to the south. Do you see the helicopter?"

"No, they must be low as there are no clouds to use as cover."

Tyler spoke up as the camera on the water tower picked up the helicopter in night vision mode. "He's two hundred yards from the end of the runway coming directly towards him. They'll be over the ground in ten seconds."

Steve's partner flipped his night goggles down over his eyes. He whispered, "I see four men at the end of the hanger. They are waiting on something."

Steve whispered back, "They are either scared from the booby trap or waiting on the helicopter. I see the chopper. Get down low in case they have night vision."

The helicopter came over the trees and dropped immediately downward to just ten feet above the ground as it came down the runway towards the hanger. Steve flipped the safety on the missile-launcher to off, aimed while following the chopper carefully, and moving with it until finally just a little bit ahead. Slowly, he squeezed the trigger.

He didn't wait to see the kill shot, but instead immediately loaded a second missile in case he missed, but he hadn't. The helicopter saw the lightning flame of the rocket a split second before impact, sending six men and a pilot to their deaths.

Unfortunately, the fire trail from the launcher gave away their position. They began receiving machine gun fire, as well as the sound of a hunting rifle from the south end group. His partner sprayed them with his UZI, wounding two before they hustled back around the corner of the building.

Steve spoke into his radio, "Chopper down. Two more men down near south end, there should two or more fellows left."

"Roger, good job," replied Eric. "Dock team. Your boat is forty yards out."

"Roger," whispered Tom into his radio. He and his partner were hidden behind rocks overlooking the dock. They had set up numerous grenade traps, including a flash grenade that would light up the dock and run the night vision of assailants. Tom set two grenades on the rock in front of him. They turned all the shore lights out, making it easier for them to stay hidden, while using top quality, night goggles to see their enemy.

Stephen was in the back of the boat issuing orders. Tonto was with him. Stephen carried an old Uzi that Tonto took from a drug lord his men killed. Tonto carried a shotgun and all his men brought machetes. Some had AKG rifles or shotguns. All their weapons were old, but their bullets could still kill. They cut off their engine and coasted in silence towards the dock.

217

They heard the helicopter explosion, filling all the men with anxiety, but all were either high on drugs or drunk, and ready for blood. Stephen promised a hundred dollars for each man's participation and another hundred for the severed head of each white man.

They tied up the boat and began slowly creeping down the dock. Just as Stephen was about to debark from the boat, the first man hit a trip wire that set off two more explosions killing three men, and wounding a fourth. Tom instantly pulled the pins on a stun grenade and flash grenade to light up the dock. He threw both in the middle of the group.

The inexperienced farmers froze where they were instead of diving for cover. Tom and his partner picked off two men on the dock leaving only two men plus Tonto and Stephen. Cautiously, they moved down the dock, with the team firing at them. Two minutes later, another man went down, and the remaining man, Tonto, and Stephen jumped off the dock into waist deep water fearing another grenade. They moved quickly from boat to boat with the team firing at them with each opportunity.

"Bunkhouse team, report?" Eric waited before he heard clicks.

Tyler asked," What is that?"

"Morse code. The enemy is too near for them to speak."

Ronnie spoke, "I see them on the camera. There are eight of them. They are as black as night, but the camera's infrared ability is amazing."

Eric whispered into his radio the count to his team. Seconds later, a booby trap went off. The group was so scared that they ran towards the team, firing their weapons wildly, preferring to take on their enemy instead of running into more bombs.

Tim and his partner began cutting them down. Four minutes later, there were only two alive, and they quickly moved inside a building and out of sight. Tim and his partner immediately ran to a second protected site about twenty yards away.

Eric realized that everything on the island was suddenly quiet. Stephen, Tonto, and the farmers had gone to ground. He knew they were probably afraid, but they also wanted the cash, and this first experience with Eric's teams scared them.

Tonto made his way up the hill, pulling his last man along with him. Stephen took another well-known path towards the house, assuming Eric would be there, but as he got closer, he began to think about the booby traps, and veered off the trail and into the woods.

Stephen grew up in the city and normally the thought of walking through the jungle during the night terrified him. However, his anger at Eric, and is overall need for cash, allowed him to put aside his fears for now.

In the command center, Eric asked, "Do you see any movement?"

218

Ronnie and Tyler were scanning all the cameras and saw nothing. The remaining men at the airport backed away from the hanger, and slowly made their way around it while moving towards the house.

Two of Tonto's gang decided to climb onto the bunkhouse roof, fearing other booby-traps if they continued moving on the ground.

Tonto began to creep up on Tom and his partner from behind. What he didn't know is that like the other teams, after each explosion and the firing of their weapons, they quickly and silently moved to their second position of offense.

Just as Tonto was about to leap down on their first position, he stopped and ducked down. Somehow, he sensed that either they were not there, or they were about to run into more booby traps, so he held his man back.

Using his night vision goggles, Tom and his partner could easily see the movement of Tonto and his man. He waited for them to rush into the open, and fire on their first location. When he realized they were backing off, he immediately took a shot at them. Tonto and his man quickly backed off into the woods, while Tom and his partner once again moved secretly to their next planned post.

Eric spoke up on COM1 to everyone, "We've whittled down their force by at least sixty-five percent, which probably scared the shit out of them, and now they are hiding. I suspect running into a military force was not something they planned for. They're scared and probably mad. I prefer a shootout that we would easily win." He checked his watch. "Three hours to sunrise. It is going to be a cat and mouse game until then."

Eric spoke to his men, "Be careful out there. They will move far slower now that we have taken out over half their men. Stay low, use your night vision goggles. We'll get them one at a time."

Tyler spoke up, "Someone is near the house." He pointed at the projected image.

Stephen was about twenty feet from the house, moving extremely slow and cautious, and he was off any paths, and afraid of the booby traps. He was surprised to see the lights out, but as he thought about it, he realized it would have been dumb to leave the lights on. He saw no movement in the house, but waited almost fifteen minutes to be sure. He moved closer to the kitchen door. He put his ear to the door and heard nothing. He quietly gave the door a push, but it would not budge. He tried his key in the door, and though the lock would turn, the door would not move. Without a flashlight, he couldn't see the wood screws holding the door tight.

He wanted to get inside to get his cash and passports, and given a chance, he would shoot and kill Eric, or at the worst escape. He moved around the house to his bedroom, broke a window, and waited for shouts or shots inside, but heard nothing. He waited a while longer, fearing a trap, but finally, he decided to move inside with the Uzi in front of him and ready to fire at anything that moved. His heart was racing. He could feel it beating in his temples.

Tyler said, "Stephen is in the house and in his bedroom. He's looking for the cash and documents. He'll be looking a long time," laughed Tyler.

Upon arrival, Eric and Gil moved everything of value to their tents. He radioed to his men that Stephen was in the house.

Ronnie spoke quickly, "Two men moving to the back of the house."

Eric replied, "They're probably the remains of the force from the hanger assault. Keep an eye on them." Eric once again relayed the new information to his teams, while Tyler put dots on the map on the screen as to the location of the bad guys. Two men were on the roof of the bunkhouse. Tonto and another man were in the woods between the dock and the house, and now two men were coming to the rear of the house from the hanger, and of course Stephen. Seven to go, thought Eric.

Stephen pulled the hidden lever to allow him to pull the bookcase away from the wall on casters. Behind the shelves was his safe. He immediately noted something was wrong as he found the steel door slightly opened. His heart sank as he reached in and found it empty, except for one envelope. Half afraid of a booby trap, he gingerly pulled the envelope out. He walked to his side of the bed and opened the top drawer of the nightstand, removing a penlight. He sat down on the bed, turned the small flashlight on, and held it in his mouth, while carefully opening the envelope. He began to read. "Dear Stephen, you're too late. We took all your money, burned all your passports, credit cards, and took all the keys, and we took your jewelry, too. You have nothing because you are nothing. Your jail cell awaits you. See you soon. Eric."

"Damn!" he screamed. "Damn, damn, damn!"

Then he caught himself, now afraid he had alerted Eric's men to his whereabouts.

Tyler was laughing. "That was priceless. This is the first time I felt like I have my revenge."

Eric was busy alerting the team so they could move in on Stephen, but quietly, they were all busy, except for the team at the hanger. He told them to stay there to protect the jet."

Tyler gave him a puzzled look. "Where are you going?"

Eric was busy adjusting his uniform, checking his weapons, his ammunition, and he put a pair of night vision goggles over his head. "I'm going to get the bad guy." He said to Gil, "You're in charge. Hold the fort down."

"The teams will get him," protested Tyler.

"I can handle him, don't worry."

Tyler grinned as he replied, "I was only worried that Stephen might bleed all over your new uniform."

Eric laughed. "I will try to stay far enough away from him."

"Yeah right, I bet you want to beat the crap out of him instead of just shooting him. He will not fight fair. He is not honorable."

Tyler had been right in his assumption, and Eric knew it. He smiled at Tyler. "Gil, tell this young agent how I took out twenty men with only fifteen shots in Africa. Tell him how I stopped a tank in Panama. Tell him how I diffused a bomb, while returning fire at a host of terrorists in Pakistan."

Gil said, "You just told him. Go, but be careful, and keep your head down. It only takes one lucky bullet to stop you, so be smart."

"Roger that," replied Eric as he turned on his heels and left the tent.

Stephen felt for the 9mm pistol he brought in from San Jose, but it was not in the makeshift holster. He had lost it in the assault at the dock or in the woods. He searched the nightstand for the 9mm pistol he kept there, but it was gone as well. He retrieved the UZI he had left on the bed while moving the bookshelf. He carefully walked through the house until he was sure none of Eric's men were there. Just as he returned to the bedroom, he saw two figures walk past the window. He frantically ducked down and watched them, but soon he realized they were Tonto's men. He moved to the window and tapped. They lurched around with their guns, but Stephen opened the window, and spoke a few words of Spanish to them.

He climbed out of the window just as he heard shots near the bunkhouse. All three men ducked down behind a bush. Stephen spotted two of Eric's men hidden between some barrels and an old truck. He pointed at them and urged the two men to go to the right and attack them. Stephen went around the other way with his gun ready. They crept forward.

Bill and his partner scanned the roof of the bunkhouse where the last shots had come from. They heard movement but saw nothing.

Tonto and his man slowly and carefully made their way up the hill towards the house, while moving to the left and out of the sight of Bill. Stephen's two men did not see Tonto approaching. Bill and his partner quickly moved to their next defensive position. Suddenly, one of the men on the roof spotted their movement. He stood and fired at them. Bill easily spun and took him out, but the moment his gun flashed, Tonto fired, hitting Bill in the back, while Stephen's two men fired wildly from the left. Bill went down like a rock.

Staying low, Tim grabbed the collar of Bill's flak jacket, and pulled Bill out of the firefight and behind the barrels. Bill was groaning, but his Kevlar vest caught the bullet, but it still hurt and nearly scarred the shit out of

221

him. Getting his breath back, he rolled into a crouch position and picked up his weapon. Tim smiled, patted him on the shoulder, feeling thankful his partner was okay.

Tonto and his worker began firing at them, as did Stephen's men.

Tom and Larry reacted to the gunfire from twenty-five yards away, as they spotted Tonto. They began firing from behind a tractor, taking out his worker with a headshot, and wounding Tonto in his left arm. The big guy dropped down out of sight, as his anger began boiling. He quickly tried to wrap the bleeding wound with his red bandana. Tom and Larry crept up the hill while whispering into their headset, letting Bill's team know where they were, so they wouldn't shoot them.

Bill managed to spot the last man on the roof, but he ducked back down. Without hesitation, he pulled a grenade from the hook on his vest, pulled the pin, and threw it hard. It arched in the air and exploded about four feet above the roof, sending thousands of metal shards into the last man, killing him instantly as the hot metal pieces cut through his flesh, while opening his exposed veins, and taking out his eyes and windpipe. The blast knocked him off the roof, and his body hit the ground on his head with the awful sound of his neck breaking along with vertebrate and echoing through the yard. He lay there in an awkward heap of blood and guts oozing onto the ground.

The bunkhouse roof was now secure, allowing better movement for Tom and Larry. Not sure if Tonto was down for good or just wounded, Tom and Larry crept up the hill. Eric ran carefully through the jungle until he reached the opening. He began cautiously making his way around the pool, spotting Stephen's men. He failed to see Stephen. He crept closer to them until he had a clear shot. Just as they rose up to fire at Bill, Eric fired two lethal shots into each man's chest, and they dropped to the ground like sacks of potatoes.

The bullets from Eric's gun literally flew over Stephen's head, as he remained flat on the ground between bushes on the other side of the pool. He watched as Eric moved quickly from side to side like a soldier. His persona puzzled Stephen, leaving him wondering why a squad of soldiers from America would attack him so viciously in Costa Rica.

Suddenly, Tonto began firing from his position at Bill and Tim, but Tom and Larry began firing at Tonto, but they couldn't get him. Eric turned his attention to Tonto after scanning the area looking for Stephen. He felt sure they could take out the last of the local would be warriors, but he had to find Stephen.

He moved again, then stopped and began scanning the area. Just as he moved again, Stephen realized he had what he thought would be a kill shot, as he carefully aimed the Uzi and pulled the trigger.

Eric heard the unmistakable click of the trigger, then instantly dove into a roll away from what he assumed would be Stephen's trail of bullets, and came up to his feet in a military-style crouch firing position, while bringing his gun up, but no bullets were actually fired.

In his frantic move off the dock, dodging through the jungle, Stephen had accidentally slipped the safety on. Unfamiliar with the weapon, it remained still and quiet, and in the dark, he didn't know what was wrong. He began quickly feeling and pulling as every possible button or slide.

Eric took advantage of Stephen's inability to fire and moved quickly around to his right, looking for Stephen in the bushes.

Tonto abruptly ran out of bullets. He set the gun down and removed his machete. He was angry with Stephen for getting him into this situation, angry with himself for going along for some cash, and most of all, angry with the man in the forest firing at him. He paused for his anger to boil deep inside, took a deep breath, and betrayed his position and intent as he screamed and charged Tim.

He ran only a few feet before Bill popped up and put two kill shots in Tonto's chest. Bill didn't wait for the large man to fall. He hit Tonto with a final but deadly headshot. Tonto's body flew against a stack of barrels and fell limp to the ground.

Eric glanced their way and then returned to his endeavor of finding Stephen, but he was gone from the bushes. Suddenly, Stephen sprang from his hiding place, and sprinted down the length of the pool deck. Eric turned in a flash at the movement and fired, catching Stephen just slightly in the top of his left shoulder. Eric heard Stephen curse.

Eric quickly spoke into his microphone. "I nicked Stephen in his left shoulder and I'm in pursuit. Secure the area around the house and then approach the house with caution."

Stephen got around the house, took the penlight from his pocket, and though in great pain from his wound, he studied the gun until he finally realized he had the safety on.

Eric took the opposite side of the house and sprinted around to the backside of the house. The four, team members began coming around the pool in the other direction as Eric whispered his location in his wrist microphone. Tyler could hear everything and it scared him. As much as he wanted Stephen dead, he did not want Eric hurt.

From the other side of the house, Stephen saw the soldiers approaching and fired at them, but with no previous practice with the gun, his shots went wide, but gradually he moved his aim upward as Eric's men scattered. As they returned with a heavy barrage of fire, Stephen dove around the corner of the house and began running.

Eric turned the corner at the back of the house with his weapon ready. Suddenly, he saw Stephen running towards him. He waited for him to get a little closer before yelling. "Stop where you are, or I'll shoot! Drop your weapon!"

Stephen hesitated for just a split second, stopped his run, but then brought his weapon up to fire wildly. Missing Eric, he dove into the breakfast window, crashing on to the table, cracking his chin, falling to the floor, and skidding across the tile, while bleeding from numerous cuts from the shards of glass.

Eric jumped back out of the line of fire. He spoke into his microphone ordering the nearby teams to the front of the house. He then spoke to Ronnie. "Throw the remote switch for the breaker box to house. Light it up right now!"

Ronnie picked up a remote control device and hit the button. He had installed the wireless relay device on the breaker box to the house upon their arrival.

Stephen could see soldiers running to the front as he sprinted down the hall. He heard a crash at the back of the house as Eric broke into the house via window into a guest bedroom.

Stephen leaped against the wall as every light in the house suddenly came on and blinding his night adjusted eyes as the teams to the front broke in and came inside firing in all directions. The flying wood splinters forced Stephen to cover his face and move backwards away from them. Eric made it to the hall. Stephen lifted his gun and began firing at the soldiers who just located his position and were sending hundreds of bullets in the wall near him, ripping the wood and sheetrock to shreds.

Stephen began working his way farther down the hall and away from the barrage at the front of the house. Eric turned the corner and caught sight of Stephen's leg. He fired one shot hitting him hard in the calf. Stephen screamed out at the pain. The soldiers up front ceased fire, but kept their aim on the hall.

Eric could hear Stephen curse as he turned to fire towards Eric, but Eric wisely changed his location by leaping across the hall into an opposite door frame. Stephen brought his gun up to fire, so Eric again shot him in the left arm just above the elbow. Stephen screamed again. Blood splattered Stephen's face, but somehow he managed to hang on to the gun with his right hand. Blood was pouring down his left arm and down his leg from his wounds.

He was hurt more than anytime in his life, but he was so furious at Eric, he gathered his wits about him, brought the gun up, took a deep breath, and prepared to mount a suicide charge towards Eric. He leaped out from the wall with the gun up and pulled the trigger. Eric ducked back into the doorframe dodging his wild shots, waiting and hoping he would run out of bullets, but as Stephen's aim improved, Eric dropped down, leaned out quickly, and fired one single shot dead center of Stephen's forehead. The force of the lead slammed Stephen's bloody body head first into the wall behind him. The gun fell away harmlessly to the floor, followed by the distinctive thud of the lifeless body of Stephen.

"Clear!" yelled Eric down the hall and into his sleeve microphone on COM1 so all could hear. "Stephen and the men are dead." Then he said to Gil, "Gil, allow the men to reload, and then I want them to search the island to make sure we have no more targets. The sun will be up soon, making the job easier."

"Roger that."

Eric kicked the Uzi away from Stephen, picked it up and went on down the hall. "Is everybody okay?"

Bill spoke up first. "Tim took a round in the body armor vest that I'm sure he will whine about for weeks, but other than that we're fine." The team laughed.

"You did excellent work and a great job. Okay, reload and let's make sure they're all dead."

Eric made his way back up the hill to the tent. He set his weapons down on the table and smiled at Tyler. "It's over. He's dead."

Tears were sliding down from Tyler's eyes, slipping down his cheeks, but looking up into Eric's smiling face, he slowly smiled. "I'm not crying for him. I'm crying because I thought you were going to be shot, and now these are tears of joy, and I am so thankful you're safe."

"Me, too, but he wasn't much of a shot."

"He had an Uzi. He could have gotten lucky."

"He hasn't been lucky since the day he met you!"

The shock of Eric's unexpected sentence totally stunned Tyler as his mouth dropped open and then Eric smiled. "And you haven't been lucky until you met me!"

Ronnie and Gil laughed. Tyler blushed. Eric laughed as well.

Tyler replied, "You forget that George has taught me well, and I can kick your ass if need be!" Tyler was laughing while wiping away his tears.

Eric noted his simple ploy helped Tyler through the moment, but he felt in the days to come that Tyler might still need a shoulder to lean on.

"Hey, boss," began Gil. "This island would make a great training base. It's out of the states, we can shoot all we want, and we can fly in and out at will."

"That's true, but it would also make a great place for some R & R," replied Eric.

Gil and Ronnie agreed. Tyler asked, "What is R & R? It's not like S & M is it?"

Eric laughed hard. "It means rest and relaxation. All soldiers need a place to safely unwind. The sun is coming up. Let's get the search over with and pack up. I'm ready to head home."

"Me, too," replied Tyler.

"Don't go getting lazy on me. We have a job in Morocco coming soon. We have a senator to protect. Do you want to be on the team?"

Tyler grinned. "Roger that. Hell, yes."

"Maybe we can stop in Cadiz on the way back and check out our new European safe house."

Tyler laughed. "You're going to love the view of the bay and..." he paused and leaned into Eric so only he could hear. "The view of the sailors down below, well, it's breath taking. Some of them lie naked in the sun."

"You're bad," teased Eric.

"Maybe true, but I'm very much in love with you."

Eric smiled. "I love you, too. Let's get busy."

EPILOGUE

They used a four –wheeler from the storage shed that Tyler managed to start, and hauled all the bodies to Tonto's boat. They also loaded all their old weapons, including guns and machetes as well hats. Tim cranked the boat's engine and let it begin warming up. Larry started the motor on one of Stephen's boats. Eric and Ronnie studied the maps, and along with Tyler's personal knowledge, they steered the boats about twenty miles away, heading east into the ocean where the water depth was over a mile. Using binoculars, they scanned the horizon in all directions, but saw nothing on the water.

Larry tied up alongside Tim's boat. Using ropes they tied the bodies together, then looped the anchor chain around the bodies as well, and tied off the chain to the engine frame, just in case the pending explosion should separate the motor from the hull.

Once satisfied, Larry returned to his boat, and called Ronnie on COM1. "This is L1, are the pineapples fresh?" It was their code phrase, indicating they saw nothing from the island, and Oscar found nothing on the government satellites.

"Roger, that. Lunch is coming up."

"Thanks. Out."

Tim took a prepared plastic explosives bomb, set the timer, and dropped it down into the engine well. He made a hasty retreat to Larry's boat and they quickly moved away. A half mile later, the boat exploded through the hull, scattering the bottom of the boat into the sea. The barely seaworthy craft sank instantly. In less than twenty seconds, it disappeared forever beneath the waters, descending to the permanent grave at the bottom of the ocean. No one would ever see the likes of Stephen or Tonto and his men again.

Satisfied with their work, they turned the boat towards the island.

Meanwhile, the men cleaned up the blood in the house, around the pool area, the docks, and anywhere they found a single drop. Eric's orders were to remove all evidence the attackers were killed on the island. They couldn't repair the wood and structure damage, but they left no evidence of killings. It took a while, but they picked up all the shell casings.

Eric spent a half-hour on the secure phone to Washington, talking to his friend Gary Roberts about the situation. They discussed various outcomes for handling the attack on foreign soil, though arguably a private island. Ted and the firm's lawyer were researching to find out if the island was part of Costa Rica or not. Gary hung up, called a friend in the CIA, who then spoke with a field agent in Costa Rica, and then made yet another call to an operative in Quepos. Minutes later, the command center received several faxes and emails from various American offices.

After much discussion, Eric smiled at the conclusion of their advice and set about a plan. The operative told him the locals feared everyone from the island because the drug lord and his thugs caused lots of pain and havoc in Quepos, and then after Stephen and Jim took over, they weren't pleased of their attitude, nor the reports of having sex with young men on the island. Eric obtained the name of the town's official. Taking Tyler and Jim for support, he left Gil in charge, and took a boat to Quepos, carrying no visible weapons, and his briefcase. The three changed into civilian clothes to appear as harmless as possible.

The ride over to the mainland took about an hour, and they docked alongside numerous fishing boats. Tyler knew where the city offices were located, and they began walking towards them. Eric noted that the dockworkers and the townspeople appeared to be wary of them. He told Eric and Jim to smile and nod politely as they continued the two-block walk.

Eric had memorized the name he was given by the operative in Quepos. They entered the office with Jim hanging back near the door in case he spotted trouble. Eric walked to the counter and smiled at the young lady behind the counter. "May I speak with Señor Buros?"

"One moment," she replied using her new English skills. She left the desk, went to a rear office, and returned with an elderly gentleman.

Eric and Tyler smiled broadly, as Eric said, "Good morning, Señor Buros. How are you today?"

Skittish, the man replied, "Well, thank you. And you are?"

"My name is Eric Hansen, and these are my friends Tyler and Jim. I was wondering if I may have a word with you in private?"

He waited while Buros looked at Tyler and Jim, and then nodded. "Yes, of course. Please come this way."

They closed the door to the man's office, and sat across from the mayor. Tyler carried the briefcase. Eric began his little speech by saying, "I thank you for your time, and I'll be as brief as possible. Recently, I purchased an island across the water east from Quepos known as Turtle Island, though I have yet to see one." Eric smiled at his little joke, but the official just nodded. Eric continued, "I understand the island has a terrible history, first with the drug lords, and then some bad Americans by the name of Stephen and Jim. Are you aware of this?"

"Yes, I am." He did not betray his feelings one-way or the other.

Tyler opened the briefcase, handed the man a copy of the purchase of the island, and waited for him to scan the papers. Once he finished reading, he nodded that he understood the transaction, and handed the papers back to Tyler.

Tyler gave Eric a small stack of the emails and faxes he received. He also included the highlights of his service record, including references for various government officials including an admiral, and current Joint Chiefs of

Staff. The official appeared to be impressed, but Eric thought he would make a great poker player.

Surprisingly, the man suddenly asked, "What are your intentions?"

Eric smiled slightly. "Only noble ones. We do not use or sell drugs, we behave with great honor, and we'll make sure you never have a problem with anyone from the island again. We will employ your people for construction and help, and will pay them well. I looked into health insurance, but there is none for your country. Therefore, we'll set up a health clinic for all your citizens. We will buy lots of produce, lumber, and supplies that will stimulate your economy.

"I can assure you there be no drugs on the island, nor will there be any more sex parties. We will not employ anyone under the age of twenty-one, but we do wish to built a new school and sports field in our city for your children." Eric stopped and let the news of his plans become absorbed by the man.

"What must we do in return?"

Eric smiled. "Absolutely nothing. We believe in becoming good neighbors. We wish only to live in peace, and though the island will not be our permanent home, we will visit it often. The families of my American workers will vacation there, enjoying the beauty and peaceful setting."

Eric nodded to Tyler, as he brought out a thick sack from the briefcase. Eric removed stacks of bank bound cash from the bag and set them on the man's desk. Tyler handed him a form.

"Sir, this is two hundred thousand dollars. This form says I'm giving it to you for the sole purpose of building a school and playground for your children. It is not to be used for any other purpose without my permission. It says you will provide proper accounting for all expenditures. This will allow you to choose your workers and pay them well. You can design the school anyway you wish. If you need help, I can provide it. I will stock the school with thousands of books and school supplies. I can provide building plans and a construction supervisor if you wish. Otherwise, I will stay out of your way.

"This also states that this money is not a bribe. It does not go to you, or anyone one else as compensation. It is merely a gift to the townspeople. Do you accept?"

Eric handed him the document and the man carefully read every word. After decades of deceit and mistrust, this offer seemed amazing to him. He smiled slightly, and signed the form beneath Eric's signature. Eric handed him another signed copy for his records.

The man finally spoke, "We are pleased to have you enjoy our paradise. I hope we can work well together but safely."

"Very good. Do you want us to escort the money to your bank?"

"Yes, I would. We don't want a riot. No one here has ever seen this much cash." Tyler put the money in the sack, and handed it to the mayor.

Eric said, "I will have a group fly in immediately to make plans for your new health clinic." Eric gave him a card. "This is my contact information. On this card you'll find numerous ways for you to get in touch with me on the card. If there is problem, please don't hesitate to call."

The man stood and they warmly shook hands, his face was now beaming with excitement. Together, they walked across the street to the bank and made the deposit into the town's account. Eric smiled when the clerk handed the official a receipt and new current balance. It was for two hundred thousand and twelve dollars. The poor town previously only had twelve dollars in their bank account.

They stopped half way to the office as the mayor had a question "I am told that a two nights ago, the previous owner obtained the services of some bad men led by Tonto. They have caused this town much trouble with their drunken brawls. They were hired to kill you and your friends. I am pleased they were not successful."

Eric smiled, while choosing his words carefully. "Those who attack in the night often learn that a blade has two sharp sides." He paused and waited for the man to take in the meaning of his statement. Eric continued, "I never met this man Tonto, but I understand and suspect he will no longer be a burden to anyone."

The mayor stood stoically while thinking through the hidden meaning, and then smiled slightly. "Very good. Very good indeed."

They shook hands with broad smiles from all. Eric and his men returned to the dock after buying baskets of fresh fruit from venders and paying cash. They filled up the boat with fuel by paying cash again.

On the return trip to the island, Tyler and Eric stood in the front of the boat while Jim took the helm.

Tyler said, "I think we made a very good first impression with the town's mayor."

Eric replied, "Yes, I agree. The CIA operative reported the man to be honorable and beyond bribes. I believe he was right. I want to build a first-rate health facility here, and free for everyone to take advantage of. In six months, Quepos will be in much better shape. I hired a friend of mine to take charge of remodeling of Turtle Island. I will make some sketches when we return. I want to rebuild everything, hire a local crew to take care of it, and then we'll use it for the firm and for us. It'll be our little paradise away from home."

"I will look forward to returning. I always liked it here, but now I just want to have sex with you."

"I have some news for you. Gary said that Jim agreed to a plea deal, turning against Stephen, but after I informed him of Stephen's demise, he tore up the deal. I sent him footage of Jim fucking the underage Juan, plus we found a book of child pornography in the safe room, and we found more

230

pictures down here. I'm sending them all to Gary. This will more than strengthen their case against Jim. You'll never have to worry about him or should I say them, again."

"I'm no longer worried about anything. You made me the happiest man in the world when you picked me to talk to and love. I never really knew what love felt like until you gave it to me. I owe you my life and my future."

"You owe me nothing. I love you very much. However, there is one little thing."

Tyler's face became a puzzled frown. "What?"

"Just one tiny thing."

Tyler laughed. "What?"

"When we get home, we'll enjoy a great dinner, we'll soak in the Jacuzzi, and then we'll go to bed, and then I, Eric Hansen, will be the TOP tonight!"

Tyler laughed and swatted his shoulder playfully, and then said slyly, "Simon says you may enter freely!"

Together, they laughed all the way back to the island. Tyler's new life without fear began the moment Stephen died. He was happy, really happy for the first time since before he came out to his mother. He learned so many things from the time he hustled on the street thru robbing the rich around the world. However, he had not learned about the joy of pure love, of being in love, and feeling loved, until he met Eric.

Before Tyler, a few times a year, Eric enjoyed sex with various partners since retiring from the Navy Seals, and building his security firm, but he, too, had not yet found love with a life-long partner. Together, they traveled the world on the behalf of the firm, as well as for vacations that were always filled with adventure. Hiking to mountain peaks, scuba diving in the Cayman Islands, parasailing in Cozumel, chasing kangaroos in Australia, riding horses in Glacier National Park, roaming with buffalo in Yellowstone, and returning to Annapolis fully revived and refreshed, and ready to go to work once again.

Once a month, Tyler fulfilled Eric's request to 'pay' for his crimes by speaking to a group of young people at local schools. He told the students how his crimes nearly killed him, and how thankful he was to be an honest person with a good job. Eric was proud of him.

Six months later, they returned to Quepos at the mayor's personal invitation to attend a festival in Eric's honor. Eric flew the entire team down including Oscar and Marti. They toured the new school and playground. The children performed several songs for them, and then they walked to what started out as a clinic, but once inspired, Eric spent even more money building a hospital for them. He also staffed the hospital with retired Navy medical personnel and paid their salaries and housing. He and Tyler smiled with pride at the fine facility. The mayor made a speech and then they all sat down to eat under the shade of the town's large trees. Eric said this was by far the best investment he had ever made.

It was good life they enjoyed, a good love they felt, and strong trust they developed. Eric and Tyler had never been happier, and everyone that knew them, felt happiness for them.

TJ Johnson
April 25, 2009

Revised March 13, 2010 while setting up Part II Crosshairs & Part III Rock Solid. Visit www.ItsFiction.com for release dates.

Author TJ Johnson

TJ began writing his stories in the eighties, mostly for fun and for friends. He was still working full-time for someone else and the career took up more time than he wished. In 2005, he began working for himself with hopes of spending more time on his writing. On the computer were several novels not yet produced, so while writing new material, he began searching for outlets for the books he'd completed. His favorite part of writing is the crafting of the rough draft, a period in the process when the words fly from the storage center deep in his brain like a movie stuck on fast-forward. The agonizing part begins with the painstaking restructuring as the editing begins, but it is a joy when the tale is finally finished. TJ often works on three stories at once, each in different stages of production. He does this to keep his creative skills at peak performance, and because he believes fiction is just too much fun!

His most recent releases: **The Raceboys** about a national champion forced to come out as a gay driver, and **A Writer's Fantasy** about his favorite college basketball team and their handsome star player. Also available is **The Will** and **Stranded. The Blackfeet Boys** set in the northwest in a time when two young warriors must abandon their home with the most feared and blood thirsty tribe in North America, and search for a safe and isolated world together.

Fans of the War Series (**The War Apart - Part 1**, **The War Ahead - Part 2**) will be pleased to know that the research is finished, and the writing has begun on **The War Beyond - Part 3**.

Currently, TJ is editing **Crosshairs,** a continuing story with the cast of Gay Grifters – an Eric and Tyler Story, and **Almost Identical**, set during WWII about twins, one gay and the other straight and their breathtaking fight for survival amongst the Nazis.

Requests for additional information and Inquiries can be obtain from **Hard Title Publishing,** at **Info@ItsFiction.com**

You may also signup for free publication notices at:

WWW.ItsFiction.Com

Contact TJ Johnson at:

Info@ItsFiction.com

1. I try to answer all my email myself; however please read "Bio & Info" at www.ItsFiction.com before writing as your question – saving time for all! Many readers ask the same questions repeatedly.

2. Please do not add my email address to any group for jokes, thoughts, prayers, or riddles, etc. I always delete these without reading.

3. I do not open any emails with attachments as these may contain viruses or other nonsense!

4. Please do NOT write suggesting plot lines as I delete these quickly, too. I like to write my own stories. If your plot is good, write it yourself! Do not send your manuscript to me – I am a writer, not a publisher, and I do not have the time.

5. All characters and names are part of my imagination and indicate no one particular. If I like a person's name, I may use the first or the last name but never both at the same time. It is true some of the events in my books are historical in nature but many are not. Choosing which to believe is your job, but this is why fiction is fun.

6. If you do not receive a reply, perhaps "Bio & Info" contain the answer already, or your email address is not functioning correctly.

7. If you have read all the above, I cannot wait to hear from you!

8. If you think a sequel should be added to your favorite story, please send me an email to the above address!

www.ingramcontent.com/pod-product-compliance
Lightning Source LLC
Chambersburg PA
CBHW070058260626
47160CB00004B/1247